Of INK and ALCHEMY

Of Ink and Alchemy

SLOANE ST. JAMES

All rights reserved. No part of this publication may be reproduced, stored in a retrieval system, or transmitted in any form or by any means electronic, mechanical, photocopying, recording, or otherwise without prior written permission from Podium Publishing.

This is a work of fiction. Names, characters, places, and incidents are either products of the author's imagination or used fictitiously. Any resemblance to actual events, locales, or persons, living, dead, or undead, is entirely coincidental.

Copyright © 2026 by Sloane St. James

Cover design by Yessy Baeza

ISBN: 979-8-3470-1871-0

Published in 2026 by Podium Publishing
www.podiumentertainment.com

CONTENT WARNING

Of Ink and Alchemy is a friends-to-lovers dark romance containing graphic and sexually explicit scenes that readers may find disturbing or triggering. Themes include manipulation, stalking, violence, intentional drugging, and kidnapping. It is intended for mature readers. If you are trigged by any of these situations, please skip this one.

Of INK and ALCHEMY

PROLOGUE

LOGAN

"Oh." The courthouse clerk, Connie, pauses, staring at the piece of paper in her hand. Her bright-red frames match the lipstick on her teeth. A phone rings in a cubicle somewhere behind her.

"Is there a problem?"

"Active military?" she asks.

"No, ma'am."

"Then I will need to see your driver's license or proof of residence."

I pull my wallet from my back pocket and slide my new, shiny license from the aged leather card slot. It lists the address of the condo I recently purchased, burning up what little was left of my inheritance and savings account. It will all be worth it. She accepts the ID with pursed lips. *I can't tell if she's skeptical or curious?* Bracing my elbow on the desk, I ask, "Hey, I heard your brother was selling his Camaro. He get any buyers yet?"

She cocks her head to the side, trying to place my face. "Not yet."

"I might have to give him a holler, yellow is my favorite color." When I picked up my application a couple weeks ago, I eavesdropped on her telling another clerk about her brother Jerome selling his beloved car.

"Yeah . . . I'm sure he'd love to talk about it."

"Oh, I bet he would," I say with a chuckle. "Jerome would talk to a brick wall."

That gets a loud laugh out of her, and her shoulders relax. "So true!"

May as well go for broke. "Did you see they're putting in another Village Pump on 191?"

She sucks her teeth and shakes her head. "Ugh, I heard."

"I swear they're the closest we get to the mafia," I mutter—convincing her with every word. "They're trying to put up a bunch of hotels too."

She glances from left to right, then leans forward and lowers her voice. "They've been buying up everything lately."

Setting my other elbow on the desk, I lean down. "I always say they're casinos disguised as gas stations."

"Well, when you hold all the town's liquor licenses . . ."

I chuckle. "Don't let 'em hear you, Connie. They'll come after you next," I joke.

She laughs and passes me my license with a smile. I resist running my tongue over my front teeth where she has lipstick on hers.

"Okay, do you have the rest of your paperwork? And have you arranged for a representative?"

I push the folder across the desk to her. She opens it and flips through the papers with practiced efficiency. A copy of her driver's license—that I stole from her purse a few months back—her legal form, Thor's paperwork, and finally, the affidavit that was written in flawless imitation. It took me a couple weeks to perfect her handwriting, but now I have no problem swirling my *G*'s and *Y*'s the same way she does. It wouldn't be the first time I had to forge documents. All notarized by Casper, of course, who is patiently waiting in the car outside.

"Well, aren't you organized!"

"Oh, Connie. *She's* organized. I'm just the delivery boy."

That earns me another laugh. She turns one of the forms around to face me. "Initial here."

I do.

Then she points to another line. "Signature."

I scribble my name.

She plucks a self-inking stamp next to her computer and sets it on top of the paperwork, then presses down with a mechanical *thunk*. "You've got one hundred and eighty days to—"

"Oh, I wouldn't miss it for the world. My representative and I will be here with bells on."

"Excellent," she says, peering down at the paperwork and double-checking my name before handing it over to me. "Well, Logan. I'll get this filed and you'll be all set."

She holds out the document and I take it from her with a smile—it's the first thing I haven't faked—then fold it in half and slip it into the pocket inside my jacket.

"Great, thanks, Connie. Take care of yourself." I nod. "And say hi to Jerome for me."

She grins. "Will do!"

I turn on my heel and walk out the door. The clouds hang low over the Bridger Range, and the snowy peaks stay hidden behind the late winter haze. A glimpse at my watch tells me we've got a few hours before we need to catch our flight home, which is good because I'm hungry and hoping we can grab a bite before we head to the airport.

White exhaust puffs from the tailpipe of the rental car that's idling on the curb outside the courthouse. Casper sits in the driver's seat, texting on his phone. Opening the door, I slip into the heated passenger seat. "Let's get some food," I say.

"All good?" he asks, not lifting his eyes from the screen.

"Got it."

He nods, then tucks the phone in his jacket and shifts the car into gear before we pull away from the curb.

1

LOGAN

"Are you staying late?" With hands planted on her hips, she leans back and stretches, cracking her spine after a full day of work. Seven o'clock, closing time. The setting sun shines through the two big picture windows on either side of the front door, casting a warm glow inside the shop. She chuckles. "What am I saying, of course you are."

I grin and return to the shop's overflowing inbox asking when our artists' books are reopening and if they would make any exceptions. I'm willing to take commissions on the days we're closed if the client is willing to pay one and a half times my normal rate.

"I was thinking of ordering some food . . . Wanna get in on that?" she asks.

When I glance up, she's got her elbows planted on the front desk, hands propping up her chin. She bats her lashes, showing off her bright-green eyes, and tosses me a hopeful smile.

The corner of my mouth turns up, and I sigh. "Yeah. I suppose," I grumble, typing out replies to hopeful client emails at the front desk. I could be doing this from my office, but she just finished up with her last client of the day, so I was covering the desk until we closed at seven o'clock p.m.

These days I only tattoo four days a week, but still, I find myself here almost seven to make sure things are running smoothly. I inherited the shop almost five years ago and still haven't mastered the work-life balance. Not sure I ever will. Maybe someday I'll hire a shop manager, but it would have to be someone worthy, and I doubt I'll ever trust anyone enough to give them control of the reins. This is too important, and I can't risk it ending up in the wrong hands again.

This isn't just any tattoo shop, it's Clyde Everhart's studio, Black Rabbit—and the woman standing in front of me is his one and only descendant, Kelly.

She rounds the desk and looks over my shoulder. "Hey, are you going through emails? That's my job, get outta here." She shoos me away and slips into the chair I was sitting in.

Kelly is still wrapping up her apprenticeship, so she previously managed our inbox as one of her duties, but technically, Francesca—*Frankie*—handles the front desk on the days we're open, Tuesday through Saturday. I hired her about eight months ago to answer phones and schedule appointments. She is great at keeping us organized. However, her work days usually end around six o'clock, so anything important outside those hours is done by me or Kelly.

"But first, I'm putting in a dinner order," she announces, pulling out her phone.

"Expense it," I tell her.

She spins in the chair to beam at me and says, "Don't worry, I am," then rotates away from me.

I hover behind her as she scrolls through restaurants listed on one of those food delivery apps.

A text notification pops up at the top of her screen.

Jason: Hey beautiful. How was your day?

She squeals.

This fuckin' guy.

"I love that he texts me to ask how my day was," she says, opening the text thread and tapping out a response.

"Yeah, Chaos, his chivalry is really breaking new ground," I grumble. She doesn't even hear me.

I can't watch this shit, so I step away and cut open the boxes from our earlier delivery. This woman occupies way too much real estate in my brain, especially considering she has a new boyfriend—the man is a complete waste of her time. He doesn't know how to handle a woman like Kelly Everhart.

Kelly is five feet, two inches of pure edgy adorableness, with her black hair, black nails, tattooed arms, and nipple piercings that occasionally poke through her shirt just to torture me. Not to mention those thick thighs and hips that I'm dying to sink my teeth into. *Jason, you lucky son of a bitch.*

She's kind and sweet, always making sure everyone she comes in contact with feels appreciated and welcome. Though if it were up to me, her gorgeous smiles would be exclusively mine.

Jason is the most milquetoast motherfucker I've had the displeasure of meeting. Unfortunately, she's been with so many clowns over the years, this guy's stock features—*like asking about her day*—have somehow been twisted into grand romantic gestures. I have no idea why she puts up with him. He's a cold sore personified, annoying, and hopefully just as temporary.

She giggles, smiling at her phone screen, and I roll my eyes, pulling out the boxes of blue shop towels from the shipment.

They've only been seeing each other for a month and a half. Eventually, she'll come to her senses. Until then, I will continue to bide my time as her best friend. Our close friendship provides me with special privileges, which is enough to hold me over. The line of *more than friends* has never been breached outside of my thoughts. I'm pretty sure she sees me as an older brother—or worse, an extension of her dad.

"Okay, we're getting burritos," she announces. Kelly leans back in the chair until her head is practically upside down, plush lips slightly parted as she glances up at me. "What do you want?"

To see your head hanging off the edge of my bed, just like this, before I fuck your pretty mouth.

The scent of her perfume wafts in my direction, and my gaze finds hers before returning to those goddamn lips. I envision grasping her chin and taking her in a firm kiss. What does she taste like? Is she eager and greedy or shy and submissive? Are her lips as soft as I imagine them to be?

"I've got to put this stock away. Order me whatever you're having." I retreat a couple steps to keep from doing something stupid.

"You don't even know what I'm getting," she counters while I load the remaining boxes into my arms and put some distance between us.

"Carne asada, beans, rice, cilantro, lime, onion, salsa," I call in her direction as I head toward my office.

She laughs. "Freak!"

As if we haven't had enough burritos at this point for me to not memorize her order, as if I didn't commit it to memory the first time she placed it.

In the stock room, I stack the boxes of towels on the shelf, then take a deep breath, dropping my head and shaking it. We've been friends for years, and friends know things about each other—but there's nothing friendly about the way I feel toward her.

We first met when she was a teenager, and it was like having a goofy kid sister in the shop. Being Clyde's kid, she earned the nickname Junior, which still carries on with our other two tattoo artists, Casper and Thor. It was fitting. She made me smile with her stupid jokes and quirky antics. After she left Minnesota for college, I continued to focus on my apprenticeship with Clyde, occasionally seeing her when she came home during breaks and holidays from art school in New York.

It wasn't until she graduated and moved back home that we really became friends. I had gotten out of a toxic relationship that almost ended my career, and despite Kelly being six years younger, she had matured a lot over the years.

She learned to hone her natural talent in art school, returning home with remarkable dexterity compared to when I'd first met her years prior. She'd also completed a piercing apprenticeship while out east and convinced Clyde to let her pierce at Black Rabbit. It was an easy sell; he was always so proud of his daughter, and rightfully so. She's a skilled body piercer, but when armed with a pencil and pen, the woman is fearless—which is why she became Clyde's newest tattoo apprentice almost immediately.

Despite being only twenty-one years old and having her dad as her mentor, she understood the significance of the opportunity and made every effort to practice her technique. Kelly may float through life as carefree and lively as a leaf in the wind, but she doesn't fuck around when it comes to art.

The shop was always chill whenever Kelly and I worked the same shift. Clyde loved having her around too. We talked mostly about our favorite artists, tattooing, and random shit. Our friendship was exactly what I needed. Her heart of gold was so bright in comparison to my dull black one—and she possessed the same creative mind Clyde had. It was inspiring to watch her genius unfold. Her style had evolved into something beautiful, reminiscent of her dad's early work.

After a few months, I began to notice her more. Paying attention to things I hadn't previously cared about, like the small birthmark on the back of her neck, or that her natural hair color is a warm chestnut brown—not the black she dyes it every eight weeks—or her burrito order. That was when I stopped calling her Junior and started referring to her as Chaos. Because that's what she was, my own personal chaos.

Somehow, the girl who was once like a kid sister had returned from school a completely different woman. One who sent my head spinning with how confident, creative, and gorgeous she was.

Apparently, I wasn't good at hiding it back then either, because I'll never forget the day Clyde cornered me in his office.

"What's going on with you and Kelly?" he asks, shutting the door behind him.

"What?" I've been asking myself that same question for weeks.

"I've seen the way you watch her . . . In case no one's told you, you're about as subtle as a shotgun."

"You're losing it, old man." I avert my eyes and chuckle, then try to change the subject. *"Hey, I've got some questions about those forms Billy is supposed to be submitting. Can we chat later today?"*

He stares at me, and I gather every ounce of denial I have to stare right back. Our standoff seems to last forever, but once he's decided I've been tortured enough, he speaks. *"Give her a chance to grow up first, yeah?"*

The son of a bitch is astute, I'll give him that.

He coughs a couple times and clears his throat. His cough has gotten so much worse in the last couple weeks. *"She's too young. She's not ready for someone like you."*

Someone like me. Not someone my age, not someone who shares a resemblance, someone like me. I raise a brow and cross my arms over my chest. What the hell is that supposed to mean?

"Don't look at me like that. You know as well as I do that still waters run deep."

I shake my head. *"I'm not interested in your daughter."*

His eyes gleam with emotion in the overhead fluorescent lights. Whoa. This might be the closest I'll ever be to seeing Clyde Everhart get choked up. *"I won't be around forever. I'm going to need you to look after her. Based on this conversation, I'll probably be a bag of charred dust bunnies by the time you're ready to admit it. But when that day comes . . . be good to her. Promise me you'll let her choose."*

"Clyde—"

With a shaky grip, he fists my shirt, yanking me down so we're eye level. *"And if you ever break her heart, I'll claw my way outta the great beyond and drag you back to hell with me just to bask in your infinite misery."*

He releases me from his hold and brushes past me, where I'm left standing alone in his office.

"I promise."

* * *

We sit across from each other in my office as we eat our meal. I swear food tastes better when I eat with Kelly.

"I finalized my design for the Bozeman expo. Wanna see?" she asks.

I nod, taking a bite. *More than anything.*

Kelly grabs her tablet from beside her and taps the screen to wake it up, then swipes a couple times and leans forward to hand the device to me across the desk. When I take it from her, she returns to her meal, and I look away before I witness how well she can fit her mouth around the massive burrito.

Swallowing, I adjust my glasses while inspecting her artwork. It's a realism piece. Her gaze is hot on my skin as I examine the casually floating astronaut. The buoyant posing is fantastic. Across from the astronaut is a deep-sea diver. My lips turn up in a smile. "Talk to me about it," I say, keeping my eyes on the piece while she speaks.

"I was thinking about Dad. I wanted something that evokes the idea of being caught between worlds, because that's how it feels sometimes. Like we're still together but just stuck on different planes."

I exhale through my nose and glimpse at her briefly.

"Then if you zoom into their visors . . ."

My fingers pinch and stretch on the screen over the astronaut's helmet, and I see she's added the reflection of the deep-sea diver's helmet, and vice versa.

"You have your model already, right?" I'm sure it wasn't hard for her to find someone to volunteer to be her canvas for the event.

"Yeah, she's actually local to Bozeman. So we're going to have one on her left thigh and the other on her right, facing each other . . . I thought about putting them on the same part of the body, it might get me more points if I have to curve them around a leg or something, but I kind of like the idea of the distance changing between them throughout the day, whether walking or sitting still . . . So, yeah . . . What do you think?"

When I look up, she's biting the corner of her lip, her eyes darting back and forth between the screen and me. I fucking love the way this woman's brain works. I zoom in and out of different areas, admiring the detail and use of shadows. "This is rad, Kelly."

A slow smile spreads. "Really?"

She holds her hand out for the tablet, and I give it back to her, smiling. "I love it. It's going to show a lot of skill. Keeping your lines and shading clean will give it the biggest impact."

"I'm nervous, realism is so hard. And I don't have any faces. The winners almost always show faces. Maybe I should just do something simple, enter one of the smaller competitions."

"Are you doing it for your dad?"

She nods.

I point my finger at her tablet. "Then do it for your dad."

Kelly has a unique style. I'm confident that in a lineup of five hundred tattoos, I'd spot hers in a heartbeat. It's expressive. Sharp. Bold, yet somehow delicate—and always whimsical. Clyde was always a little cheeky in his designs, that's something they have in common. He was a stoic man, but the joy he had for tattooing was always present.

"Have you come up with any ideas for flash at the event?"

Each of us is designing a few sheets of exclusive flash designs for Bozeman. Keeping the designs we're offering limited helps us know how much time will be spent on each client so we can fit more people into the schedule.

She chews while nodding, then swallows. "Yeah, I'm thinking of doing like western-themed centaurs. Like cowgirls and cowboys, except half horse. Get it?"

Like I said, whimsical.

"Very cool," I say, with a small chuckle. "Is that what you're practicing tonight?"

"Nah, tonight I gotta ask the hat."

The hat is one of Clyde's old trucker caps she keeps in my office; in it are a bunch of small crumpled pieces of paper. Each paper has a different tattoo style and subject, and she uses the random picks from the hat as a prompt because it takes away the decision fatigue. It's very Kelly to do it this way, leaving things to fate. She's into crystals and tarot and all that witchy shit. It's frustrating as hell sometimes, but it's part of her charm.

When I was Clyde's apprentice, he made me practice so many different styles before I landed on what my specialties were: traditional, black and gray, blackwork, and to my own surprise, surrealism. Adding realism to my repertoire was challenging. In the beginning, I was annoyed with Clyde for making me learn styles I didn't ever plan on using professionally. I was a fan of *his* work, I wanted him to teach me *his* style of tattooing. He was quick to correct me in saying no one would ever tattoo exactly like him, and no one would ever tattoo exactly like me, either— and every artist had a responsibility to find that out for themself.

Art was a journey and couldn't be kept in a box. Learning various mediums and styles would make me a more well-rounded artist. And he was right. Black and gray taught me how to master smooth shading, traditional taught me about design and silhouette, Japanese helped me understand composition, realism helped me conquer light sources and shadow. It was in this that I discovered my passion for painting. And I plan to teach Kelly the same way her dad taught me.

Leaning over, I grab the brim of the hat and hold it out in front of her to pick from. She makes a big display of covering her eyes with one hand while she takes a big pinch and draws three papers with the other.

Pick one: Anatomy
Pick two: Food
Pick three: Woodcut

"Hearts."

I shake my head. She's done hundreds of anatomical hearts already.

"Skulls," she counters.

"No." She knows what she needs to practice.

She groans. "But I hate hands!"

"Maybe if you sign more, they won't seem so foreign," I say, signing in American Sign Language. Kelly asked me to teach her how to sign because she wants to contribute to making our shop more inclusive. I've signed since I was little, so we often cater to deaf clients, and she wants to be able to communicate with everyone we work with—she's a chatty little thing by nature. Spending extra time teaching her ASL was a no-brainer.

"*I hate hands,*" she signs back with an unamused expression. Then pauses a moment to roughly sign that "*the knuckles always look like shit.*"

"*Stop bitching and get to work.*"

My mother was deaf. She died after being hit by a drunk driver, but I've never stopped practicing ASL. She's the one who taught me to sign. We have several clients who sign, so I encourage the other artists to learn. I even taught Clyde a little. It's a good skill to have either way. Kelly is a quick study; she's picked up a lot just from watching me talk to deaf clients, and the rest we cover with lessons or by making her sign while she speaks in our casual conversations.

Her phone dings, and she grins at the screen. *God, what on earth could this guy be saying to make her look so smitten?*

"What now?" I ask.

"Jason." She sighs all dreamily. *Give me a fucking break.* "I dunno, I just really like him. He's so sweet. Since Dad died, it's really nice to have somebody to make me feel good about myself. And who knows, maybe this will turn serious. I know that sounds crazy, but—"

"It doesn't sound crazy, it *is* crazy. You've only been with him a month."

This is the first time I've ever heard her express interest in something long-term with a guy. Usually, she's just dating and keeps it casual, or I scare him off before he gets any ideas. I'm letting her get it out of her system because once she's mine, I'm not giving her back. The level of restraint I show even letting her go out with other men is beyond generous, and only because of a stupid fucking promise I made to her dad, who I, unfortunately, have great respect for. My patience should be studied.

"Six weeks," she argues.

My jaw tenses. "You're only twenty-five."

"I'm turning twenty-six soon. Half of the people I graduated high school with are engaged or married—"

Marriage? Is she fucking serious?

"So what?" I snap. "Do you really think you're ready to settle down with somebody?"

She flinches, but I still see the remnants of stars in her eyes. Holy shit. Have I not been paying attention? Somehow it snuck past me that she's actually developing feelings for this poster child of mediocrity.

"I'm not saying I'm ready to recite vows with Jason. I'm just ready for something more serious. I feel like I've had my fun, but now I'm ready for the next step. I'm not saying I'm there yet, but I think this guy has . . . I don't know, *potential*. It's time for me to grow up, ya know?"

"If you wanna settle down, that's great. But you're not going to find it with that guy."

Well, Clyde, I waited. Kelly may like to leave her decisions up to fate, but when it comes to this, I control the strings. I've invested too much. I gave her freedom, but just because I let her wander doesn't mean I'll let her get lost.

"How would you know?"

I scoff. "Because I know you. You're dressing him up to be something worth wanting. That's not love, that's settling. If you have to chase love that hard, you won't find it."

Knowing she wants to be locked down is all the confirmation I need. It would be cruel to stand by and watch her look for the thing she wants most while I hold it behind my back. Love isn't something she needs to chase.

Her phone chimes, and she smiles down at the screen again. "I told him I had to work. He's pouting."

He's *pouting*? "Three-year-olds pout, Chaos." This guy is a clown.

She rolls her eyes at me and switches her phone to silent, then tosses it up on the countertop.

That's right, you piece of shit. Pout all you want. I get your girl tonight.

2

KELLY

"You still dating that fella with the bad haircut?" Herb mutters, grabbing a block of cheese from his fridge. Herb is my neighbor, a gruff old veteran with a soft heart, a firm handshake, and a voice that came from whiskey, war, and too many Pall Mall cigarettes. Most nights, I'm working at the tattoo shop, but once a month, we get together at his house and cook dinner. Tonight, we're making grilled cheese and tomato soup, one of his favorites.

Halting my stirring of the roasted tomatoes and peppers that have been pureed into a smooth liquid, I look over at him and blow out a breath. "His name is Jason." He knows my boyfriend's name, he's just being a dick. "And he doesn't have a bad haircut. That's just the style."

"The style these days is 'bad'?" he asks.

I roll my eyes. "I don't choose fashion trends, Herb."

Dad always said Herb never met a silence he didn't want to ruin. I enjoy our monthly chats, even when he's being a cantankerous asshole, because deep down, the man is a big teddy bear. I've known him for as long as I can remember. He was my dad's best friend for decades. Herb was the only one who knew what my dad was going through after my mom died when I was a baby, and they bonded over widowerhood. Whether or not they would ever admit it, they'd needed each other.

"Well, it's downright ridiculous. Back when we were chasing skirts—"

"*Skirts?* You're better than that."

He clears his throat. "Forgive me. *Ladies.*" *That's better.* "Back then, we at least knew how to be presentable. We understood the art of courting a woman, we didn't need those damn phone swipers."

"Well, who needs dating apps when you have the Pony Express, right?"

"Christ, how did ol' Silent Clyde raise such a loudmouth? Hey, speaking of phones, keep stirring while I try to find mine. I'm always losing that damn thing."

I chuckle and resume stirring, then raise my voice extra loud so he can hear me in the next room over. "If you can't keep track of it, I'm going to have to buy you one of those Life Alert necklaces!"

"You can buy me one, but you can't make me wear it!" he hollers back.

After a couple minutes, he returns to the kitchen, dropping his phone—protected by a brick-sized phone case—on the kitchen table with a thud. "What about that other boy that's always coming around? Logan?"

I smirk. *Always coming around?* "That *boy* is thirty-two. And he's not at my place that often."

"Boy. Man. You know what I mean." He waves a hand in the air. "I like that one. What's his deal? He single?"

I quirk a brow at him. "Why? You want me to put in a good word for you?" I'd probably put in a name for Herb before I would any other woman. Though I'd rather not unpack that anytime soon.

"I'm just saying, maybe you should go out on a date with him."

"Are you sundowning? We're just friends. And besides, he's my boss."

"That's kinda hot."

I choke on a laugh. "*Hot?* Did you say 'hot'?"

"What, I'm only supposed to say shit like 'swell' and 'dandy' and 'neat'? I had lady friends before—*hot* ones too."

"Yeah, I bet you did." I glimpse at the framed picture on the wall of him and my dad lounging in a pair of cheap red lawn chairs with a beer can pressed to each of their palms. They look so much younger.

"It's true. If your dad was around"—he nods toward the picture that held my attention—"he'd tell you what a Casanova I was."

Grinning, I glance down at the rich red-orange sauce. "If Dad was around, he'd tell you you were full of shit." What I would give to get a peek into their wild past. Dad never remarried; in his eyes, it was Mom or no one. But Herb embraced bachelorhood after his wife passed.

"I had some good lines, even Clyde had to admit it."

I turn the dial, lowering the flame on the burner, and spin to face Herb, putting my hands on my hips. "All right, let's hear it. What was your best pickup line? 'Hi, I'm Herb. I survived smallpox'?"

"Hey, I wrote them poetry, like a gentleman."

He is a romantic despite his gruff appearance. I've read some of his work, and it's true, the man's lexicon is lethal.

I step aside so he can taste the sauce and decide what he wants to add. He's particular when it comes to cooking. "You are a poet, I'll give you that." He beams, adding more salt, then some smoked paprika. I rest my elbows on the counter and cradle my chin in my hands while I watch him work. "Ever accidentally use the same poem on different girls?"

His silence is dripping with guilt.

The smile on my face spreads ear to ear. "You rascal."

"Only got busted once. I didn't know they knew each other." He raises his eyebrows. "Now, let's get back to your bad taste in men. All I'm sayin' is, Logan seems like a better match for you."

I groan. He's only saying that because Jason doesn't have tattoos. Logan and I are tattoo artists, it's different.

"Yeah, well, Logan doesn't date."

"Oh, like hell," he croaks, popping the lid on a jar of cayenne.

"I'm serious! And it's a shame because he could probably have his pick of anyone he wanted."

Once he finishes fine-tuning the soup with spices, I take over stirring again, and he shuffles back to the cutting board, selecting a serrated knife and the fresh loaf of sourdough he baked earlier.

"Including you?" he asks.

I roll my eyes. "When Logan and I first met, I was sixteen and he was twenty-two. I had an instant crush on him. Because of course I did, have you seen him?"

"Girl."

I chuckle at his imitation of one of my girlfriends. "We worked together in the evenings. I helped out in the shop after school, cleaning and taking care of whatever tasks Dad assigned me to. He was the apprentice, so we were in the same boat." I smile at the memory. "Let me tell you, Herb, for two years, I basically lived in that shop."

"Oh, I heard all about that. Clyde said you followed him around like a little puppy dog. Said your crush was about as—"

"Subtle as a shotgun," we say in unison.

I grin. "Anyway, before I left for college, I got up the nerve to ask Logan if he would ever see me as anything other than a friend."

"What did he say?"

"He laughed at me, saying I was far too young for him and that while he was flattered, he simply wasn't attracted to me in that way. I was like his kid sister. I played it off as a joke, but my teenage heart was crushed. Oof, that one stung." Knowing Logan the way I do now, I should have seen it coming.

He saws through the crust of the sourdough loaf. "What about the next time you asked him?"

Huh? I cock my head to the side. "What do you mean? I didn't ask him again."

Herb releases a frustrated sigh. "Then how do you know he's not interested?"

"Because he already said no," I repeat.

"Well, of course he said no! You were still a kid!"

Laughing, I reply, "Trust me, he's not interested. We literally joke about my silly teenage declaration. I'm not opening that door again. It's not worth it. Besides, I never see him with other women."

While I was in New York, the distance withered my feelings toward him, but if I'm being honest with myself, they never *fully* vanished. However, I've worked hard over the years to curb any . . . *temptation* I've felt toward him.

"You're being foolish."

"Okay, okay. Let's say for argument's sake I did want something more than friendship with Logan. What happens if he says 'I'm still not interested in you,' huh? He owns Black Rabbit, Herb! It's not like I'll ever walk away from Dad's shop. There would be an uncomfortable awkwardness lingering over us forever. I can blame the first time on puppy love; if I get rejected twice, then shit gets weird. It would not only ruin our work relationship, it would destroy our friendship."

"And what if he said 'Gee, Kelly, I think you're a real swell gal and would love to go out with you?'"

"It would still be weird. Business and pleasure don't mix. It could end disastrously. What happens when we break up? Again, I'm stuck working in Dad's shop, with my ex as my boss? Forget it. Someday I want to own Black Rabbit. It's not worth jeopardizing that. Sure, there will probably always be a small part of me that wonders what could have been, but we'll only ever be friends, and I'm *fine* with that . . . Besides, I have Jason!" I shake my head. *What the fuck have I even been doing considering all these hypotheticals when I have a boyfriend?*

"So you're just going to remain friends and wonder what could have been? For the rest of your life?"

His hopeless romantic is showing.

"Yes. That's all he's ever been and all he ever will be." *Despite the many nights I once spent imagining more.* "Sometimes a person can change your life in the most amazing ways without ever being a part of it the way you want them to. For me, that person is Logan—and I'm okay with that. Really."

After Dad died, Herb looked out for me, but it was Logan who stepped in and became my rock. That was when I realized I could count on him for anything. He's protective of me, and I don't know what I'd do if I lost that. Without him, I'm not sure I'd have gotten through those dark days alone.

Thankfully, this new relationship with Jason might be the thing to finally put an end to that stubborn-as-hell childhood crush.

"Do you want bacon on yours?" I ask, spreading butter over the sourdough bread and adding a hefty pat of butter to the hot skillet.

He inhales and blows out a breath, like he's frustrated by my answer. "Nah, I'm good, supposed to be watching my cholesterol . . . Add more butter."

"What about your chole—"

"It's a dairy product, it's good for my bones. Do you want me to end up with osteoporosis?"

I chuckle and add another pat.

By the time we sit down to eat, my mouth is watering. The loud crunch of the buttery, toasted bread fills the room when we bite into our sandwiches.

"Goddamn," he mutters.

"Mm-hmm."

I dip the corner of my sandwich into the soup and take another delicious bite, letting the melted cheese and tangy tomato soup meld together on my tongue. This is heavenly.

"I think you should ask him out."

I drop my chin. He's going to ruin my sandwich if he doesn't quit with the nonsense. "You talk too much."

"You sound like your father."

I'll never get sick of hearing that from his best friend. I hope I always keep part of my dad with me. "I miss him, Herb."

"Me too, kiddo."

3

LOGAN

As usual, I'm working late. Kelly often keeps me company, but this week is different. This week she hasn't been in as often. The other night, she had dinner with her neighbor across the street, and tonight, she's got a date with her toolbag of a boyfriend. Normally, I could escape into my art as a distraction, but ordering swag for the upcoming tattoo convention in Bozeman, Montana, makes for a shitty diversion. Stickers, drink koozies, hats—everybody loves free shit. I still have to put in the T-shirt order and secure a rental van big enough to haul us and our supplies. *God, I'm never gonna get out of here.*

The chime of the studio's after-hours doorbell breaks my concentration, and I amble out of my office to the front of the shop. Then I see my stepbrother, Camden, standing outside with a six-pack of beer. His furry Alaskan shepherd sits at his feet, wagging her tail. Originally, she was his wife Jordan's dog, but Camden has fallen in love with her too.

I unlock the door and shove it open. "Chicken Salad has to stay outside." *Such a stupid name for a dog.* Only service animals are allowed in the shop. There's too much we need to keep clean and sanitized in here; there can't be dogs walking around.

"Nice to see you too. I've already got her tied up on the sidewalk. Just picked her up from Mom and Dad's, they watched her while we played in Denver."

"Better not tell Kelly, she'll be jealous." Kelly loves their dog and will sometimes watch her when they're out of town. "Come on in." I push the door open wider for him to enter. I'm not sure why he's here so late. "Need a touch-up or something?"

"No, I'm actually here to ask for a favor."

Great. "What do you want?"

"We've got the annual gala coming up for Safehouse." That's the organization Camden founded to help people experiencing domestic abuse. "Wondering if you would be willing to part with any of Clyde's flash for an auction item."

He gazes along the wall of Clyde Everhart's original work—his flash designs. He painted each and every tattoo by hand. They stay up in his memory, and people come through just to take selfies in front of his art.

"I'll handle getting it framed," he assures.

"I've gotta check with Kelly first."

He furrows his brow. "Isn't it your shop?"

It's not about whose shop it is. "She's sentimental. I can't just give away her dad's art without asking her. I'll talk to her. If she doesn't have anything, I'll donate twelve hours of tattooing. Fair?"

He nods. "I can text her about it if you want me to."

"I said I would talk to her," I reply firmly.

He grins. "Still on your bullshit, I see."

I raise an eyebrow. "Feeling lucky, or just loud?"

Camden plays in the NHL, and I may be taller than him, but he's probably got forty pounds of muscle on me. He could kick my ass if he wanted to, and is known for being an enforcer on the ice, but even when we were kids he cowered from a fight with me, so now it's become part of our stepsibling banter.

A wicked grin spreads across his face. "Always . . . Hey, speaking of Kelly. I'm currently winning the betting pool for when you decide to make a move, so if you could do it sometime this month, that would be awesome for me."

I blink at him. "There's a bet?"

"Obviously!"

"Who's in on it?" I ask out of curiosity.

"Mom, Dad, Jordan, Hailey, and Alexis." I love them, but my parents, sister-in-law, and stepsisters have too much time on their hands.

Camden holds up his palms. "Don't shoot the messenger." He glances out at Chicken Salad on the other side of the glass, where she's flopped on her side, her belly gently rising and falling in relaxed breaths as she snoozes.

I roll my eyes. "So, was that all you needed, or . . . ?"

"Jesus. Can I just sit down for one goddamn second and catch up?"

I drop into one of the upholstered chairs in the waiting area. He grabs a beer and twists off the top before handing it to me. Then opens another for himself.

"So . . ." he begins.

"So . . ." I echo. I'm not sure what to say. I know he's about to bring up Kelly. I can feel it.

Camden sits across from me, leveling me with a stare and taking a pull from his beer.

I glare right back.

"You realize you're wasting time, right?" he asks.

He's always giving me shit about this. I don't know why he cares so much about Kelly and me getting together. I'm extra annoyed tonight because she's with Jason when she should still be here with me. I can't help but imagine her in his bed, and it pisses me off.

I bring the lip of the bottle to my mouth. "I'm biding my time. That's different," I say, before taking a sip.

"I heard she has a new boyfriend."

I scoff. "Yeah, he's a fucking idiot."

"Of course you'd think that. He's taking *your* job," he says. "She like him?"

"Does it matter?" I reply.

He furrows his brow. "Yeah, I'd say that it matters a lot."

That makes me laugh.

"What's funny?"

Leaning forward, I rest my elbows on my knees. "There's no universe that exists where we don't end up together in the end."

Cam shakes his head. "You fucker. I knew it."

"I've just been waiting for the right moment." Which I've recently learned is *right fucking now*.

He slouches in his seat, stretching his arms over the back of the sofa like he owns it. "Well, you better figure that shit out. Kelly's a great girl; if she likes this guy, then you better make your move before the two of them get too comfortable."

My jaw clenches. "What does it look like I'm doing?"

He tips his bottle toward me. "It looks like you're plotting all the ways to turn her boyfriend into a hashtag."

He's not wrong.

Camden glimpses at the furry mutt on the other side of the glass. "You could always do what I did . . ."

"That's cute, sport, but I don't play hockey. I can't just steal center ice and make some big proclamation." It was all over the news when he did it with Jordan. He's a walking cliché.

"No shit." He points at Chicken Salad. "I'm talking about a dog, dumbass."

I chuckle. "I'm not surprising her with a pet."

"Why not? I did."

My head rolls to the side. "No, Chicken Salad was already Jordan's. You just returned her to her."

He groans. "Fine, then *you* get a dog. Hell, you could pick up some stray off the street and she'll be all over you. She'll wanna spend every minute with the dog, and by the transitive property, she'll want to spend every minute with you. Or . . . and hear me out . . . you quit being a little bitch and just tell her how you feel."

"You realize Kelly and I are friends, right? I don't have to lure her with animals," I remind him. "But a dog isn't the worst idea in the world."

He throws his hands up and, thankfully, none of the beer in his drink spills on the sofa. "God, you're fucking pathetic. This whole intimidating, dark vibe you have going on is such a sham. Can't even tell a girl how you feel. Jesus Christ."

I smile and take a sip of my beer. He seems genuinely irritated about it, which I find amusing. She'll know soon enough, but this isn't something I'm leaving to chance. In order to keep the situation under control, I can't become hasty and skip any steps. The timing is essential. I promised Clyde I'd let her choose—*or at least give her the illusion of choice*. She has to come to the conclusion on her own that Jason isn't good for her . . . but that doesn't mean I can't speed up the process.

After Camden left, I was able to finish ordering all the promotional gear for the expo. I went through our quarterly profits to make sure we're on track and, as usual, we are. When I exit out of the spreadsheet, the last open window is the shop's calendar. *Kelly's birthday is next week.* I'm almost finished with her gift.

My eyes catch on the wooden lockbox along the shelf. Clyde gave it to me about a month before he passed. I stare at it for a moment before pulling it down and turning the six numbered dials to the right combination—his late wife's measurements. If I were to guess, I'd say they're probably the same as Kelly's—fucking stacked.

Clyde had lots of pictures of Nancy in his office, most from before Kelly was born. The similarities between mother and daughter are staggering. Alberto Vargas is probably rolling in his fucking grave that he didn't get a chance to paint either of the Everhart women. Kelly is all curves with a pretty face, the perfect pinup model.

I open the box to the stack of sealed envelopes. The sight of his penmanship is a heavy blow. He entrusted me with these handwritten letters to give to Kelly as she got older. There's one for every birthday until she's fifty. The man squeezed every drop of life out of his time on earth.

He lost the love of his life early, and even through his grief, he somehow managed to raise an incredible daughter on his own. I wish he were here to give these letters to Kelly himself. I flip through some of the nonbirthday ones.

WHEN KELLY FINISHES HER APPRENTICESHIP
WHEN KELLY SELLS MY HOUSE

I chuckle. Kelly will never sell that house; it's her most prized possession, and she sees it as a literal connection to her dad. I read on and my shoulders tense.

WHEN KELLY GETS ENGAGED
WHEN KELLY GETS MARRIED
WHEN KELLY BECOMES A MOM

These are the ones that make me nervous. It wasn't until a few months ago, when I found a letter from Clyde reminding me that my time with Kelly was finite, that I realized it was time to put my plan in motion. That was when I went out to Bozeman.

I can't stop her life from moving forward, but I can slow it down and make it work in my favor.

Behind the stack is the open envelope that reads:

FOR LOGAN: WHEN YOU'RE READY TO ADMIT I WAS RIGHT

In typical Clyde fashion, he gave me sage advice at the exact moment I needed it. I pluck out the note and read it again:

Stop being a pussy. Take care of my girl.
—Clyde

"You're a poet, old man." I tuck the letter back in the envelope and put it behind the stack, then close the lid and swipe my fingers across the numbered dials. *Stick to the plan. Be patient.*

I grab my jacket, my phone, and the cardboard box containing her birthday gift, then head toward the rear employee exit. I'm just setting the security code when a car whizzes by, honking their horn twice in quick succession. I smile and shake my head, dragging my phone from my pocket, anticipating the text. Sure enough, four seconds later, her message comes through.

> **Kelly: Go home!**
> **Me: Heading out now.**
> **Kelly: About time. I'm gonna swing by the coffee shop in the morning. Medium Earl Grey?**
> **Me: That would be great. Thanks.**
> **Kelly: Good night!**
> **Me: Night.**

At least the date didn't end with her staying at his place. Silver lining.

4

KELLY

I stretch plastic wrap across my dad's old workstation and set up for some fake skin practice. Logan promised one of the organizers I'd submit a piece for competition at the Bozeman Tattoo Festival in a few weeks. It's my first time having my work judged, and being Clyde's daughter, that's apparently a big deal.

Logan's won countless awards over the years; his training with my father was extensive, and now he's ensuring that my apprenticeship has the same strong foundation. He's an extraordinary mentor and teaches me the same way my dad taught him. It's a longer and more demanding apprenticeship than most, but carrying the Everhart name means I'm held to higher standards. I have a legacy to uphold.

Having my first competitive submission be a realism piece is daunting if I think about it too much, so I don't. Logan convinced me to ignore the voice of doubt. I'll always fall back on trusting him in the moments I don't trust myself.

After all my ink caps are filled, I start working on the flat canvas of practice skin. The fake stuff isn't the same as actual flesh, but it's as close to the real thing as I can get for experimenting and practicing techniques.

Peeling off the stencil, I do a quick inspection of its placement, then gaze across the shop at Logan while wrapping gauze around the grip of my tattoo machine. Just because I have a boyfriend doesn't mean I can't admire how attractive Logan Teller is. He's hot as hell and just as welcoming. If anything, it's safer to appreciate him now that we've friend-zoned each other.

Most women would take out a second mortgage for the natural highlights in his shaggy blond hair. He keeps it just long enough that he can run his fingers through it and tuck it behind his ears, where it stays out of the way during his tattoo sessions. His facial hair is normally trimmed up neat, but every once in a while he neglects it, and the scruffy, unkempt version of him is just as attractive.

Crinkles frame his hazel eyes at the corners, which is usually evident of someone who smiles a lot, but Logan's were likely earned with glares. He's more . . . reserved. Only a select handful of people get to see his gorgeous smile, and I'm honored to be one of the lucky few.

At six feet, four inches, he's over a foot taller than I am, which leaves him with a lot of real estate for tattoos. His left arm is a vibrant patchwork sleeve my dad did; he idolized the man.

His right forearm is blacked out, but he's bare from his elbow to his shoulder. His neck, back, legs, stomach, and chest are all filled with art he's accumulated over the years.

Everywhere except for that bicep.

From the outside, he appears threatening, but I've seen his softer side. Logan prefers tea over coffee, novels over television, and oil paint over a night on the town. He loves to create. When he's not at the shop, he paints stunning portraits in his loft. He's quiet and a bit of a recluse, which makes many people uneasy. Well, it's his scowl that unnerves them. Dad always said his still waters run deep, but that's never deterred me from wanting to swim in them.

And those glasses? *Fuck me.*

"The meteor that killed the dinosaurs was hot, too. Get back to work," I murmur under my breath while bringing my focus back to the task at hand.

In my peripheral, my phone lights up on the countertop, and I smile. I lean toward the screen to peek at it without having to take off my gloves. Another text from Jason.

Jason: Thinking of you.

He says the right things, but I find myself regarding it with the same appreciation as one would a generic greeting card. There's a certain predictability to his words—which should be a good thing, right? It shows he's stable. Relationships need stability.

Across the room, the wrinkle on Logan's forehead deepens as he locks in the tablet in front of him. I know that look, he's sketching. He presses the pad of each finger to his thumb while he studies his tablet.

It reminds me of my dad; he used to do the same finger tap thing when he was deep in thought. Logan is so similar to him it's spooky, which is probably why they got along so well. Both were quiet men, possessing their own unique charm. They didn't need to speak to understand each other. Their passion for art and tattooing was evident in their work rather than words. I swear, one time I watched them have an entire conversation that consisted of grunts, nods, and facial expressions. They had a special bond from the beginning. Which is why my dad's shop, Black Rabbit, was left to him. I had barely even started my apprenticeship when Dad passed, so I wasn't prepared to run an empire. Like my father, he's a bit rough around the edges, but his energy is calm. He's secure in himself, and I find comfort in his presence.

Once I'm set to begin, the buzz of the tattoo machine comes alive in my hand, and I dip the needle into the ink, ready to pull my first line.

Clyde Everhart is a household name in the tattoo industry; he's one of the greats, right up there with Norman Collins, Rick Walters, and Stoney St. Clair. The shop name is worth millions, but Logan has always been in it for the art, not the profits. I was a little surprised some of the ownership didn't go to me, but it made sense for Logan to take it over. Besides, there's no one I would trust more to carry on my dad's business. Someday, I hope to be part owner, but I want to finish my training first and spend a few years improving my craft.

I was twelve when my dad caught me hunched over, gritting my teeth, with a tattoo needle pressed to my flesh. He didn't yell, he simply sat down, took the machine from my hands, and helped me finish the flower on my calf—and then he gave me some antibiotics, and I wasn't allowed to even look in the direction of another machine until I finished college.

After graduation, I returned home and started my tattoo apprenticeship. Dad was my first teacher, but he was diagnosed with stage IV lung cancer. He was given four months and lived six. I tried to talk him into treatment, but he resisted. Personally, I think he was ready to see Mom again. His mentorship only lasted a few months before he died. After that, I didn't want to step foot in the shop for a while.

Behind me, I feel Logan's presence towering over me.

"What do you think?" I ask.

"Nice lettering," he murmurs, commenting on the tattoo of two fists that read *BURR* and *ITOS* across the knuckles.

"It's supposed to be funny."

"It *is* funny," he states.

"As is evident by your boisterous laughter."

That gets a small chuckle out of him, and I return to my work. The hours with Logan after closing time are my favorite. It's not uncommon for our conversations to slip into the early hours without either of us looking at the clock. However, even the evenings with him when we work alongside each other in silence are enjoyable. Being around each other has always been easy. The platonic intimacy Logan and I share is special; we belong to each other in a way most people wouldn't understand. Sometimes I don't understand.

He's seen me at my lowest, so I've got nothing to hide or prove when it comes to him. I need to depend less on Logan, but when I'm having a rough patch, he's who I rely on. He lets me have my feelings and work through them on my own timeline. I don't feel awkward or isolated when I'm emotional around him. He's helped me go through Dad's belongings at least a dozen times already. Hell, sometimes he even shows up without me asking. It's like he has a sixth sense for when I'm in the attic and need company.

Logan plops down on one of the rolling stools from Casper's station across the aisle from mine and slides up beside me. *Why does he have to smell so good?* His chin cocks toward my phone lighting up on the countertop.

The buzz of my machine eats up the dead air. I can practically hear the smart remark he's holding behind his teeth.

"Is he pouting again?" he finally asks, not bothering to hide the annoyance in his tone.

I grin and shake my head. *He's baiting me.* "Your condescension is showing."

"Who said I was hiding it?" Logan leans forward, resting his forearms on his knees as he watches me work.

"Tell me . . ." I begin. "When Jason moved into your brain rent-free, did you already have the place furnished and decorated?"

"I don't allow roaches."

What the hell's his problem?

"Wowww," I say, stretching out the word. "Was that cathartic for you?"

"It was. Thanks for asking."

I scoff. "God, Logan. Want to make fun of his appearance while you're at it?"

"I would, except his haircut beat me to it."

What, are Herb and Logan having secret meetings behind my back? I roll my lips, refusing to laugh at the coincidence . . . Maybe it isn't the best haircut. The corner of my mouth twitches, and smug glee rolls off him in waves.

Jason isn't perfect, but damn, how about giving the guy a chance? "It's almost like you can tell the exact moment he insulted the barber . . ."

"Logan!" I shout, spinning around and pointing a gloved finger in his direction. "Stop being an asshole."

He isn't generally the first one to start a conversation, but one thing he keeps his pulse on is the state of my relationship. It's part of his whole protective-older-brother thing. Knowing Dad, he probably made Logan promise to keep tabs on me, and now Logan's taking the job way too seriously.

"He's not—"

I cut him off. "Look, I've spent years casually dating and enjoying different people, but how long can I really get away with that? Those were temporary flings. I want a love like my parents had. Not every romance needs to be cinematic, bursting with grand gestures and fireworks. The best relationships are the ones that *last*. Every sparkler fizzles out eventually. Jason and I have an adult relationship—we don't need performative razzle-dazzle bullshit, we've got something better.

"Jason is nice. He's ambitious. He's responsible. He texts back. He asks about my day—"

"He asks about your day? Wow, give that man a medal!" His words bite.

On paper, Jason is a catch, so why the fuck does Logan have to keep scrutinizing our relationship? He's never this hostile with me. I've briefly dated assholes in the past and Logan never blinked. Now, all of a sudden I have something halfway decent and he wants to bust my chops?

"Just because you don't want love doesn't mean the rest of us don't," I snap.

He sets his jaw, glowering at me. I hope he sees the same blazing fury in my eyes as I see in his. *Shit, are we fighting?* I don't have time for this. I return to the tattoo, unwilling to let any irritation interfere with my work.

"How are you feeling about the con?" He asks it like a truce.

I take a deep breath and count to ten before answering.

"Nervous."

I've been to conventions before, but this will be the first time I submit a piece for the show's judges.

"Why?"

He knows why. "Because I'm expected to be as good as my dad was, which is impossible." My bloodline has garnered me a large following on social media, where I post my work. However, the comment sections are often filled with strangers comparing my art to my dad's.

Logan doesn't say anything, so I continue. "The industry has me under a microscope. I'm accused of riding his coattails, which is true in some respects, but I want to be judged on my own merit. Sure, he's Clyde Everhart to the masses, but to me, he's always been Dad. Just because I'm his daughter doesn't mean I can compete with a legend—and I don't want to." I huff. "I'm stuck straddling the line between wanting to stand out on my own and keeping his spirit alive by following in his footsteps to make him proud. But damn, his shoes are big."

"What did Clyde tell you?"

"Let the art lead. Ignore the critics and create for yourself."

"Do that. You can't control what others say or do, just do your own thing. If it's received well, great. If not, fuck 'em."

"Doesn't make me any less nervous."

He laughs.

"Anyway—new topic. Hey, I've got a good idea," I announce, wanting to change the subject. "You should let me give you a tarot reading."

I'm genuinely curious what the cards might say about Logan.

"Oh yeah? Why's that?"

"Well, for one, it can give you some clarity."

"And two?"

I shrug. "Might improve your love life."

He groans. "Can we go back to you being pissed?"

"I'm just saying, maybe there's somebody right in front of you, but you can't see the opportunity because you don't know what to look for. You could be missing out."

When he doesn't reply, I glance up to find him staring at me. I can't tell if he's even listening to what I'm saying or dreaming up some new tattoo design.

Classic creative behavior. I return to my work and leave him to his thoughts. However, he interrupts by asking, "Who says I'm not dating already?"

Laughter bursts out of me and I quickly whip the end of my line to make sure my shaking shoulders don't fuck up the ink. "Everybody?" I answer. "You never leave the shop. You're turning into a hermit, dude."

"I'm a perpetual bachelor."

"You're *celibate*," I tease. *When was the last time he had sex?*

"I've had relationships."

"Operative word, *had*. What about that girl you were seeing while I was in New York? What happened with her?"

"We broke up."

I wait for him to give me more, but he doesn't. He's never offered up the details of his relationship history, and I haven't pried. Logan doesn't share that part of his life with me, and I respect his privacy, but sometimes it feels a little unbalanced because I share everything with him.

"So, one bad breakup and you're done for life?"

There are times he seems lonely under his hard exterior. Everybody needs to feel loved.

I've considered setting him up with friends, but there's a part of me that doesn't want to. It's not that I don't want him to be happy, but I don't think any of them are good enough. Whoever inevitably steals his heart needs to be the best, someone I approve of. I suppose I'm a little protective of him too. That said, he'd benefit from having love in his life. Someone to help him loosen up every now and then. Let people see his less serious side, the side he shows me. Then again, maybe he should adopt a dog.

"Not saying I'm done for life. But I'd rather be single than date the wrong person." He raises a judgmental eyebrow at me.

"I get it, you don't like Jason," I huff. "But he's the first truly decent guy I've dated. Why are you giving me so much shit?"

"I just think you can do better."

Annoyance takes hold, and I force myself to relax my arms so it doesn't affect my grip.

"Well, good thing who I date isn't up to you."

He smirks and grumbles something under his breath that I can't make out.

"Can I read your cards?" I give him my best pouty lip. "Please? It will be fun."

He releases a long exhale. "Fine."

Yes! I turn off the machine and set it aside.

"Not right this second. Jesus. Finish this and then we'll see."

* * *

Almost done. I pull a line through the practice skin, concentrating on keeping my speed, depth, and pressure consistent, ensuring precise and delicate lines. Fine-line work is meticulous and requires a steady hand. It's very zen.

I dab away excess ink and continue to build up the color, keeping a close watch on the imagery coming together. Whenever I tattoo a person, I'm much more focused on how their skin is taking the ink, how the ink is flowing, making sure it's as close to absolute as I can get. However, with fake skin, I don't have to check in on the client's comfort, which allows my mind to wander.

As soon as I'm finished, I sit back and scan the tattoo for flaws. I touch up two small weak spots, but overall, the lines are clean and smooth.

I feel him hovering.

"See anything?" I ask, my eyes glued to the piece, sweeping over each detail for imperfections.

"Nope." He rests a palm on my shoulder and leans forward, using his other hand to draw attention to the piece. "Good detail here." He points out a couple wrinkles I added to the knuckles. He squeezes three times, like always. "Nice work."

"Thanks." I nod, setting down the machine and peeling off my gloves. "Okay, ready for that tarot reading?"

He sighs. "If you insist . . . But only because I know you're too stubborn to take no for an answer."

I smile. "Proud of you for choosing peace, I'm exhausting to argue with."

"Well aware," he quips.

In record speed, I straighten up my station and disassemble the tattoo machine for cleaning. I'm eager to do a reading for the self-proclaimed perpetual bachelor.

After wiping down my table, I gesture for him to sit across from me while I grab my cards. Once I sit down, he pushes his sweater to his elbows, exposing his brawny tatted forearms that I struggle to tear my gaze from. Logan takes the deck from me; it looks miniature in his massive hands.

"Shuffle and cut the cards," I instruct. "But while you're doing it—"

"I know, I know," he drawls. "Think of a specific question. Go put your things in the autoclave while I do this."

Works for me. He smirks while dividing the deck in two as I gather my things and head to the sterile room in the back. The whir of the machine drowns out the swish and slap of shuffling that echoes through the empty shop.

When I return, the cards are stacked neatly in the center of the table.

"I shuffled them with extra mysticism."

I give him a sharp look, and he returns it with his mischievous hazel gaze. "This deck is powerful. It does not enjoy being mocked," I warn.

He places his hand over his heart. "I wouldn't dare."

"What's your question?"

His expression turns serious. My body leans forward while I await his response. "Will the food I ate for dinner give me heartburn?"

I reach across the table to shove his chest. "Be serious. Did you think of a real question?"

"Yes." He smiles, seemingly amused with himself.

I blink at him. "So . . . ?"

"Should Kelly break up with her boyfriend?"

"Logan!"

"That's what I placed my intent on. I can't change it." He folds his arms and nods for me to continue. "Come on, let's see what your powerful deck has to say."

I roll my eyes. This isn't the reading I wanted to do for him. I knew he wasn't a fan of Jason, but what a waste. This thing with Jason *is* something, I just know it, and I'm going to let the cards put him in his place.

The first lay represents the situation. I place down the Two of Swords, which tells me things are not working out very well. Okay, not a great start. I set the second card horizontally across the first, forming a cross. The second card represents the challenge that's impacting the first one. Seven of Cups, which means there's too much wishful thinking going on.

I gingerly flip the third card, placing it below the cross. This one represents the foundation of the situation. I draw the Emperor, which means it's time to make a decision. Be assertive and forge ahead.

I know my decision and feel very solid in it, thank you very much.

"You're being awfully quiet over there," Logan comments. "Want to translate what you're seeing?"

I huff. "It says . . . it says maybe things aren't as great as they seem and that there's a decision to make."

"Does it now?" A slow grin spreads across his face. "What else do the cards have to say?"

I flip the fourth card and lay it to the left of the first two, which tells me how the past is relevant to the situation, and the deck reveals an inverted Judgement.

I swallow. "There's been a history of trusting people who might be dishonest." I don't like this, it feels like I'm being set up.

The fifth card, an inverted Temperance, is placed above the others, representing the present. "Right now there's a sense of discord. Certain things aren't fitting together and—"

"Certain things as in *Jason and Kelly* aren't fitting together?"

"*And*," I continue, "there are areas of distraction and neglect."

"Is that true?" he asks, his voice dropping an octave, taking on a more sensual tone. "Is he neglecting you, Chaos?"

"No!" He's giving me shit, but it almost sounded like he was flirting. "In fact, he's *very* generous. Besides, he's been texting me all night, I wouldn't call that neglect."

"It sure is distracting, though . . ." he mutters.

"Can I continue?"

He nods.

Next comes the Page of Cups. "New beginnings are coming . . . trust your intuition and find courage to love again."

"This is so cool," he says, sitting back and threading his fingers behind his head.

"You're being smug," I hiss.

"Are the cards saying that or are you?"

"I am."

He chuckles. "From my point of view, I'd say it's pretty fucking justified."

I can't help but laugh, it's almost comical the way this is playing out in his favor. The universe has a sense of humor.

"Come on, keep going. I'm having fun," he says.

"The following three draws are about *you*. So maybe stop acting like such a dick." The seventh pull forms the base of the four-card staff that sits to the right of the other six. I flip the inverted King of Wands and my eyes narrow; *now I've got him*. My finger taps the imagery. "This represents your subconscious motivations . . . *you have ill intentions*. When I look at this in relation to the first card, it says you're meddling where you ought not to and—"

"Hey, now—"

"*And* manipulating the situation!"

The corner of his mouth tugs into a sexy smirk. "What else does it say?"

The eighth card, the Queen of Pentacles, is placed above the upside-down Magician. "The deck says you're stable and grounded, reliable and nurturing to those you care about." *To be fair, that's an accurate read of Logan.*

"That's nice."

"Mm-hmm. Moving on," I announce. "This next card is a representation of your hopes and fears."

Two of Cups. "*You* want to be in a relationship. You want to find someone, you crave connection."

He scoffs. "Who doesn't?"

His feeble attempts at remaining aloof have me choking back laughter. I can see right through his bullshit.

Finally, we're down to the last card—which represents the outcome. I flip it over and my laughter stops. *Death.* He raises an eyebrow.

"It's not literal," I assure him. But I don't like it. "It means you're about to experience profound change. Something is coming to an end, and something new is about to begin. When it happens, there's no going back."

This worries me. I believe in progress and self-growth, but I'm really happy where I am in life. I don't want anything to change for either of us.

"Fascinating."

Maybe he's about to find the one he's looking for. *I should be thrilled, right?*

"Readings aren't always accurate," I remind him as a disclaimer. "Everything is subjective."

I gather my cards and swallow down the energy vibrating off Logan. I thought for sure it was going to say that Jason was a good match and I should stay with him. It's not like I'm going to pick up my phone and break up with him after one tarot spread. After all, everything is up for interpretation. However, something tells me this is going to be wedged in my thoughts like a stubborn splinter.

"Or . . ." he says, with his stare burning into me, "it's all true."

The shop's back door swings open with a loud groan, then closes quietly. I can tell it's Thor by the way he slammed the door. "Goddamn. We need to throw some WD-40 on these hinges," he barks from the back.

"Joining us for poker tonight, Junior?"

I gather my deck of cards into a pile and slide them back into the case. Logan's gaze finds mine. "Can't. I'm meeting up with Jason," I reply.

"You sure? We could use you to distract him while we clean out his bank accounts. We'll make sure you get a cut."

"I'm not sure he finds me distracting enough." The words fall out of my mouth before I can stop them. "To take his money," I add quickly. *Yikes, what's wrong with me?* Thor's footsteps grow louder as he walks down the hallway.

Logan smirks at me. "You want to empty my pockets, Chaos? Put your hands in and see if I notice."

5

LOGAN

Thor leans against the doorframe while I drag the card table to the middle of the break room. "The fuck are you so smiley about?" Thor crosses over the threshold and grabs a chair, flips it around, and places it next to the table before straddling it backward and crossing his arms over the back.

"Kelly gave me a tarot reading," I reply, dropping into the chair across from him, still grinning like a bastard over that tarot read from Kelly and the uncertainty I painted on her face. Tonight, I saw the doubt. She takes all that mysticism shit as gospel. It's one thing for me to tell her she should dump her boyfriend, but to watch her face in real time as the oracle backed me up? Glorious. I didn't even have to push, just stacked the deck and let her convince herself I was right.

"Did the cards tell you I was going to take all your money?" Casper asks, walking in with a bag of food tucked under his arm. For somebody who eats all the fucking time, he never seems to put on any weight. Like a goddamn tapeworm, good at hiding and usually up somebody's ass.

I raise a brow. "Pretty bold talk for somebody who still owes me twenty bucks for lunch last week."

Casper slides into the chair adjacent to me and crosses his arms. "Pretty bold talk for someone who still owes me six hundred from Vegas."

I scrunch up my nose. "Motherfucker, do I look like someone who goes to Vegas?"

Casper narrows his eyes at me for a beat, then relaxes and sits back, rubbing his forehead. "Shit. Who the fuck owes me money from Vegas?"

I do, but he was so blitzed I'm taking six hundred as an inconvenience fee. Nothing inconvenienced me more than making sure he didn't die that weekend.

"Probably some sketch client," Thor replies. He and I split the six hundred. "Quit bringing degenerates in here."

Casper barks out a laugh. "Says the felon who tattoos gang members."

Thor doesn't blink. He has a little side gig where he covers up gang tats for guys wanting to get a fresh start. He keeps it under the radar, and as he's not bringing me trouble, I don't care what he does with his free time. His clients know if they snitch about who does their work, he'll give their location to the wrong people. He still stays in contact with a lot of the guys he met in prison.

"Be honest, though, are you doing it out of the goodness of your heart or because you just want karma to stop kicking your ass?"

"Are you actually billing them?" I ask. "Or is this one of those 'good deed' things I keep hearing about?"

Thor shakes his head and begins shuffling the cards for stud poker.

"I mean, if you want to call pro bono identity fraud a good deed . . ." Casper mutters.

"For real, though, do you make any money on this?" The ex-con stares at me with a tired gaze, like he's waiting for me to finish cracking jokes so we can get on with the game—*he really takes the fun out of it.* "Or do they pay you in butterfly kisses?"

"He takes money for it," Casper answers.

"Uh-oh, lost some moral high ground there, Hawthorne," I tsk, using his full first name. "Might want to consider starting a Hugs for Thugs mentorship program to make up for it."

"Or free touch-ups on Mafia Makeover Mondays."

"Fuck both of you," Thor replies, dealing our hands. "If anybody fucks with mob bosses, it's Casper. How many favors have you racked up now?"

"Please, I deal in cash only. You're the only one dumb enough to keep them on fucking retainer."

"Favors are worth more than cash," Thor grunts. After years in prison, cash is just paper to him. Favors, on the other hand, that's leverage money can't buy.

I roll my eyes and turn toward Casper. "Speaking of, that guy still reaching out to you?"

He groans. "No, but his girlfriend is. Luckily, I'm not stupid."

Casper isn't swayed by pussy, never has been, probably because he's got the uncanny ability to charm the literal panties off women. However, he doesn't just take the first girl to fall in his lap, he's far too selective for that. It's all about the chase for him—anything that'll give him a rush. He lives for an adrenaline rush.

We throw some money in the pot and begin.

Casper peeks at his cards. "Wow, this is gonna hurt." He glimpses up at us. "You, not me."

"Why do we keep inviting him?" I ask, my question directed at Thor.

"Because if we played with two people," Thor starts, fishing a burger from the bag of food next to Casper, "we'd be playing Go Fish."

"Great game," Casper muses, gazing at his cards. I can't tell if he's serious or not. We ignore him.

"So, Kelly gave you a tarot reading," Thor says. "Still letting the cards do what your spine won't?"

I level him with an unimpressed stare.

Thor chuckles. "Rig the cards again?"

"Obviously," I murmur, looking at my hand.

I almost always stack her deck. I'd rather put my thumb on the scale than give fate the opportunity to be lazy.

She thinks I don't pay attention to that shit, but she's sweet-talked me into at least three dozen tarot readings over the years. Not to mention, the side project I've been working on for the last six months or so has given me a lot of time to learn about all her divination stuff. It's almost too easy.

At least I was honest in saying I've been manipulating the situation between her and Jason. That has to count for something.

If that weren't enough amusement, she also gave me the image of her pupils dilating right at the end there. She felt the tension between us and might finally be admitting it to herself. Whenever we're together, everything feels *right*. I hope the rest of her night with Jason is spent questioning every last word out of his mouth.

"Wow." Casper sucks his teeth and shakes his head, then glances at Thor. "So that's what rock bottom looks like, huh?" He nods in my direction.

Thor smirks.

"A loaded tarot deck? Next you'll tell me you jaywalked."

"Oh, fuck off. I've tried telling her to break up with Jason, but she doesn't listen to me. She'll take advice from a fucking deck of cards before the guy who actually gives a shit." I fold my cards and huff out a breath. "So yeah, I planted the seed that she needs to get rid of him."

"Hey, instead of manipulating a deck of cards, why don't you manipulate her pussy and be done with this fucking friend zone bullshit?"

Thor spits. "Try planting *that* seed in her next time. I guarantee it'll yield better results."

"He's such a Scorpio," Casper adds, showing his hand.

I collect and shuffle the cards while Casper neatly folds his winnings in front of him, then unwraps one of the burgers and takes a huge bite.

"Soon, it won't matter anyway," I add, dealing everyone another round.

Thor makes a disgruntled sound. He wasn't thrilled about the idea, but I will owe him a favor, and as previously established, favors are high currency for outlaws.

More cash is thrown in the middle of the table. I swap out two cards, hoping for a jack. Nada. Fold.

"That's your redemption arc," Casper says, pointing at me with his already half-eaten burger.

Thor sighs. "She's going to hate you for this. Hell, *I* hate you for this."

"She doesn't have to know."

Casper smirks. "Ah, yes, the plan to make her fall in love with you. Something you haven't been able to accomplish for the last three years, but sure, add a hard deadline, that ought to help."

"I haven't been trying the last three years, I've been keeping my word to Clyde."

Thor tosses in more cash, upping the ante. "If you keep going about it like this, you'll be buried next to Clyde before that ever happens. You're too old for this shit—but hey, maybe in twenty more fake tarot spreads, you'll earn her crystal privileges."

Casper's expression is laced with faux amusement. "Then you're only eighty tea leaf readings away from a séance. Sixty of those and she'll hold your hand."

"Yeah, for a fucking palm reading," Thor snorts.

They give Kelly shit for her esoteric rituals, looking for omens and signs from the universe, but they love her.

"How many palm readings until you get to first base?" Casper asks, shaking his head. "At least I know how to talk to women. You two are pathetic."

"I talk to women," Thor argues. "You're the one running thirteen background checks before introducing yourself."

"Asking 'You like that, baby?' and her yelling 'Harder' is not a conversation," he replies.

I cross my arms over my chest. "Thor's got a point. What's even left to talk about after you've hacked into her ISP and mapped her jogging route through traffic cams?"

"Oh, you're one to fucking talk," Casper replies, nodding to the pot. "All in."

"You sure you wanna go all in with that?" I ask.

Casper scoffs. "I've gone in on worse things."

"We know."

6

LOGAN

Water seeps into my shirt as I lie on my back on the unforgiving kitchen floor, my shoulder jammed against a cabinet while I inspect the water line to my dishwasher. *Shit.* I turned off the water main and threw down a couple towels to soak up the leak, but this place is a mess.

My phone chimes on the counter—a specific chime that only plays for one alert: *Attic door open.* Kelly doesn't know I installed a security feature in her attic.

In the early days of her going through Clyde's things, she would vanish from the world for entire weekends, drowning in her grief—dismissing calls, texts, food, and sleep. Then she'd walk into work after her days off like an empty, discarded shell of who we all knew her to be. It was bad.

I told her to let me know when she was going through his possessions, but it was always met with dead air, so I installed a device that would tell me what she wouldn't. It's not like I've placed hidden cameras around the house—though I'm not opposed to it—I simply want to know when she's in the attic, where she's possibly engaging in an emotionally draining task I can conveniently assist with.

I hop off the floor and head to my closet, changing into a pair of dry jeans and a new shirt. My phone chimes again, this time with a text message from Kelly.

Kelly: What are you doing right now?

It's her way of saying she needs help—*needs me.* If she calls, I'll be there, no questions asked. A flooded kitchen and busted dishwasher can wait.

Me: Nothing. You?
Kelly: Going through Dad's artwork.

That's a big deal.

I quickly tap out a reply.

Me: On my way.
Kelly: Better prepare yourself. I'm throwing a rager of a pity party right now.
Me: I'll pick up a keg.

She needs to get better about locking her doors; I didn't even need to use my key. Walking through the kitchen, I tuck a fresh pack of her favorite Australian licorice in the cupboard and head for the hall when I hear the music. She's playing his old Bob Dylan albums. The wood creaks under my weight as I climb up the attic ladder.

When I reach the top, I find her on the right side of the room, surrounded by piles of sketchbooks, framed paintings, and loose artwork. I raise an arm and brace myself against one of the ceiling trusses, then lean forward, scanning the length of the attic. It's a large space; there's a window at one end, but the rest is illuminated by two bare bulbs in the ceiling, each with a dangling pull cord. This is where she spends her weekends—well, Sundays and Mondays, when the shop is closed. Wonder if she'll ever turn it into a bonus room rather than a mausoleum for his belongings.

With the music playing and her thoughts distracted, she hasn't noticed me yet. A wave of dust motes swirls when she drops a cardboard box that reads *CLOTHES* on the floor and nudges it snugly beside a twin box. It appears to be a donation pile. *Good start.*

"Wow, Chaos." I whistle, looking around. "Really went all out on the pity party, I see. No food . . . No drinks . . . Damn, not even a single half-deflated balloon rolling around."

A small smile tugs her lips. She sighs with big soft eyes and tearstained cheeks, seeming totally overwhelmed but somehow still drop-dead gorgeous.

"If you're going to mope, at least put in some effort. This is just lazy."

Her face cracks and she chuckles, rising to her feet. I stride over, dragging her into a bear hug and breathing deep. Years ago, I frequently held her. One embrace in particular let me believe we had something more, but she was still hollow from the loss. I was just imagining what I wanted to see—convinced myself of a story that didn't exist. The timing wasn't right. *But now . . .*

"How are you doing?"

She shrugs. "I've separated his shirts and flannels, I'm keeping his favorites."

"In addition to the one you're wearing?" I comment, appreciating Clyde's old Jimi Hendrix tee she's sporting.

Kelly glances down and tugs the hem, holding it out in front of her. "I just wanted to wear it for a little while."

I hold her gaze. "You wear it well."

"Thanks. I wanted to wait until you got here before I started on his art."

She releases the fabric and inhales through her nose, blowing out a slow breath as she looks at the daunting task surrounding her, unsure where to start.

"It's like purgatory's garage sale. Can't bear to look at his things but can't let them go."

"Nobody is rushing you to do this," I assure her. After he passed, I helped her move some of his things into the attic so she could deal with them when she was ready, without the torment of facing them daily in the meantime. She said living within the walls was one type of grief, but looking at his artwork was another hell entirely.

She sits back down among the clutter. "Grieving is weird. Some days I feel at peace, other days it's as if a boulder is sitting on my chest and I'm being crushed under the weight of it. And his art? This is all I have left of him. Dad's soul is still alive in every brushstroke. *How do I get rid of that?* They're more than just his sketches and paintings—they're the most beautiful parts of him. His creativity, inspiration, and emotions. The way he saw the world. The essence of who he was as a person and how he expressed himself. I want to hoard all of his things like a dragon."

Towers of sketchbooks and artwork he's done in the past fill this section of the attic. It's everywhere, even his old dusty posters stapled to the angled ceiling.

"Logically, I know I can't keep it all, and it's not like I'd ever throw it away, it's gotta be worth something to someone, even sentimentally. There are more than a few tattoo museums and other shops that would be thrilled to have some of his stuff on their walls, right?"

"Absolutely. Nothing will be thrown away," I promise. "How about we go through the framed pieces first?"

"Yeah." She nods. "That sounds good."

She picks up a frame and holds it at arm's length, smirking.

"Can I see?" I ask, stepping closer. I move a box to the side so I can sit on the dusty floorboards adjacent to her. She angles the painting to show me.

My brow scrunches at the abstract piece. "This isn't his." I remember this from the last time I was up here helping her when she let me take photos of all his flash.

"No, it's mine," she says, handing it over with a chuckle. "I was probably five or six."

"Oh, well then, this is *definitely* a keeper," I reply, setting it aside in a keep pile. "Remind me to have you sign it later so it's worth something."

She grins, making a *tsk* sound at the suggestion. The next one she holds up is a watercolor portrait of her mom.

"Keep," we say in unison.

After that, it's an assortment of various framed flash sheets. "Cap did this one," she says, passing it to me. My eyebrows shoot up and I survey the aged paper in the frame. Wow. August "Cap" Coleman is known as the godfather of American tattooing. I set it in the keep pile.

The next dozen or so are Clyde's. We have the majority of them at Black Rabbit, but it appears he's squirreled away some extras at home.

"We could hang them in the shop?" she muses while shrugging.

I nod. "Camden came by the shop the other night. The Safehouse gala is coming up, and he was wondering if there was any of your dad's work we could donate to the auction."

"Oh." She pauses and looks back at the framed piece.

"You don't have to say yes," I remind her.

She smiles. "If Dad were still alive, he'd donate it." Sitting crisscross, she angles her body toward me, holding up both of the framed flash pieces. "Which one?"

"The tigers and roses will sell for more," I reply.

"Actually . . . let's put them together as a set."

I raise my eyebrows, didn't see that coming.

"You sure?"

She nods, smiling. "Yeah . . . It makes it easier knowing it'll be appreciated by whoever offers the highest bid."

"Atta girl." I take the two framed pieces and set them in a new pile. Now he'll get off my dick about that donation.

"Oh, this one would be cool in the shop!" She hands me a large painting of a panther Clyde did.

It's bold. She's right, it'd be a fantastic addition. The brick wall by the office would be perfect.

"Maybe that brick wall—"

"By the office." I smile, finishing her sentence.

"Great minds."

I nod and set it with the two she's donating to the Safehouse auction.

She hands me a framed jigsaw puzzle he glued together. "Don't need this one."

I nod and set it in a new donation pile. She struggles making a decision on the next three, but in the end, she donates two and only keeps one. Kelly pauses, gathering her hair in both hands, twisting the locks into a messy bun. She swipes the back of her arm across her forehead and scrutinizes the stacks we have yet to go through.

"Proud of you," I say.

"What?" she mutters, moving another stack aside.

"You're doing a good job. It's not easy."

Her shoulders relax, and she offers me a soft smile. "Thanks for being here. This probably isn't how you wanted to spend your day off, but it's really nice to not be alone."

"Not that I ever mind doing this with you, but just out of curiosity, is there a reason you don't ask Jason?"

"Come on." She huffs out a breath. "Don't start with me, Logan."

"I'm asking in good faith. I just want to hear your answer." I want *her* to admit it, that I'm better at taking care of her than he is.

She sighs. "I almost called Jason. My finger hovered over his name. You know I've been putting off this part because it's the hardest—figured I'd start crying at some point."

"He's never seen you cry?"

"Once, when I was telling him about Dad. It was clear he was uncomfortable. He kept looking around, like he was hoping for something he could use as a distraction. It's not his fault, some people just aren't great at dealing with other people's emotions. He tries. He's a sweet guy, and he has good intentions, but perhaps I'm not yet ready to share all of this with him."

I open my mouth to tell her he's insecure but then decide better of it. After all, I gave my word. "I'm glad you share it with me."

"Well, you have a knack for helping me decipher what is actually valuable, and you're a good sounding board when I'm trying to justify keeping something, even when it's not the logical decision." She grins, poking me in the side. "You're an enabler."

"Oh yeah?"

She shrugs. "In many ways, you loved my dad as much as I did, so part of me feels like you should have a say in it too. I trust you to handle his items with care and respect. You get it."

"You know, I needed you too after he died. We had to lean on each other a lot to survive those early months."

She scoffs. "I leaned on you a lot more than you leaned on me. That's probably when our friendship was taken to the next level—"

"Next level?" I question.

"I just mean . . . You were my silent strength when Dad died. You've always been steadfast and reliable. You're a rock."

A grin spreads across my face. "I'm your rock."

She rolls her eyes. "Don't let it go to your head. Jason is trying, and that counts. He'll get better."

Ugh.

While she goes through a few more, I pop the lid off a box of photos and thumb through them. Some are Kelly's baby photos. She was a cute kid. I wonder if she wants to be a mom someday . . . *How have I never asked her before?*

I continue flipping, then pause on one; she appears to be about five years old, with both arms wrapped around an absolutely massive dog that's as tall as she is. Her face presses into its fur, both of them wearing huge grins. This hellhound must be patient zero of her obsession with dogs and why she squeals at every pup on the sidewalk and asks the owners if she can pet them. I smile and place the stack of photos back in the box, then slide the lid into place.

"How are you feeling about the competition coming up?"

She snorts. "Petrified."

"You're good under pressure."

"I am?"

"Yeah." My lips twitch. "Remember when you pierced that woman's ear and she started screaming bloody murder? Pretty sure the other customers in the shop thought you were harvesting organs."

Laughter bubbles out of her.

"You barely flinched. The rest of us were ready to duck and cover. I don't know how you talked her down after that."

"Yeah, she was fun." Kelly sighs happily. "Hey, is this Dad's?" She angles another frame toward me.

It's similar, but she's right, it's not his work. I take it from her. "This looks like Scrotum's work."

"*Scrotum?* Who the fuck is Scrotum?"

I chuckle. "He's a fellow artist, Jeremiah." I point to the corner of the canvas. It's tiny, but I can see a portion of the signature before it disappears behind the frame. "Yeah. Right here. J. Yelnatz."

"Oh, I remember that guy!"

Kelly shifts her body against mine. Damn, she smells good, like fresh iris and orange. "Why do they call him Scrotum?" she asks.

"Because he was pretty close to being a dick, but not quite."

She's sent into a fit of giggles, and I pause, taking a second to admire how damn pretty she is when she laughs. My fingers itch to touch her, tilt that delicate chin toward me, and claim her lips. Instead, I force myself to look away and pick up a nearby sketchbook, opening the cover.

I turn the page, and Kelly calms her laughter, leaning over to take a peek.

"I love that one," she says.

Her mom is posed with legs tucked up, head resting on her knees as she looks out a window.

"It's achingly beautiful . . . in the best way possible."

She smiles down at it, nodding.

The next page is different. It's a portrait of teenage Kelly, standing barefoot in rolled-up jeans and an oversized shirt, painting on an easel and wearing a smile on her face as she dips her brush into the watercolor palette.

"That's me."

As if I wouldn't recognize her. It's like a black-and-white snapshot in time, back to when I first met Kelly. She was so young then.

I flip another page.

"Whoa." I bring the whole book into my lap.

She tilts toward me, straining her neck to get another look. When she recognizes the image, she smiles and sits back. "Aren't those great?"

They're realism sketches of her mom as a pinup model. "Damn," I murmur, turning the page. I've never snooped in his sketchbooks. "Man, he was down *bad* for your mom."

There are so many in here.

She laughs. "Yeah, the first time I saw it, I slammed it shut. Felt like I was looking at my mom's nudes, but he drew her the way he saw her. Each stroke was drawn with adoration, one line at a time."

She laces her fingers together and rests them on my shoulder, leaning in while we marvel at the provocative imagery together. "Do you ever think of doing stuff like this?" she whispers.

If I turned my head right now, I'd have her lips on mine. The air feels thicker. I swallow and pull back, staring straight into her big green eyes. *Fuck.* My dick stiffens before I can stop it, forcing me to tear away my gaze and think of Clyde. That does the trick.

"You mean when I paint?" I rub the back of my neck. "Yeah. I'd like to."

She traces her fingers over the paper in a way that shouldn't be as sexy as it is.

"What's stopping you?"

I shrug. "Finding the right subject." She's giving me an opening to ask for a favor I've had on my mind for some time now. "Will you pose for me?" My voice comes out rougher than intended.

Her eyebrows rise. "Me?"

"You don't need to be nude, just posing, emoting, et cetera." My throat tightens as I imagine putting her in different positions.

"Sure, whatever you need," she says, leaning forward and dragging a new stack of frames closer to us. She passes me one, and I cock my head to the side as I admire the bright use of color.

"Jason has asked to take photos of me." She nods to the sketchbook in my lap. "Kind of like those."

It's like a bucket of cold water dumped over my head.

Fuck Jason.

All I can think of is her naked and sprawled out, looking like living art, and him cheapening her by taking a picture with his phone so he can rub one out later.

"Of course he did," I bite.

She furrows her brow. "What?"

I shake my head. "Nothing."

"No." She rotates toward me and puts her hands on her hips. "Say it."

"Fine. Imagine he takes your photograph. Do you think he'll point his phone at your body and snap something he can show off to his buddies? Or will he actually capture you? Will he even understand what he has in front of him?" I jab my finger into the sketchbook, open to the stunning piece of her. "Like *this*."

Her throat bobs when she swallows.

"That's the difference between him and me," I snarl, sounding bitter—because fuck it, I am. I withdraw my finger from the page. "*I* understand the distinction."

She purses her lips. "He may not be as artistic as you, Logan, but not everything has to be buried under layers of creative critique. Sometimes, it's for fun, or maybe he just likes the way I look from behind."

There it is. My jaw clicks as I clench harder.

She claps the cover shut on the sketchbook and sets it aside. "You're being a dick."

"You're selling yourself short." I inhale and scrub a palm down my face.

"Why?" Kelly scoffs and reaches for another painting. "Because I enjoy sex?"

My lip curls. "No, but maybe I don't want to think about you having sex." *Lie. I have spent countless hours speculating that exact question, specifically* how *she likes to be fucked—usually with my dick in my hand.*

"Oh." She winces and looks away from me, appearing almost *insulted*—which piques my interest. "Sorry."

I pick up a few small framed prints and sift through them. "For?"

She shrugs. "I didn't know that bothered you."

"It doesn't *bother* me." I set the prints aside and look at her. "I just don't like thinking about you with other men."

We stare at each other; it's the most I've ever revealed about my feelings—and I know she senses it this time because her face pinkens with a blush, making my heart hammer against my chest.

She blinks a few times, then crosses her arms and tucks her legs in, retreating from me. "I-I think we've gotten enough accomplished for the day. It's getting stuffy up here. Besides, I don't want to keep you from enjoying the rest of your day off. We both know you need to take more time for yourself."

Shit.

My head drops between my shoulders before I lift my chin again, forcing myself to meet her gaze. "I don't mind staying."

She averts her eyes. "No, I'm good."

This is why I don't skip steps. I should have kept my fucking mouth shut.

"Okay." I sigh.

"Here, um, don't forget these." She hands me the three framed pieces: two for Camden and the panther that's going in the shop. "I'll bring the rest next week."

"Your birthday's on Tuesday, have any plans?"

"Yeah."

She doesn't offer more than that. Ouch.

Rising to my feet, I shuffle toward the center of the attic where there's more headroom. "You sure you're all right here?"

"Mm-hmm." She stands, brushing dust off the Hendrix shirt. "Yup. All set."

"Hey . . . are we good?" I ask. That's the more important question.

She pastes on a fake smile. "Of course."

"Make sure you eat something soon, yeah?"

"'Kay."

'Kay.

I maneuver the paintings at an angle while climbing back down the ladder and she doesn't follow me. *Fuck.*

On the way home, I make a stop at the hardware store to get the piece I need for the dishwasher. While standing in line at the checkout, I spot a three-pack of pink velvet hair scrunchies in various shades next to the candy, lighters, and other random shit, then toss them on the conveyor belt with my item.

7

LOGAN

By Tuesday, it's been crickets from Kelly. It's not uncommon for us to text over the weekend, especially if we haven't seen each other, but even when I checked in on her, it was met with silence. It puts me on edge. My more basic instincts are dying to corner her. I want to crawl into her head and read her thoughts. I'd like to know how much work I have ahead of me.

Casper is wrapping up a big session with one of his repeat clients. It's a massive back piece. I pause by his station and check out the work. A lifelike python is curled up, waiting to strike, spanning from the guy's neck down to his waist. He's putting the final touches on it with white ink to brighten up where light reflects off the serpent's scales.

"Damn. Well done," I comment, appreciating his work.

Casper straightens his back and inspects the piece. "Yeah, it turned out great." He returns to his hunched-over position to finish working. "You wanna grab lunch later?"

"I gotta wrap up some stuff in the office. My next appointment is in thirty minutes." With my fist, I thump the top of the partition wall dividing his space from mine. "Have you seen Kelly?"

He sits up and nods toward the piercing bay. I should have figured. I resist looking in the doorway as I walk past, but I eavesdrop on the conversation she's having with her client.

"Any plans for your birthday?" the woman asks.

"Yeah, I'm actually getting off work a few hours early because my boyfriend is taking me out to dinner."

"Aww," the woman squeals. "That's so sweet!"

Is it? Sounds like bare-minimum behavior to me.

"Where's he taking you?"

"Lupa."

The rest of her response fades when I shut the door to my office. That's enough of *that*. I plop down in my office chair and lean back, staring at the ceiling.

My jaw clenches. I grab the phone from the cradle and hit the button to connect to the front desk.

Frankie answers. "What's up?"

"Hey, I need you to cancel my appointments after four o'clock, I've got an errand to run."

Jason doesn't know it yet, but his time's already up.

8

KELLY

I wish this client were more of a chatterbox. I've never wished for it so much in my life. Some people love to talk while I work, others meditate, some just want to focus on the meaning of their tattoo, and others throw their earbuds in and listen to music. Whatever their choice, I'll always respect it. But right now the last thing I want to do is sit with my thoughts.

I blot away the excess ink from the skin and take more into the needle. Focusing on the tattoo proves much more difficult when my mind won't stop thinking about my last conversation with Logan; not even the steady hum of the machine can quiet my thoughts. There was more to his words than he was saying, but I should have pushed him more—instead, I changed the subject and sent him home like a coward. *What was I afraid of anyway?*

I've replayed our conversation on an endless loop. Each time, my mind seems to manipulate the memory into believing that his words meant more than they probably do. Like a lie you repeat over and over until it becomes the truth. I've even written it down on paper. All he said was that he doesn't like to think about me with other men—which could mean he's jealous, or the more likely scenario is that it's because he sees me as family. *He's protective.*

So why does the prospect of Logan's interest excite me? Probably because I spent years focusing on my attraction toward him and now the remnants from that teenage crush are being resurrected—I need to bury them deeper this time. *Which isn't easy when he understands me better than anyone.* I would love if Jason could show the same patience with my grief that he does.

I wish I'd never given Logan that stupid tarot reading the other night. Since then, all of Jason's shortcomings and our incompatibilities have been put under a magnifying glass. My relationship was fine last week! Until Logan started poking holes in it and saying words I find myself wanting to twist.

Nobody is perfect, I remind myself. Jason can't be everything. I blot away the excess ink from the tattoo. "Okay, I'm ready to start shading. Would you like to take a break first? Stretch? Use the restroom?"

The client shakes his head.

"Sounds good."

I swap out the shader. If this were a custom piece, I'd likely be paying more attention to the tattoo itself. However, I've already done six of these sexy maritime mermen in the last four days. I posted a flash sale promotion on Instagram. I'm not taking any commissions so I can spend my free time practicing for the upcoming convention in Montana.

Today, the Bozeman Tattoo Festival made a post on social media announcing that Black Rabbit would be in attendance. Casper said one of the judges commented that they were looking forward to seeing my growth as an artist. *No pressure or anything.*

My thoughts wander as I fill in color on the merman's tail, but eventually they circle back to Logan. I can't escape it.

How do I feel about Logan?

I don't have an answer. I don't know.

Sure, he's physically attractive, it's an objective fact, but I've always been able to separate his good looks from our friendship. Now I can hardly make eye contact with him before the butterflies stir in my stomach—which are quickly replaced by a heavy stone of shame.

When Jason takes me out for my birthday dinner tonight, I plan to count all the ways he's better suited for me. I need to stop entertaining ideas of being more to Logan. Especially when I'm not even sure what he meant in the first place by that stupid comment regarding me with other men. I'm lucky to have Jason. Other women would be thrilled to have a partner like him. Besides, it's a moot point, Logan doesn't do relationships. *He doesn't seem to do anything.*

Jason is optimistic and animated. He's a golden retriever—essentially the polar opposite of Logan.

Logan's more like a wolf. Many accuse him of being grumpy, but that's not entirely accurate, he's just . . . stoic. Spends a lot of his time in his thoughts, a place I'd love to vacation. I'm forever fascinated by the way his brain works. How he can sit in silence before creating an utter masterpiece.

There's nothing wrong with Jason—and there's nothing going on with Logan.

We're friends—*just* friends.

"Are you comfortable in this position?" I ask, before starting again.

They nod.

"Good, if that changes, just let me know. You're doing a great job!"

Yes, this birthday dinner is exactly what I need. Once we're sitting down at the restaurant, I'll be reminded of how great Jason is, and why I should be investing into our relationship—instead of searching for deeper meaning in Logan's words. A possibility isn't worth tearing up weeks of groundwork. Possibilities aren't a strong foundation.

Regardless, the best part of my birthday is yet to come: today I get a letter from Dad.

As soon as I wrap up with my client and clean my station, Logan walks up to me, holding a small box and an envelope. I smile . . . *my letter.*

"Happy Birthday, Chaos," he says, giving it to me.

I stare at the envelope, my fingers tracing the familiar handwriting, which reads:

WHEN KELLY TURNS 26

I press the paper to my chest.

"Thank you."

Then he hands me a small black box tied with ribbon around it. "And this is from me; wait until you get home to open it."

My head cocks to the side with an easy smile. "You didn't have to do that."

"I wanted to."

Frankie's voice cuts in. "Logan, your two o'clock is here."

He gives me a small nod and heads toward the front.

I have another twenty minutes before my next client, so I quickly tuck the black gift box into my purse and take my letter into Logan's office.

All the sounds of the shop are muffled when I close the door. I sit in his upholstered chair and delicately open the envelope, the one my fingers itch to tear into.

My lower lip quivers as soon as I unfold the paper to reveal the block of his handwriting.

New words.

As much as I love to see them, they're a stark reminder of his absence, and that ink and paper is the closest I'll ever be to him from now on. We're one-way pen pals. His words are just an echo.

Hey kid—

Happy birthday! Congratulations on your 26th trip around the sun. You better be celebrating and not wasting any time missing me today, because let me tell you, I'm doing fucking great!

I hope you know that I'm still so damn proud of you. I trust y'all are keeping the place afloat. Don't be afraid to keep Logan in line, I have a feeling you're the only one he'd let boss him around anyway. I'm guessing you're wrapping up your apprenticeship. Wish I were there to see your work, I'm sure it's stellar.

Twenty-six was one of the best years of my life, that's when I married your mom. She says hi, by the way. I'm going to give you some relationship advice since I'm not there to tell it to your face. I'm not even sure if you're dating, but if you are, whoever you're with better be top notch. You're Kelly fucking Everhart—never forget that. Your name carries weight, find someone strong enough to carry it. I'm sure you'll meet a lot of great guys, but you only have one soul mate. When you're young, it might be hard to tell the difference. And that's my gift for you today: the difference.

First, don't be expecting fireworks or rainbows or any of that bullshit. Your heart skipping a beat isn't love, it's cardiac arrhythmia. Second, you aren't going to recognize them right away, because the funny thing about soul mates is that they look a lot like you. You're going to be expecting some new face to waltz into your life and sweep you off your feet, but it doesn't work like that. Soul mates grow together. When you look into their eyes, you're going to see yourself. Got it?

Find a partner worthy of your heart. The one who reflects who you are. Someone who takes in the strays and observes beauty without taking a photograph. Who has art in their soul and fire in their veins the same way you do. Who inspires you to be the best version of yourself but treasures the worst of you just as much. Find your equal. Your second self. And someone who can raise hell just as much as you.

I'll leave you with this. There are certain things that every human should experience before they leave the earth: sex, art, music, and most of all, love. And when you find your person, that's the real deal, kid. That's what life is all about. You'll see.

Love you.

Dad

I look up at the ceiling, blinking, trying to contain the tears. I'm sure mascara is already smeared across my cheeks.

"I miss you, Dad. That was one hell of a birthday card . . . I really wish you were here for me to talk to. Things have been weird lately."

Glancing back down at the note, I start at the top and read it again.

•

"I got you something," Jason says, pulling out a long and skinny jewelry box covered in gray velvet. "Happy birthday."

I smile and take the gift from him, opening it. It's a beautiful necklace with a red ruby pendant.

"Wow!"

"It's your birthstone."

I pause a moment. *He thinks this is my birthstone? But it's May.*

"Oh? Actually my birthstone is emerald, but I still love it! Thank you!"

It's not exactly my style, but it is very pretty, and it's the effort that matters. I could be with one of those guys who doesn't even remember my birthday at all.

"Look, it even matches my nails." I chose a simple red dress and painted my nails with a matching glitter polish—I firmly believe in wearing sparkles on your birthday, and now I have jewelry to match.

"No, your birthstone is ruby."

"I love the necklace," I repeat, not wanting to argue.

I spent an extra half hour on my makeup, and tonight is supposed to be fun—I'm going to have fun. I'm done thinking about Dad's letter or the messy conversation in the attic with Logan . . . And I'm definitely not entertaining the tarot reading that basically told me my relationship was a sham. I just want to enjoy my birthday, eat a nice dinner, and have a good time.

He seems satisfied with that answer, and the tension between us dissipates.

"Excellent, because there's something else I got you."

My lips curl into a smile. "What?"

He swallows a bite and points at me with his fork. "I found this really great company. I made a few phone calls, and normally they have a waiting list a month long, but I was able to fit you in."

My brows crease. "A company for what?"

"It's an estate liquidator. They can come by your place and just take it all away. Everything in the attic. They have a bunch of experts who will appraise the items, find out how much something is worth, manage the art and the selling. They do all the work. You can finally get your weekends back, babe!"

What the fuck?

My chest feels too tight, too hot. His words finally register, and panic coils as I imagine strangers rifling through my dad's things. *No way!* My breaths quicken, but I force myself to drop the tension in my shoulders. *He's only trying to help.* Just like that, my mind is back to comparing Jason to Logan. I wish Jason understood that I need to process this in my own way. I wish he'd be supportive instead of just trying to take it away. Logan gets it, why can't he?

"Jason, that is a really thoughtful gift, and I appreciate the hoops you probably jumped through to arrange it, but I can't just let someone else come in and go through his things." I roll my lips together. "Some of it might not be worth anything, but it's sentimental. I have to do it at my own pace."

"I'm trying to make your life easier. You said you were stressed, this would take away the stress!" He pulls out his phone, checking his messages.

"I know . . ." I reach across the table to grasp his hand, stealing his attention back. "I know your intentions are good, but I'm not ready to move that fast yet."

"Just thought you might want to spend more time together."

He stares at me, the friction growing between us. I don't want to ruin the night. Maybe he's right, this is why we're feeling off, we don't have enough time together. We haven't had time to bond and maintain our relationship, and these things take work.

"How is your steak?" I ask, smiling.

He shrugs. "Fine. I've probably cooked better at home." He checks his phone again.

"What do you want to do after this? We could watch a movie at your place?" I suggest.

"I dunno, I've got an early morning."

Disappointment. I took off work early for this dinner because I was hoping for the extra time together.

His phone buzzes, and he checks it one last time before shaking his head. "No, let's do the movie. You're right. We have this time, we should use it."

I smile. "Yeah?"

"Yup. Let's grab the check and get out of here. You got all dressed up for me, I wouldn't want to waste it."

9

KELLY

We're lying in Jason's bed watching one of the Bond movies; it's nice, lying together. About twenty minutes in, he's kissing my neck and I find myself still focused on the movie. This is his signature move. If I don't seize the opportunity of half-assed foreplay now, I'll end up watching James Bond get *my* birthday sex—while I celebrate at home with a cupcake and a vibrator.

"You should take off that dress," he whispers. "Grab a condom."

They're in the drawer of the nightstand on my side. I roll over while he nudges down his boxers and strokes his dick.

My back stiffens when I grab the box—it's empty.

The fuck?

It was at least half full the last time we had sex.

The voice that comes out of my mouth sounds hollow. "Why are you out of condoms?"

"Huh?" He keeps jacking off as if nothing's wrong. "I dunno. Who cares, you're on birth control, right?"

"Jason, the box is empty. There were at least a dozen in here last time we had sex. Where did they go?"

He's clearly used them, and not with me. Sure, my schedule has been crazy lately, and we haven't had a ton of time together, but we agreed to be exclusive.

He pauses and shrugs. "I dunno. Are you sure the box didn't just tip over?"

My fingers probe the empty drawer. "No, you are out."

"Well, I didn't use them!"

"So, you just threw away all of our condoms, then?" He lives alone, it's not like a roommate walked in and took them.

"Well, no, but—"

"Are you sleeping with other people?" I ask.

"Of course not!"

I blink at him. "Then where did they go?"

"I don't fucking know!"

Is this really happening?

Burying my face in my palms, I push back the tears, then scoot off the bed and straighten my dress. "I want you to drive me home."

"Are you fucking serious?"

"Yes!" I shout at him. He's too good at lying. His surprise is almost genuine, except it doesn't explain the missing condoms. I can't ignore the facts sitting right in front of me.

The ride to my house is completely silent. I spared a glance at him once, and he looked even more mad than I was, as if this is all *my* fault and *I'm* being an inconvenience. *Unreal.* I'm done. Clearly I judged this situation all wrong.

Mentally, I catalog all the items I might have left at Jason's house, and thankfully, it's nothing important because I'm never going back. My bottom lip trembles. *Twenty-six sucks.*

As soon as he pulls into my driveway, I pop the door handle and out tumbles a pink velvet scrunchie. *That's definitely not mine.* I crouch down, pick it up, and stare at the object that doesn't belong to me.

I look him right in the eye . . . and I don't see myself. Logan was right, I've been chasing the version of him I want to see, but that's not who he is.

The scrunchie bounces off his chest when I hurl it at him. "We're done," I say calmly, then slam the car door and march toward the back entrance of my house.

"Fine, fuck you, then!" His shout is muffled through the windshield. "Enjoy your fucking necklace!"

When I get inside, I whip the door closed and toss my purse on the floor, sending its contents careening across the tile into the kitchen—including the small black box from Logan.

My arms drop to my sides. *Shit.* I didn't even open his gift yet. I was so excited about Dad's letter I forgot about the present.

I remove my heels where I stand, then slump onto the floor next to the gift, my back slouching against the kitchen cupboards as I pick the box up off the floor.

The bow unravels when I tug on the loose ribbon, and I gingerly pry the rectangular lid off; it tumbles from my fingers, hitting the floor with a hollow *thunk*. The air is sucked from my lungs all at once. I stare for a long while, unable to move.

With careful hands, I remove the stack of tarot cards from the box.

I flip through them one at a time; each has been painted with a piece of Dad's artwork that's fitting to the card. Every single card—*all seventy-eight*—hand-painted by Logan, richly detailed with bold colors and meticulous brushstrokes. I'm speechless.

This must have taken him months. How did he even get all the artwork? He must have gone through hundreds of pages of flash in my dad's old catalogs. Some of these we only saw for the first time the other day!

This is unbelievable.

Confusing feelings or not, the only person I want to see right now is him.

My phone sits a couple feet away, where it landed after throwing my purse. I crawl over to it and check the time. It's past eight, which means he should be off work by now. I tap out a text message.

Me: Wanna come over for ice cream?
Logan: Always.

10

LOGAN

I stare at the screen. She reached out. *Thank fuck.*

When I arrive at her house, I find her in the kitchen and do a double take. *Damn.* I'm not used to seeing her all dressed up and wasn't prepared for the wicked vision of her in that dress, with her bare back on display. She's a smokeshow. Kelly's too busy taking out her aggression on some Oreos with a meat tenderizing mallet to notice me staring. One after another, she pulverizes the cookies between two layers of paper towel.

Something must have gone down at Jason's place. Pity.

Thoughts and prayers, asshole.

"Wow, look at you," I comment.

Kelly spins around when she hears my voice. Her makeup is a little smudged; it has me imagining all the ways I could smear it more. This woman is a fucking bombshell. Her head tips to the side with a wistful smile. "Logan, those tarot cards . . ."

She trudges over to me and wraps her arms around my middle and holds me in a hug. I rest my hands on her lower back, brushing my knuckles over the exposed skin; she's softer than silk.

"Only you know how much that means to me," she says, her voice muffled into my shirt. "Thank you." I don't remember the last time anyone has held me like this before. The scent of fresh oranges in her hair is intoxicating.

"I'm glad you liked them."

"I love them." She withdraws from my arms.

My eyes catch on the open bottle of wine on the countertop behind her. I was too distracted by her figure to see it earlier, but there's not a glass to be found. I nod to the cabernet and scattered cookie crumbs. "Wanna talk about all that?"

"Ugh!" she grunts, spinning around and walking back toward the scene of the crime. "Not really." She wraps her plump lips around the rim of the wine bottle and takes a pull, then hands it to me. I take a sip of the half-full bottle.

"I'm not even that upset we broke up!" She raises the mallet. "Isn't that fucked?" She slams it back down, obliterating the cookies. They never stood a fucking chance.

Kelly broke up with him. I've had plenty of practice hiding my emotions over the years, and right now, it's paying off. Hell, I'm out performing half of Hollywood right now.

Stepping forward and brushing up against her back, I delicately pry the weapon from her clenched fingers. "How about I handle this and you grab us some bowls?"

"Yeah," she says, nodding. "Yeah, okay."

She goes up on her tiptoes, and the delicious shape of her ass is put on display as she reaches for the ceramic dishes in the overhead cabinet. *Not tonight.*

Doesn't stop me from appreciating her curves, though. It's almost as if the universe is rewarding me for taking their breakup off its to-do list. A spectacular view in exchange for services rendered.

Dusk—that magical hour of the day where everything is bathed in the summer sun's last golden rays. We sit shoulder to shoulder on her front stoop enjoying our ice cream. Vanilla with crushed Oreos. Oreos she pulverized in a rage-spiral over Jason—which is my new favorite flavor.

I nod toward the wine bottle next to her, the one she's been toting around like a security blanket. "You shouldn't drink alone when you're sad."

"I'm not sad, I'm angry. And besides, that's why you're here." She tips the bottle in my direction. "Are you trying to be my human wine stopper?"

"Maybe . . . Tight fit. Goes in deep. Shoved in at just the right moment when you think you just can't take anymore . . ." I muse.

She snorts, covering her mouth with the back of her hand. Drunk giggles spill out of her to the point that she starts tipping sideways, and I have to wrap an arm around her middle to keep her from falling.

Good. The less heartbreak I need to remedy, the smoother this will go.

She's hurting, and I should probably feel bad about that—but I can't help but revel in the beauty of it all.

Frankly, I'm thriving.

The cool evening breeze rolls in, sending a wave of goose bumps up her arms. I shrug off my jacket and drape it over her shoulders. She tugs it closer to her body.

"He didn't even have an excuse!" she argues, recalling the events of tonight and plunging her spoon back into the bowl. "I think I'm more annoyed with myself."

"Why? You didn't do anything wrong."

"I should have seen it coming. Been more aware. You told me he wasn't good enough. You saw it. Hell, the fucking tarot spread even knew he couldn't be trusted. I really thought he was going to turn into something more. We were barely together a couple months. Isn't that pathetic?"

"No. Jason is pathetic."

She sighs. "I think my bar is too low."

"Yeah," I scoff. "You need to remember you're Kelly fucking Everhart and stop settling for less."

She gives me a funny look, tilting her head to the side.

"What?" I chuckle.

Her eyes narrow, and she returns to her ice cream. "Nothing."

"The bar for men is in hell . . ." She groans, scraping at her bowl. "Did you know he bought me the wrong birthstone?"

There was a necklace sitting on the counter; that must be from him. I can't take credit there, he fucked that one up all on his own. "Seriously? One Google search to know it's emerald."

"Yup." She takes another drink of wine. "And doubled down when I corrected him, like, full conviction." She does a little shiver. "Ugh, I just want to wash him off me."

I set down my bowl, leaning back to fish my phone and stylus from my pocket, then open my drawing app.

"Maybe you need a break from dating . . ." I sketch out a penis, then turn the screen toward her. "Don't swipe on them if they look like this."

Her lips slowly curl into a smile as she savors the bite of ice cream in her mouth. She sets down her dish and holds out her hand, gesturing for the device. I pass it to her, and she turns her back to me so I'm unable to watch.

Raising an eyebrow, I pick up my bowl and take another bite, peering down the street. A car is parked along the side, facing us. It pulled up a little bit ago, but I don't think anyone has exited the vehicle; unfortunately, it's too dark to make out the driver. *Are we being watched?*

Kelly spins around and shows me her masterpiece. It's a much more realistic penis than the one I drew, though she's dramatically shortened it.

"Mm-hmm," I say, acknowledging her artwork while swallowing. "This Jason?"

"Part of Jason," she mumbles under her breath.

"My condolences . . . On the bright side, much bigger and better things await you."

She chuckles.

I glance at the drawing again. "All jokes aside, I can tell you've been practicing. You've got some talent when it comes to the male sexual organ."

She takes a big spoonful of ice cream and signs, "*My drawing skills are pretty good too.*" I shake my head. Goddamn it, Chaos. She likes to sign while eating because *It's fun to talk with your mouth full.*

"*You're going to get a brain freeze,*" I sign my reply right as she scrunches her face and makes a painful noise. She leans into me, laughing. It's contagious.

When it passes, she sits up and sighs, letting the silence stretch between us.

"Stop messing around with these *temporary bros* when you were built for a soul mate," I mutter.

She slowly turns her head. "What did you just say?"

"Quit wasting your time with those bros you always go for."

Kelly shakes her head. "No, the soul mate thing. It's the second time you've mentioned something Dad brought up in his letter."

"What was the other thing?"

"The Kelly fucking Everhart thing."

I lift my shoulders. "Maybe fate thinks you need a reminder."

She nods. "Yeah . . . maybe. Odd timing is all."

"Got any plans this weekend?" I ask, changing the subject.

She shakes her head. "Nothing. Probably just get some stuff done in the attic."

"Well, if you need a break from the fun, would you want to come by my place? I'd still like to photograph you for that series of paintings I have planned . . . That is, if you're feeling up to it."

Her eyes widen. "*Sunday work?*" she signs, chewing a piece of cookie.

"*Sunday's perfect,*" I reply with my hands.

She grins down at her bowl, pushing around the last bites of ice cream. Without thinking, I cup her chin, turning her face toward me, and use my thumb to wipe away the bits of cookie dust at the corner of her mouth before sucking them off my finger.

Her lips are soft. *Fuck, I can't wait to kiss her.* I've spent years watching her, learning her habits, likes, and dislikes, yet there are still so many unknowns. I'm desperate to know how she tastes . . . the sounds she makes when she's turned on . . . the rhythm she prefers when she's on top . . . how long she can be edged before she shatters . . .

So many damn unknowns.

If I were to kiss her now, I'd only be an alcohol-induced rebound and our friendship would be fucked. That said, as soon as her gaze drops to my mouth, I can't pull away. I'm drawn to her like a flame. I lean in a half centimeter and she does the same. That's when the car I was watching earlier peels out with a loud screech. She jolts at the noise and jerks away. *Shit.*

"What the fuck was that?" she asks, looking in the direction of the blur that's already out of sight.

That was way too close. I scrub a hand down my face. "I dunno."

If it weren't for that car, I might have risked it all and regretted it forever. I gotta get out of here.

One of these days, I'll be able to kiss her gorgeous lips until they bruise under mine. However, I'm not a bandage for her temporary hurt over some passive distraction. I'm the reason she'll never know heartbreak again.

"You've had a long day," I say, clearing my throat. "I'll clean up the killing field in the kitchen."

She avoids eye contact with me. "You're a great friend."

I resist groaning. My favorite title—emotional support staff.

"So are you. Come on." I nudge her and we stand together. After we stack our bowls on top of each other, she gives me another long hug. My palm cups the back of her neck, my thumb pressing three squeezes. "Go take a shower. You'll feel better."

Inside, I go to the left toward the mess, and she heads down the hallway on the right toward the bathroom and bedroom. It's not long before the sound of the shower echoes down the hall. I smile, listening to her hum a song while I wash our dishes in the sink and wipe up the abundance of crumbs littering the countertop.

As soon as the kitchen is sparkling, I make my way to the bathroom. Steam pours from the cracked opening. I poke my finger against the hollow wood door enough to widen the gap and watch her blurred silhouette through the textured glass as she rinses her hair. My dick strains against my zipper as if there's something I can do about it.

Her beauty is cruel. The kind that could ruin a man—and I'm on my knees begging to be destroyed.

Kelly's phone sits within reach on the bathroom counter, so I swipe it and unlock it with her code: Clyde's birthday. She uses it for everything. I block Jason's phone number and any other method he might have of contacting her. Then I add a location tracker. Once I've finished syncing it to my phone, I lock her screen and place it on the bathroom counter exactly how she had it. I spy on her until she turns off the water, and then I back out of the hallway and slip out the door.

11

KELLY

"Dad, I could really use your help right now," I say into the still air. "Do you want to keep your Blues Traveler albums?"

No answer.

Thumbing through the record sleeves, I admire the variety he collected. Celine Dion . . . Talking Heads . . . King Gizzard and the Lizard Wizard. "Your taste is eclectic, that's for sure," I mutter.

I raise my voice louder—so he can hear me. "Okay, I'll save these for next week, but I want you to think about them until then. I need an answer by end of day Saturday, got it?" I should probably check to see what time—*oh fuck!* It's after six o'clock, and I told Logan I would help him with that photo shoot. I open my text thread with Logan.

Me: I'm so sorry! I lost track of time, is it too late for photos?

If he was hoping to shoot using natural light, I won't get there in time before the sun starts to set. Especially since I still need to clean up before I go since I'm covered in dust.

Logan: Never too late. I've got enough lighting.
Me: I'm going to take a quick shower and I'll head over. Does it matter what I wear?
Logan: Nothing baggy, something comfortable.

My stomach growls. I haven't eaten since this morning.

Me: Have you eaten yet?

Logan: No, we can order in though.
Me: I'll pick up dinner. Burgers from Matt's?
Logan: Sounds great.

A little over an hour later, I'm pressing the buzzer at his loft with a brown bag of greasy food in hand. "It's me," I say into the speaker. The door unlocks and I pull it open, then press the 6 to the top floor once I'm in the elevator. The round white button glows as the lift climbs higher.

Once I exit, I make my way to his front door and let myself in. I don't know when we started just walking into each other's houses, but we've been doing it for years.

Stepping over the threshold, I enter his loft and my gaze rises to the tall elevated ceiling that reaches above both floors. His place suits him, artsy and rough around the edges, but not in a pretentious kind of way. Large area rugs sprawl across the aged wooden floorboards, softening up the living spaces. The interior walls are a mix of concrete and red brick, showcasing a few large pieces from his favorite artists. On the adjacent wall, gridded windows rise to meet the industrial ceiling. The older glass is divided by black mullions, and fresh air wafts through a few of the panels that are tilted outward, bringing with it the smell of spring.

His bedroom loft and art studio are accessible by a curved metal staircase that climbs to the second level; the foot of the bed faces the windows and skyline and is just barely visible from where I stand.

Tonight's sunset is stunning, spilling rays of warm light across the floorboards. It must be incredible to wake up with a panorama of the city every morning. It's not a huge space, but the open floor stretches it wider, and the view takes care of the rest.

He gives me a quick hug. "Hi."

"Sorry I'm late," I say, handing him the food.

"How was your epic quest in the attic?" he asks over his shoulder, heading toward the kitchen.

As usual, time slipped away from me. Logan texted earlier that morning confirming our plans and asking if I needed help with Dad's collection of vinyl, but I told him I was fine and that I'd catch up with him later.

"Actually . . . really good." I hooked up his record player and an old banged-up speaker, then danced in circles among the dust and memories, jamming out the way we used to when he was still around. "It was more therapeutic than I expected."

He smiles, and I toe off my shoes, following him into the kitchen. I spot the tall studio lights he's set up for later. I decided to go with a pair of black leggings and a fitted white tee to ensure that he can easily reference my figure later, when he starts painting. I skipped the bra in case he's planning on painting nudes. Depending on the poses he has in mind, I don't want it to impact the natural human form. At least, that's the professional justification I'm going with. I posed nude in art school for the extra cash, it's no big deal.

Padding around the granite island, I open the fridge for something to drink.

"Ooh, you got one of the barrel-aged stouts from Citra?" The brewery only made a limited batch, and it's sold out everywhere. I've been dying to get my hands on one.

"All yours," he replies, dumping out the signature crispy tater tots onto the plates. "I had one yesterday. They're pretty good."

"Rain check. I'm not ready to jump into something that heavy. What are you drinking?"

"Old-fashioned. You want one?" He plucks an orange from the bowl, already knowing my answer.

"If you're making them, I can't say no."

I perch on the wooden barstool across from him, leaning forward with my elbows on the counter, and admire the way he muddles the sugar, citrus, and bitters—the way his forearms tense and tighten is like a performance all on its own.

"What kind of whiskey are we drinking tonight?"

He smirks, pulling the stopper from the glass decanter. "The good stuff."

After pouring, Logan grips the orange in one hand while slicing the paring knife through the peel, forming a slow, precise spiral. He twists it over the glass, releasing the oils and dropping it into the smoky amber liquor.

"Beautiful."

He slides the cocktail in front of me. "Cheers."

"Cheers." I bring the drink to my lips, letting the warmth of the whiskey coat my tongue, savoring it as it rolls down my throat. *It's delicious.* He seems satisfied by my appreciative sigh.

Setting my glass down, I arrange our food on the plates he laid out for us while he finishes wiping down the counter. "Let's eat. I'm starving."

He raises a brow. "Forget to eat lunch again?"

"Hey, you're guilty of it too." It's not uncommon for us to become caught up in our work once we begin. One of the many similarities we share.

We catch up on our days while devouring our burgers. His gaze seems to track my mouth between bites. It's the same easy, casual conversation we've had a hundred times before, but now there's a hum beneath it that quickens my pulse.

After dinner, I find myself staring at Logan as he preps the space, all six feet, four inches of quiet dominance. He adjusts one of the lights, dimming it to create a softer ambiance. He's focused and controlled as he works. His calculating eyes are framed by those goddamn glasses that drive women wild—and I'm no exception.

While he sets up his camera and tests the lighting, I wander toward the giant windows, drawn to the towering buildings silhouetted by a technicolor sky. The cocktail in my hand expertly balances the ratio of smoke and citrus—the flavors lingering on my taste buds. With each sip, I grow more relaxed. As darkness falls over the city, it's transformed into something magical, sparkling like a night sky.

He brushes up behind me, and I almost lean back into his broad chest. My cheeks heat with embarrassment when I realize he's reaching for the open windows—not me. The temperature has dipped since the sun melted below the horizon.

"Ready?" he asks.

"Mm-hmm," I answer, lowering my chin. I recall the other night when, for a split second, I thought he might kiss me. Between the wine and the breakup, I probably wouldn't have stopped him; my emotions were all over the place. I shake away the intrusive thoughts and remind myself what I'm here to do.

"Where should I be?" Waiting for direction, I peel off my socks and toss them toward my shoes at the front door.

"First, I want you on the sofa," he instructs, moving the coffee table out of the way. "Lay on your back." His voice takes a deeper tone. I've teased him in the past that he should use his bossy voice around women more, it's sexy. But at this moment, I'm glad he's using it with me and not someone else.

I point to the left side of the firm leather sofa. "My head at this end?"

He nods while I get settled.

"So, what kind of mood are we going for?" I ask, letting down my hair from the ponytail. "Something somber? Some bleak chic?"

"Seductive."

I swallow.

"Just you," he adds.

Damn.

When it comes to men, there's not many who can compete with Logan. He's a terrific friend and probably an even better partner—if he were to give love half a chance. He watches out for the ones he cares about, protective with an edge of danger.

Does he take women home? Despite how often I joke about him being celibate, I can't imagine that's actually true. He's far too attractive. His sex life isn't any of my business, but that doesn't stop it from slipping into my thoughts anyway. It steals my attention more than I'd like to admit.

He snaps a few quick shots, then tweaks the settings on his camera before crouching on his knees. "Turn your head toward me a little more," he says, then adjusts the lens. The shutter clicks a few times.

"Arch your back for me."

I chuckle. "For you, huh?"

"Kelly . . ." He draws out my name like a warning.

"Yes, sir," I purr, flashing him my best sex eyes in an attempt to fluster him.

His tone sharpens. "Do that again."

So commanding.

"What? Call you *sir*?"

He tilts his chin. "You know what. Give me that look again."

I swallow, the charged air settling as I meet his suggestive gaze once more. Warmth washes over my cheeks and I don't shy away—I bathe in it. I've posed before, but never has it felt so . . . intoxicating. The way I'm able to hold his attention is like wielding a powerful weapon I didn't know I possessed. It's addicting and I like it.

Maybe it's the warm cocktail in my veins or the soft lighting, but this time, I don't bother pretending. I drop my guard and give him a good look at the temptation I've kept buried for too long.

"Your eyes are so fucking perfect," he whispers.

There's no way I'm not visibly blushing. He snaps a few more photos. "Are you comfortable laying on the floor?"

"Sure!" I shoot off the sofa, my voice way too loud. *Be more obvious.*

"Right here." He points to the rug.

Once I'm on my back, he sinks to his knees and straddles my midsection. *Whoa.*

"This okay?" he asks.

I bob my head up and down.

He sets his camera on the floor. "Do you mind if I adjust your hair?"

"No." I lift my head, and he plants a palm next to my ear, using his free hand to fan out the strands to his liking. Then he picks up his camera again, aiming it at me.

"Look right into the lens, Kelly."

My chest rises and falls as I peer up at him.

"Stunning." He smiles and gives a subtle shake of his head behind the camera. "You're so good at that."

My laugh is awkward and forced. He smiles wider.

"You don't have to be shy," he says. "It's just me."

I nod. "I know."

"Are you uncomfortable?"

In the best way. "No."

Quit sexualizing him. You're making it weird.

"Good."

This is one of the most arousing nights I've experienced in a while. It's hotter than any foreplay I had with Jason, yet Logan and I are both fully clothed. I remind myself that the tension between us is in my imagination only. Dad always said I was great at playing make-believe.

My gaze travels to his neck and broad shoulders, tracing the tattoos that peek out of his collar. "Eyes on me, remember."

I refocus. "Sorry."

"Don't apologize. You're doing great."

My inhibitions lower every time he praises me. He pauses shooting to stand, retreating a few steps. "Okay, now sit up, lean back on your palms, and pull your knees up."

I switch to a sitting position, and he drops to a crouch in front of me.

"Have you ever considered doing boudoir photography?" He can create a vibe, that's for sure.

He smirks. "Inviting women over to strip down and let me take my time with them? No, but it sounds like fun. I like where your head's at."

I huff a breath, ignoring the tinge of jealousy. "You just ruined it."

"I'm only teasing you." He laughs. "It's cute you think I'd photograph anyone else like this." His massive hand cups the back of my calf, and he slides it over a few inches, then winks at me. "Keep your thighs open."

Logan is sexy as hell when he's behind a lens, bossing me around. Especially when he uses that calm, controlled tone—the one that makes me want to push back, just to see what happens.

He lowers his camera, eyes fixed on me. It's not professional, hell, it's predatory, like he's been imagining stripping me down and taking his time. *What is he waiting for?*

"Aren't you going to take the photo?" I mumble.

"This one's not for the camera. This one stays with me—safe in my head, where I can look at it whenever I want."

Holy hell.

His voice is quiet but rough. It's what I imagine he sounds like first thing in the morning, that sexy rasp after a night of little sleep. The image of waking up naked next to him forms in my thoughts. *No, no way.* I shake my head. Blistering heat and nervous giggles bubble to the surface, which only adds to my embarrassment.

"You're such a freak."

My laughter seems to break Logan out of his silly trance. He raises his camera again, taking a couple photos.

"You like it," he whispers from behind the lens.

My teeth bite into my lower lip as a flutter spreads throughout my chest. He's right . . . *I kinda do.* Logan hits the shutter at least half a dozen times in quick succession. I blink out of the haze. Shit. I shouldn't have had that old-fashioned. I'm *far* too relaxed. This is getting out of control, he must be messing with me.

Logan delves a hand into my hair again, fluffing it up. It's hard to resist closing my eyes and giving in to the sensation. "When was the last time you posed?"

I clear my throat. "Not since college, for figure painting."

"Nude?"

"Sometimes."

"Hm." His jaw tightens along with the rest of his features.

"Oh, don't be like that. It's not sexual." *We're back to that conversation from the attic.*

"I just don't like the idea of you on display for a room full of people."

"Why, 'cause I'm like your sister?" I avert my gaze.

He smirks. "If I thought of you like a sister, we wouldn't be here right now." I swear a record scratches. *What did he just say?*

My face slackens. "You don't?"

"No." He clicks the shutter. "Keep right like that."

Oh. I hold still while he works. My thoughts are racing, but none will hold still long enough for me to give them attention.

"Why do you seem so shocked?" He chuckles from behind the camera. "Focus on me, Chaos."

Wait—what the hell is happening right now?

"There she is . . . Those are the eyes I want." His grin is wicked. "Fuck, the way you're staring has me almost believing it."

There's no way he just said what I think he said. I must have misheard him. I blink a few times. "You once said I was like a sister to you. You used to call me Junior . . ."

It was easier to pose for him when there wasn't a chance in hell of him being attracted to me. But . . . what is he saying?

Earlier, I brushed off his flirtation as him helping to set the mood for photos or trying to get a rise out of me, but now I can't help but wonder if it was more than that.

I gaze into the camera lens.

"Why do you think I started calling you Chaos?"

Jesus Christ.

He snaps more photos.

Nope. *Nope, nope, nope.* I ignore the intrusive thoughts of him. This is the product of alcohol and an inconvenient ovulation schedule. I can't let him muddy my emotions. Thankfully, I don't need to speak to him, I just need to complete the task at hand: hold still and take direction. So that's exactly what I do.

He remains quiet and professional for the rest of the shoot. If I didn't know any better, I'd say it was by design, forcing me to sit with my thoughts. After two hours, we wrap up.

"Thanks, Kel. You did a fantastic job," he comments, flipping through the shots he took on the small camera screen. "I think these will turn out perfect."

He sounds so pragmatic. *Was that it? Was it all for show?*

"Anything . . . for a friend." I put on my socks and shoes, waiting for him to say something. Correct me, laugh at the statement, shake his head—*anything.*

He doesn't so much as glance in my direction.

Logan simply hands me my jacket to send me on my way. "I'll edit these tomorrow. Let me know if you need any help moving boxes out of the attic this weekend."

He seems completely unfazed by my phrasing, and I hate the sinking feeling in my stomach. We've only ever just been friends. He's made that clear over and over, yet I keep seeking more. The tendrils of my teenage crush have me in their clutch again.

Logan and I walk to my car parked outside, and I climb into the driver's seat.

"Drive safe," he says.

I nod and shut my door, eager to get out of here. As soon as I pull out of my parking space and turn the block, a lump forms in my throat and my eyes swell with tears.

12

LOGAN

Fuck me, these photos are incredible. Being on the receiving end of her intoxicating gaze, when she was close enough to touch, had my self-control stretched thinner than ever before. Straddling her body was an exercise of pure restraint. I work through one photo at a time at my home desk with editing software, adjusting the lighting to highlight her curves. *Unreal.*

I click through a few, until the one of her staring up at me while on the floor stops me in my tracks—those emerald eyes destroy me with one glance. It's not even a pose I plan on painting; I just wanted to see how she would react. Not to mention, get a preview of what it'll look like someday when I'm between her legs, right before she takes every inch. The need in her expression, her hard pierced nipples poking through the shirt, the hitch in her breath—she wasn't just acting, she was aroused, and these shots are proof. Putting her in those positions like she was my plaything had my pulse pounding.

I've got her right where I want her . . . and she has no fucking idea.

The comment about me seeing her as a sibling was icing on the cake. That couldn't have been better timed. I haven't seen her like a sister since not long after she returned from college. That's when I stopped calling her Junior and started referring to her as Chaos. That's what she felt like. She left a kid and returned a goddamn siren. A woman I didn't recognize. She dressed differently: Black pants hugged her thick thighs—thighs I wanted to sink my teeth into. Crop tops that left little to the imagination, especially when her nipples—*that are pierced*—peeked through the fabric. Her hair and nails were a glossy black, but it wasn't some bullshit edgy art-grad persona she invented. She was sexy and sure of herself like

I'd never seen before, like she'd found who she was and embraced every ounce of it unapologetically. Not to mention, her talent as a burgeoning artist was off the charts. It was whiplash. My entire life I've had no problem maintaining discipline and control. *Until Kelly.* Kelly is my own personal Chaos.

I've honored Clyde's wishes for three years, giving her the opportunity to live a little, grow up, and experience what life had to offer her, but now she's going to find out what *I* have to offer.

He's given me his blessing. And she's twenty-six, the same age Clyde was when he met Kelly's mom, and I plan to follow in his footsteps, making her my bride before she's twenty-seven.

With each photo I swipe through, my dick strains harder against the fly of my jeans. When I can hardly stand it any longer, I unzip, shove my boxers out of the way, and wrap a fist around my aching cock, stroking it to the vision of her. *Fuck.* I'm throbbing, swollen, and desperate for release.

My imagination runs rampant with our future together, all the ways I plan to mark her and make her mine—especially on her knees, gazing up at me like she is on my screen. It won't be long before I can look into her gorgeous eyes and bury a hand into her lush, black tousled hair as I relish the pouty red lips begging to be used. She'll open her mouth, so soft and inviting, stick out her tongue, and I'll slap the head against it while she whimpers for more. My grip will tighten around a fistful of hair while I guide her lips over me. She'll swallow every inch like she was made for it, her bare tits bouncing as I fuck her pretty face. *Fucking Chaos.*

When I've had my fill of her mouth, I'll flip her around and make her ride my tongue, grinding her sweet pussy against me—her little body trembling and shaking when she comes. She'll gasp and moan until she forgets every name but mine.

I'll have her paying off the debt of our years spent as "friends" by wringing one orgasm at a time from her needy cunt.

My palm works my cock, every pass more demanding than the last, feeling the burn in my forearm, as I keep myself close to the edge just long enough to savor the control and hot-as-fuck fantasy. I squeeze tighter, until my knuckles bloom white as pre-cum leaks from the tip. My dick twitches in my hand, and I twist my wrist, bringing myself to the verge of climax.

I'm not ashamed of my obsession with her or the many ways I plan to possess her body. I've been hers for years, and it's time she repays the favor. It won't be long before she peers up at me with the same hungry look she has on my monitor—craving sex. Craving me. Not someone like me . . . *Me.*

She's the only woman who's ever made me feel this alive—this *real*. I'm done worshipping her from a distance, I want to hold her, protect her, and claim her in my bed. Brutally show her she's mine, every fucking day.

My fist pumps faster and my muscles tense as I imagine towering over her kneeled at my feet. Her posture perfect because she's such a fucking good girl.

"That's it, Chaos. Make me come."

Her lashes flutter and her green eyes roll back when I fill up her greedy mouth with cum, her throat bobbing to swallow every drop, glancing up like it's not enough. My back arches against the chair and I release into my hand, grunting as hot ropes spurt from the tip and roll down my knuckles. When I'm completely spent, I slump into the chair with my chest heaving.

My phone buzzes on the desk with a text notification. From her.

"Your timing is impeccable, sweetheart," I mutter, grabbing the phone with my left since my right is still covered in the cum she earned.

Kelly: Hey, I wanted to ask you about that photo shoot we did . . .

My smile grows wider. *It's about time.*

Me: Yes?

An ellipsis dances across the screen for what feels like ten minutes. I eventually set the phone down and clean off my hand while I wait for her to finish whatever she's about to confess, hopefully something she's been stewing on since last night. My intent was to force her to question things—question *us*. I want to see her come to that conclusion on her own, even if it is a roundabout way to not break my promise to him.

"Go on, ask me, Chaos. Ask me what you want to know."

The dots stop moving, and I hold my breath waiting for it. For a split second, I consider whether she's about to reject me. I shake my head. No fucking way. Chemistry as strong as ours is two-sided.

Then the dots start up again, and I throw my head back and groan. "What, is she typing out a fucking novel?"

A notification chimes, and my gaze darts to the screen.

Kelly: How did the pictures turn out?

I can't help but bark out a laugh and shake my head. "Oh, come on." She's still too scared to admit it. *So am I*, my thoughts echo back. I type my response.

Me: They turned out incredible.
Kelly: Glad to hear it.
Me: That's all you want to ask?
Kelly: Yeah.

13

LOGAN

My client Hunter and I haven't spoken more than three words to each other the entire session. He might be as tight-lipped as I am. Fine by me, I don't need conversation. As soon as I finish the last line and wipe him down, I kill the machine and nod.

He leans forward in my black leather chair, checking the piece in the mirror, then gives his version of what a smile would be before making a noise that's somewhere between a grunt and a satisfied sigh.

"Is that a good sound?" I double-check to be sure.

"Mm."

Right.

I wrap up his arm and hand him the aftercare sheet, giving him the spiel. "Wash it. Don't pick at it. Moisturize. No hot tubs. Don't be an idiot."

"Mm."

That could mean he understands or "go to hell." Either way, I think we're done here.

At the front desk, I take the payment since Frankie is out to lunch. Hunter digs a few hundreds from his wallet and drops them on the counter like we're making a shady drug deal.

"Change?"

He shakes his head, then heads for the door, holding up his hand in a wave, and I return the gesture.

I think we bonded.

Once he exits, I check in Casper's next client. He's got a consultation with Anna Kucera next. I give her a nod. We've met previously, since her brother, Rhys, plays for the Minnesota Lakes with Camden, so I've seen her around at various Lakes Hockey events we're expected to attend as families of the team, mostly just the big games and galas. I don't recall ever seeing ink on her.

"First tattoo?" I ask.

"Yeah," she replies, her voice soft and shy. She sounds nervous.

"Casper does great work. He'll take good care of ya."

She nods and sits on the edge of the sofa in the waiting area. Anna reminds me of a deer. Untrusting and skittish.

As soon as Casper comes to the front to get her, her shoulders relax. Everybody likes Casper, he's warm and hospitable. Make no mistake, there are parts of him that live in the shadows, but very rarely does he reveal that side of himself. He's a charming golden retriever the majority of the time, making friends everywhere he goes.

He greets her with a warm smile. "Anna?"

She nods and stands.

"Hi, I'm Casper." He shakes her hand. "You can follow me back to my chair and let's talk more about what you have in mind." Then he leads her toward the back of the shop near his workstation.

I glance down at my watch. Frankie still has ten more minutes before she returns. Thor is in the back painting a custom sign for the shop. His hand lettering is unparalleled; people come from all over to get his script tattooed on their bodies.

Laughter comes from the piercing bay where Kelly is doing nose piercings for a group of four friends. One of them gushes, "It looks so good!" The rest chime in with positive affirmations and excited nervous energy.

"You did great!" Kelly cheers; her happy sound carries through the shop.

I chuckle and check the trash cans to see if they need to be emptied, but it looks like she already did it this morning. Plants appear to be watered. Frankie's got everything taken care of. I check the mailbox, freezing when I see a letter addressed to Kelly from Billy Akers. I tear into the envelope as my blood pressure soars.

Junior,

Long time! Hope you're well . . .

I mutter under my breath, *Fuck this guy.*

My eyes dart across the lines of text, reading as fast as I possibly can. He wants to know "how it's going" since I took over Black Rabbit. *That's nice.* As if he didn't almost destroy the Everhart name and drown the business Clyde built from the ground up. After I fired Billy and nearly bankrupted myself trying to clean up the mess he left, he had enough money to retire out west like he always wanted—and that's where I hoped he would stay.

The fact that he's reaching out to Kelly has me seeing red.

My molars grind as I finish the note. It seems friendly, but Billy is a fucking snake. He's fishing for information. I wouldn't doubt if he fucked up whatever scheme he was running out there and now thinks he can slither back here and manipulate Kelly the way he did Clyde... Not a chance in hell. Not that any of us even knew it was happening until it was too late—and to this day, Billy, Casper, and Thor are the only ones who know the truth. I've worked hard to keep it that way.

I stuff the letter back in the envelope, folding it in half and tucking it into my back pocket. Billy is up to something. Especially because he sent it to the shop. If he really wanted to reach out to her, he would have sent it to her house directly—this feels like a message for me. Testing me and reminding me he's still out there. He knows Kelly is my weakness, so this is his way of hitting me where it hurts. He can try, but he'll quickly learn that this time, I'll strike back. Hard.

I figured out how to block him in every digital capacity, but nothing like the good ol' United States Postal Service to come through for him. I just need to figure out what his angle is and get ahead of it.

I can't waste any time obsessing about this since my next client will be arriving soon, and I need to get my shit together before they show up. My gaze drifts to the large picture windows at the front of the shop and the tension drains from my shoulders—until my eyes focus on a man with a bouquet of roses coming toward the shop.

Oh, fuck no.

Jason.

I'm not letting him anywhere near Kelly. Things are already in motion and I don't undo my own work. There's no way in hell I'm giving him access to her. They're done.

I stand behind the desk, his five-foot-nine height no match.

The door swings open, and his dress shoes clack as he makes his way toward me.

"Is Kelly here?"

"She's off today."

He knits his brow. "I know she works Tuesdays."

He doesn't know shit. Not even her birthstone, apparently.

"I don't know what to tell you, man," I reply with a shrug.

He sighs, clutching the red roses at his side. "Look, I just wanna talk to her for five minutes."

"It doesn't take five minutes to say goodbye, but I'll pass along the message anyway."

He takes a deep breath. "Let me talk to her, Logan."

"No. Whatever you thought you had is dead, and you're going to leave it buried."

He cocks his head to the side and narrows his eyes. "What the hell do you care anyway?" He lifts his chin. "You want my sloppy seconds?"

A grin slowly spreads across my face, and based on the way he just took a step back, I think it makes him uneasy. I chuckle.

"What?" he seethes.

"That you thought she was ever yours to begin with."

"She still *is* mine. Kelly's just hung up on some trust issue bullshit. It doesn't involve you, this is between me and her."

"No, *I'm* the one between you and her." I furrow my brow. "Besides, it sounds like you have enough side pieces to keep you busy."

He steps up to the desk and sticks his pointer finger at my face. "I never cheated on her. I have no idea where that fucking scrunchie came from!"

My smile can no longer be contained. "Funny how shit just turns up sometimes."

He withdraws a couple steps and angles his head slightly, keeping his gaze on me. "Were you . . ." He narrows his eyes. "Were you at my *house*?"

I raise my eyebrows. "That's a pretty bold accusation."

Though, in this case, an accurate one. I can't be sure if he used any of the condoms from the drawer to cheat on Kelly, but that's not the point. Thor happened to mention he'd seen Jason talking with a woman at a bar the week before her birthday, nothing more than a laugh and a handshake, but it was enough for me to build the rest of the story. I don't need proof to make her believe it. Perception is everything, and suspicion will always work harder than the truth.

Lucky for me, he cared more about his ego than his home security. I'd noticed that a water stain under one of his outdoor planters wasn't centered beneath the flower pot. A quick lift and there was his spare key just waiting for the wrong person to find it.

Jason retreats another step. "What the fuck . . ." His eyes dart in the direction of Kelly's laughter in the back of the shop, and I round the desk, blocking the path to her and standing my ground.

"This won't play out the way you think it will," he warns. "Trust me—it doesn't end in your favor. I'll tell her."

"Yes it will, and you're not going to mention my name. Remember . . . I know where you live."

He releases the flowers from his grip and lunges for me. My fist connects with his face, and the snap of bone meeting cartilage echoes off the walls.

Jason drops with a grunt, his head bouncing off the hard floor. He sucks in a breath of air and I sink to my knees, crouching over him and landing another blow to his jaw, spraying blood across his cheek. The pound of adrenaline pulses through me—I don't want to stop. He needs to learn exactly what happens when he fucks with what's mine. She's never been his, and if I have to physically remove him from the equation, I'll do it.

His hands flail as he tries to gain purchase on my shirt, eventually curling his fingers into the fabric, and rearing back his other arm to clock me in the mouth. The impact of his knuckles splits my lip, and the taste of copper floods my palate.

He spits blood in my face and I laugh—he just wrote his name on his coffin.

"You're a fucking psycho!" he stammers, blood pouring from his nose.

My palm finds his neck and I press my thumb to his windpipe, itching to feel it collapse under the stress. I increase the pressure and his eyes widen.

"You have no idea how big a psycho I can be." I grin, lower my voice. "Walk into my shop again, and I'll make you scream so fucking long the devil will ask me to keep it down."

"Whoa." Casper's voice cuts in from beside me, and he reaches under my arms and pulls me back. "Thor! Need you up front," he calls over his shoulder.

"I'll fucking expose you," Jason says through clenched, bloody teeth. He props up on his elbow and stabs a finger in my direction. "I'm not done with her. Over my dead body."

Heavy footsteps sprint from the back of the shop. "Ah, shit," Thor mutters, quickly assessing the situation.

"Have it your way." Casper tightens his hold, and Thor pushes me back.

"What's going on—Oh my God!" Kelly shrieks.

"Kel!" Jason says, wide-eyed. "Your boss is a fuckin'—"
Thor grabs Jason by the collar of his shirt, hauls him up, and guides his shuffling feet toward the door. "Time to go."

I shrug Casper off me and wipe my lip on my sleeve.

The bell rings over the door as Jason is shoved out of it. He points back at me through the window, pinning me with a scowl.

Kelly is glowering when I spin around. Not sure if it's all the testosterone, but she looks hotter than ever when she's furious.

She throws her arms out to the side and scowls. "The fuck just happened?" she whisper-shouts, trying not to attract attention from clients.

I scrub a hand over my face and wince when I hit my swollen cut lip. *Damn, that stings.* What am I supposed to say, the truth? Pass.

Her sharp stare burrows into my skin. I take back nothing. I've never had a problem exhibiting self-control, but after that letter and seeing her ex back-to-back, I didn't stand a chance.

She crosses her arms, waiting for an answer. They drop to her sides when she realizes there isn't one coming. Kelly scoffs at me with disdain, turning on her heel. As she walks away, she shakes her head, ripping off her black latex gloves and hurling them into a nearby trash can as she returns to her clients. Thankfully, all the customers stayed safely in the back of the shop and only staff saw our little scuffle.

Thor's arm shoots out toward the door that Jason was just escorted out of. "If you learned to communicate like a normal human being, you wouldn't need to orchestrate a crisis just so you can play the fucking savior."

Frankie comes skipping in the front door from her lunch break clutching an iced coffee and freezes. "Holy shit, what happened to you?" she says.

Casper clamps his mouth shut and holds up his palms. He takes a few steps backward before heading back to his consultation with Anna. He avoids drama like a bad ex-girlfriend.

Thor is the only one who speaks up. "Jason stopped by." He picks up the smashed bouquet of roses on the floor and walks over to the front desk, dumping them in the trash before he leaves too.

"Ohhh. Yeah, Kelly told me about the birthday breakup." Frankie smiles and swirls the ice in her plastic Starbucks cup, giving me a once-over. "Had a little confrontation, did you?"

"I don't want to talk about it," I gruff.

"I understand. First rule of fight club," Frankie assures me, returning to her post behind the front desk. "Hope you got a couple shots in."

I nod.

"Atta boy." She plops her purse on the counter, then begins rummaging through one of the desk drawers, procuring a first-aid kit and handing it to me. "Here, take this back to your office and get cleaned up. We can't have clients walking in and seeing this shit."

14

KELLY

I slump down into the cool black leather of my client chair, knees bent to prop up my drawing tablet. After queuing up a playlist on my phone, I recline the seat slightly and angle myself away from the aisle that runs the length of the shop. Hopefully the headphones snug over my ears will deter anyone from talking to me. My knuckles pale as I grip the stylus firmer than I should, so I take a deep breath and relax my hold until it's comfortable in my hand.

Thoughts wander as I make the first few strokes of a face. Realism has been my main priority lately; it's one of the hardest styles to master. There's so much precision and attention to detail required, not to mention a profound understanding of light and shadow, demanding daily practice.

Feminist anthems belt through the headphones, but the songs fade into the background as my concentration settles in, softening my anger. The crushed roses near the front door might as well have been a confession. They weren't a sign of Jason's remorse, they were bait. His apology should have been as loud as his disrespect, and there's no florist in town with enough stock to make up for cheating. However, my current attitude is aimed toward Logan and the way he seemingly revels in stirring up trouble in my life lately—starting with Sunday night's photo shoot.

What the hell was that?

Was he fucking with me? Was he simply creating a sexy atmosphere for our shoot? Whatever it was, it was . . . *new*. Until recently, he's never given me any reason to suspect he harbors feelings. We're close friends, for sure, but never more than that.

Oh fuck. Have I misjudged his intentions this entire time? The stylus slips from my fingers and into my lap. No. There's no way. He would have said something by now. I pick up my pen and keep working while I overanalyze every interaction we've had over the last two weeks. If it were anyone else, I'd think there was a likelihood—but this is *Logan*. He can't be held to the same standards.

My chest tightens and I swallow the lump in my throat. I should ask if Frankie wants to grab drinks after work; I could use some girl time—I need to step away from all of this so I can gain some perspective. My own feelings have made this already confusing situation even more disorienting.

Dad's letter was filled with relationship advice, but I'm done with fragile egos and bullshit. Logan can do whatever the hell he wants, it's his life. I'm not going to wait around with bated breath for him to open up to me and explain himself. It's an exercise in futility. I have enough on my plate, like getting my career off the ground and making a name for myself, and the Bozeman Tattoo Festival.

My pen glides across the screen as I add more detail and structure to the man I'm drawing, sketching out glasses over the smoldering eyes that stare back at me. *Damn it. I'm drawing Logan.*

Groaning, I tap the corner of my screen to erase the canvas.

I throw my head back against the headrest and inhale a renewing breath. Glancing down at the blank screen, I start over, this time drawing my mom. I've practiced her figure numerous times before. I only know her from photos, but I've memorized her face. She's a beauty. I wonder if she ever dealt with any of this shit with Dad. Probably not, Dad worshipped the ground she walked on. Which is the only thing I'll accept going forward.

I sigh, adding the high cheekbones I inherited from her.

Yeah, this calls for drinks. Normally, Logan is the person I talk things out with, but not this time. I need a break from him to determine how I feel before we hash out what happened—because he owes me an explanation. He's not sweeping that fight under the rug.

Climbing out of the chair, I make my way toward the front desk, where Frankie is scheduling an appointment over the phone. I move around the desk and fold my hands together. She smiles at me while finishing her call.

When she hangs up, Frankie tucks her black textured curls behind her pierced ears and angles her chair toward me. "How may I help you?" she asks sweetly, drumming her fingers on the desk. I wonder if she'd ever let me draw her. Her warm sienna skin tone is beautiful, and matches her bright brown eyes.

"Hey, what are you doing after work?" I ask.

"Nothing, why?"

"Wanna go out for drinks?"

She gives a delayed blink. "Oh my God. Yes!" Her voice lowers to a whisper. "Did you hear about what happened earlier?"

I match her hushed volume. "With Jason? I didn't see the whole thing. I'm still trying to figure out what the hell went down between them." I roll my eyes. "I need to vent."

Frankie checks the computer screen. "I'm done at six, but I'm all caught up on emails, so I'll see if I can head out in twenty. Let's go to that new place that just opened on Quail Street. I hear they have a solid happy hour, we might be able to catch the tail end of it."

My smile grows. "Excellent. I'm going to wrap up my work and then meet you over there."

As quickly as I can, I clean up my space, wiping down the countertops and chair with sanitizer, making sure everything is in its rightful place for tomorrow. By the time I'm done, I have a few minutes left, so I open Instagram while waiting for Frankie.

After some mindless scrolling, I check my DMs, which mostly consist of people haggling on prices or asking about commissions. Then I check my message requests folder: only one.

WhiteShirtBlackSkirt762: You will never replace me.

My brow furrows and I click their user name. Zero followers and zero following. Rolling my eyes at the fake profile, I block the account. After grabbing my purse from inside the cabinet, I hook it over my shoulder and get ready to walk out. That's when I catch my reflection in the large mirror—my outfit: white shirt, black skirt. *What the fuck?*

"Hey, ready to go?" Frankie asks, peeking her head into my station.

I startle, tearing my eyes away from the mirror. "Yeah, for sure. Just heading out."

The new restaurant has a modern sleek look, with living vines climbing the walls. Chic lighting fixtures illuminate the wooden tables with cozy seating—we managed to snag one just in time because a line is forming at the host stand. Tajin rims the edge of my glass, where a delightful mango margarita fills it to the brim. It's dangerously delicious, pairing perfectly with the chips, salsa flight, queso, and Mexican street corn we ordered from the happy hour menu.

"Who do you think sent it?" Frankie asks.

I scoff. "Probably Jason, if the events of today are any indicator."

"Yeah, can we please talk about that? I still can't believe Logan punched him!" Frankie gushes. "The man who barely says two words to anybody suddenly decides he's going to square up?"

He's never once shown aggression the way he did today.

"I can't make sense of it," I reply. "I've never seen him go off like that. And why won't he tell me what they were fighting about?" The way he looked earlier is burned into my memory. The fire in his eyes was savage—and completely foreign. He's the calm one, the unshakable zen artist. Before today, he could have told me he was a pacifist and I wouldn't have blinked. *So what the hell happened between him and Jason that led to fists being thrown?*

Frankie lets out a dry laugh and plucks a chip from the basket, scooping up a dollop of guacamole. "Oh gee. I wonder."

I roll my eyes. "It's not like that. He's just always been there. We *get* each other—"

"Yeah, and now he wants to get more." She cocks a brow, sitting back in her seat and crossing her arms over her chest. "With Jason out of the picture, he's making sure it stays that way."

"He's protective by nature, Logan guards everything my dad built," I say, pushing my finger through the ring of condensation on the table. "He steps in to make sure things are taken care of now that I'm on my own. He helps me out in the attic. He's my mentor. He cares about the shop, tattooing, and Dad's wishes."

Frankie rolls her lips together, nodding at me with raised brows while she holds back a smirk.

"We accept each other the way we are and offer support when the other needs it. Besides . . ."

"Besides?"

"I lend a shoulder if he needs to talk, but that's the thing—he doesn't share his life or feelings with me the same way I share mine with him. I don't know what's going on in his mind, and I never will." My voice softens. His silence hurts. "All this time, it felt like we shared some sacred connection, forged through our shared passion of art and tattooing, but almost everything I know about Logan I've learned through observation . . . Maybe I don't know him at all."

"You know him. You know him better than anyone. He even invites you to spend the holidays with him and his family."

"Yeah, because he knows I don't have anywhere to go."

She pauses, nailing me with a blank expression before brushing the salt off her fingers. "Oh come on, Kel."

"What?"

"Are you serious right now? Have you seen the way he looks at you?"

I blink at her. It's like she's not listening to a word I'm saying.

We stare at each other for a beat. Her eyes relax and she cocks her head to the side. I startle when she slaps both palms on the table. "Wait, do you seriously not realize he's into you?"

"Did he say something to somebody?" I sip the cold, sweet margarita.

She scrunches up her nose, scooping salsa onto a chip. "Please, Logan doesn't say anything to anybody. He's practically mute . . . unless he's talking to *you*. Which should have been your first clue. *Think about it.* He punched your ex for bringing you roses. I'm tellin' ya, he's not going to let another man near you." She pops the chip in her mouth.

I consider her argument, his words still echoing in my mind . . . Recalling the set of his jaw when he said he doesn't like thinking about me with other men. Our photo shoot, and the way his strong thighs bracketed my hips—hell, that alone has had me crossing and uncrossing my legs all week. And those piercing hazel eyes didn't give off "friends." No, his stare pinned me to the floor, unrelenting and . . . ravenous.

The heavy air in the restaurant is suffocating. My pulse pounds in my ears, drowning out the ambient noise around us. My gaze snaps to Frankie's, and her face splits in a wide smile, like she just witnessed the realization slam into me.

"What am I gonna do now?" I ask.

"*Oh no. My super-hot best friend has a crush on me, whatever will I do?*" she mocks, cupping her cheeks in faux shock.

I drop my face into my hands, mumbling "Thanks for your support," before lifting my chin to see her finishing a bite.

She waves as if to clear the air. "You know what you need? A good book," Frankie suggests, then takes a sip of her margarita.

"Like a self-help book?"

"Basically." She nods. "Charge your vibe, read some smut, rub one out, and then get a good night's rest."

"Call the doctor in the morning?" I chuckle, swirling the straw in my drink. "I don't think I can masturbate my way out of this problem."

Ironically, Logan is essentially both my problem *and* my solution.

"No, but it'll give you a clear mind so you can listen to your feelings without sexual tension influencing your decision. Because, whew, that man . . ."

She makes a solid point.

"I can't jump into a relationship the second I get out of one, that's insanity."

"Is it, though? In some ways, it's like y'all were already dating. You hang out all the time, talk about everything, work together . . . You're basically in a relationship without the sex. Which is a travesty if you ask me."

I shake my head. "No way, that's different. It was platonic. This would change everything. If it didn't work out, it could put the shop at risk."

"Sometimes change is good . . ." She spoons more of the street corn onto a small plate. "Do you think it would be for the better?"

"I don't know." My head falls back and I stare at the ceiling as if the answers are scrawled on the plaster above us. "I'm still trying to come to terms with the concept of it. I don't know what to think about anything." When I look down, I snatch up my margarita, bringing it to my lips and taking a substantial gulp.

"I bet he's good in bed. Controlled . . . calculating . . . *firm*—"

I choke on my drink. "Okay, okay, okay. That's enough," I sputter.

Forming a small circle with my lips, I blow out the matchstick after lighting the last candle. My *Now That's What I Call Fucking, Volume 6* playlist hums through the Bluetooth speakers in the background. With my e-reader in one hand and a vibrator in the other, I focus on releasing the pent-up sexual tension that's been swelling since the photo shoot with Logan. He's kept me in a steady state of arousal since our night together. It's as irritating as it is erotic—provocative, in every sense of the word. Leaning back into my pillows, I take a deep cleansing breath to relax, returning to my "self-help."

With the touch of a button, the silicone toy whirs to life; I drag it over my flesh, skating across my inner thighs, and climbing higher, where all my tension lies. My cheeks flush with heat as the words on the illuminated page play out in vivid detail. I lean into the sensation, focusing on the book, the characters, and nothing else. Letting my brain empty of questioning his intentions. My only goal is to relieve stress and let go of the events that occurred over the past week. My legs extend, heels pressing into the mattress as my back arches. *Don't think, just feel.* My pulse quickens and my breaths come faster as the vibrations hum over my clit. Heat curls inside me, my stomach tightening and ass clenching as I concentrate on the needy ache between my spread thighs. The need to come grows more urgent by the second. My jaw relaxes as I surrender to the thrum of pleasure.

And then the buzzing ceases.

Dead air.

My battery-operated boyfriend dies.

"No!"

Frankie was right, I should have charged my toys ahead of time. Frustrated, I toss the useless tool and e-reader aside, taking over manually. I resort to my go-to mental imagery with the highest success rate. A tall, faceless stranger stands before me. I've fucked him countless times in my fantasies—he's top notch. Tosses me around like I weigh nothing, fucks with abandon, and edges mercilessly.

He's rough and obsessive. Demanding.

"Hands and knees, sweetheart. Let's see how well you follow directions."

He forces me onto all fours and spreads my cheeks, his fingers digging in—hard. He spanks my ass, like *really* spanks me, until it hurts. With each brutal strike of his palm to my sensitive flesh, my pussy contracts.

"Aww, are you blushing, Chaos?"

My eyes shoot open. *That voice.* Fuck, all these years it's been *his* voice. It wasn't until that nickname that I was able to place it. Realized. He's not the faceless stranger anymore.

Fuck it. I'm too close. My conscience warns me this is a bad idea, I won't be able to take it back, but I crash that train of thought before it gets too far down the track. My need to come is stronger, and what's the harm in indulging in a little fantasy?

As soon as the voice of reason shuts up, my thoughts run wild—shameless and starved. He flips me on my back, teases, taunts, and marks me with handprints before devouring every inch. He's the cruelest form of bliss.

My abs tighten and my thighs stretch wider as I approach the finish line. Almost there . . .

Figments of him become clearer as I ride my hand; he gives that sinful smirk of his, amused by the power he holds over me. His mouth finds my neck and he licks and sucks while viciously fucking my body.

The pressure builds and builds, with the thrill slowly overtaking me. My back arches into the pillows cradling me and I moan, coming to the image of him braced above, working me over with a wicked grin. But it's more than his masculine voice, appearance, and stellar imaginary performance. I get off to who he is as a whole; his stoicism, his artistry, his natural dominance. I want it all.

The tension in my shoulders dissipates, and I lie there, soft and spent, gradually coming to terms with my own feelings toward Logan. If post-nut clarity exists, then pre-nut psychosis must also. This isn't that. There's no regret. I'm physically satisfied but could go another round with the same daydream.

This was supposed to stop me from thinking about him that way, clear the persistent hormones that hijacked my control panel. Somehow, I've gone and done the opposite, and I'm left even more confused than before.

Fuck . . .

Fuck!

15

LOGAN

He had it coming—he had it coming for a long time, and landing those blows felt so fucking satisfying. As soon as he insinuated there was anything "sloppy" about Kelly, it was over for him.

However, the response from her, or lack thereof, has not been ideal. I pull my phone out of my pocket and reread the text thread between us.

Me: You okay?
Me: I can tell you're mad.
Kelly: I think it's best if we put some distance between us right now. I need time to think.
Me: About Jason?
Kelly: It's not your business.
Me: When I help you pick up the pieces after your breakups, you make it my business.
Kelly: Fine, then let's talk about it. Why don't you tell me why you got into a fight with Jason?

There are a million things I want to tell her, but I don't know how to say any of them. Not over text.

Kelly: Typical.
Kelly: Stop acting like you're some innocent bystander in this. You want to be involved less? Give me the space I'm asking for.

I grit my teeth. That was last Tuesday, a week ago—a whole goddamn week—and she has barely said two words to me since. I've practically been rocking in my seat with all the shit that's been piling up in my head for the last seven days. I'd grab a drink, but there isn't enough bourbon in the world strong enough to soothe the choke hold that anxiety has on me. Even at work, her answers are short and clipped. She keeps her head down. It's so unlike Kelly, and her behavior scares me—it's unnerving. A few days ago, she went into the attic, and it took everything in me to stay put. I always help her with Clyde's stuff. How long does she need to think?

With my phone shoved back in my pocket, I try to focus on the book in front of me. I'll be making up my days off today and tomorrow since I did some commission pieces on Sunday and Monday, and I'm trying to relax like a normal person even though I want to crawl out of my skin. After a few sentences, my mind wanders and I have to start over again.

Maybe I should go into the shop . . . However, knowing our friendship is on the rocks has me distracted, and I can't sit still. I close the hardcover and toss it beside me on the sofa. The same one she was arching her back on during our photo shoot.

I don't expect her to be ready to jump into a new relationship overnight, even though that would make my life a lot easier. She thinks she has a choice in the matter, which is by design, but the truth is, I'm the only outcome. When it comes to me, there's no escape clause and no expiration date. When we do this, it's permanent.

I crave her smile. The way it melts my stress away. I could use it now. She's been so distant, it's never been like this between us. I need to do something to get her back on track. Remind her why we're good together. My foot bounces as I rack my brain. I need something that will bust down her walls . . . *There is one thing.*

I pull out my phone again and open the search engine, hoping I'll find what I'm looking for.

After making a few calls yesterday, I hit the jackpot. At least I think I did. This morning, I woke up at three o'clock a.m., packed up my truck, and drove seven hours to South Dakota, all the way to the April Valley Rescue.

After turning into the parking lot, I get out and stretch my arms over my head, leaning to the left and right until I hear the satisfying crack from my spine. Better.

Right on time. I wasn't taking any chances.

Inside, I'm greeted by a friendly staff member with short brown hair and a buffalo plaid vest. She's probably who I'm looking for.

"Are you Carol?" I ask.

"Yes, I am!" she says brightly.

I extend my hand across the desk. "Hi. I'm Logan. We spoke on the phone yesterday."

"Logan! Yes, right! We received your application, and everything looks great." She rounds the front desk, gesturing for me to follow. "Come on, I'll introduce you to the little guy you were interested in."

Raising an eyebrow, I fall in step behind her, and she leads me through a heavy metal door into a larger room filled with kennels. Each one appears to be six feet by ten feet, separated with blue walls that are about six feet tall, and chain-link doors. Barks echo off the walls as she guides me to the dog. There's one in particular I'm interested in, but I have no idea how dog adoptions work. From what I hear, you're supposed to *just know*, whatever the hell that means. We pass by a Chihuahua, and he stands on his hind legs and rests his miniature paws on the chain link, yipping at me. *Is it normal for it to shake like that?*

I follow her down another row of kennels and she pauses, unlocking one of the doors and waving me in with an open palm.

"Here we are! I'll let you two get acquainted, take as much time as you like. If you think he's a good match and you're still interested in adoption, come find me at the front desk and we'll finish your paperwork. If not, let me know if there're any other dogs you would like to meet, and we can set that up."

I nod, and enter the kennel with the beast. *Holy shit.* "That's for sure a dog, right?" I ask, unwilling to risk taking my eyes off it.

She chuckles. "Yes."

"Okay . . . just making sure. Thanks."

Carol leaves us be, and I study him with my hands on my hips.

He doesn't bother to greet me, just lies there with his chin pressed to the cold concrete. He tracks my movements as I step closer and crouch in front of him. We lock eyes, staring each other down. Interesting.

"Sorry, I had to ask," I say, apologizing to him. He looks more wolf than dog and is the size of a small horse. Thick black fur covers his body, except for around his muzzle, which is more gray, and the parts of his jaw that are patched with white. He's charming in a might-rip-out-my-spine kinda way.

Carol said he was a stray and they weren't sure of his age but estimated him to be around five years old. She didn't know his breed either, but if I had to take a stab at it, I'd say he's a cross between a Great Dane and a werewolf. Apparently, he's been here for over a year.

"So . . ."

He glances away from me, I take a look at the sign on the wall.

Name: Dogmeat.

I shake my head. "Christ, that's the worst name I've ever heard. And I know an Alaskan shepherd named Chicken Salad."

He blinks slowly, like he's offended.

"Yeah, I'd be pissed too. Your PR team did you dirty, man."

The big guy huffs out a breath at the same time I do. His ears twitch, and he looks at me again.

"You're right, you don't exactly scream 'emotional support animal'," I muse. "Nothing says *calm* like a hundred-pound hellhound in row eight . . . Lucky for you, that's okay."

The dog raises an eyebrow at me, then lowers it again, like he's given up on everyone.

"Dude, if I bring you home . . . you gotta be cool, all right? You can't be terrorizing the neighborhood, or dragging dead cats and shit into my place."

He lifts his chin weakly from the ground, and I offer a few scratches and pets. His coarse fur is much softer than it looks.

"My house isn't huge, but there's a dog park across the street." I scan his kennel. "You'll have a hell of a lot more room than you do here."

His tail begins slapping the gray unforgiving floor.

"And I'm not calling you Dogmeat. You're not a walking joke, that bullshit stays here."

He stands to his full height and I blink.

"Goddamn, you're massive." I shake my head. "Just when I thought you couldn't appear any bigger." I'm not crouched all the way down, yet I find myself looking up to meet his vacant stare. He's easily over a hundred and fifty pounds.

His gaze burrows into mine, but there's an emptiness in his eyes, like he's given up hope. I recognize that kind of surrender. He's been to hell and back.

This is my dog.

After forty-five minutes of paperwork with Carol, I'm walking out the door with a new dog. My truck jerks when he hops up into the cab, giving my suspension a run for its money. With the way his tongue is lolled out of his mouth, it almost looks like he's smiling. This started because of Kelly, but maybe this will be good for me too. Kelly has always said I should adopt a dog.

"Wanna get something to eat?"

His tail thumps.

"Yeah, me too. I'm fuckin' starving."

Before we get on the highway, I swing through the drive-thru of a fast-food joint and order four burgers—two for each of us—a cup of water, and a shake. When we park to eat, I expect him to snarf them down in a single gulp, but he eats at a respectable pace, almost like he's savoring every bite. I'm well aware this is bad for him, but damn, poor guy has been in jail for a year.

"I've tattooed a few guys who've been in prison," I tell him, swallowing. "One of them told me that the second thing he did when he was released was get a burger."

The dog looks at me with raised eyebrows, ears twitching.

"The first thing? The first thing he did was blow out his girlfriend's back. I don't know who your girlfriend is, but I hope you enjoy these bail burgers as a consolation."

I finish my first burger and crumple up the wrapper, tossing it in the brown bag. Then I unwrap the second one and hold it out for him. He takes it from me, biting it clumsily. The bottom part of the bun drops onto the seat, but he manages to finish the rest of it before dipping his head to gobble up the remainder.

"Thirsty?" Gingerly, I remove the lid from the paper cup filled with water. My new buddy leans down and slurps up a few gulps, then sits up straight. Water drips from his muzzle when he pants.

"Life is good on the outside, huh?" I take another bite of my burger and shift into gear. "Ready to roll?"

With us back on the highway, he smears his snot all over the passenger glass as he watches the world pass by. "Aw, come on, man." I lower the window, and he thrusts his giant head into the fresh air, letting his tongue flap in the wind. The corner of my mouth turns up in a smirk. He needs a name, but I might leave that to Kelly.

"Tomorrow is going to be a little weird . . ." He's not listening to me, far too interested in the cornfields. "I'm going to need you to play along. You're just gonna have to trust me. At first you're gonna think I'm a huge asshole, but I promise it's not what you think it is."

The big brute pulls his head back in and faces me. Oh, now he wants to listen. I roll up the window. We've got six and a half hours to kill before we get home.

"So, there's this girl . . ."

16

KELLY

"Oh come on!" I shout when my hair dryer trips the breaker, causing my house to fall silent. I forgot to unplug the microwave first. The old wiring in this house is going to drive me mad. I once had a guy come out and do an estimate and the number was so big I almost pulled a muscle laughing.

"Ugh!" I stomp my foot like a toddler. "I don't have time for this. I have a client at eleven!" As if whatever gods are controlling my day can somehow fix it because it's inconvenient for my schedule.

After the world's fastest shower, I just want to dry my hair. I try to brush through the knots while racing out of the bathroom. Working little sections at a time toward the ends doesn't even seem to make a difference, because I ran out of conditioner and now the texture is all wrong. Maybe I didn't rinse all the shampoo out. Or maybe the water softener is busted again. Great.

Last night I was up late working on the realism drawing of my mom. Something was off with the shadows and I spent far too much time trying to fix it—without any luck. This morning I looked at it again, hoping fresh eyes would help, but it was no use. I lost track of time, and now I'm running late for work. I hate being late, it throws off my whole groove. I make a note to ask Casper to help me with my drawing when I get to work. He'll know what to do.

I bolt down the hall, skidding on one foot to stop in front of the breaker box. *Flip. Click. Slam.* The lights turn on again. Detouring through the kitchen on the way back, I yank the microwave cord from the wall, producing a small pop of a spark, and sprint back into the bathroom to resume drying my hair, this time with success.

Flipping my head upside down, I hold the hair dryer in one hand and my phone in the other to check the traffic report. There's an accident on the highway, *because of course there is*. Looks like I'll be taking the back roads until I get ahead of it.

Black jeans, black tee. My usual uniform. Someday I'll start wearing more color, but today is not that day. I grab my hairbrush and tear it through the tangles. Close enough.

Three more minutes before I need to be walking out the door. I might actually make it on time!

With toothpaste globbed onto my toothbrush, I brush while scanning my bedroom floor for shoes. I spot my combat boots and clumsily step into them.

Hurrying back to the bathroom to spit, I lean forward in the mirror and notice the white smear of toothpaste that dripped onto my shirt.

"Fuh!"

After rinsing my mouth, I dash to the bedroom, swap shirts, and haul ass through the house, throwing open the back door and grabbing my purse off the table on the way out. I'm only a minute behind when I back out of the driveway. Amazing.

Sadly, I missed my opportunity to make coffee this morning, but at least I won't be late.

Halfway down the road, I turn down the radio when I hear a funny clanking sound from the car. *What now?*

"Ugh!"

What, is everything in my life going on fucking strike? Relationships, vibrators, and as of this recent development, my car. Something is in retrograde.

I miss Logan. Normally, I would text him I was running behind, and he'd have a few words to chill me out and a fresh coffee waiting for me when I arrived. However, that won't be today. I'm going through a cleanse, taking a break from men—or at least, attractive, emotionally unavailable men.

Another light turns red. It's starting to feel less like a drive to work and more like a scenic tour of every intersection in the fucking city. I pull out my phone and quickly shoot off a text to Thor.

Me: Hey, are you at the studio? I'm running behind. So sorry.

Hawthorne: Nah, I swapped with Casper, he's opening. Who cares anyway, you don't have a client until 11:30.

Me: 11:30? I thought it was 11!

Now, I'm remembering, I think he's right. I was so distracted yesterday, Frankie was telling me something before I left and I totally spaced. Why does my life feel like such a mess?

Hawthorne: Schedule says 11:30. Casper can double check. Or Logan, he's probably there already.

That's because he practically lives at the studio.
Doesn't matter now, looks like karma has decided to bless me with coffee after all! I should have probably saved that money to go toward the car fund in case it's extra fucked, but I really could use a pick-me-up. Self-care matters.

After swinging through the drive-thru for an iced Americano, I flip on the radio to sing the rest of the way to work. No need to hurry if it's just Casper and me . . . and probably Logan, but he usually stays in his office in the mornings.

I pull into the parking lot behind the shop in a spot next to Casper. Doesn't look like Logan has arrived yet; he must be having a morning too. I grab my coffee and bag and climb out of my car, locking it up and heading for the rear employee entrance.

Inside, I make my way through the shop, nodding to Casper as I pass by the sterilization room. "Morning."

"Hey," he calls over his shoulder.

I set down my coffee and purse in my booth, heading toward the front of the shop to unlock the door and turn on the *OPEN* sign. That's when I notice something outside the right picture window.

"What in the hell?"

I spot a . . . black bear? I squint and continue my way toward the front. *No, it's a dog!* Oh my God, who would leave their dog out here all on their own?

My eyes widen when I unlock the front door and step out onto the sidewalk, where I'm quickly made aware just how massive this animal is. I blink a few times; *it looks almost like Loki.*

"Oh, you're a *big* puppy."

Massive. With shaggy black fur and friendly golden eyes.

I glance from left to right. We're sandwiched on the city block between a trendy wine bar and a hair salon. The salon won't open for another two hours, and the wine bar doesn't open until four. There are no cars around. The dog stares at me. As I close the distance between us, it begins to slap its tail on the sidewalk.

"Where is your owner, baby?"

I hold out the back of my hand for the dog to sniff before scratching . . . *him* under the chin.

"You're a sweetheart."

My fingers probe around his collar for any tags, but there's nothing. "How long have you been out here? Are you thirsty? I'm going to get you some water."

I swing open the shop door and go back inside.

"Casper!" I yell. "Whose dog is out front?"

Casper pops his head out of the sterilization doorway as I head for the employee lounge.

"I dunno. He was there when I rolled up."

What if the poor thing's been out there all night? "Do you think he's hungry?"

"Nah, he looks like he ate his owner, so he'll probably be good till dinner."

I wave a hand. "Oh, he does not."

"Well, Logan should be here any minute, you can ask him what he wants to do with it."

The employee lounge is small but sufficient. It contains a tiny kitchen space with a fridge, sink, and microwave for people to heat up food during their breaks. I find an old Tupperware container in one of the cabinets and fill it with water, then walk back outside and place the dish next to his fuzzy front paws. The dog looks down at the water dish, then back up to me.

"Aren't you thirsty?" He leans into me when I scratch him behind the ears. "Aww, you're a good boy."

I untie his leash from the pole and walk him around to the back of the shop where we have a patch of grass so he can do his business. He sniffs around for a while but doesn't seem to need to relieve himself. Then I spot Logan driving into the back lot.

I sigh. "Shit. Okay, look, my boss can be kind of a stickler about animals in the shop, so you're gonna need to give the best big puppy-dog eyes you can muster, got it?"

His golden orbs shine when he looks up, and nostalgia washes over me. He reminds me so much of the dog I had when I was a little girl.

Same color, same eyes, same size. I rest my palm on his tall back. "Yes, exactly like that!"

Logan hops out of his truck and strides over to me as I step onto the sidewalk. "Did you get a dog?"

It's the first thing he's said to me in a week that isn't work-related. It's nice to hear his conversational voice again, but I wish he'd use it to open up to me.

"No, some asshole tied him up out front and left him there," I say, glancing down at the pretty canine.

"Kelly, what the fuck? Go tie him back up again. You have no idea what that dog is capable of. That thing looks like he only knows German attack phrases."

My arms shoot out to cover the dog's soft ears with my hands. "Be nice!" I whisper. My furry friend wags his tail and glances up at me with his tongue lolling out. Oh, my heart. "See? He likes me!"

Logan rolls his eyes. "You don't even know who he belongs to."

I cross my arms. "Whoever the owner is doesn't deserve this sweet boy. Why would they just leave him out here like this all night?"

He shrugs. "Maybe because he looks like a—"

Rising to my tiptoes, I clap a palm over his mouth. "Is your comment constructive or critical?"

Logan purses his lips when I pull my hand away.

I've always wanted a dog. Now might be the time, it seems the universe has put one right in my path. Maybe it's just my hormones or the fact that this one reminds me of the dog I had when I was little, but the words fall out before I can stop them. "I'm going to adopt him!"

"Absolutely not." He crosses his arms.

That was the wrong thing to say to me. Not when I've already had the morning from hell. "You don't get to tell me what dogs I'm allowed to save!"

"He's not a dog. He's a direwolf."

I pet the dog's head. He *is* a bit wolfy, but he's got a collar, clearly he was somebody's pet. "He's very docile."

"He looks dangerous. And pissed off."

I huff under my breath. "Yeah, well, apparently that's how I like 'em."

"What was that?" Logan cocks his chin to the side.

I ignore his question when the wolf-dog's tail starts thwapping the ground. "Look, he's not mad. He's a perfect little angel! He's adorable!"

"Kelly, that hellhound has murder mitts the size of dinner plates and you're talking to it like it's some roly-poly kitten. We need to call animal control."

"No!" I shout. I inhale a lungful of air and slowly release it, fanning my fingers at my sides, attempting to stave off a hissy fit. "Okay," I say with a calm voice. "How about I take the dog to the vet and let them scan for a microchip. Just really quick. At least let me do that."

He glimpses at his watch. "You're going to be covered in stencil ink and telling someone to relax their arm in like . . . twenty minutes." He scrubs a hand over his face and sighs. "I'll take him to see if he's chipped."

"And if he's not?"

He purses his lips and stares at me. My eyes plead with him to let me keep this delightful furry monster.

"Then I'll adopt him," he declares.

Excuse me? I blink several times. "You mean, *I'll* adopt him?"

"No. I mean me."

"*You?*" I grimace. "You don't even like dogs!"

He cocks his head to the side, eyeing my new fuzzy best friend. "I like this one," he states.

What the fuck is happening? I survey the parking lot, hoping somebody else is nearby so they can confirm that yes, Logan has done a total one-eighty. Has he lost his mind?

Squaring my shoulders, I plant my feet in front of him, prepared to go toe-to-toe with a giant. "I have a house!"

"I have more square footage," he counters.

"You don't have a yard!"

Logan raises a brow. "There's a dog park across the street."

I cross my arms. "You complain when people eat too loud."

"I'll wear noise-canceling headphones."

My voice raises an octave. "You work too much."

He shrugs. "I'll work less."

I shove at his chest. "Logan!"

"Yes, Chaos?" He smiles and I flinch.

I narrow my eyes. "Why are you being such a dick right now?"

"This is too much dog for someone your size."

"That's bullshit, and we both know it," I say with a scoff.

"Maybe."

I look down at the adorable pup and sigh. If anybody needs a dog in their life, it's Logan. He needs a companion, someone to keep him company and form a quiet bond with. Someone to be with him when I can't. There's something about this sweet animal that reminds me of him, and it's not just the size. I probably can't afford to take care of a dog of this size anyway, at least not until I start tattooing full time. The food bill alone would bankrupt me.

"Shop dog?" I say, hoping for a compromise.

"We can't have a dog in the shop."

I sigh. It was worth a shot.

"Okay." I hand him the leash. "You can adopt him."

"If he's not already chipped," Logan adds.

He takes the leash from my fingers, gives a sharp whistle, and the dog falls right into step beside him as they march to his truck.

They're kind of a perfect match.

Logan is driving out of the parking lot when I swing the door to the shop open and return to my tattoo bay and iced Americano. My phone buzzes in my back pocket.

BlackShirtBlackPants554: You will never replace me.

"Oh, fuck off," I grumble, then lock the screen and stuff it back in my pocket. I roll my neck, trying to shake off the stress. My phone buzzes again, and I catch the notification at the top of the screen.

I clutch my drink, but condensation has built up around the sides of the plastic to-go cup, making it slick. As soon as I bring it to my mouth and sip from the straw, the drink slips from my fingers and lands at my feet, exploding on impact and spraying all of my clothes and every visible inch of my workstation.

I nod at the mess. "Cool."

Sighing, I trudge back to the kitchen area and wet some paper towels, then tuck a canister of Lysol wipes under my arm to get to work cleaning my space before my client arrives. I was hoping to ask Casper about my drawing, but it looks like that will have to wait until this afternoon because with the way my luck is going, I've got my work cut out for me today.

Every time I hear the shop's door open, I'm on my feet, checking to see if Logan is back. He's gone for over an hour before he returns. The back door opens, and I step out of my booth just in time to catch him sneaking in the back entrance—dog in tow—now sporting a fresh new collar fitted with a couple metal tags.

He actually fucking did it.

I stop at the end of the hallway and plant my hands on my hips. "What happened to no dogs allowed in the shop?"

His eyes catch mine, and he holds up a finger to his lips while sneaking the massive beast into his office.

"What did you name him?" I ask.

"Dogmeat."

My lips part. That's the most heinous name I've ever heard.

He chuckles, probably at the shock I'm wearing all over my face. "Relax. Thought I'd give you the honors. Pick something good."

17

LOGAN

Sitting in the chair across from my desk, Casper speaks with a hushed voice, even though the door is closed. "Are you sure you aren't taking this too far?"

That's rich coming from him; a house of cards has more stability than Casper.

Thor leans against the wall of my office with his arms crossed over his chest. He swivels his gaze to Casper and shoots an open palm in my direction. "Of course he's taking it too far!"

He grins ear to ear at Thor's outburst; he loves getting a rise out of him. Thankfully, Kelly is out taking the unnamed dog for a short walk. I've just finished going over the upcoming travel plans for the expo in Bozeman. I have no idea if she'll even be speaking to me by then.

Pinching the bridge of my nose, I sigh. This was always the plan. Did they think I wouldn't follow through? The hard part is over; Casper and I went out to Bozeman a few months ago and took care of everything. The only thing left to do is show up.

"I need you to trust me on this," I say, repeating myself from earlier.

Thor scoffs at that answer.

"Are you telling me you wouldn't have done the same with Salem if given half the chance?" I've struck a nerve. Hell, I've probably fucked up his entire nervous system by just mentioning her name. Casper oscillates back and forth between us while we have a mini stare-down.

Thor's jaw tics. "That's different," he growls.

"How?"

Casper gives a half-hearted laugh and waves his hand lazily. "I mean . . ."

Thor's situation wasn't anything like this. But still, he knows I'm right. He's just pissed I thought of it first.

Thor glares at Casper and then me. "Why me?"

"Insurance."

"If this ever—"

"It won't," I assure him. "I give you my word."

He gives me a long look. "You're being fucking reckless."

I shrug. He's right, but that doesn't change anything. "The ends justify the means. It stays between us," I remind him. "I'll owe you one."

Thor pushes off the wall and nearly rips the door off its hinges when he yanks it open. "Yeah, you will," he says, storming out and making the loose papers on my desk flutter. The door bounces off the wall and shudders while gently swinging.

Casper leans back in the chair and calls out the door. "That was your best dramatic exit yet!"

"I knew I shouldn't have brought her up." Mentioning her name was like tossing a grenade. It worked as I intended, but a dick move nonetheless.

"And yet you did it anyway." He smiles. "So . . . you ready for this?"

I smirk, turning my chair toward my screen and getting back to work. "What do you think?"

"I think you might be crazier than me," he says, grinning wider. *Impossible.*

I nod to the door. "Can you shut that? I have something else I want to show you."

He leans over, grabbing the edge of the door and nudging it shut. As soon as it clicks again, I remove the folded envelope from my drawer.

"Billy tried reaching out to Kelly."

I heard Kelly telling Thor she was staying late tonight, so I asked if she could watch the stray until I got back from running an errand. The more time they spend together, the better. I want her to become attached. Can't imagine it will take much, considering I'm already bonded and it's been less than forty-eight hours since I brought him home from the shelter.

The night Camden showed up with Chicken Salad, I was rock solid in my no-animals-allowed policy. But one look at Kelly with my dog and I'm bending the rules for her. Pathetic.

My "errand" is purchasing dog food, as if I didn't just do it yesterday. However, with the sour mood Kelly's been in the last week—which seems to have reached a crescendo today—it's a no-brainer to pick up her favorite pad thai from the restaurant on the other side of town. Took me a bit longer, but she needs to eat something. It's such a rare occasion to see her irritable. *I'm supposed to be the grumpy one.*

When I pull into the rear lot of Black Rabbit, I park next to the only car left—Kelly's. I snatch the plastic bag of Thai food with one hand, tucking the kibble under my arm before hopping out.

The autoclave is noisily running in the sterilization room when I return, but as I walk down the hall closer to her station, her voice becomes more audible. It sounds like she's talking to someone on the phone. I soften my footsteps and carefully set down the food in my office, then tiptoe closer so I can eavesdrop.

Even better, the mirror in Casper's workstation across from Kelly's offers a perfect view of her, but I don't like what I see reflected back. Her eyes are heavy the way they are when she's been thinking for too long. And she's not on the phone, she's talking to my dog.

Kelly sits on the backless stool and scratches behind his ears. "Over a week. No calls, no voice notes, no memes, nothing . . . I saw him at work, but I was careful to hold my boundaries and keep my space. It's this cleanse thing I'm doing." She speaks while signing at the same time. She's made a lot of improvement in the last few months.

"I don't think he's even noticed," she says.

I've noticed—every day, every hour, every fucking minute that passed has been done in misery.

I've played her little game all week. I kept myself occupied with work and went to bed early every night. It was easier to keep busy and sleep than admit she's stopped talking to me, and seeing her day after day and wondering what she's thinking.

"Then *you* show up. And he decides he's going to keep you. Not gonna lie, I was mad at first, but you seem like kindred spirits. Unfortunately, now it makes it harder for me too."

Our dog yawns and rests his head on her knee. Her fingers delve into the long fur on his shoulder blades. She withdraws her hands to sign, but this time she doesn't speak while doing it. Like saying the words out loud is too difficult. Her movements are a little fumbled, but I'm able to piece together what she's trying to say.

"I was hoping for some clarity, ya know? Thought if I had a break from him, I'd realize I was confusing his comfort for something else. Maybe I'd discover that my feelings toward him were simply . . . codependence."

Her eyes soften, and she looks so fucking . . . dejected. She's been masking her sadness with anger. I'd rather carve out my kneecaps than see her hurting like this. Fuck.

"I wanted to ignore the feelings so they would just go away."

The dog huffs out a big sigh.

"I know, that shit never works, but I had to try," she says aloud.

A small smile crosses my lips.

"You want to know what hurts the most?" Hearing her voice crack is like a knife in my chest.

She wipes her fingers under her eyes that I now realize are brimming with tears. "He's fine!" She laughs.

Guilt clogs my throat.

The dog lifts his head.

"What kind of bullshit is that, anyway?" She groans. "Ignoring my feelings for him hurts more than my split with Jason did. Isn't that fucked? And the longer we go without speaking, the harder it is." She wipes away a tear. "Now when he's around, he makes the job I love feel like servitude . . . I'll never be able to truly let go when he owns my family's shop. But breakups don't last forever, eventually the pain fades."

She's not talking about her ex, she's talking about me.

Our dog lifts a paw to rest on her knee, and I appreciate him comforting her in a way I can't right now. Well, I could, but I'm too selfish. I'd rather get caught up on what's going on in her head, since she's been keeping me in the dark.

"You know what it feels like? It's like being locked in a room with only two exits. Behind one door is inevitable heartbreak, and behind the other is endless longing . . . and neither is an escape. So I just keep staying in the room, trapped."

He lowers his paw to the floor, and she holds him captive again with her hands as she signs more. "I hate having a crush in adulthood. It's way worse than when I was a teenager, because now there's thick forearms and hot, broody demeanors. And your new dad has them both in spades. He's not as gorgeous as you are, but he's still . . . Damn, he's *something*, that's for sure."

My chin drops to my chest and I grin in amusement. I could not be happier with her admission. We're finally getting on the same page at the same time. The furry menace lifts his head and licks her palm.

"I'm gonna get over it," she vows. "You'll see."

I roll my eyes. *Like hell.*

"Or I won't, and I'll be cursed to live out the rest of my days miserable and horny. Ugh, this is so unconstructive!" She furrows her brow. "No, not you. You're terrific. In fact, you should look into getting your therapy license."

Looks like ol' Dogmeat can be an emotional support dog after all.

With her head cocked to the side, she strokes his fur. Kelly gazes at him thoughtfully. I'm about to interrupt when she speaks.

"Wanna know something crazy?" she asks. "I got a letter from my dad the other day, and he told me to 'find someone who takes in the strays. Who observes beauty without taking a photograph. Who has art in their soul and fire in their veins the same way you do.'" She continues, whispering, "That's Logan . . . *He described Logan.*"

I glance at the ceiling and sign *thank you* to Clyde. For being dead, the old man is doing some serious heavy lifting. He can't take full credit, I'd already read his letter the night of her birthday while cleaning up the kitchen, but I appreciate the playbook nonetheless. *Why else would I have gone through all this trouble?* Clyde would have done the same thing for Nancy, so I consider that a stamp of approval.

"Do you think he'd be a good partner?" she asks.

The dog groans. *Way to help, asshole.*

"What? I'm serious. He's a great friend, so probably. He dated someone years ago, I never met her, but I guess they had a bad breakup or something because he doesn't talk about it. To be honest, I've never seen him with another woman . . . ever. Wait a minute . . ." Her eyes grow wide. "What if he's—"

All right, we're done here.

I step into the light, interrupting that thought before she can finish it. "Come up with a name for him yet?"

18

KELLY

His voice catches me off guard, and I yelp, pressing a hand to my heaving chest. I blink a few times, catching my breath. "What the fuck, Logan?" I shout. "You can't just sneak up on people in an empty shop!"

He offers a bemused smile, as if my fear is idle entertainment for him. "My dog is here. Did you think I wasn't coming back?"

"No, just hoping," I mutter, waving my crossed fingers.

I was having a perfectly lovely evening without him. Confessing all my inner thoughts to his dog was therapeutic, almost like practice for when I inevitably have to say them to his face. But I'm not ready yet. The possibility of rejection is too high, and the dismissal itself is too much to bear. *Oh, did you think I was* actually *flirting with you?* he'll ask.

Logan steps into my station and pats the dog—that was *supposed* to be mine—on his haunches with a couple thumps. "I was half expecting you to kidnap him while I was gone."

"It crossed my mind," I admit with a raised chin.

"So, what's the name?"

I glance down at the pretty animal. "I wanted to name him Logan. Just so you would look like a jackass if you ever tried to use him as bait to pick up women . . . Also, if he ever tried to run away, the image of you jogging down the street, screaming your own name, is pure comedy. But that felt like punishing the dog, so . . ."

He crosses his arms. "Aren't you a funny girl . . ."

"I think you should name him Odin, after the Norse god. The first tattoo you ever did was of Odin's two wolves."

Logan narrows his eyes curiously. He's probably wondering how I know that. My dad took a candid photo of him tattooing his first client—he was so proud of him.

I marvel at the dog while stroking the fur behind his ears, where it's softest. *He looks so similar.* "I used to have a dog like this when I was a little girl named Loki. In Norse mythology, Odin and Loki have a sort of brotherhood thing, so I figure that gives me partial custody."

Logan raises an eyebrow. "So—just to be clear—in this scenario, you're his mom?"

Then it hits me. I didn't actually *hear* Logan come in. A wave of heat rises up my neck as the panic sets in. "How long were you standing there before you walked in?" I blurt.

He leans back onto the half wall and crosses his arms, boring his hazel eyes into mine.

My lips part at the same time my arms fall lifeless at my sides. *Please, no.*

"Answer me, Logan." I want the ground to open up and swallow me whole. Let me live out the rest of my days among the floor joists and asbestos.

He doesn't respond. His gaze strips me bare, and my heart gallops faster and faster. The vulnerability terrifies me, but not as much as the kernel of hope that wants to unfold in my chest. I'm not ready to do this.

His continued silence transforms my fear to anger. This isn't fair. Logan has always been the one to think in silence, whereas I do my thinking out loud. For our entire friendship, I've always given him my words. Sarcastic ones, vulnerable ones, aimless rambling ones. For years he's gotten them for free, stuffing his face at *Kelly's all-you-can-eat buffet of feelings.* Not anymore, the kitchen is closed.

The ones he heard tonight weren't for him—not for free. If he wants any more, he's going to have to earn them, and if he wants to play the quiet game, then so be it.

"I want to be alone," I demand, standing and brushing the black dog hair off my thighs, pleased to avoid his eye contact.

"Why?"

"Because I want it!" I snap. "That's the point. I don't owe you any more of an explanation."

"You do when it's space from me."

My palms stop swiping at my jeans and I freeze, giving him a long blink. My face reddens, this time not from embarrassment but fury. *Did he really just say that?*

"We"—I wag my finger between us—"need time apart."

He has the nerve to smirk at me. "A week wasn't enough for you?"

"No."

He steps closer, towering over me, and I push my shoulders back.

"Why not?" he asks, again.

I scoff. "What are you, a fucking toddler? Because I said so." I turn my back to him and busy myself with cleaning my workstation so I can get out of here.

"Look at me."

I shake my head. I'm more than happy to sit this one out.

"Damn it, Kelly. Look at me!" he roars.

"Fine!" I yell, spinning in his direction and placing my hands on my hips, noticing that Odin is standing between us defensively. He stares Logan down, and for a brief second I relish the smug satisfaction of his protection. "What?"

His voice levels out. "Talk to me."

I laugh and throw my arms up—the audacity of this man. "All I fucking do is talk to you, Logan! And all you do is stare back. The little you do say is stuck in my head for days while I try to make sense of what you meant. I'm tired of it! I'm done being the one who goes first. Spill your own guts for once."

My chest heaves and tears rise to the surface. Somehow I got the gene that makes me cry when I get really angry. It's so inconvenient. I don't want him to think I'm weak, because I'm not.

His stiff jaw releases when he opens his mouth to speak, and I hold my breath. Then he closes it. Like he always does. We stare at each other, waiting. With every second that passes, the kernel in my chest hardens. *It will always be this way.* He's never going to let me in. He's never going to trust me with his thoughts and feelings. A tear slips, and I turn away from him because tears say just as much as words do.

Odin sits, his anxiety eased by the calmer tones.

This is such a waste of time. His silence takes away some of the pain and replaces it with numbness. I'm calling in sick tomorrow.

He breaks the silence. "I like you."

I scoff. "But?" I continue for him, moving to the counter and stuffing my tablet into my bag. Every cell in my body is yelling to flee from this humiliation.

He grabs me by the hips and spins me around, pressing my back against the counter. His hands brace the hard surface on either side of me, caging me in, and he leans down until we're face-to-face. Odin barks, and I flinch at the deep warning growl that follows.

Logan turns his head slightly to ease the dog's worries. "Odin, sit." Surprisingly, he follows the command.

Cornered by him, Logan drags his attention back to me and his deliberate eyes search mine.

"If you want me to talk, then you're going to fucking listen."

I give a subtle nod, unsure of what's about to happen. He has that wild look in his eyes again, the one he had after Casper and Thor hauled him off Jason.

"I've been your friend out of respect for Clyde, but the things I imagine doing with you are so fucking unfriendly."

I forget how to breathe.

He releases a ragged sigh, like the words have been echoing in his chest for years. We study each other until he stands to his full height again and brings his hands to my waist, his thumbs grazing back and forth over my stomach. I can't move.

"Inhale," he instructs.

His command makes me suddenly aware of the way my lungs are burning for oxygen, and I suck in a breath. The silence that stretches between us might be the most we've ever shared.

"Since when?" I ask.

"Before Clyde died, he made me promise to let you grow up before I made any move."

"My dad knew?"

He nods, giving a small chuckle. "Before I did."

Something about Dad giving Logan his blessing, even if it wasn't immediate, offers me peace. It calms the swirling chaos in my thoughts. Dad saw the good in him, and knew that it was good for me, too. My feelings aren't as confusing as they once were, but they don't explain where we go from here.

"So, now what?"

His grip on me tightens as he lifts me onto the edge of the countertop. My palms press to the cold surface, and I grasp the edge. He smirks and steps between my thighs, cupping my face in his hands.

My pulse roars in my ears, his woodsy scent enveloping me as he leans in and brushes his lips against mine. They curve into an arrogant smile, his movements uttering *I told you so*, like this kiss is everything he already knew it would be, and he just won the battle he's been fighting for years.

Our lips fall into a perfectly matched rhythm, convincing me our mouths were made for each other; kissing him is the most natural thing in the world, and I commit every second of it to memory. His actions are hungry and deliberate, as if after years of anticipation he's determined to take his time with me and savor every second.

My heart hammers as he seizes my jaw, tilting my chin higher until I have no choice but to surrender to him as he deepens the kiss. I'm intoxicated by the heady mix of raw need and adrenaline coursing through me. His tongue teases mine, and I taste his restraint with every pass. The more he holds back, the greedier I become, stoking the fire that licks at my core. My fingers curl into his shirt, and I fist the material, drawing him closer.

His lips are controlled and commanding, much like him.

"Logan," I say, catching my breath. "Be unfriendly with me."

19

LOGAN

Fucking hell. The moment her mouth touched mine, the wall between us came crashing down. It was about time, I'd been slowly chipping away at it for years, waiting for the inevitable collapse. No other woman could bring me to my knees the way she has. Our kiss has proven what I knew all along—*she's it*. We've officially crossed the line, and I'll scorch the path we took to get here to make sure we never go back to just friends.

I've been patient for years, and her plea to be *unfriendly* has me wanting to rip her clothes off with my teeth. She tastes like mint gum and my future wife, because I'm never letting go of this.

She nips my bottom lip, the small act of aggression spurs me on, I grip her tighter and she moans against my mouth, tugging at my self-control. Nothing could have prepared me for her. Her sweet tongue, that seductive sound, I'm one more desperate whimper away from losing control. My palms find her ass as I deepen our kiss and tug her into me. She instinctively lifts her knees, wrapping them around me. Goddamn, she's perfect.

Her fingertips slip under the hem of my shirt, brushing over the bare skin at my waist. My cock twitches and I press her against it so she can feel exactly what she does to me. Her teasing touch travels up my chest. I have wanted this, wanted her, for too long.

Kelly grinds against me, and I furrow my brow, groaning because I know this next part is going to kill me. She sighs on my lips. *Fuck, doesn't she realize I'm fighting for my life here?* As much as I want to take her right here on this counter—I gotta slow us down. Way down.

"Hold up," I rasp, regretting the words already.

"What's wrong?" she asks, breathless.
She's not making this easy.
"We can't."
Her fingers trail down my stomach and drop at her sides. *Don't pull away.* I circle my arms behind her back, refusing to let her. I've been waiting to fuck this woman for years and now she's got her legs wrapped around me and I have to say no. My dick may never forgive me.

When it comes to Kelly, I feel the same way Clyde did about Nancy, it was her or nothing. There was no point in trying to go after anyone else because I already knew what I wanted, I just had to bide my time until she was mine. I am not a very patient man, but for her? For her I'd wait a goddamn lifetime.

I fold her into my chest, tucking my head down to whisper in her ear. "It's not a question of want," I promise. "I want you so fucking bad. But this won't be something we do because the opportunity presented itself. This isn't a onetime thing. I'm not temporary. You're barely out of the breakup with the guy you said you could see a future with."

I retreat a step, and she winces with remorse reflecting in her gaze.

"It's okay," I say, chuckling. I palm the back of her neck and squeeze three times, assuring her I'm fine. "Give me time to prove to you that *I'm* the one you have a future with. I need to know you're all in. When I finally work you over," I say. Her bruised lips part, and I run my thumb over her lower pout. "I want you begging for it. Begging for me, for us, for everything."

She makes a frustrated sound. "You're kinda killing the mood."

"I'm not killing it, Chaos. I'm winding you tighter."

Her laugh is the last sound she makes before I press my mouth to hers again, kissing her slow and deep, letting my kiss say all the words I couldn't—that she's mine now and I'm never giving her up.

Kelly looks behind me and her eyes widen. "Where's the dog?"

I turn around, and she scurries off the counter.

"Shit," I mutter. "Odin!"

Then I hear it, the swoosh of the plastic bag. I rush to my office, catching him trying to paw his way into the disposable Thai food containers that are half covered in slobber.

"Oh my God," Kelly says, laughing—her face still glowing from the kiss, that blush on her cheeks has me biting my knuckles.

I crouch down and snatch the not-yet-breached pad thai containers, passing them to Kelly.

"I'll go wash these off," she says, walking out the doorway.

I plant hands on my hips, scolding him with a look. "Dude . . . Did you see what I had going on? You couldn't have waited ten minutes?" I pick up the mess of napkins, battered sauce packets, and everything else he tore apart. "I'm out there trying to get you a mom, and you're in here eating our dinner. Those bail burgers were a onetime thing, man. The least you could've done is claw into your dog food," I whisper-shout.

He eyes the bag of dog food, then tries tearing into that as if I just gave him permission. "Easy, easy!"

I toss everything in my hands into the trash can, then wrench the bag of kibble out of his stiff jaws. "Let me get a damn dish first. You're behaving like an animal."

Kelly waltzes back into my office with two clean containers of pad thai. "Good as new!"

"You get started on yours, it's probably getting cold. I'm gonna feed this hound before he begins eating my desk too."

I find some old Tupperware in the employee lounge and fill it up for him. I'm not sure how much I'm supposed to feed him, but I assume big motherfuckers need big-motherfucker-sized portions. As soon as the dish touches the floor, he goes to town, gobbling it up.

"Christ, bud. Don't forget to come up for air."

The sight of Odin devouring his food reminds me of a piece of wisdom Clyde imparted on me when I first began apprenticing for him in my early twenties. He once told me that eating pussy was an art form, it should start like a butterfly landing on a flower and end like a bulldog eating a bowl of oatmeal.

I pat Odin on the back. Good thing the old man had the foresight to be cremated, because he'd be flopping around in his grave if he learned his advice would someday be used on his daughter.

20

KELLY

I expected him to be here early, but apparently he's taking his oath to dog parenting seriously. I'm proud of him. He strode into Black Rabbit this morning whistling like he didn't just have his cock pressed between my thighs a mere fourteen hours earlier. My stomach flutters as soon as he makes eye contact and smirks. Darting my gaze away, I scurry into my workstation to get ready for the appointments lined up today. I swear the events of last night are written on my face for the whole shop to see.

He strides down the aisle, heading toward the front of the building, and then I hear him talking to Thor. I can't hear what they're saying, but Thor laughs. *He's not talking about me, he's not talking about me.* Even though this is my family business, I don't want to be known as the girl who sleeps with her boss. Technically, we didn't have sex—though not for lack of effort on my part.

I never felt intimidated by Logan the way other people were, but I'm starting to get it now. He wields authority at his discretion. Even Odin doesn't think twice before following his commands.

"Morning," he says, on his way back to his office. I lift my hand in a wave without looking, and he chuckles, pausing in front of my tattoo bay. "Your client is here."

"Huh? Oh. Thanks." They're early. I was going to grab a new box of latex gloves from the stock room, but I've got enough to get me through the next appointment. I'll grab a new pack afterward.

He nods, then turns into his station that sits across the aisle from mine, and up one, so we're diagonal from one another. From the right angle, we can see each other if we're working at the same time. Which it looks like we'll be doing today.

* * *

"I love it," Jane gushes when I wipe away the excess ink. I've been working on her for the last forty-five minutes, inking a sexy merman on her arm.

"Thanks, me too!" I beam, offering a brief smile before returning to the tattoo. I peer at Logan across the way. He's hunched over his prone client, tattooing the back of their shoulder. As usual, he's working in silence.

Stop staring.

Tearing my eyes away, I anchor my elbow and continue on. I've already outlined the piece and am currently adding miniature sailor tattoos to his chest with fine blue lines. The machine buzzes against my grip. Normally the steady vibration is enough to put me into a trance so I can zone out while tattooing, but not today. Today, Logan occupies my thoughts.

We made out less than a foot away from where I sit now. I can practically smell his clean, woodsy cologne lingering from the night before.

I wrap my latex-gloved hand around my client's wrist and adjust her forearm, stretching the skin to get a finer line while adding a simplified ship tattoo to the merman's chest.

Focus on your work. It's difficult when I feel his eyes on me; I suspect he's playing the same game I am. How can I not look at him when he altered my brain chemistry with that kiss?

"We're almost finished," I say.

"I love it."

That makes me smile as I work. I'm very satisfied with this one; all my curves are smooth and clean, the colors are vibrant, the placement on her inner forearm is flawless. Shading even. When I'm finished, I wipe the piece and sit back to inspect my work. Dad was a firm believer in *bold will hold* when it came to any American style. Rich colors and strong linework make all the difference. These mermen are a nod to the mermaids he used to do but with my own little twist. Dad would approve.

I glance at Logan, and for the first time, he looks up at the same time I do. His eyes glow like hot embers, like he's been tattooing fifteen feet away with the same wicked thoughts in his head. However, it's his sexy wink that makes me forget how to breathe.

After Jane leaves, I get my station cleaned up and check the notification on my phone.

RedShirtBlackPants11: You won't replace me.

I roll my eyes.

KellyEverhartTattoo: Fuck off, Jason. You replaced me first.

I can't prove he's the one who has been leaving these creepy messages, but it doesn't take a rocket scientist to figure it out when they started coming in the night he got into that fight with Logan. I toss my phone on the counter, then head to the stock room to grab a fresh box of black latex gloves before my next appointment arrives. On my tiptoes, I probe the top shelf for a box of my size. There's supposed to be a step stool in here, but nobody ever puts it back where it belongs.

"Damn it. Where are they?" It's times like this I find my short five-two height annoying.

"Need help?"

Before I can answer, he's brushing up behind me. He grabs the box from the top shelf and lowers it in front of me and drops his lips to my ear. "You look really good today." His voice is low—*predatory*.

Trapped against the shelf, my pulse races. I suck in a breath. "If you fluster me and I botch someone's tattoo, I'm sending them your way so you can explain why my ink is crooked."

"If you can't pull a clean line, that's on you," he says playfully. "I can't be held responsible for your shoddy work."

A nervous laugh escapes me. "Aren't you supposed to be my mentor? I can feel your eyes on me out there. It's distracting."

"Yes, and as your mentor, I get to study you. I notice every shake of your hands and every slip of your needle." I hear the smirk in his voice as he continues, "And I'll teach you how to keep going even when those hands are trembling so much you can barely hold the machine."

I swallow. The way his intense gaze follows me around the shop is thrilling. I'm impressed by how much my senses pick up on his proximity. The tension we share—even from a distance—is scorching. Like tortuous foreplay.

"Does that mean you're going to put a move on me today the way you did last night?" I've been wanting to ask him more about that kiss. *Was he caught up in the moment? Was it premeditated? Was it even real, or did I imagine the whole thing?*

"No."

The rejection stings the smile right off my face.

"Not yet," he adds.

We've been friends long enough that he should know how much that kiss has been occupying my thoughts, how I've been overanalyzing it. The only relief I've found is the way his eyes have been undressing me all day. He deserves a little payback.

"Might do you some good." I rotate the box of gloves in my hands. "Overworked and underfucked is bad for your prostate."

He huffs out a laugh. "Chaos."

I smile. He says the nickname like a warning.

"What?" I shrug. "It's important to take care of your health. We can lock the door so nobody sees."

He jerks me tight against his front, and I let the box of gloves fall at my feet. Wow, he's strong.

"If you don't stop flirting with me like this, I'm going to lay you down and invite them to watch."

I bite my lip.

He spins me to face him, then slides a palm under my shirt, snaking it up my side until his thumb is just brushing the underside of my breast. Cunning eyes pierce mine like he's already conquered me. The knuckles on his other hand caress the underside of my chin, tilting my face up to meet his. "And when I finally hold you down and break you in, I'm going to show you the difference between playmates and soul mates."

His words knock the air from my chest.

He simply smiles, then backs away. "Have a good afternoon, Kelly," he says. "Oh, and I need you to come in on Monday. I'm on your books."

He's on my books? "You want me to tattoo you?"

He turns on his heel and walks out, throwing a "Yup" over his shoulder and leaving me standing there with my arms at my sides, a box of latex gloves at my feet, and a thrashing heart in my throat.

Hours after the accosting he gave me in the supply closet, I'm cleaning up my station after a busy day. I spray disinfectant on the counter, sweeping the towel over the surface. Logan casually leans into the opening of my bay and tells me his request for the tattoo he has in mind. It nearly has me doubling over in laughter. But he's not joining in.

The smile fades from my lips. I turn, narrowing my eyes in disbelief and shaking my head; there's no way I heard that right. He's kicked back in my client chair with his feet up, threading his fingers behind his head, as if he was simply asking about the weather.

"Absolutely not," I scoff. "Are you fucking nuts?"

Casper huffs out a laugh from across the aisle. Besides me and Logan, he's the only one left in the shop. He's sketching out a commission for his new client Anna. Casper seems pretty jazzed about whatever idea they came up with together.

My eyes refocus on Logan. I lean back against the countertops, gesturing to him with open palms. "Why would you even want that?"

"Because it's permanent."

"Exactly!" I counter. "This isn't like some rose or eagle or whatever."

"I know, that's why I'm asking you to do it." He glances up at me with sincerity in his eyes.

"Even if it wasn't totally insane—which it is, by the way—what you're describing is too intricate. I haven't done large portraits."

"Maybe not with tattoo ink, but you've done at least fifty with a pen and pencil."

"Yeah, that's a flat surface!" I argue, crossing my arms.

"Use a stencil," he says. "Your piece for Bozeman is more intricate than this one." *How can he have so much confidence in me?* This is way above my pay grade.

"I don't think I'm ready for a project like this."

"You are," he presses.

His bare bicep holds my attention as I size up the area. "I've never done a piece that big before."

"I never did a full leg wrap until I did one," he argues, then raises his voice louder. "Casper, can Kelly do a black-and-gray portrait?"

He wanders over and leans against the half wall at the entrance of my workstation. "Where's it going?"

"There." I point at his arm.

"Yeah, I think she could do it."

They're both crazy.

Logan raises a smug eyebrow. "You're not some brand-new apprentice anymore. You can do this."

Casper smiles and pushes off the wall to return to his work.

With a furrowed brow, I close the distance between me and the lunatic sitting in my chair. I extract his hand from behind his head, straightening his elbow, and the muscle in his forearm twitches as if he's resisting the urge to touch me. His hazel eyes track the way my fingers travel over his skin as I rotate his arm and inspect the area. *If I did take on this project, what would be the best strategy?* My lips purse as I think it through.

My gaze darts between his stare and the blank canvas on his bicep. "Can I do something not based in realism?"

He gives a single nod, but those eyes don't leave mine for a second.

I swallow. "What if it's ugly?" I whisper. "What if it doesn't work out?"

He curls his fingers in the waistband of my jeans and tugs me close. A shiver ripples across my skin. "Are we talking about the tattoo or something else?"

Yes.

I gulp down the hesitation and brush over his bicep. "What if you regret it?"

Our eyes meet, and the corners of his crinkle with a smile—not cocky or smug, just unequivocal certainty. "I've wanted you to mark me permanently for longer than you know. I'll never regret having something that ties me to you."

21

LOGAN

"Hope you're ready for this, because it's too late to change your mind," she mutters, setting up her supplies. We've come in on Monday to knock out the first session, or as much as she can get done. She didn't back down from the challenge; maybe she knew I wouldn't let her walk away from it.

I provided her with the candid photo, taken before we began our photo shoot, the one of her gazing out the window. Of course she looked beautiful, but that's no different from any other photo of her. However, in this one, she was *real*—unguarded and raw in a way that could never be replicated no matter what direction I gave her. It captured who she is in every way—her softness with sharp edges. It's not just her looks I want tattooed on me, it's her soul. She was given free rein and full creative control. Two days later she handed me a masterpiece.

Grabbing the collar of my shirt at the nape of my neck, I pull it over my head. She pauses for a moment, dragging her eyes from my waist, up my stomach and chest, and finally to the arm she's going to tattoo to gawk like a true professional. I find great amusement in the way she stares at me like I'm something she plans to devour.

She's modified her portrait into a wild frenzy of black lines, giving the tattoo a hand-sketched appearance. The intent of sketch tattoos isn't to appear flawless but rather to highlight the natural evolution of shapes coming together to make art.

The piece starts with fewer lines on top near my shoulder, making her face appear brighter with a light source from above. From there, it continues toward my elbow, where the lines become heavier and unruly with shading and shadows, until they mesh into total coverage. She's drawn her long raven hair with a few pieces blowing across her face, but the rest of it flows down my biceps until it bleeds into my blacked-out forearm. The incomplete strokes, the bold, rough lines, the use of negative space, it all comes together in magnificent contrast. I'm in awe.

I wanted Kelly as she sees herself, in whatever style she wanted . . . but what she designed is beyond anything I could have done. Beautiful, chaotic, and complex—and all the ways she's tangled herself into my life.

"This is going to be great in your portfolio."

She barks out a laugh. "Ha! Like I'm putting my own face in my portfolio . . . Talk about a vanity piece," she grumbles.

She studies the full coverage below my elbow, running her fingertips over the ink. "Are you cool with me going into this with white? Just to make sure it flows . . . And I think we should touch up some of your black too, so it blends naturally."

"Whatever you want, Chaos. I trust you."

She grasps my wrist with her gloved hand and sanitizes my bicep and forearm with green soap before going in with a disposable razor to remove any hair. Afterward, she wipes it with antiseptic. The stencil sits on her clean station cart in four different pieces.

After she gets the first three stencils placed, the last one on the bottom proves difficult to match up with the other pieces, so she has to cut and adjust it to get it to cooperate. Kelly doesn't speak, just furrows her brow, determined to make it work. She peels off the final stencil from my arm, offering a preview of the finished product in bright indigo. I'm in love.

"Okay, stand up, take a look in the mirror."

The way she's created it to blend in with the ink on my forearm is so fucking cool. My smile nearly splits my face. "Incredible."

She shakes her head with a half grin. She knows it's awesome but is too preoccupied by pretending to be annoyed with me. When she's finished filling her ink caps and has arranged her everything to her liking—my arm included—she takes ink into her 5 round liner needle. The illustrative sketch is made up of different line weights; some mimic the slash of a pen, varying in size up to thick paintbrush strokes. She has an array of needles arranged by size in unopened pouches on her tray. She'll be switching these up during the session, but she's starting with the more delicate sections toward the top.

Her eyes find mine. "Ready?"

I nod, and she exhales. As soon as she pulls that first line on my shoulder, I sigh with relief. Putting her face on such a prominent part of my body, one I'd been saving for her, is my offering—and she's taken it.

Over the years, I've watched her tattoo hundreds of times, but this is different because I am the one under her needle. She's done work on her friends and the other guys at the shop with little things for practice, but I didn't want her to mark me until she was ready for more than just practice. This is about permanence.

"You could have had anything here. Why my face?" she asks.

She's not ready for that answer, so I sidestep the question, letting her focus. "Don't think of it as your face. You're tattooing a piece you made. It's art . . . that just happens to be your face."

Pride fills my chest while watching Kelly work on me. Her lines are clean and sure. I've witnessed her progression over the years, seen her struggle through the days of riding the tube and uneven shading to the sharp lines and smooth curves she makes on me today.

She lifts the machine and anchors her elbow, ensuring she has the correct depth.

"Nice pressure," I mutter.

She flicks her eyes to mine for a brief second. "You're not allowed to critique me while I work."

I smirk. She's more confident than she was the other day when I presented her with my request. "That wasn't a critique, it was praise."

"It was a *positive critique*," she argues. "You chose to have my face on you forever, which means you forfeit your right to any commentary."

I chuckle. "That's not really how apprenticeships work."

"That's how this is going to work."

"Yes, ma'am," I reply.

The corner of her mouth tilts into an amused grin. She works in silence for the next twenty minutes or so, and I get to stare all I want.

"Are you all packed for Bozeman?" I ask. We fly out Friday morning—only four days away. I'm very familiar with how my body heals when it comes to ink, which means I'll only be able to show off her work for a day or two at the expo before the scabbing begins to form. The timing is going to be tight.

"Yeah, I spent most of yesterday packing, just have to get my gear together."

"Model still good to go?" I ask.

"Yup. She's all set. If anything, I'm the one who's getting cold feet."

That surprises me. "Why?"

She shrugs while switching needles. "I've never tattooed for an audience before; what if I can't focus? Not to mention, comparing my work to other artists... My impostor syndrome is going to flare up. Plus, you know, judges."

"You've got a great piece planned. Forget the other artists, forget the judges, you're competing against yourself."

She blots away the ink. "I love that you think I'm less critical when I compete against myself. That's when I question everything. Should I add more contrast? Can my lines be tighter? Are my shadows where they need to be?"

"Every artist sees flaws in their work, but you gotta remember that it's art. Art doesn't have rules, it's a lawless, subjective beast. You have good instincts, trust your gut. You're going to kill it."

She chuckles, taking more ink into her needle. "You're biased." She presses it to my upper arm, continuing along the lines she's stenciled.

"Perhaps... I also know talent when I see it."

She's too busy concentrating on a particularly long line that she has to whip in and out of to reply. As soon as she completes it, I open my mouth to tell her she did an excellent job in the places she had to pick up and stop.

"Speaking of Bozeman, who is watching Odie?" That's become her newest nickname for him.

"Jordan is taking him. He was introduced to Chicken Salad yesterday, and they're already thick as thieves."

"I hate that we're leaving him so soon," she says.

"We, huh?"

She shakes her head. "You know what I mean. You just adopted him. What if he thinks he's getting abandoned again?"

That's why I'm not boarding him. The last thing I want to do is put him in another kennel after he just got busted out. "Already ahead of you. Jordan is house-sitting so he doesn't have to leave his familiar home. It works out since Camden is in Canada this weekend for the playoffs anyway."

Her shoulders seem to relax with that news. "Look at you already being a good daddy."

I cock an eyebrow at the suggestive title and she blushes. "Too bad he can't be a shop dog."

"He's happier taking a nap on the couch and barking at squirrels across the street at home than he would be waiting around on this cold tile floor or in my cramped office."

I once did a guest spot at a tattoo shop that allowed artists to bring their dogs to work, and I'll never do it again. The floors were filthy, twice a dog hair floated into one of my ink caps, and I had to start all over again with a clean setup. Outside of having a service animal, it's a major health hazard for everyone involved.

The first hour passes quickly, which mostly consists of her peppering me with questions regarding Odin and how he and I are adjusting to our new cohabitation. I can't deny it, there's something fantastic about coming home to a happy dog at the end of the day. He's very chill. It's an ideal arrangement.

I smile, savoring the feel of her touch as she works.

"Sooo . . ." she says. "Are we going to talk about that kiss?"

My chin drops and I smile. "Sure."

"I'm just making sure it wasn't a heat-of-the-moment thing or—"

"It wasn't," I answer, cutting her off.

The only sound between us is the buzz of her machine.

"How do you feel?" I ask.

"I'm a little nervous. I think we should start slow. I'm recently out of a relationship, I just want to make sure I'm not jumping into something too soon. Especially with you."

I examine her cautious expression. "Do you trust me?"

"Of course," she says, pulling a thicker line with her new needle.

"Good. Look, I'm not going to lie to you, if the kind of slow you're talking about is rooted in hesitancy, then I'm not interested. I want you all in."

She scoffs. "I'm not allowed to be nervous?"

"You're allowed to feel anything you want, but you also need to understand my intentions. That's why we're talking about it."

Kelly takes more ink into her needle. "So what are your intentions?"

I gather my words carefully. "This will never be a 'see what happens' thing for me. I'm not built that way—not when it comes to you."

"We've known each other for a long time, don't you think we should start casually?"

I bark out a laugh. "We've known each other too long for us to ever be casual. Us and casual will never coexist."

"You've thought about this a lot, haven't you?" she asks.

Years. It wasn't until she expressed that Jason could be something long-term that I realized she had reached that point in her maturity when she was ready for more. When I learned she desired something more than dating and was planning for something that didn't have an end date.

"Yes."

"You sound like an intense boyfriend." She chuckles.

A smile spreads across my face. *Wait till you see how I am as your husband.*

"I'm not a boy, Chaos—and I'm not your friend." *Not after feeling her lips on mine.*

She stops tattooing and sits up straight, looking me in the eye.

"I'm a man who knows what he wants. For years I've stood in the background, biding my time while you chased flings. It wasn't patience, it was discipline. The way I wanted you never grew stronger—it grew darker. There's no one else for me. You're it."

It's not a coincidence I haven't dated anyone all this time.

Her lips part. "Why didn't you ever say anything?"

"Because you weren't ready to want me back—not in the way I did. Your dad knew that, and made me promise to give you time to live your life freely without being tied down to someone like me." I rest my palm on her warm thigh. "But now you're a big girl who can make her own decisions. So, what is it going to be . . . are you ready for me, or do you need a couple more years to figure out what you don't want?"

Her cheeks darken into a beautiful rosy hue.

For years, this woman has silently crawled up my sides, growing like wild, untamed vines, wrapping around my neck and rib cage. There's no use in trying to cut away my desire for her. I've tried, and every time, it grew back stronger. It's too late to slow down or scale back. Our lives are too tangled together—our relationship is inevitable.

"Logan . . ."

"I'm just asking you to continue to trust me." This time with her heart.

"Okay."

I smile. "You're ready?"

She attempts to stifle a grin. "I've already kissed you. I think we both know there's no going back after that."

Cradling her face, I draw her lips to mine and kiss her again. She sighs softly. I no longer have to wonder what she tastes like or how her mouth feels on mine. I can finally kiss her whenever the thought crosses my mind.

With flushed cheeks, she presses her elbow into my chest and nudges me to sit back into her client chair, narrowing her eyes at my smug grin. She draws more ink into the needle and returns her focus to my arm.

"Stop distracting me. I'm trying to work."

"Wouldn't dream of it." I grin.

"Yeah, right . . . How's everything feeling, by the way?" she asks.

"Great. You have a light touch."

"Just wait until I start blacking out your elbow," she mutters under her breath. "Think you'll be able to keep up your intensity when you start crying in my chair?"

I wink at her. "I like when it hurts." I'm convinced any pain inflicted by her hand will feel like pleasure. She's claiming me with ink, it should hurt. This is forever.

She speaks softly as she pulls line after line on my arm. "I think you're going to cry."

"I look cute when I cry."

Someday, she'll give me her tears too, and I'll earn them. One thrust at a time.

"Are you ready for a rest?" she asks at the two-hour mark. The past couple hours have flown by, thanks to conversation. Though even in the spans of silence where I simply watch her work, the minutes pass like seconds.

"Why? Is your hand getting tired?"

She sits up and raises an eyebrow with a little feistiness. "Are you patronizing me?"

I chuckle. "No, just asking if you want a break."

She returns to my lower bicep. "Please. You'll break before I do," she says slowly, keeping her anchor point while she shades the lower part of my arm. She's right, the elbow is going to hurt like a motherfucker.

Her phone buzzes from across the way. I know it's not Jason because I took care of that. I can see the notification that pops up on the screen from here.

"Someone sent you a DM on Instagram." I glance over at her. "Have you been getting a lot of requests for Bozeman openings?"

She gives an exaggerated huff. "Yeah."

I cock my head to the side. "Then why the big sigh?"

"Nothing," she says, but there's an awkward pause after her words. *What is she not telling me?* "I've been getting these weird messages lately. They are starting to get on my nerves."

That has my attention. My shoulders automatically square, my molars compressing until my jaw aches. Every muscle is coiled tight as I attempt to remain calm.

"What do you mean? Who are they from?"

"I dunno, they come from different accounts. I block them and then a few days later, there's another message. They all say the same thing: *You will never replace me.* Might be Jason, or who knows, maybe somebody's trying to fuck with me before the convention or something. You know they bumped us up the list at the expo, maybe we took someone's place and they're pissed about it? I know it's a long shot, but those are the only things I can come up with."

What the fuck? "How long has this been going on?"

She shrugs, swapping out needles for a bigger shader. "Few weeks."

"A few *weeks?*"

"Since we split up."

Would Jason really be that fucking dumb to send her messages after the warning I gave him? Looks like I might have to pay him a visit after all . . . The organizers for Bozeman moved Black Rabbit into a headliner spot on the website, noting Kelly's name. It's her first time tattooing at a convention in front of an audience, and with tattoo royalty in her bloodline, of course the organizers wanted to showcase it. The posts have been spreading like wildfire. Kelly is hot news right now. The other option is . . . *Billy.*

"I'll look into it," I assure her.

"It's fine, Logan. Really. They'll probably stop after we return from Bozeman . . . Just don't do anything until after. Please don't give me more to think about. I'm sure it's nothing."

I purse my lips at the request, annoyingly aware that if I push too hard right now, it might scare her away. I'll give her till we return, but after that, I'm taking it into my own hands.

"All right, time for the elbow," she warns, adjusting the armrest and putting me in a new position that gives her better access. "Deep breath."

I lean back in my seat. The only thing bringing me unease are these messages—and the occasional tweaked nerve that shoots up my spine while she paints the cluster of needles over my bone. I stare down at her thick black lashes as she works with laser focus, letting her beauty distract me from the protective impulse to hide her away from the world.

After crisscrossing lines again and again until they blend in with my blackout, Kelly goes in with white ink to touch up areas where there should be more brightness. When she uses it on top of my existing ink, I give her some direction, as the white is simply mixing with the black pigment already deposited into my skin, giving the appearance of slices of negative space cutting into the once-covered area. She takes my instruction and implements the design like a pro. The white on black has a bit of a learning curve—it forces you to invert the design in your head, sort of like figuring out if zebras are white with black stripes or vice versa. She manages just fine, like I knew she would.

After eleven hours, with a few intermissions in between, she finally sits back, peels off her gloves, and gives the finished piece a once-over. A few tremors roll through my sensitive flesh. It's been a while since I've had a session this long; I'm probably going to feel like shit later once the tattoo flu sets in.

The silence settles between us, and I catch the moment she realizes how beautiful it is. Her eyes soften and her lips part. "Wow."

"See it now?"

Her eyes find mine, and her smile widens. "You know, I wasn't sure at first, but . . . Damn, I'm into it. I actually kinda love it."

"Me too."

22

LOGAN

Kelly is wedged between Thor and me on the flight to Bozeman, her eyes glued to her tablet. She's been sketching nonstop since we took our seats, even during takeoff, cramming in every bit of preparation she can before the event.

I tilt my chin down, whispering in her ear. "It's okay to take a break, you know."

"Mm-hmm," she hums, her gaze still fixed on the screen.

The pilot's voice crackles on the overhead speaker, announcing our descent into Bozeman. As we slice through the clouds, the peaks of the Bridger Range are made visible. Kelly's stylus moves with quick, precise strokes, doing her best to fight against the occasional jerks of the plane. Her jaw is set—focused but not tense.

Closing my tray table, I smirk. "You're gonna do great, Chaos."

Apparently, that's enough to pause her furious scribbling, and she tilts her head to face me. "What's with that nickname, anyway? Why Chaos?" She stabs a finger into her chest. "By the way, I'll have you know that this is literally the least chaotic I've ever been in my life."

I cock a brow, taking in her messy, disheveled hair tied up in a loose bun, and her sweatshirt, littered with cookie crumbs and a cranberry juice stain from when the flight attendants passed out drinks earlier.

"This is different," she snaps. Kelly points to the stain on her shirt. "This is nerves."

I raise my palms in surrender. When she relaxes back in her seat, I continue. "You earned the nickname Junior because—"

"Because I'm Clyde's kid," she huffs.

I shake my head. "Maybe that's how it began, but you've earned your place at Black Rabbit—the guys might still call you Junior, but it's not by default because you're living in his shadow, it's because you've proven strong enough to shoulder the legacy."

"And Chaos?"

"I wanted to call you something nobody else could." *Junior belonged to the shop. Chaos belonged to me.* "When you returned from college, you sent my world into a tailspin. It seemed fitting. You'll always be my Chaos."

She narrows her eyes. Then slowly turns her focus back to the tablet. "Well, knowing how serious you can be, I'm taking it as a compliment."

"I meant it as one."

Even though she's looking down again, her pink cheeks lift slightly, telling me that she's wearing a smile—until it fades. "What if they lost our bags? Put them on a plane going to Cincinnati or something?"

I huff out a laugh. "They didn't lose our bags. Everything is going to be fine."

She nods. "You're right. Sorry."

"Our flight is early. Our gear is going to be riding around the carousel when we get to baggage claim. Thor double-checked the van rental reservation, and it's waiting for us at the airport. Your hotel room is booked—" I assure her.

"Yeah, about that. I really think you should be staying at the hotel with the rest of us. What if we can't get ahold of you or something?" she insists.

I'm staying at the condo I bought last year. I rented it out last winter for skiers and snowboarders since it's not too far from Big Sky. It's a small one-bedroom, so the rest of the guys are staying at the hotel where the Bozeman Tattoo Festival is taking place.

"I'm like fifteen minutes away. It'll be fine."

She shakes her head. "I dunno, I just have a weird feeling. Like something unexpected is going to happen."

Another scratchy announcement blares through the speakers, reminding passengers to put away any electronics and prepare for landing. She tucks away her tablet into the backpack stowed under the seat in front of her. The plane makes a shallow bank as our elevation decreases and we close the gap between us and the tarmac below.

Interesting that she's picked up on that. "Everything will be fine."

* * *

After dropping Kelly, Casper, Thor, and all of our gear off at the hotel, I take the rental van down the street to a nearby coffee shop, where I place an order for two iced drinks and a couple sandwiches to kill some time while I wait for her call.

I smile when my phone rings. She's punctual.

"Miss me already?" I answer.

Her voice pitches with panic. "They don't have my hotel reservation. I told you something weird was gonna happen, Logan! I did this! I jinxed myself!"

I roll my eyes. *Other people are always taking credit for the things I do.*

"Whoa, slow down. What are you talking about?" I ask, using my calmest voice.

A young toddler sitting with his parents not far from me enthusiastically face-plants into the giant blueberry muffin placed in front of him. I keep my laughter at bay while playing the role of Concerned Friend No. 1.

She takes a deep breath and exhales, speaking slower this time. "We went to check in at the front desk. Casper and Thor got their rooms. However, there wasn't any reservation in my name. So I had them check under yours. They said only two rooms were purchased. Did you forget to book mine?"

"Of course I didn't forget. Give me a minute, I'll phone the hotel and get this straightened out."

I end the call and check the weather report for Bozeman while waiting for my order. Blue skies for our whole trip. Beautiful.

"Logan!" The barista sets a brown paper bag on the counter and a drink holder with one iced tea and one iced Americano—*decaf*. The last thing she needs is more jet fuel.

After depositing a couple bucks in the tip jar, I gather my food and drinks, then head back to the rental van to return her call.

"Hey. I just spoke with them. Unfortunately, they've been having some glitch in their reservation system. They don't have any vacancy, so I'm going to come pick you up and you can crash at my place."

"Don't you only have one bed?"

"I'll take the sofa." *I'm not taking the sofa.*

"I don't want to make you—"

"I want to."

"What about—"

"Don't even start with me, Kelly. I'll update Casper and Thor. All you need to do is meet me in front of the hotel in two minutes."

"Okay."

I hang up before she can argue any more.

That was easy.

"Oh—Oh my God!" she says. Dropping her backpack at the door, she beelines across the condo to the large picture windows. "Logan, this view is unreal!"

I would have bought any dump that allowed me to become an official Montana resident. A condo was the ideal situation. Monthly dues cover building maintenance, making it easy to manage, and they allow occasional short-term rentals. On paper, it appears nothing more than a diversified portfolio . . . In practice, I'm building a backstory.

After the real estate agent showed me the gorgeous panorama, I was sold. What can I say, I'm a sucker for a view. Seeing her curves silhouetted against the big blue sky and white-capped mountains has me appreciating it even more.

I set our food in the open kitchen. "There's a couple sandwiches in the bag, why don't you pick one out while I bring in our suitcases."

"Mm-hmm," she mumbles, still staring out the window.

It only takes two trips to carry in the remaining bags from the van. When I'm bringing in the last of them, I find her still standing in the same spot as I left her. I toe off my shoes and push them aside.

"Hey. Chaos. Time to eat," I say, removing our food from the brown paper bag.

"Huh? Oh, sorry!" She spins around with a soft smile, throwing a thumb over her shoulder. "Those mountains are hypnotizing." I'm relieved to see her carrying much less tension as she eases her way toward the kitchen.

The guys were aware Kelly didn't have a room. However, I didn't anticipate that she'd be so anxious on the trip, which makes me feel a little guilty for adding an extra layer of mayhem to her day.

She bellies up next to me at the island and unwraps a sandwich. After a few bites, Kelly's eyes drift from the majestic mountains to the interior space. She nods in approval while swallowing. "You didn't tell me you had such a great place."

I've only been out here a couple times since I bought it. Once to furnish the condo, and a second time to wrap up paperwork with the county. It's a corner unit, so the natural lighting is fantastic, with a wall and a half of floor-to-ceiling windows in the living room. The countertop faces out, so we're able to admire the spectacular landscape while we eat.

A small balcony, barely big enough for a table and two chairs, is accessible from a glass door near where we sit. The times I've visited, it's never been warm enough for me to utilize, but it faces the northwest, so I imagine it's an ideal spot for watching the sunset with a drink in hand. On the other side of the condo is a straight iron staircase that stretches to the upstairs loft. It's an open-concept bedroom with an enclosed bathroom—somewhat similar to my place in Minneapolis, only smaller.

"Thanks."

"So," she begins. "What do we have planned for tonight?"

"Nothing." I lean forward, propping my elbows on the kitchen island and checking my watch. It's just after four o'clock.

"Should we go out on the town?" she asks. "I heard Casper mention going out to some bars."

"Or . . ." I turn to look at her. "I could make us an old-fashioned and we can watch the sun go down behind the mountains."

Our eyes meet, and we regard each other for a moment. I press my tongue into my cheek.

Her mischievous gaze has me rooted in place, like she's already imagining the things I plan to do to her. "I like your idea better."

23

KELLY

I feel so . . . content. After stocking the fridge and showering off the hectic day, we're finally alone on his balcony, sipping old-fashioneds. The warm bourbon softens the mood as we settle into our cushioned chairs, watching the vibrant pink sky sink below the peaks.

The mountains almost don't look real. They sprawl across the entire horizon, shooting out of the earth, mingling with the clouds like giant snow-capped castles in the sky. Pine trees cover the lower ridges, caught between valleys and foothills with pops of green. It's like a postcard one might find at a gift shop—*wish you were here*. Except the only person I want with me is already by my side.

The peaks possess an untamed wilderness that doesn't answer to anyone. The beauty that exists in Montana isn't something you can claim, regardless of whether you were raised here or are just passing through—it tolerates your presence the same way it tolerates the sunrises and sunsets.

Even with the occasional chilled breeze, I'm perfectly comfortable in my leggings and T-shirt—I opted not to wear anything underneath in hopes he might notice. *It seemed to work during our photo shoot.* Logan must have had a similar idea, because he threw on a pair of sweatpants—and I noticed, I *definitely* noticed.

I've always been someone who believes in fate, and it seemed like the universe chose to force us together when my hotel reservation got screwed up. Earlier, when he suggested we spend the night alone with stiff drinks and a gorgeous view, there was a flicker of something mischievous dancing in his eyes, enough to spark the hope of another kiss—one similar to our first, but this time I don't want to stop.

I inhale, filling my lungs with fresh mountain air. Montana is stunning. "I can't believe you don't come out here more often."

He shrugs. "Black Rabbit is there."

"Is that what's keeping you from leaving? I mean, who wouldn't want to see this every day?"

"No."

"You could probably open another shop if you wanted to . . ." *What the fuck? Why would I even suggest that?*

He shakes his head. "The way you feel about your dad's house is the way I feel about his shop. It has to stay there. That's where he started it, that's where it'll remain. It wouldn't feel right, it's a piece of history."

Butterflies swarm my stomach. There's something so sexy about the way he respects my father, even though I'm the only one left. He's protective and proud of what my dad built, and even though it's been years since his death, every decision Logan's made regarding the shop has been done with that consideration in mind.

"I'm not sure I'll ever be able to express how grateful I am to have someone like you taking the reins, helping it thrive while still preserving the reputation of my family's name."

He nods. "It's an honor I don't take lightly." The atmosphere feels more charged as we lift our cocktails in sync, letting the smooth liquor slip down our throats concurrently.

I roll the glass between my palms. "Dad always was a good judge of character."

He chuckles.

I smile. "What's funny?"

Logan shakes his head. "Nothing. How are your nerves doing after that?" He nods to my drink.

"Much better, thank you." I take another sip. "I confirmed with my model, my stencils are ready, but I probably won't sleep a wink until it's over . . . How's your tattoo recovery going? Any regrets?"

He pushes up his sleeve to show me; it's healing nicely. The more I look at it, the more I've come to love it. I can admire the beauty of it the way he does.

"Never."

My attention returns to the mountains. I stand, step up to the edge of the balcony, and soak up the panorama. Logan's gaze sears my skin; even in the crisp evening air, I feel him.

He shifts in my peripheral, punctuated by the scrape of his chair and his presence closing in; his broad chest is firm against my back. He sets his glass on the drink rail before cupping the ledge and boxing me in; *this is becoming a trend with him*—he must enjoy seeing me trapped with nowhere to run. I peer down at those damn hands of his. As if he notices me leering, he grips the rail tightly, making the veins swell under his inked skin—it's practically lewd.

I've watched those skilled, calloused fingers create art on everything from flesh to canvas, but what else are they capable of? *Are they powerful enough to steady my hips? Wrap around my throat?*

"I like seeing you on my balcony."

"Oh yeah?" I reply, turning my head and giving him a sideways glance. The quiet stretches between us, but it's not awkward—it never has been. "Is it strange that this doesn't feel . . . new?"

"We both know this isn't new."

"Yeah." I swallow down some of the fear in my confession.

Releasing the ledge, his hands settle on my hips, firm and deliberate. He spins me to face him, then guides us back to his chair. Standing in front of him, I brace a knee on the cushion between his thighs and set my drink on the small table wedged between the two chairs. Logan's palms move up to my waist and he guides me closer, tugging me into his warm lap.

I twist sideways, pressing my lips to his throat, before he dips his chin and takes my mouth in a deeper kiss. He tastes of warmth, the bourbon and citrus lingering on his tongue. For someone who seemingly hasn't dated in years, he doesn't seem to have lost any skill.

We snuggle close on the quaint balcony, my head relaxing on his shoulder while we enjoy the sunset. "It's weird kissing you."

He laughs. "It's *weird* kissing me?"

I squeeze my eyes shut and shake my head. "That was a poor choice of words. I mean, it's just . . . surreal. I can't count the number of times I've wondered what it would be like. I imagined it all the time as a teenager," I say, with a small chuckle. "I always assumed it would be one of those things that only ever existed in my imagination."

His hand travels up my spine, stopping at my neck. "Ah, I see." He squeezes my nape three times. The familiarity is nice, like bringing silly little things from our friendship over into something more serious.

"Did you ever feel like that?" I ask.

He shakes his head. "There was never any doubt in my mind it would happen. But yeah, I thought about it a lot, definitely fantasized."

Fantasized? "You fantasized about kissing me?"

I glance up at his jaw; he's so damn attractive. "In my tamest daydreams, yes."

That has me straightening in his lap. "And in your wildest ones?" I bounce my eyebrows.

He rolls his eyes, adjusting my position so we're facing the mountains. He lazily massages behind my knees—his touch coiling the tension in my core. "I can't tell you that," he murmurs, his voice low and husky.

"Come on," I pout. "Say it."

He lifts behind my thighs, tilting me back into his chest, then lowers my legs to settle on either side of his. With one arm wrapped around my middle, Logan swipes my glass off the table, bringing it to his lips.

"Hey, that's mine."

"What are you going to do about it?" he asks.

The sexual tension between us has been smoldering ever since he suggested a night in. It's like he's waiting for me to make the first move—which is what I thought I was doing when I skipped the bra.

My frustration wins over. "Do you feel nothing right now?"

I'm practically squirming in his lap, and he seems maddeningly unaffected. I want to steal his attention, just a little.

He clamps tighter around my waist, pulling me into his hips and letting me feel how hard he is. I suck in a breath, my pulse thrumming faster.

"You think I don't notice?" he asks.

"Then why don't you take control?"

A low chuckle rumbles in his chest, dark enough to raise goose bumps. "You're the one writhing on my cock, sweetheart." He sips from his drink like he has all the time in the world. "Tell me, which one of us seems more in control?"

If he wants to play games, so be it. Let's see how far I can push him before that composed demeanor snaps.

I thread my fingers over his, prying his hold from around my middle, then guide his hand under my shirt and up to my breast. A rough groan is drawn from his throat as I arch into his touch and whimper softly.

"Fuck," he says on a breath.

I jut out my chin with a satisfied smile, biting my bottom lip when he takes over. His fingers work absent-mindedly, plucking my piercings; idly toying with my body with one hand while the other rests on the arm of the chair, clutching his old-fashioned. My slow exhale is the only sound between us.

"I can't sleep with you tonight." His voice is gruff.

I roll my eyes. "Then let's not sleep . . . please, just act like you want me." I'm about two rejections away from being offended.

"*Act* like I want you?"

I swallow. *One rejection away.*

His lips graze the shell of my ear. "I could spend every day fucking you for the rest of my life, and it still wouldn't be enough. Want is useless. The way I feel about you . . . It's addiction . . . obsession . . ."

He takes the breath right out of my lungs. "I didn't know you imagined us like that."

"If I told you the things I imagined, you wouldn't still be sitting in my lap."

"Care to test that theory?"

"I've seen the boys you've dated. I've seen your mornings after a night with them. You've never looked exhausted, or weak, or *quenched*. You've never yelped when trying to sit. They underestimated you. Chaos can't be tamed with a gentle hand."

Oh my God. Anticipation and lust swirl in my chest and I roll my hips, loving the way his touch feels when it collides with a threat.

"*That's* what I fantasize about. Taming you. Watching you bend to my will with a sweet moan on your lips."

I've never experienced someone like Logan—never experienced anyone in the same *tier* as Logan. He's a category all his own. How is this the same man who barely speaks to anyone, and suddenly, he comes out with *that?*

He proved his point, making all the other guys I've dated seem like immature fuckboys in comparison. I'll never go back.

I angle my head, skimming my teeth along his neck and tracing the tip of my tongue over his stuttering pulse. Releasing my piercing, he snakes his hand higher under my shirt until he wraps it around my throat. He takes one final swig from his cocktail before setting it down, then slips his cold hand into my underwear.

"Logan . . ." There are so many words, but my brain can't find any of them. He's right, this is more than mere *want*. This is pure need.

I'm mumbling nonsense when his fingers spread into a V, caressing just outside of where I need it most.

"What do you want, Chaos?"

"More. Don't stop." My rushed words aren't nearly as restrained as his, but it's all I'm capable of at this moment.

"Who said we were stopping?" His thumb sweeps over my clit, and I shudder. *So good.*

"Feel that?" he whispers, lightly brushing his lips over my temple—a complete contradiction to the way he's squeezing my neck, reminding me that my size and strength are nothing compared to his. I'm at his mercy. Below, his fingers slip inside, making me gasp. "I bet I could hold you like this all night, and you'd let me, wouldn't you?"

I nod, whimpering when I want to scream. He tightens the hand around my throat while he finger-fucks me with the other.

"So fucking wet . . . feel yourself."

"Huh?"

He drags my trembling fingers to where his were a moment ago, sliding over my slick arousal. "Touch your pussy for me." I melt into him as he guides me deeper. The way he takes over is so sexy.

"Feel how wet you are? Get it all for me."

"Logan . . ." I want his hands back, his are so much bigger compared to mine.

He nudges me out of the way and rubs circles over my clit.

I clasp behind his neck, gripping his shirt and rolling my hips for more.

He plunges deeper; I should be embarrassed by my audible gulp, but I don't care. I don't give a fuck about anything outside this moment with him. I sigh his name as he teases and pets. "Aww, does that feel good?" His voice is patronizing. *God, he's conceited.*

"Your cunt belongs to me." His cock flexes. "Do you like the way I play with my girl?"

I nod, and a shiver shoots up my spine. *Why is that so hot? The way he rules me so easily has me stunned into submission.*

He chuckles in my ear. "Then you're going to love the way I eat her . . ." He adds another finger, and I writhe in his arms. "Let me taste you."

My chest heaves as I brush the backs of my still-wet knuckles over his lips, and he draws them into his mouth. He releases my neck to rub my clit while his other hand keeps time stroking inside me. His tongue is greedy, licking and sucking my fingers. The competing sensations wash over me, and I arch my back. "L-Logan, I'm going to come!"

I feel a wicked smile form on his lips.

"No, I'm serious." The orgasm building feels too big. I don't know what's going to happen. "We have to go inside, I'm going to come."

Withdrawing from his mouth, I grasp the arms of the chair, trying to stave off the impending climax.

"What's the matter? Worried someone might hear you? Why don't you introduce us to the neighbors?"

"We can't—" My hips jerk and the orgasm rolls over me. I cry out, my face flooding with heat in embarrassment, but I can't stop it. He's rendered me helpless.

He laughs, and claps a hand over my mouth, smothering my moan. "Uh-huh, that's a good girl. Give it all to me. All of it."

I groan, clenching harder at his praise.

"Fuck, you're tight. Can't wait to feel how selfish your pussy is when you're taking every inch." My sounds are muffled by his palm; the more he speaks, the longer my orgasm draws out. "Keep coming. Just a little longer . . . Don't you dare stop until I say so. Not until you give me everything."

As soon as the flutters ease and my muscles relax, I collapse against him with heaving breaths. *That just happened.*

He nuzzles my neck, pressing a kiss behind my ear. "You did so good for me . . . so fucking good."

I'm floating.

I nod, unable to speak. He fixes my underwear back in place, and I stand on shaky legs. Gravity is kicking my ass. He made good on that threat earlier. Reaching ahead of me to open the door, he chuckles. I stumble in with an embarrassed laugh.

"Let's get you upstairs so I can bury my head between your thighs."

24

LOGAN

She managed to get up the stairs on her own but held that handrail like it was the only thing keeping her upright. She's great for my ego.

When we reach the upstairs bedroom, I remove my glasses and place them on the nightstand. "I'll help you relax before tomorrow."

She huffs out a laugh. "Mission accomplished." Sitting on the edge of the bed, she peels off her leggings, preparing to crawl under the covers. *Not so fast.*

I tear off my shirt and clear my throat, shaking my head when she begins to pull back the duvet. "Lie back, Chaos."

She gapes at me, looking between me and the bed. "You were serious?"

"Lie. Back." I won't be satisfied until she's limp in my arms. Her eyes stay on mine as she obeys, reclining in her little crop top and cute boy shorts, resting her arms above her, offering herself on a silver platter.

Jesus Christ.

I straddle her waist and shimmy the rest of her shirt up her body, tugging it over her head but leaving it around her elbows like a loose restraint.

"These fucking piercings," I growl, my gaze fixed on her gorgeous tits.

My lips find hers, and I kiss her slowly, nipping and becoming more desperate as she makes those sweet noises.

The sounds that come from this woman could ruin me. So fucking sexy. After pressing one last kiss to her lips, I smile against her mouth, then move to her neck, kissing down her body.

"Are you wearing a T-shirt tomorrow?" I mutter against her skin.

"What?" She sighs. "Yeah, why?"

My teeth sink into her shoulder, and she yelps. "Logan!"

"I'll keep them hidden," I vow, though I want to brand her for every man to see. For now, I'll be discreet, but there's some primal part of me that needs to see the indent of my teeth on her skin.

"I'm the only one who gets to mark you like this," I say.

I suck her pierced nipples into my mouth, feeling the metal bar press against my tongue before releasing, and I continue my path down her body, biting the soft flesh on her breasts and stomach, slowly burying my teeth in until I feel her twitch. I take my time, slowing down rather than speeding up, building the anticipation and forcing her breaths to come quicker.

Moving lower, I hook my fingers in the sides of her underwear, slipping them off and returning to bite the exposed skin at her hip. My palms cover her knees, pushing her thighs apart so I can lick the sensitive inner flesh. She tenses as if preparing for another nip. This time she rolls her hips when she feels the sharp sting of pain.

From between her legs, our gazes meet. Her green eyes are glazed with lust, her lips swollen from my kiss. Perhaps most beautiful of all are the red indentations in the shape of half moons that decorate her body from shoulder to thigh—tangible proof that she's mine now.

My hungry stare takes in her slick pussy. "Fuck, look at you."

With a feather touch, my tongue grazes over her clit, and she jerks at the sensation. Kelly plants her heels into the bed, arching her back, I flatten my tongue and drag it over her again, slower this time. I've waited years for this, wondering what she would taste like. She doesn't taste like strawberries or cotton candy, she tastes like mine—like the only woman I want to eat from now until they bury me in the earth. A satisfied smirk tugs at my lips. Then I do what every starving man does, I devour the meal in front of me.

Each breathy moan fuels my frenzy. I lap up her arousal as I take my time torturing her. She lifts her hips, pressing herself against my mouth, and causing me to drive my hips into the soft mattress. I want her to suffocate me with her pleasure.

I slip two fingers in, curling them, feeling how close she is. Her body contracts as if she's about to come. *Too soon.* When her legs begin to tremble, I pull away at the last second and bite her thigh. She jerks her hips and thrashes. "No, don't stop. I was so close!"

"I know. Straddle me." Grabbing the shirt that's still wrapped around her elbows, I yank it off and toss it behind me. Then I flip onto my back, sweeping a few of the pillows out of my way. She crawls over me, straddling my hips and grinding against my cock. It would be so fucking easy to yank my sweatpants down and fuck her stupid. Instead, I shake my head. "No, Chaos. On my face."

She furrows her brow. "What? I can't."

"Why?" I hiss, exasperated.

"I don't know, I—"

I sit up, gripping her hips, then drag her up my body before she can argue. She plants a hand on the headboard as I gently lie back, but this time with her pussy against my mouth. As soon as I shove my tongue inside, her jaw drops, and she releases a whimper that has me wrapping my arms around her thighs and yanking her flush against my face. *That's what I'm fucking talking about.*

I groan, humming against her flesh while I ravage her, until she tries to retreat. I refuse to allow that when I've waited this long. I nudge her to the side, giving me just enough room to turn and bite her on the inner thigh again—this time it's disciplinary. She yelps at the sting.

"Did you just try to take my meal away before I was finished?"

She blinks down at me, panting. "What? I-I just—I didn't—"

"Stop." I cut her off. "When my head's between your thighs, this pussy is mine. You sit still until I say otherwise. Is that understood?"

"Holy fuck," she mumbles, staring at me in a haze.

I give her a gentle swat on the cheek, just enough to grab her attention. "Is that understood, Chaos?" I repeat.

Her breath catches. "Yes, sir."

Those two words have my mouth curving into a smile, and I press a soothing kiss to the bite. "Good girl. Don't ever interrupt me when I'm eating." She's soon going to learn just how feral and greedy I am when it comes to her. Eventually, she'll learn to love my danger. She'll even mistake it for safety.

I lick her sensitive clit, and she tentatively rocks against me. My lips cover the bundle of nerves and suck. She startles with a jolt, but quickly corrects herself and stays in place. "Sorry, sorry, sorry . . ." she quickly utters.

Our eyes meet, and my hummed forgiveness vibrates against her pussy. Next time I won't be as nice. A shiver rolls through her. *Almost there . . .*

"Fuck, Logan. You do that so well—I'm close. I'm really close."

I keep sucking, not changing a thing. Her legs tremble, telling me she's right on the edge. My lips stay locked on her and the quake in her legs crescendos until she finds that edge of ecstasy . . . and leaps.

"Fuck, Logan!" she shouts, and I tip her forward so she drips onto my tongue. Her hand delves into my hair, holding her steady as she grinds against my mouth. The way she continues muttering my name through her climax, so pathetic and needy, triggers something in me and I snap. My cock twitches, and before I can stop it, I'm coming. My hips jerk as I groan against her, swallowing her arousal as mine continues to pump out of me. *Fuck!* I spear my tongue inside, feeling her pulse—then I lap up every trace of her before releasing her thighs.

When we're finished, we both sit motionless, except for our heaving chests.

"Now I'm done," I say.

She slides off me, flopping on her back like a rag doll.

I sit up, head swimming as my vision dots in the corners. I crawl in front of her, spreading her legs, and kissing her cunt one last time. As soon as I'm finished, I drag my bottom lip from between her thighs, higher and higher, over her skin until I reach her navel. She looks down at me, her heart hammering against her chest. A slow smile creeps onto my face, and she mirrors it before dropping her head to the pillows.

"That was . . ." She pauses.

"Yeah."

She's made for me, the piece that makes everything shift into place.

I make my way up her body and press my lips to hers before drawing back just enough to take in her beautiful flushed cheeks. She's glowing. *I did that.* Her gaze settles on mine, soft and serene; we share a moment of silence that's heavy with unspoken words.

It's getting late.

After cleaning up, I fall on my side next to her and pull her body into mine. She hums when I brush her hair to the side and press a kiss to her bare shoulder. Her breaths turn steady within minutes, and I know she's asleep. In my arms. Where she belongs.

25

KELLY

I'm walking back to our booth with a cup of coffee and nervous energy. "You can do this," I whisper to myself. We've just finished setting up our tattoo stations and are going through power checks. With over a hundred artists in one space, and that many tattoo machines running, it's crucial we don't have any issues.

As soon as I exit the restroom, I'm confronted with my first glimpse of the hallway where attendees have lined up for entry.

I can't see the end of it. "Holy shit," I mutter.

It's not like I've never been to a tattoo expo, but I've always attended as an apprentice. My dad mentored both Logan and Casper. Thor met my dad a few times, but he didn't start working at Black Rabbit until after Logan took over. Anytime I've gone to one of these, I've acted as an assistant, making sure Dad, Logan, or Casper had all their supplies, and handled transactions for merchandise. We sell a lot of T-shirts with the Black Rabbit logo and prints of various flash art.

On occasion, I've conducted body piercings at events, and while it's more nerve-racking to do it while others watch, it's still not as scary as being an Everhart and inking another person with an audience. I get enough criticism on my Instagram posts accusing me of either being too similar or too different.

Not today. Today, I'm doing my art the way I want, the way Dad taught me. I walk across the hallway to the event center doors; the security staff member's gaze drops to the badge on a lanyard around my neck, and he nods for me to pass through.

The massive room is filled with various booths and tattoo stations for people to watch. The buzz of tattoo machines in every direction forms a steady hum, and it takes almost no time at all to settle into the background like white noise. The air is thick with anticipation and excitement, which feeds my already anxious nerves.

Our booth looks similar to the others; every vendor—or artist and/or shop—is given a ten-by-ten booth. Because of Black Rabbit's notoriety, we tend to have more foot traffic, so we opted for extra tables to extend our space. We pushed our four eight-foot tables end-to-end at the front of our double booth, and Thor is currently steaming the wrinkles from the black linens draped over them. I've already made sure our three tablets are fully charged and connected to the Wi-Fi, and that the software we use for our client waiver forms is functioning properly.

Besides the tattoo models and appointments we've arranged ahead of time, everyone is first come, first served, which means our table could get rushed as soon as the doors open. Logan, Casper, and Thor are all award-winning artists who are usually booked out a year in advance. These tattoo events are filled with top dogs tattooing all under one roof, giving attendees the opportunity to meet and be inked by their favorite artists—but they have to get their name on the list first.

We have three tattoo stations set up behind us; each has a padded table and a cart with all the supplies we might need during our sessions. It'll be cramped, but I've seen other booths working in much tighter quarters than this.

Casper kneels on the floor, unpacking our ink boxes and loading up each cart.

All four of us have created flash specific for this Bozeman event; mine are sexy cowgirls, ranch hands, and western centaurs done in an American style. A few have features similar to what I used in my sexy mermen series back home. I'm glad I had the foresight to do that, because I'm going into the day feeling much more prepared. But my first tattoo of the day is the one I have spent weeks practicing, the astronaut and deep-sea diver. The stencils are ready to go at my station.

"Casper, what side of the booth do you want?" Everybody helps everybody during setup.

He glances up at the wall and shrugs. "I'll take the left."

I nod and get to work, pinning up the various sheets of flash to our black fabric backdrop.

"Thor, are you okay being in the center?"

"Yup."

My height is making this task a little harder. Thor must see the way I'm struggling on my tiptoes because he chuckles from behind me. "Wanna trade, Junior? I've only got this corner left to steam. I can pin the ones on top for you."

"Yes, please!" My heels meet the floor again, and we trade places, so I get to work steaming while he hangs up our flash. All the guys are well over six feet, so it's no trouble at all for them.

Crouching on the floor with the steamer, I spot Logan across the room talking with one of the organizers wearing a headset. His outfit today is simple, black jeans and a solid flannel with the sleeves rolled up his forearms. His clothes are casual, but he wears them with a confidence that makes him appear so much more collected and put together than the black jeans and plain white tee I'm sporting. He'll probably switch to a short-sleeve shirt later too. The temperature always heats up once doors open and attendees flood the event space.

He mostly nods and gestures, rarely speaking unless he has to—which is so contradictory to the Logan I shared a bed with last night. In the bedroom—or balcony—he is a completely different animal, in every sense of the word.

And his mouth. He talks dirty like nothing I've ever heard, but he knows how to back it up. Logan's talents stretch far beyond art and tattooing. The way his tongue teased and licked and probed . . . *Fuck.*

The best part, the highlight of it all, is that when I was about to come, *he maintained*. He didn't suddenly switch it up. He kept the same pace, same speed, same motion, same intensity, all of it. In my previous experience, as soon as I hinted I was about to cross the finish line, my partner would throw a wild card and change positions, then wonder why I didn't come.

Steam puffs in front of me while I watch him from a distance. He nods to another man, looking so professional and not at all unhinged.

He showed me the possessive side of him, the one I only ever caught a glimpse of the day he hit my ex. Logan was savage last night. The way his eyes darkened when I rode his face and he warned me not to move . . . It was equally unsettling as it was attractive. Part of me wondered what he would have done if I had pulled away from him a second time—*taken his meal away*. What would he do to me? How far would he go?

I'm not sure I have the guts to find out.

* * *

"Still good?" I ask, glancing at my model, Valerie, who is spread out on the padded table, while I tattoo the deep-sea diver on her left thigh. Months ago, I made a post on my social media that I was seeking a volunteer for the Bozeman Tattoo Festival. I had given a loose sketch and received a ton of applicants. Val had written that she had lost her dad last year and my piece reminded her of him. I knew instantly she was the perfect model for the astronaut and diver. It was kismet.

I add detail to the heavy boots of his diving suit. I'm struggling to know whether I should increase the shading to make it *more* bold. I didn't do it in the original because I wanted more focus to be on his helmet, but now I'm unsure. I want to effectively illustrate the way he's weighted down on the ocean floor. The whole competition aspect of it has me second-guessing. I remind myself I'm only competing to get seen by judges, some of whom are artists I really respect. I'm not trying to win.

"Golden," she answers through clenched teeth.

"Do you want a break? Need to stretch?" She shakes her head, picking up her metal water bottle and taking a sip.

"You got this, Val," I say with a smile, turning back to work.

The lighting and shadows aren't what I'm used to back at the shop, but using a headlamp has made this so much easier.

His deep voice rasps from behind me. "You're on pace."

I smile. Logan's words help me relax. I've been nervous about taking too long.

"Where am I at for time?" I've got appointments scheduled after this, so I don't want to get behind.

The buzz of tattoo machines and chatter is white noise at this point. However, I could probably pick out Logan's voice no matter how loud it was in here. He's working the table, occasionally checking on me, but mostly speaking with attendees and answering questions. This is his ninth circle of hell. A full day of talking with people and getting attention. Poor grump.

"Which of your tattoos is your favorite?" someone asks.

Logan doesn't hesitate for a second. "This one. The portrait on my arm. Kelly Everhart just did it this week, it's pretty fresh."

I whip the end of my line and pop my head up to make sure I heard him correctly. He's unbuttoning his shirt and sliding his arm out of the sleeve. Logan has many tattoos, but his favorite is the owl my dad inked on him. It's *always* been the owl. My father designed it custom as if he was bestowing a gift; it represented Logan's quiet nature and cunning mind. A silent bird of prey. A predator.

As he shows off my work, I feel the blush rising to my face, then quickly return to the task in front of me. *His favorite tattoo is the one I did? It's not even his usual style!* My dad's owl, on the other hand, *that's* Logan. That tattoo is sacred to him.

"Nice!" the attendee comments. "Love that it incorporated your blackout."

"That was all her idea. She's fucking brilliant."

A new voice cuts in. "I read in an article that your favorite tattoo was the owl Clyde did."

Thank you, kind stranger! I, too, would love to know what he has to say about that.

"It kinda looks like her," the same person comments. *Fuck, I was hoping it wasn't obvious.*

"Yeah, it does," the first person agrees, their gaze bouncing back and forth between me and his arm. "Is there a reason it's your favorite?"

"I still love the owl Clyde did—it's an honor to have a one-of-a-kind piece from him based on how he saw me. He chose it for me. However, the woman on my arm is something I chose for myself. It's dark and beautiful, there are so many layers to it."

What the fuck is happening right now?

The machine in my hand is running, but my mind is still. He wasn't trying to be romantic or impress me, he doesn't even know I'm listening. He meant it. He answers a few more of their questions, and then they move on to the next booth.

"Keep going," he says, his voice low—only for me. "Don't second-guess your instincts. Remember why you chose this."

It's for Dad, a dual narrative piece. One person anchored to the ocean floor by immense pressure, the other weightlessly floating above earth. Two explorers unable to breathe freely, separated by water and space.

I nod. "Thanks, Logan."

He steps to the side, arms folded, eyes tracking my movements. Not judging my technique, just quietly supporting me from the sideline. Ever-present, like he always is. People stop to watch and ask questions, lots of pictures are taken. At first it was a little scary, but after a while, they faded into the background, just like Logan promised this morning.

Two hours passed. Then three. Then five.

Nearing the end, I switch to a smaller needle, using white to highlight the edges and add detail to the reflection of the astronaut's helmet—which is already finished on her right thigh. Then I take a few more passes, adding detail and cleaning up edges where I can. I sit back and scrutinize my work, tracing every line, every edge, every shadow. Double-checking light sources, line weights, and shading. It's beautiful.

"Finished," I say, peeling off my black latex gloves and taking a deep, restoring breath. My fingers are a little tingly; my grip tension was a bit strong, but that was mostly nerves.

"Holy shit," Val beams. "I fucking love it."

"He'd be really proud of you, Kelly," Logan adds.

I nod. The hours I put into this piece were worth it.

I wipe both thighs; the contrast between the two pieces is remarkable. It conveys the loneliness of separation, but they balance each other so perfectly that it feels whole. At this moment, I realize that it doesn't matter what other people think about my art. I love it, Val loves it, Logan loves it—who the fuck cares about the rest of them? This is *my* art.

Toward the end of the day, they announce it's the last chance to turn in the tattoos that judges will look at. There's a competition at the end of each day for the fresh pieces that were completed at the convention, and then at the end of the event weekend, there's a final competition for best of show. Logan tells me to head over to submit my piece and stay to watch the judging.

"Do you want to come with me?" I ask.

"I can't. Thor and I have to head out for a bit."

I furrow my brow. "Why?"

"Just some Bozeman paperwork I have to take care of that I didn't last time I was in town."

Probably condo stuff. Damn.

"Oh. Okay. What time will you be back?"

"Shouldn't take too long. Go have a drink at the hotel bar when you get done here, and I'll text you when I'm nearby to pick you up," he says. "You did great today. I'm proud of you."

He wraps me up in a hug, holding me for a moment, like it's hard for him to let me go. Our embrace is interrupted by another announcement for the last call. Then he presses a kiss to the top of my head before releasing me.

At our booth, I hand over the contest submission form to my model and follow her toward the judging area. I stay behind when she turns in the paperwork; artists can watch from a distance, but they aren't allowed to submit the forms as an attempt to keep the judges unbiased. It's important they judge the piece and not the artist.

Every convention has different categories split up by style: black and gray, color, anime, realism, abstract, American trad, et cetera. After that, the groups are usually broken down by size: small, medium, and large. I am entering the medium black-and-gray contest.

Casper is submitting a realism tattoo he did earlier this year. His client agreed to come to the convention so he could enter it into the competition. They are judging realism tattoos on the last day. A lot of the realism artists submit pieces that were completed at their own shops. Realism tattoos sometimes take several sessions to complete, so there's not enough time in a weekend to finish a tattoo like that with as much detail and shading as the style requires to make it look hyperrealistic. Casper's is an entire leg piece that took about six sessions to complete.

Different conventions have different ways of judging, and for this one, the judges have comment sheets and appear to be taking notes on each one. The judges are meticulous as they analyze each piece. They are judging numerous aspects of the work: shading, composition, saturation, linework, and probably a million other things I'm not even aware of. Watching them is as intimidating as it is fascinating.

When they get to my piece, my nerves are firing on all cylinders. I watch the judges' expressions and the various areas they point to. They scribble notes on their clipboards. From nearby, I hear a spectator compliment my piece, so I smile. The other submissions in my category are incredible.

I don't expect to place, not with as many seasoned, award-winning artists who are entering the same contest as mine. I'm still learning, but I'm honored to be able to compete alongside many of the artists I admire. I'm not doing it for approval; I just want to be seen. Judged by people who know what they're looking at and understand the art and the effort that goes into each and every tattoo.

Third place goes to the local shop that Logan has done a few guest spots at, a hauntingly beautiful Medusa. Second place is a detailed octopus, and first place goes to someone who did a high-contrast Batman. Their artwork is stunning, and the awards are well deserved.

The announcements crackle as the crowd nearby claps. I'm about to head back to my booth, feeling happy and satisfied, when they make another announcement. "We do have an honorable mention for fresh medium black and gray. Kelly Everhart of Black Rabbit."

Holy fuck.

My stomach flips. I glance behind me toward our booth, wishing Logan were standing here with me. I wish Dad were here too.

I accept my handshake and red ribbon from one of the event staff, who compliments my excellent composition and clean technique.

Before heading back to our tables, I take a moment to stare at my piece. I can't wait to show the rest of the guys. The ribbon is cool, but it's nothing in comparison to feeling seen. To be *noticed* by some of the most respected and experienced tattoo artists in the country.

They liked it enough to mention—and that's everything.

26

KELLY

I'm washing at the bathroom sink when a woman sidles up beside me; she's wearing a tank top and is fully inked out, like most of the attendees here. There's a stunning black cat tattooed on her shoulder. Two sections of her bleach-blond hair are streaked with vibrant purple. The diamond Marilyn stud near her cheek pulls up slightly when she smiles at me.

"I like your ink," she says, holding my gaze.

"Oh, thanks. Yeah, I've had this one for a long time . . ."

"Sorry, I have to say something, it's probably nothing, but when I was out there earlier, I noticed a guy watching you from across the room. He gave me a weird vibe. Do you know him or should I flag a security agent or something?"

I furrow my brows and glance at the bathroom exit. Logan already left as far as I know, and he's the only one who would be watching me that closely.

"Are you sure it was me?"

"Yeah. He's about this tall." She holds her hand above me but it's still too short for Logan. "Brown hair, average build. Kinda clean-cut . . ." *Definitely not Logan.* "Anything like that sound like someone you know?"

I shake my head, my thoughts circling back to everyone I tattooed today, but that description doesn't match any of them. "I don't think so."

"Do you have friends around?" she asks. "I don't feel comfortable leaving you alone out there with that guy. He's giving me the ick."

What the fuck? "Um—yeah. Well—no, actually." I take a deep breath and try again, this time pretending like I'm less flustered. "Yes, I have friends, but they had to leave for a few minutes. I was just going to head to the bar for a drink."

"By yourself?"

I nod, no longer keen on the idea. I can't help but wonder if it has anything to do with those weird messages I've been getting on Instagram. *Is it another artist?*

"Hm . . . well, we're about to become friends." She holds out her palm. "Hi, I'm Rosa!"

I grin, shaking her hand. "I'm Kelly."

"Okay, Kelly. Here's the deal, I just came from the bar, and that place is way too crowded anyway. Wanna head across the street and get a drink instead?"

I nod. "Yeah, let me just text somebody quick." I dig out my phone.

"Sure! I'm gonna go outside and make sure that guy isn't around."

"Oh, hey. If he is, would you mind getting a photo of him?"

"You better fucking believe I will," she says, nodding before exiting the bathroom.

I open my text thread with Logan and begin typing.

Me: Hey, I was just in the bathroom and some girl said

Fuck, he's gonna freak if he thinks there's some guy stalking me. It's probably just some creep trying to get my number. I delete the message and start over.

Me: The bar here is too crowded, I met a girl in the bathroom and we're going to go across the street.

Rosa reenters just as I'm sliding my phone into my back pocket.

"I can't find him." She shakes her head. "Let's hurry before he shows up again. Ready?"

"Yup." We fall in stride and make our way out the door, beelining for the lobby and exiting the main doors toward the other bar.

"A scrunchie? And he still tried to deny it?"

"Right?" I throw my hands up in the air and chuckle. "Thank you!"

"God, men are such fucking idiots!"

I lift my second drink to my lips. Rosa is hilarious, she's definitely a girl's girl. I have a lot of clients who are women, but the only women at Black Rabbit are Frankie and I, and we're usually too busy working to chat during the day. Rosa and I have a lot in common when it comes to our taste in tattoos and history in men. After a wild day packed with excitement, this little cocktail hour is just what I needed, and hey, I made a new friend! I already plan on telling Logan we have to come back next year just so Rosa and I can meet up again.

I shrug. "Honestly? I think it was a gift from the universe. It opened me up to a much better opportunity."

She raises her eyebrows. "Oh yeah? Does this opportunity have a bigger dick?"

Not sure how to even answer that. I've felt it but haven't technically *experienced* Logan yet. Not like that. I wipe away the condensation on the side of my glass, trying to avoid the question.

Rosa cocks her head to the side. "Don't tell me you haven't slept together yet."

"It's new!" I answer, laughing.

"How new?"

"I mean, we've been friends for a long time, he and I go way, way back. When I first met him, I had a crush, but that was so long ago, and he was a bit older than me at the time. But after Jason and I split, things shifted between us."

"Who initiated it?" she asks, fully invested.

"At first, I couldn't tell if I was just making it up in my head. He's a quiet guy, sometimes talking to him is like pulling teeth. But once I realized what was happening, I called him out on it—well, I kinda snapped—and then . . . he kissed me."

The memory makes me all warm and fuzzy inside, granted that might just be the altitude.

She gapes at me. "Holy shit."

"Wanna hear the craziest part?"

"Obviously!"

I lean in. "He's felt this way for years and never said anything!" I set my drink down.

With her glass in hand, she squints and points at me. "See? They're fucking idiots."

I shake my head and chuckle.

"Has it been weird going from friends to this?"

I shrug. "Not really? It's the same, but just with a *ton* of sexual tension added."

"Sounds like you need to release some of that tension . . ." She eyes me while taking a drink.

I raise my glass. "Cheers to that. So, what do you do for a living?"

"I'm a corporate girlie. Pitch decks, modeling spreadsheets, quarterly reports, blah, blah, blah." She waves it off.

"Really?" I chuckle. "I wouldn't have pegged you as someone who worked in an office. You have some great ink." I compliment her, my eyes drifting toward the cat again.

"Oh." Rosa juts out her shoulder and tilts her head toward it. "It's actually a cover-up. Used to say my ex's name." She holds up a hand. "I know, I know. I learned my lesson."

"Well, the cat is beautiful." I take a sip. "Since we're swapping tales of our exes' greatest hits, what's yours?"

She laughs. "Actually, it's a boring story." She huffs. "Young and dumb. He just . . . grew tired of me." She cocks her head to the side. "If it's meant to be, we'll find our way back, right?"

Her words make me wince; it sounds like her heart is still broken and I've been going on and on about my new relationship with Logan.

"That's true. And if not, men are shit," I proclaim, holding up my drink in a toast.

"Hear, hear," she cheers, clinking her glass against mine with a smile and a wink. "Okay, enough about boys—how long have you been tattooing?" she asks.

My brow furrows. "How did you know that?"

She reaches out and jiggles my lanyard. "It's on your badge."

"Shit, I forgot I was wearing it." I remove it from around my neck and stuff it in my purse. "I'm finishing up my apprenticeship, but got my license a little over a year ago."

My phone vibrates on the bar top, and the screen lights up with Logan's face.

"Whoa!" Rosa exclaims, using her finger to turn my screen to face her. "Please tell me this is the new guy."

My heart beats a little faster as I swipe the screen and pick up the phone. "Hey," I answer, with a laugh.

"Staying out of trouble?" His voice is deep and gravelly, and I have the impulse to kick my feet. Aside from his sporadic comments throughout the day, we haven't spoken about anything from last night. After traveling and all the extracurriculars in Logan's bed, I crashed hard. Today was so busy, even though we were in close proximity, it wasn't like we had any quality time during the convention.

"No."

Rosa bounces her eyebrows up and down.

"Uh-oh. Sounds like it's time for me to take you home," he teases. "Where are you?"

"The bar across the street from the convention entrance." I glance down at my coaster with the establishment's logo on it. "The Griffin."

"I'm pulling up now. Get out here."

"You're here now?" *That was fast.*

Rosa sets her drink down, then digs in her purse for her wallet. I cover my hand over hers. I'm buying this round.

"I'm here now."

I bite my lip and smile. "'Kay. Be out in a minute."

He ends the call, and Rosa looks at me with a big smile, chewing her straw knowingly. "Who was that?"

I open my mouth but am unsure how to answer. I haven't actually said it out loud yet. "That's Logan" is my response.

"Atta girl!" She slaps her credit card on the bar top. "You got the last one, this round is mine. With a man like that, you have much more important things to do," she says with a chuckle. "It's way past my bedtime anyway."

"Are you sure?"

"Absolutely! Have fun!" She shoos me off. "Oh, wait—let's exchange info! Work sends me all over the place, and I'm in Minneapolis occasionally. We should grab a drink when I'm in town."

"I'd love that! What's your Instagram handle?"

She cringes. "Actually, I'm not on social media. I can't doomscroll responsibly, had to give it up. What's your number? I'll put it in my phone."

I nod. If I didn't have to rely on social media for a source of income, I'd probably do the same. I rattle off my number as she types it in.

"I'll text you!" she says, and I quickly shove my phone back in my bag. After a quick hug and promises for future drinks, I throw back the last of my cocktail and hurry out the door.

I feel his gaze on me before I spot him.

When our eyes meet, my desire is drawn taut—all-consuming and possessive. It feels inevitable, like lust and friendship have joined forces. This is where I belong. As I close the distance between us, my body clenches with anticipation for him.

"Hi," I say, hopping in the passenger seat and closing the door.

"Where's Thor?"

"Dropped him off at the hotel . . . Show it to me," he says, grinning.

"Show what?"

"You know what—when were you going to tell me you got honorable mention?"

"Who snitched?" I ask, while fishing the ribbon out of my purse.

"Casper couldn't wait to brag about it."

I hold out the ribbon for him to see. He leans over the console and gives me a big bear hug. "So fucking proud of you."

"Wild, huh?" I muse.

"Well deserved. You designed an incredible piece and executed it beautifully."

The blush rises in my cheeks. He's not saying it as a friend or someone I'm romantically involved with—he says it as a peer, as my mentor. Pride fills my chest as I accept the compliment. It means so much coming from someone with as much talent as Logan Teller.

"Thank you." I nod. "Everything go well with your mysterious errand?"

I didn't come out and ask him what he needed to do, but he didn't offer.

His grin is practically cheek to cheek. "It did."

I tilt my head with a small smile. "Gonna tell me what it was?"

He shifts the car into drive and pulls away from the curb. "Just some boring paperwork."

27

LOGAN

My wife believes in soul mates. I, on the other hand, believe in taking what's mine. There isn't a lifetime she could hide in where I wouldn't hunt her down. Fate didn't marry us today—*I did*.

It's not that I did it without her permission so much as she just hasn't been formally notified yet.

It wasn't even that hard. All I had to do was purchase property in Montana, make it my primary residence, establish a little trust with the locals, and get the county to perform a proxy marriage—which is a walk in the fucking park once you forge the paperwork.

Kelly showers with her head tilted back, water sluicing off her inked skin. She's so goddamn beautiful I can hardly speak. I lean against the doorframe, admiring the way the steam winds itself around every luscious curve. Bringing the lowball glass to my lips, I let the smooth smoky Foxx Bourbon coat my tongue, while my fist tightens around the plain white shirt in my other hand.

I didn't even know proxy marriage existed until a couple years ago. That was when the wheels in my head began to turn. Apparently, residents of Montana have the option where one or both parties are able to marry each other by representing someone as their proxy—*in this case, Thor*.

"Are you going to join me or just stand there and watch?" Kelly asks.

I smirk and push off the doorjamb, setting my things on the bathroom counter. Well played. After shucking off my clothes, I swing the shower door open and step inside, letting the warm steam envelop me.

As soon as her eyes flick briefly to my cock, her plush lips part. The hitch in her breath has the corner of my mouth tilting up. That sultry gaze of hers drags over every inch like she's already plotting a hundred ways to ruin me. I could stand here for days, watching her try and fail to hide her hunger without ever growing tired.

She hauls me into her, delicate fingers linking behind my neck and bringing my mouth to hers. Soft, starving lips brush mine while her nails scrape my skin. Breaking the kiss briefly, she searches my eyes, then kisses me again, running her fingers through my wet hair. "I have wanted you like this for so long," she whispers, melting me into a fucking puddle.

I chuckle, allowing myself to succumb to the pure happiness bursting in my chest. "Is it everything you imagined?"

"Not exactly." She glances down, sinking her teeth into that full bottom lip as she stares at my hardening length.

My hands slip down her sides and reach behind, filling both my palms with her ass. "No?"

She releases a gentle sigh. "When I imagined it, you were buried in my throat."

My head flops back, and I squeeze my lids tight. "Jesus, Kelly."

Lowering my chin, I cup her neck, tilting her jaw up while my lips cover hers. She smiles against me. "Please?"

I nod, and she falls to her knees. *Fuck, yes.* Widening my stance, I make every effort to adjust my height, then brace a palm against the tile wall. I'm defenseless against her pleading.

"Stick your tongue out."

With soaked hair plastered to her neck and shoulders, she peers up at me, holding me captive with those big green eyes. Mascara smudges beneath her lashes—and she follows directions, while tracing the tips of her fingers up and down my calves. My sights are set on her creamy tits; those pierced tits brush my thighs.

I fist the base of my cock, slapping it on her tongue, *and she fucking whimpers.*

"Fuck, you're perfect."

"Let me prove it first," she purrs.

My head shakes in disbelief. This must be a dream. Grabbing her by the throat, I tilt her head back and spit into her mouth. "Suck."

She gasps, regarding me in awe like I built the universe with my bare hands just for her.

Her plump lips encircle me like she was made for it, sliding up and down my length, and I blow out a breath—wrecked by the image of her. How fucking gorgeous she looks with me in her throat. The way she tongues the underside of my cock, as if memorizing every vein, has a groan working its way up from my lungs.

My free hand delves into her hair and tugs it at the base. Her salacious gaze tangles with mine, and I nod, encouraging her while bobbing that sinful mouth faster over my dick. Her eyes roll back and flutter closed as she submits. *Fuck me.*

"You're doing so good, Chaos. So fucking good."

She hums around me, and I pump in and out. Dropping her hand, she grants me control to take over, then digs her fingers into my thighs.

"Can you take more?" I ask.

She mumbles an "*Mm-hmm.*"

"That's my girl." I guide myself deeper until she gags, and I hold her head steady. Tears form at the edges of her pleading eyes, mascara staining her cheeks. "I've got you."

She cups her palms behind my thighs, coasting them higher until she sinks her claws in my ass, hauling me closer. The way she marvels up at me proves she believes every word without hesitation, that sacred trust spurs me on more than lust ever could. Trusting me not to take it too far, to not hurt her. That trust means everything because our relationship will need it when she discovers what I've done.

I release her wet tresses, and she inhales, drool spilling from the corner of her mouth. She moves quickly, dipping her head to wrap her lips around one of my balls. Her hand works up and down, stroking my cock while she sucks. *Christ.*

She moans—the vibration shoots through me, and the heat in my core coils tighter. White spots dot the corners of my vision, and I curl my toes, doing my damnedest to keep from coming.

Not yet.

I pop out of her mouth, and she locks her plump lips around the crown, giving all the attention to my sensitive tip. Kelly fists my length with both hands stacked on top of each other; she tears a rumble from deep in my chest when she rotates them in opposite directions. *Fucking hell.*

"Get up here." I'm not ready to finish yet.

She subtly shakes her head defiantly, not stopping.

"Goddamn it, Kelly . . ."

She releases me with a wicked smile. "Yes, dear?" she asks, like my doting, domesticated slut.

"I'm going to finish all over your fucking hand if you don't stop."

"You better not."

With her fingers circling the base of my balls, she takes the rest of me down her throat like it's her personal mission to make me suffer. I should pull away, but I physically can't do it. The message from my brain is denied by my need to come down her throat. I want to see her swallow me; I've imagined it too many times.

The hand wrapped around me tugs downward, forcing my knees to lock. "Sit up straight, Chaos," I command. The release hits me like a freight train, and I growl, bracing myself against the shower wall. "That's it. Look at you, such a messy girl. Show me how fucking thirsty you are for my cum."

Her eyes sparkle while she worships me on her knees, her throat bobbing as she swallows. I empty myself into her with her name on my lips, and she takes it with so much eagerness I have to remind myself she's real—*my fucking wife*. This is so much better than any fantasy.

Once the blood returns to my brain, I turn off the water and wring the droplets from her hair. We exit the shower, and I run a warm, fluffy towel along every inch of her body, then do the same for myself. My cock is starting to relax, but I'll be back in no time, I'm sure.

I plug in the blow dryer sitting on the counter and begin combing my fingers through her locks, letting the dryer fill the silence. Goose bumps spread across her naked flesh as the warm air hits her skin, and she shivers occasionally. Every time I catch her gaze on me, I hold it. Each glance is charged with anticipation. I don't break eye contact, I want to see her just as affected as I am.

We've exchanged looks countless times in the past, but this is different.

She may think it's just another night, but I know better. Tonight, there will be no waiting and no mercy. I don't worship softly. Peace will only come after we've fucked ourselves into submission—and we'll have to tear each other apart to get there.

When her hair is dry, I brush the silky strands for any remaining tangles. My focus falls on my plain white shirt sitting on the counter where I left it next to the glass of bourbon. Then I hold it in front of her. "Put this on."

She cocks her head to the side, furrowing her brow quizzically, but draws it over her head. When she looks in the mirror, she holds her arms out at her sides and laughs. She's practically swimming in white cotton.

"This thing fits me like a dress," she comments.

I grin.

Without saying a word, I grasp under her thighs, pick her up, and pin her against the bathroom wall. "You're mine now."

She presses her forehead to mine, encircling her arms around my neck. "I like the sound of that."

My mouth crashes against hers—she parts her lips, demanding more. Her legs wrap around me as if they've done it a thousand times before. I knead her thighs with my palms, digging my fingers into the curves just under her ass.

Her soft body is pliable in my arms. The way her warm skin feels against mine overwhelms me with a sense of nostalgia, like home. She pauses our kiss by pressing her forehead against mine, catching her breath. "Please don't make me wait any longer."

I shake my head and swallow. "I won't."

She relaxes into me like I've finally granted her the right to breathe.

As I carry her into the bedroom, my cock hardens, and her thighs start to tremble before I even place her onto the downy mattress and climb on top of her.

And then I kiss her.

It reminds me of the first one we shared. Slow and aching. She parts her lips for me, like she's welcoming me home. Sealing my mouth over hers like a vow, I will honor and cherish this woman until the stars burn out.

Drawing back, I am in awe at my wife's beauty. Her heavy-lidded eyes blink up at me, lips swollen and craving more. I catalog this moment, searing it into my memory. The clean scent of iris and orange, the way my body so easily eclipses her small frame, her touch ghosting up my spine, her shallow inhales, her seductive expression . . . curious and soft, but also deprived and wanting—how I've wanted her for years.

She looks every bit the bride she is, laid out on ivory sheets, my white shirt riding halfway up her stomach, her soft, bare thighs on display and caged around my waist.

Her gaze searches mine. "You're staring."

"I've waited too long not to," I rasp. "I'll look as long as I please."

Her face warms.

"I finally have you," I add.

Her skating fingertips pause on my back, and she lightly jabs my shoulder blade. "Don't be ridiculous. You had me before tonight."

No, I didn't. Not like this. Not legally. She's always been mine, but now there's paperwork to prove it.

My straining cock is poised at her entrance.

"You haven't asked if I'm on birth control," she observes.

I chuckle. "I know your burrito order. Do you think I don't know if you're on birth control or not?" *What she doesn't know is that I don't care.*

She blinks up at me, somehow surprised.

"Do you want this?"

She studies me with eyes deep as an ocean. "Of course I do."

Her answer sends me over the edge; my wife just said *I do* on our wedding day. The context is irrelevant, I'm not about to get distracted by facts.

Leaning on one elbow, I cradle the back of her neck, squeezing thrice, a gesture to remind her how far we go back, how it's all led to this.

I drag my palm down her rib cage, savoring the shiver that rolls through her. The thick head of my cock notches at her entrance, and she braces for more. I watch her face, searching her gaze as I push inside—slow and reverent. Her breath catches, halting the way her chest rises and falls with anticipation as she focuses on the sensation. I pause halfway, then plunge deeper, making her take the full length and loving the way her lips part.

"Logan," she sighs.

I'm possessive of her—every utterance of my name, every muffled moan, every raw scream is mine now. *She* belongs to me, even if she doesn't fully understand how yet.

Her thighs tremble. She stiffens her muscles, as if trying to dampen the tremors.

"Let me feel you shake." My hand glides from her waist to her hips to under her thigh.

She relaxes, easing the tension, and her knees quiver against my sides. A rosy hue blooms on her cheeks—*fuck, I love when she blushes.* There's something so sexy about seeing this woman shy and nervous.

She's one of the strongest, most outgoing women I know, yet she completely submits under me. I pull out and thrust in again; her sounds are angelic.

"Just like that," I coax.

Every caress is met with another round of shakes. I grip her flesh, driving inside again and again, and she arches her back.

Sitting on the balls of my feet, I rest her legs on my shoulders and her white shirt rides up as I watch my length disappear into her.

"Every inch of me was made to fuck you exactly like this."

"Maybe I was made for you too," she says, her voice breathy.

Fuck. Clutching the white shirt collar, I tear it open, the sound of ripping fabric echoing around us. She startles and then laughs.

"Show me how your pretty pierced tits bounce when I pound into you."

Her grin splits her face. "So savage," she purrs.

"For you I am," I pant, snapping my hips into her. "Do you like having that control over me?"

"I love it."

I draw her into my chest, pressing my teeth into her shoulder, and roll us, putting her on top of me. She yelps at the brief bite of pain, then steadies herself, letting the remains of my tattered shirt fall from her delicate frame. Planting her palms on my chest, she grinds on my cock, every movement languid and unhurried as she teases me.

This is a punishment, she's purposefully torturing me, and I'm relishing every second.

Her hips lazily roll, and I can't take my sight off her body. "How's this?" she taunts. The ache inside me grows. I want her bouncing on my dick and crying my name. I'm fucking greedy. "Why so quiet, Logan?"

I shake my head, grinning at her adorable, naïve display of boldness. "Goddamn it, Kelly."

My hands find her soft hips, and I grip the flesh before gliding over her ass, lifting a palm and striking down with a loud clap. She yelps, her pussy throttling me. I'm obsessed with this woman.

"Aw, Chaos. You think you can play me, huh?"

She retreats, letting me slip out. Without blinking, I clasp each of her nipple piercings and tug her forward. "Sweetheart, I've been practicing. I've been celibate for three goddamn years waiting to fuck you—"

She gasps, eyes wide.

I haven't dated, how is this a surprise? Either way, it makes me smile. "That's right. You can mess with me all you want, but you'll lose control long before I do. I'm better at this than you."

"You weren't the only one who had to keep their hands to themselves," she says, hovering above me.

I smirk. "Is that what you did, Chaos? Think about how I'd fuck you, then go home and keep your hands to yourself?" I flick her piercings. The need to grab her and impale her on my cock has my fingers twitching.

"Sometimes," she admits.

Fucking hell. I want to see that.

"Were you secretly my filthy girl behind closed doors? Did you ever picture my face while you were being fucked by other men? You did, didn't you?"

Her lips part, and she moans.

I quirk a brow. *Interesting.*

"You moaned without me touching you."

Her face burns crimson. Her coy demeanor is irresistible.

"Why are you blushing?" I grin wider, savoring the surrender of her body. "Are you embarrassed by how often you got off to the image of me fucking you when we were *just friends* or is it because I can make you whimper with my words? See, I control you too, Chaos . . . I have since that first filthy thought of me crossed your mind. Have you always been this easy to manipulate, or is it me? Are you so impatient to be my slut already?"

She rolls her lips together, not wanting to admit it, but she can't keep secrets from me.

"Your cunt is a dripping mess. Every shallow breath is begging me to finish you off."

She's practically panting. She can lie to herself, but the way her body begs says everything.

"*You're just aching to come on my fat cock, aren't you?*"

Using my knuckles, I brush the underside of her breasts and travel down her stomach. Lower and lower. She doesn't push me away as my thumb drifts between her slick folds, and her legs start to shake again, lashes fluttering. "So fucking wet. Such a desperate girl."

I press my thumb to her clit, and she rolls her hips. She's losing her nerve. Christ, she'll be humping the air to get off any minute. My dick jerks in anticipation. "Is this what you need?"

She sighs, lowering herself and letting her head fall back as she rocks against my cock with abandon.

"Oh, Chaos . . . Does this pussy need to come?"

Kelly's noises are so sexy.

"Come on, you can tell me."

She glances at me with big pleading eyes. Normally, they would be enough to drown me, but not tonight. I shove her off me, flipping her onto her back, and stuff my entire length inside. She cries for mercy, but she won't find any from her husband.

"Too fucking bad." My hand wraps around her throat, and I fuck her with long, deep strokes. "Now it's your turn to wait."

Her cries are so lovely when they're caught in between gasps for air.

"This is what you wanted, isn't it? To provoke me on purpose? You've got a smart mouth and a weakness for the way I fill your cunt. What a dangerous little combination."

She merely sobs in response. Overstimulated Kelly is so fucking hot.

"You know what I used to think about? Fucking you in the shop." I pump into her steady and rough. "In front of Thor and Casper, in front of clients, but mostly in front of your boyfriends—I fantasized about forcing them to watch me break you in ways they couldn't. I wanted everyone to see Black Rabbit's legacy turn into my needy little slut who cries and begs. They all saw your strength, but I wanted them to see the surrender in your eyes as they rolled back."

Her lips part as she hangs on every word.

"I wanted the darkest parts of you. The side you hid from them."

Her gaze fills with tears, with the raw vulnerability of finally being seen.

Kelly is a kind, sweet, bubbly ray of sunshine—she was raised to be all these things. But there are parts of her the sun's warm rays can't reach . . . and that's something we have in common. It's why we've always been drawn to each other. She thinks it's fate, but it's familiarity. The depraved parts of me live in her too. I've caught glimpses of them, but she hides hers better than I do.

She arches her back, pushing her chest toward me. I tuck my chin to bite her shoulder.

"Don't stop!"

I chuckle at her helpless plea, digging my teeth deeper. "But more than anything, I wanted you to be mine."

Kelly blinks up at me, finally focusing. "I'm yours."

I drop my mouth to hers, and she nips my lower lip, tugging it until it releases from her teeth. Those two words form a lump in my throat. *Fuck, I need to get it together.* I concentrate on her warm breath on my skin as she unravels.

"I'm going to come." Her voice trembles. "Come with me . . . please?"

Her request has me smiling. "Anything for you."

My vision tunnels as she tenses beneath me—*there she is*.

"Hold it," I warn. "Keep it right there for me, pretty girl. You come when I say."

Heat builds low and fierce. I slow each thrust as we're swallowed up by the wave, lost in each other. With shaking thighs, she pants.

"Now."

She exhales hard, her release choking my cock, and the feel of her pulsing around me is all it takes. I lock down, buried deep, forcing her to take everything I have as pleasure rips through me. The release of spilling inside her is like nothing I've ever experienced.

My name sounds like a prayer when she comes. I pull all the way out and inch back in—she matches my movement, drawing out her orgasm. It feels so . . . *right*.

She's ruined me. Any lingering guilt from forging her name earlier is gone. This was inevitable. Knowing it's done helps me sleep at night.

When her body softens, I draw back so I can see her more clearly. Her silky hair is disheveled and fanned out over the pillow. She looks up through her lashes with glazed-over bedroom eyes. Her lips swollen and bruised, that gorgeous face wrecked and radiant—glowing from ecstasy.

My wife.

Unreal.

I set the tea on her nightstand, honey for her and lemon for me. She's curled up in bed, with wild hair, soft eyes, and freshly fucked bliss still warm on her cheeks.

That wasn't just sex, it was our beginning. She just doesn't know it yet.

I settle in behind her, wrapping my arms around her waist and folding her into my chest. She fits so perfectly, beyond what's physical. I press my lips to her shoulder, echoing her words. "I've wanted you like *this* for so long."

She sighs contently, tea forgotten on the nightstand.

"Was it everything you imagined?" she asks.

"So much more."

But she doesn't know why. She has no idea what she just gave me. What we just did. She doesn't know she just fucked her husband for the first time and consummated a marriage I made happen without her knowledge because it was the only way to make her untouchable. However, it wasn't just about protecting her, it was about making her my wife and sinking my teeth in before anyone else got the chance.

I should feel guilty, and there is a small part of me that does, but it's like a tiny knot in a long strand of thread. What I feel is full and fucking alive, because everything I care about is curled up in a white sheet and breathing heavily in my arms.

She told me she was mine.

28

LOGAN

I glance at Thor over my shoulder while loading a suitcase into the back of our rental van in the hotel's parking garage. They have a loading zone near the convention center, but there were at least twelve vehicles lined up, so this is faster. We've got ninety minutes to get to the airport, return our rental, and then get through security. After two days of tattooing all day and partying all night, the guys are a little burned out. Kelly and I are in the same boat, though our late nights are attributed to other activities.

Thankfully, the guys already boxed up some of our supplies to ship back home last night—all the shit that's too big to take on the plane. The hotel front desk printed the shipping labels for us, and it'll go out with their other packages today. "Did you get that box of signage we had on the main table?"

"Yeah, it's already in."

"Who grabbed the tablets?" Casper asks.

Kelly raises her hand. "I've got them in my carry-on."

"Thor, I met a girl you might be interested in," Kelly says. She met some woman at the bar while he and I were taking care of the proxy marriage paperwork.

"What's her Insta?" he asks. That's a trick question.

Kelly shakes her head. "She doesn't do social media."

He cocks a sly smile. "You have my attention."

She rolls her eyes. "She's not local but says she travels to Minneapolis for work sometimes. I think she's your type."

"Oh, I'm very curious to hear what you think *my type* is."

I chuckle and make my way to the driver's door to set my to-go cup of tea in the cup holder, then notice a folded piece of paper on the windshield. We haven't been parked long enough to get a ticket, and we only left it unattended for maybe fifteen minutes while retrieving bags from the guys' rooms and the event center—and a quick stop at the hotel's coffee shop. I snatch it out from under the windshield wiper and open it up.

You will never replace me.

I crumple it in my fist and do a three-sixty, raking my gaze over the area in hopes I'll see somebody lurking. There's a few people walking down the sidewalk, a woman with a stroller and some teenagers. A few of the hotel security staff stand around on their phones, but nobody looks suspicious. I scrub a hand down my face.

"You good?" Casper grumbles from behind me. I glance toward Kelly; she's still laughing with Thor and, likely, poorly describing what she thinks his type of woman is.

I pass the note to Casper. "Found this on the windshield."

He furrows his brow, looking around like I did.

"Kelly's been getting DMs that say the same thing," I add.

Casper cocks a brow. "How long?"

I shrug. "A few weeks."

"You think it's someone from the convention? Maybe another artist trying to shake her up?"

"No fucking clue, but why would they leave it after the event is over?"

"You sure it wasn't there earlier and you just didn't notice?" he asks. "Have you told Thor about this?"

I shake my head. There's no way I wouldn't have noticed if it was there earlier. Peering over at Kelly, I keep my voice hushed. "She was adamant it was just someone fucking with her online."

"Well, shit's offline." He scoffs. "So what are you going to do?"

I scan the parking garage a second time. "Find the asshole and rip his spine out," I say under my breath. "That letter from Billy? He had a PO box only a couple hours away."

Casper averts his eyes. "I'll help however I can. Thor will too, but—"

"Not with this. He's already stuck his neck out for me. I'm not bringing him into an uncontrolled situation. I'll deal with this."

"You don't think it's . . ."

It crossed my mind. "I don't know." The crumpled piece of paper goes into my pocket, and I toss another duffle in the van.

Kelly passes Thor one of the bags, and he loads it in the back.

"I've got it!" Kelly announces to Thor, still trying to guess. "Strippers?"

"I think you've got me confused with him," he says, nodding toward Casper—who rolls his eyes.

She laughs, appearing so relaxed and at ease. I don't want to do anything to take that smile off her face. "Okay, but really, if Rosa shows up in Minneapolis, maybe you should come out with us."

He shrugs. "You know me, normally I'd take you up on meeting one of your hot, inked-up girls—especially if she's from out of town—but . . . I'm kinda laying low right now."

She shrugs. "All right. I can respect that." Kelly's phone dings with a notification, and she digs it out of her pocket, then glimpses at the screen and shrieks.

The blood drains from my face. I hurry over to see what it is.

Kelly holds the screen in front of my face. "Look! Odin and Chicken Salad are snuggling!"

I exhale, realizing it's just a text from Jordan with a photo of the two dogs curled up together and passed out. I fake a half smile; that's the best I can do after the kick of adrenaline.

Casper pipes up. "Let's get moving, we need to have the van returned in twenty—and those late fees are a real kick in the dick."

I'm more concerned about my wife having a stalker, who is escalating, and how I'm going to tell Kelly about this. She's too chipper right now, fresh from her first expo and an honorable mention win, plus Casper took first for realism. Another trophy for that cocky fucker.

I'll break the news to her when we get back home. I don't want fear to overshadow the weekend we shared together. I'll tell her tomorrow. For now, my priority is to get her home safe.

29

KELLY

It's evening when our flight lands home in Minneapolis. It's been a long day of travel. I slept briefly on the plane, but the rest wasn't satisfying—not enough to make up for all the late nights with Logan.

I stare at the suitcases like a zombie as they go round and round on the baggage claim carousel. "You're going to stay at my place tonight," he says.

"I need to go to my house. I don't have any clean clothes . . . and I need sleep. I'm so tired."

"I am too," he says. "I'll do your laundry. You can wear something of mine to bed. I promise, you can go straight to bed when we get home."

When we get home, as if I live there or something.

I point a finger at him. "No late-night canoodling."

He smiles. "Canoodling?"

"Whatever, I'm tired. Words are hard."

"But *canoodling* was on the tip of your tongue?"

I disregard his teasing and narrow my gaze at him, signing "*No sex*" to him.

"*Heavy petting*," he signs in a counter.

A smile threatens to show through the serious face I'm putting on. My index and middle finger pinch together with my thumb. "I mean it, Logan. Tonight, sleeping together is literal."

He holds up both of his hands in concession.

I text Jordan from the baggage claim carousel and let her know we'll be home soon so she can head out, along with a big thank-you for housesitting and watching Odin while we were gone. It takes a while for the four of us to get our luggage, but eventually, we split off from Casper and Thor to head home. We're both exhausted from a weekend of too much interaction, too much caffeine, and too little sleep.

His loft is shrouded in shadows when we arrive, lit only by the lights of the city shining through the window, casting an orange glow. It smells like Logan, familiar and calming. Even the *click-clack* of Odin's paws on the aged wood floors is comforting. Logan takes our luggage to the back corner of the loft near the kitchen and unzips the bags, then begins loading dirty clothes into the washer. I unpack our water bottles, washing them at the sink, and tucking any snacks we didn't eat on the plane back into the cabinets. By the time I'm finished, Logan is carrying the empty suitcases upstairs, and I hear him start the shower soon after.

It's then I realize we're moving in sync. No rush, no words, just the soft rhythm of us existing in the same space, like we've done it for years. I pause to savor the moment, and a smile blooms on my lips.

Odin whines, pulling me from my amusement, and I snatch his leash. Just need the keys so I can get back in. They aren't in their usual spot. Logan probably left them in his pocket. I call up to him, but he doesn't hear me. He must already be in the shower. Hurrying up the stairs, I find his jeans strewn on the floor and reach into the pockets.

I have a copy of his house key, but the security fob to access the exterior door is a separate thing. My fingers quickly find the cold metal key ring and fish it out, and with it falls a wrinkled piece of paper. A receipt? I pick it up and unfold it.

You will never replace me.

It looks like all the others, typed in a plain font. But this one is different; it's so much more threatening when there's not a screen between me and it. My heart gallops in my chest. *Where the hell did this come from and why does Logan have it in his pocket?*

Odin whines again. I set the note on the dresser and grab the keys to take him out.

By the time I return from taking Odin for a walk around the block, feeding him dinner, and coming up with my own theories regarding the messages, I hear Logan stepping out of the shower. Before climbing the stairs, I double-check the locks on his door. I'm not sure how to begin this conversation, but I won't be able to sleep until we discuss the piece of paper I found in his pocket. The note is still where I left it. I pick it up and sit on the edge of the bed, staring at it. The online messages were one thing, but this is fucked up. I assumed this was Jason trying to mess with me, but Bozeman? That doesn't make sense.

Steam pours out of the bathroom when Logan emerges shirtless with a towel tied low around his waist. His stride halts when he notices what I'm holding.

"Is this why you wanted me to stay the night?" I ask, studying the words on the paper, wishing they would evaporate.

Logan sighs. "It was on the windshield this morning when we were loading up the van."

"In Bozeman?"

He turns his head, his palm working the back of his neck. "Yeah."

"Why didn't you tell me?"

He shrugs. "You were in such a good mood talking to Thor, we were about to get on a flight, I didn't want to stress you out. I wasn't hiding it, I planned on showing you tomorrow."

Logan opens his top dresser drawer, drops the towel, and tugs on a clean pair of boxers.

Great, now I've got to tell him how Rosa and I really met in the bathroom. If what she said was true, it's likely he left this note. He's gonna flip his lid when he finds out I kept that info from him, but the probability of these two instances being related are too high.

I squint, rub my tired eyes, and let out an exhausted exhale. "There was something that happened in Bozeman I didn't tell you about."

His back stiffens and he turns around. "What?"

"Remember how I said I met Rosa after the convention? Well, it was because she followed me into the bathroom at the event center while we were wrapping up. She said there was some guy watching me, and it gave her a bad vibe. She questioned if he could have been someone I knew; she described him, but he was too short for anybody at our shop. I asked if she could get a picture, but he was already gone when she went back out."

"Why didn't you tell me?" I swear red flames flicker in his irises. *He can't be serious.*

I throw up my hands. "The same reason you didn't tell me about the note!"

He sits on the edge of the bed, elbows on his knees, rubbing his jaw like the news just sucker punched him.

"It crossed my mind that the two things were connected." I stand. If I don't get in the shower now, I might not have the energy soon. "But

I talked myself out of it and figured it was just a weird guy. Men can be creepy."

"You should have told me."

"I know, but Rosa stayed with me to make sure I was safe. We went to a different bar across the street as a precaution, and nothing else happened after that, so I forgot about it. I wasn't trying to keep it from you. But now that there's a note . . ."

"How did she describe him?"

I struggle to recall her words after dismissing the event in my head. "I think brown hair, average build," I say, undressing and walking into the en suite bathroom. My voice echoes off the tile walls when I open the glass door and step into the shower. "I was thinking maybe she noticed Casper or something, but then she held up her hand to show how tall he was, and it was only like five-nine or five-ten."

I turn the dial and the warm spray from the shower resolves some of the new tension in my shoulders.

Logan clears his throat and enters the steamy room, leaning against the countertop. "How old?"

"I don't remember if she said."

"You got her number, right? Can you ask?"

I nod and pop the lid open on the bottle of shampoo, squirting some into my hand. "Yeah . . . I'm going to send her a picture of Jason and ask if she recognizes him. The height matches."

"That's a good idea."

"I just have a hard time believing he would go that far. We were only together a couple months. Not to mention, he was too lazy to buy a box of condoms, so following me out of state seems out of the question."

"He also showed up at your job and started a fight. If you only dated a couple months, then maybe you don't know him as well as you think you do."

I roll my eyes, lathering the shampoo in my hair. I disagree, but I can't prove he's wrong either. *You will never replace me.* The message itself is pretty obvious, but why would Jason care? He's the one who cheated. If anyone was getting replaced, it was me.

"What if the note was there before and we just didn't see it?" I ask.

"Huh?"

"Maybe it really was somebody from the event, and they left the note early, but we only noticed it on the last day? Could that be possible?"

"Possible . . . But unlikely."

I rack my brain for other options while rinsing my hair and adding conditioner.

The note was typed and printed, which means it was premeditated. We were only away from the van for maybe twenty minutes.

"This happened at the convention. It's gotta be somebody in the industry. They have been messaging me for months, and we posted about it everywhere online." Our shop advertised it, along with all our artists. The event itself plastered my name on their marketing materials and graphics. A few of those posts went viral, it was all over social media.

Unless . . . "Do you think the person who's been sending me DMs actually left the note? Or did they use a messenger?" I ask while soaping up my skin that still has stencil ink smudged on it from over the weekend. *If they were using someone else to deliver it, why not just use the messenger's handwriting? Why the extra steps to type it up and print?*

"It's gotta be somebody I know."

"Yeah. Jason."

I wipe a clear spot on the glass door and give an exasperated sigh, and he rubs a towel over his wet hair.

"Most stalkers are previous partners, Kelly."

The hair on the back of my neck stands on end. I haven't used that word yet. *Stalker.* It makes the whole thing seem more real—*scarier.* I don't want to have to deal with this. It was so easy when I could mark the problem as spam and delete it. Out of sight, out of mind.

"You really think it's a stalker?"

"You've been harassed for over a month by somebody leaving strange messages, and now they just left the same message in person. The behavior is escalating."

It's so invasive. "So, now what? Do I go to the police?"

My question is met with dead air, and I rinse the conditioner from my hair.

"Logan?" I prompt.

"I don't see why we need to involve the police . . . I'll take care of it."

Frustrated and tired, I shut off the water in a huff. "How? You don't even know who it is!"

He speaks with a level tone. I don't know how he can be so chill right now. He holds a fluffy towel in front of him when I exit the shower and wraps it around me. Next to the sink, he's already set out a clean shirt for me to wear to bed. I shouldn't have snapped at him, he's just trying to help.

After I finish drying off, I brush my teeth, then slip the shirt over my head, pulling my wet hair from the collar, and get started on my skincare routine. I'm too tired to dry my hair tonight—I can deal with everything else in the morning.

"I'll find out who it is," he says, his voice low and lacking emotion. "And I'll take care of it."

He says it like he's got no problem making someone disappear.

I laugh, following him out of the bathroom, then draw back the covers to the bed. "What, are you gonna kill him?"

He doesn't laugh with me. He doesn't even blink. His glare is dark and calculating, as if he's gauging whether to lie to me. The sheet is limp in my hand as I study the shift in his character.

"Would it scare you if I said yes?"

I open my mouth to say *of course*—that's how a normal person should respond to a question like that—but stop short because . . . *I don't know.* "You aren't a murderer."

"No, but I won't hesitate to bury a problem if it keeps you safe."

His gaze softens slightly, and he climbs under the covers, looking like my Logan again. I take off the shirt and settle in next to him, not wanting anything between us. He hauls me into his side, and goose bumps rise on my skin. I'm unsure if they're from the loss of heat after my shower or caused by the words he uttered like a promise; regardless, his body is comforting and warm.

I nuzzle deeper into his chest and close my eyes . . . trusting him.

30

LOGAN

I'm not sure what time it is when I wake up the next morning, but the sun is much higher in the sky than it usually is. We must have needed more sleep than I realized; even Odin is still snoozing on his cushy dog bed, flopped on his back with his legs in the air.

I'm still not comfortable letting Kelly go back home alone. I can't believe she didn't tell me about the guy at the expo. I should have paid better attention to who had their eyes on her this past weekend. My stomach turns to think that even with her at my side for most of the weekend, someone was lurking in the shadows, waiting for me to step away so they could get close to her.

My tense muscles soften against the mattress at the sight of her sleeping form next to me. Curled up on her side, she looks so small and vulnerable. Her chest expands in a relaxed, even rhythm. Peaceful. Her glossy black hair and inked body contrast beautifully against the crisp white sheets. Rolling onto my side, I prop myself up on an elbow and smile at the stunning sight before me.

I trail my fingers over her bare shoulder and rib cage, stirring her, and she rolls onto her stomach. Crawling over her, I hover on all fours and sweep her hair to the side. Dipping my head, I ghost my lips over the nape of her neck. I work slowly, planting soft kisses down her spine. She stretches her arms above her head, arching her back slightly.

When I reach the dimples above her ass, I trace each one with my tongue, and she hums a raspy moan, proof she has the ability to seduce me in her sleep.

I figured after the paperwork was signed I would feel more at ease, but with a stalker on the prowl, I won't relax until I put a stop to him.

I've been on high alert ever since hearing that another man was watching her, as if she was a target—as if she was something he could take from me. Kelly is my wife, and mine to protect. Her stalker will soon find I'm not just her hunter, I'm also his.

I don't need the police, I need resources. I need time. This is personal.

When I do find him—because I will—I won't hesitate to bury him as promised. I'll make him disappear like a fucking magic trick, making him forget Kelly, and the rest of the world forget him.

There are some secrets Kelly will never learn for her own benefit. I'm a selfish bastard when it comes to her, but at the core of my actions is her.

"This is the best way to wake up," she mumbles. "Besides maybe one other thing . . ."

"Oh yeah?" I check the clock to see how fast I need to make this. Shit. We're not late, but we will be if we don't hurry. "I don't know if we have time."

She lifts her hips, and I sit up on my heels, giving her room to get to her knees and put her heart-shaped ass in the air. Covering her right cheek with my palm, I spread her apart and take in the view of her glistening pussy. I press my thumb to her tight knot and smirk when she sucks in a breath.

"Not today, but soon. If we didn't have to hurry off to work so fast, I'd probably dive tongue first into your pretty cunt too."

My cock is pointing at her as if I can't see what's right in front of me.

"Please," she whines. She must know it's my weakness. I'm a sucker for manners.

Gripping her waist, I yank her against me, sliding my cock between her soaked lips. Her whimpers are so distressed my forehead breaks out in a sweat.

"We'll have to be quick."

"Then what are you waiting for?"

She glances back at me, wearing nothing but ink and a wicked smile, like she's daring me to snap. She doesn't just make me lose control, she strips it from me, demonstrating that she's earned her moniker—*beautiful, reckless Chaos*.

I smile and shake my head, then push inside her tight, wet entrance. Goddamn. I lean back to look, and her pussy hypnotizes me the way it swallows my length.

This time it's not slow and sentimental, it's quick and dirty.

She rocks against me, fucking me back, and I crack a palm across the top of her ass. Then she constricts around me and hums.

"That's it, take it like my good fucking girl."

We selfishly steal pleasure from each other, and our rhythm is primal and demanding as we seek the gratification that only the other person can provide.

She sits up on her knees and leans into me. One hand palms her heavy breast and the other captures her throat. Her groans vibrate through me as I ravage her. She wraps an arm around the nape of my neck; the other braces us against the headboard so we don't fall over.

I hammer into her again and again, and no matter how hard I fuck her, it's like she can't get enough. I figured she had a freaky streak, but this is more than I anticipated.

"All these years."

"What?" she asks, panting.

"I wondered how you liked being fucked. Turns out you want it rough."

She chuckles, squeezing me a little more. "And you like control."

"Perfect match, then," I say between breaths, grunting when I bury deeper.

"Aren't we a pair . . ."

Devious girl.

"I knew we would be." I imagined it so many times. There's not a place in this world I haven't imagined fucking her. Like an animal that's been in a cage for too long, pacing back and forth, my thoughts about Kelly grew more and more unhinged. I tried ignoring them, but they always went back to her. Now she's mine, and this is our happy little life complete with morning fucks before work.

She turns her head to the side. "How did you know?"

"You know how."

That darkness that she has. The depravity that exists within her that's never been fully quenched. It's not a choice, it's not curiosity, it's deeper than that. There's a carnal urge inside her that begs to be ruined in the most sinful of ways. Dismantled and then pieced back together again and again.

She moans as I drive into her. "I love the way you fuck me." Her voice is raw and vulnerable, words barely intelligible. *Almost there, sweetheart.*

Gripping a handful of her hair, I jerk her head back, exposing her neck, and sink my teeth into the soft flesh near her shoulder. She comes, screaming my name, and her pussy flutters over my length, and I growl against her skin with a clenched jaw. Squeezing my eyes shut so I can focus, I make sure my next words come out in the correct order. "I love fucking you, Chaos."

"Come inside me," she begs. "*Please.*"

That goddamn word. I surrender to her without a fight, taking her trembling body and holding her tight against my chest. My cock pulses, flooding inside her. Her delicate hands cover mine, and our fingers intertwine.

We collapse into the covers, sweaty and tired.

"We"—she heaves a breath—"are so good at that."

"We are," I agree. I chuckle and sit up to check the time. Shit. "But we're going to be late."

She climbs out of bed with a smug smile on her face.

"Feeling proud of yourself?" I ask.

"Making my punctual boss late for work? Very."

31

KELLY

By the time I get to work, I'm already craving a nap. This morning wore me out, not to mention it's the first day back to work since we returned from Bozeman, which feels like a week ago instead of a few days.

I slouch in one of the upholstered lobby sofas. "Hey, Frankie, who's my first client today?" A yawn slips out before I can stop it. That shit needs to quit right now, or I'll never make it through the day.

"Let me see . . ." With a few mouse clicks, she clears her throat. "Looks like you've got a frenum piercing with Kucera."

Oh, that's right, he's coming in for his ladder.

Frankie puffs out her cheeks, then quickly releases them, cocking her head to the side. "Huh. That's weird," she mutters.

"What?"

"I dunno, the calendar shows Kucera on here twice . . ." She taps the keyboard a couple times. "Oh, never mind. Different Kucera."

"Anna?" I ask.

Frankie nods, her tight black curls bobbing.

"Oh, yeah, I remember Casper mentioning something about a session with her this week . . . By the way, I love the curls you're rocking today," I add.

"Thanks!" she says with a bright smile. "Oh! I wanted to ask you what you thought about me getting a stud right here?" Her pointy bright-blue fingernail taps on her right nostril, and her eyes narrow. "Something delicate?"

Frankie has beautiful features, so she could pull off any piercing flawlessly. "Absolutely you can. We can do it during your break if you want?"

"Yeah?"

"For sure. Let me get you a tray to look at." The excitement of giving my coworker and friend a nose piercing gives me a boost of energy. I pop out of my chair and head to the piercing bay. While I'm back there, I prep the small room for my first client, making sure my tools are laid out, along with the tray of barbell jewelry. I also select a couple trays of various stud jewelry for Frankie to consider while she's at the front desk. She's already familiar with the jewelry we offer, since we frequently have artisans stop by Black Rabbit to show us new designs. Frankie is great at selecting unique pieces for us to carry, so I'm sure she already has an idea of what she wants.

When I return, Rhys and Micky Kucera are just entering the shop. I offer them a bright smile. "Today's the day! How are you feeling?"

"Nervous," Rhys says with a chuckle. Micky appears much more enthusiastic than her male counterpart.

I set the trays of studs on the front desk next to Frankie for after she finishes getting Rhys checked in, then chat with Micky for a bit while he fills out the consent and release form. She's got a cool-as-hell cocktail lounge I've been to a handful of times, and it sounds like business is still booming over there.

When Rhys is finished, I bring them both back to the piercing room. Rhys takes a seat in the central chair, and Micky sits in one of the spectator chairs along the wall.

"So, we're doing a frenum piercing today. It's been a little bit since our consultation, but as you may remember, we'll only do three bars today. We can mark and photograph your goals for additional bars so we have that on record for the future."

"Can't be the same number as Cam, he's already giving me shit for riding his coattails."

Camden is Logan's stepbrother, and since I've attended most of the Teller family gatherings in the last few years, he's practically my stepbrother as well. I did his frenum piercings too. He's got a good heart, but being an asshole is part of his charm.

I grin and roll my eyes. "Camden didn't patent the Jacob's ladder. I've done hundreds of these. You're not riding his coattails."

"See?" Micky says to him. "And once this is done, I'll be riding your front tail!"

I snort. Micky tends to say whatever crosses her mind, often forgetting to filter her words, but she makes it endearing. "After two to four weeks," I add. "You don't want to risk infection."

"Worth the wait!" she says.

"Yeah, I figure the offseason is the best time to get started."

I scrunch my nose. "My condolences regarding the playoffs. You guys played a hell of a season." I don't keep up on hockey too much, but Logan does, especially since Cam is the captain. I don't know if it's the sport he cares about so much as it is his family. He's got a soft spot for them, so we see them every couple months. Come to think of it, it's been a while since our last trip to his dad and stepmom's place, so I make a note to schedule something.

"Thanks. So . . ." He gestures to his crotch. "How does this whole thing work again?"

I smile and recite the spiel over what the process is. "So, as you know, this piercing goes through the frenum and along the loose tissue on the shaft of the penis. We're still doing the underside, correct?"

He nods.

"Awesome. I'm going to use a twelve-gauge needle to create the holes in the tissue. Like I said, I prefer to keep it no more than three bars at a time. Anything more than that can increase your risk of infection. From your consult, it sounds like you want more than three."

"Camden has seven rungs. I want eight."

I fight back a grin; that's a lot. Not sure I can promise that, but if I can . . . way to go, Micky.

"All right. So, generally, I'll leave the room and give you a few minutes of privacy to achieve an erection. This is necessary for the marking process so it will give you the best aesthetically pleasing result—that will be the big determining factor for how many piercings we can do based on how much real estate is available. I want to make sure they aren't too close together, otherwise it won't look right and can increase your risks while healing."

That's my nice way of saying, *Okay, pal, let's see how big your dick is before we begin talking numbers.*

"If we are unable to do eight bars on the shaft, we can continue down to the lorum and scrotum—"

"Nope." He cuts me off.

"No problem." I laugh. "Okay, so once you're erect, I'll mark the locations of the piercings. If you're comfortable, I'd like to mark all of the rungs today and photograph them for future reference. It's a photo that will be taken on your personal phone for you to keep. I find planning the entire ladder in advance gives the best results. There's a much lower chance of running into issues like spacing or how even it is."

He asks every man's most important question, and the one we all hate answering. "Is it going to hurt?"

"You'll feel a quick pinch, the pain should be brief. Some clients have said it was painful, others have said they barely felt it. If I were to make a guess, I would say you'll be all right. Hockey players are used to taking some pretty hard hits, so your pain tolerance is probably on the higher end. I'll have you do some breathing exercises."

He nods. "Cool."

"I also recommend not starting out by piercing the bars near each other. Once we mark it, we can maybe do one on top, one on bottom, fill in the center as we go. Since we're doing this in sessions, it tends to look better if you space them out. No penis is perfectly straight and symmetrical, so the way we align the piercings will not be perfect either. Instead, we'll work with your natural shape to give the illusion that everything is equally spaced and lined up. Make sense?"

"So, I'm going to be hard when you pierce it?"

I shake my head. "No, no, no. It would be much more difficult to pierce otherwise, this is just to guide me where to pierce."

"What if it doesn't . . ." He nods to his lap.

I grin. "Then we wait. Most clients are flaccid by the time we finish prepping the area." *Especially once they see the needle . . .*

"At that point, I will push a hollow needle through the skin where we've marked, likely using a forceps to isolate the tissue. Then I'll hold the piercing in place while I insert the jewelry. We'll do a straight barbell today, and once you've healed, we can swap that out for a curved one in the future. Afterward, we'll go over maintenance and aftercare during the healing process."

They both nod, and Micky places her hand over his. They're adorable.

"Do either of you have any questions I can answer?"

He shakes his head. "Nope. Let's do this!"

"Great!" I clap my hands together. "I'll give you a few minutes of privacy. Micky, do you want to let me know when he's ready?"

"Deep breath in," I say.

Micky starts humming the Oscar Mayer wiener theme song. I glance up, and Rhys is shaking his head and fighting off a smile. Her attempt to relax him works.

"Little pinch," I say, inserting the needle. "Exhale."

Rhys blows out a breath.

He barely made a peep. Atta boy.

"That wasn't so bad," he says.

Micky squeezes his hand, then exhales with relief. I grin. She showed up ready to rock, but I think watching me shove a needle through her husband's penis had her a bit worried for him. I was mostly worried we weren't going to be able to fit eight, but his anatomy is quite . . . accommodating.

"You did awesome!" I screw on the barbell and clean up with saline before moving to the next mark.

"Another deep breath." I insert the needle.

"Ouch." I'm not surprised, his pain receptors are more awake after the first bar. The last one will probably be the worst.

"Sorry about that. Try to relax a bit, go to your happy place."

"I can't go to my happy place, or I'll end up hard again," he mutters, making both Micky and me laugh.

"You're doing great. You've only got one more, this one might be the worst, but then you're all done for the day."

He nods, and Micky rubs his back in slow circles, and a small band of sweat beads on his forehead.

"Release the tension from your shoulders. Deep breath in . . ."

"Fucking fuck!" he shouts. I bite my lip to keep from smiling. I can't help it, there's something about grown men experiencing brief, temporary pain—that they opted for—that will always amuse me. Maybe it's just because shoving a needle through a man's penis feels like a fun little consolation prize for putting up with the patriarchy. Thankfully, he doesn't squirm much, so I'm able to work quickly, sliding the jewelry through and getting him cleaned up.

"You did it! You're all done!"

He slumps back in the chair and exhales slowly.

"I'm so proud of you!" Mickey says, cupping his face and kissing him.

"Hellcat, I wouldn't do this for anybody but you."

They're sweet. Once he's all done, I give him the rundown on all the aftercare, and we exit the room.

Anna and Casper are walking down the aisle between the tattoo bays when she stops in her tracks. A soft smile grows on her face. "What are you doing here?" she asks, glancing behind me.

Micky whisper-shouts from behind me, "Your brother just got his di—" Her voice is suddenly muffled, and I spin around to see that Rhys has clapped his palm over his wife's mouth.

"Consult," he answers. "I'm getting a tattoo consult."

"Yeah, let's go with that." Anna wrinkles her nose. "I'd rather part my hair with a chain saw than hear the rest of what Micky had to say."

Thor and I laugh from behind our tattoo station walls, but everyone else remains professional. Logan is working on a guy's arm a few feet away, but even with his head down, I can tell he's smiling.

"Wait, what are *you* doing here?" Rhys asks Anna, cocking his head to the side.

"Consult," she blurts, fidgeting with her cotton-candy-pink hair. I know for a fact she's past the consultation phase, but that's none of my business.

Rhys narrows his eyes. "Hm."

I use the opportunity of silence to usher Rhys and Micky toward the front desk so we can settle up payment and hopefully spare her from any big-brother lecture she was about to receive. I don't know much about their sibling dynamic, but I've heard through the grapevine that Rhys is very protective of his little sister, though she's clearly in her midtwenties. I don't have any biological big brothers, but growing up in Black Rabbit, it sure felt like I did sometimes.

After they leave and I get the piercing room fully sanitized, I prep my tattoo bay for my next client. This will be one of my first cover-ups; the tattoo being covered is behind the client's ear. It's tiny, no bigger than a dime—piece of cake. We've decided to cover it up with a nautilus shell. It will look awesome when it's complete.

Logan's wearing his glasses while he works, and I bite my lip as I stare, reminiscing about all the things he said to me this morning while I was spread like an offering. The raw unhinged version of him is so different from the man he is for everyone else, and I love that he is both.

He pauses tattooing to sign to his client. "*Doing okay?*"

The client nods and I grin. Watching him sign is really . . . *hot*. The combination of compassion and knowledge will always be sexy . . . The black latex gloves on his skilled fingers and exposed sinewy forearms don't hurt either.

His eyes find mine and he smiles, signing to me this time. "*Having a good day?*" He winks.

My lips roll together to keep from breaking into laughter and reply with my hands. "*Can Twinkies have good days?*"

He chuckles and returns to the tattoo, shaking his head.

32

LOGAN

After a long week of work, I'm ready to be done. Kelly called my stepmom, Linda, who was more than delighted to hear Kelly's suggestion to get the family together for a meal. The last time Kelly and I went to my parents' was Easter. Camden couldn't make it because he had a game in Canada, and Alexis was absent because she had the flu.

Cars are already stacked in the brick driveway when we arrive at my parents' river bluff home; it's a welcoming sight with warm-cedar shakes and round dormer windows. Alexis and Camden and Jordan have already arrived. Hailey probably isn't too far behind. Odin whines in the back seat when Chicken Salad bounds out of the front door. They're best friends after spending the weekend together while we were in Bozeman.

Kelly turns her head to speak to the beast in the back seat. "Looks like your girlfriend is excited to see you, Odie."

Jordan steps onto the front porch and waves at us. As soon as we open the door in the back seat of my truck, Odin is bounding out, and then the two big dogs run off into the trees that sit on each side of the house.

"Use protection!" Jordan calls after them.

"Crazy kids," Kelly adds.

I've always been an introvert, but socializing, or at least being in the company of my family, is something I've always enjoyed. Growing up, I lost my mom early. Signing is the piece of her I still carry with me. I know what she looks like from photos, but the only memories I have left are of her hands. I will always remember them. I've drawn them several times from memory. She had fingers like an artist, wrinkled and knobby but beautiful.

Losing our moms at a young age is something Kelly and I always had in common. I was an only child like her until my dad, Bruce, met Linda, who was a single mother of three coming from an abusive relationship. Suddenly I found myself with a new mom and three new stepsiblings. Clyde, on the other hand, never remarried. His first wife was his one and only, so after that, Kelly and art were all he needed to feel complete.

"Hey, Mom . . ." I duck my head and peer into the fridge. "Do you have any fresh mozzarella?"

I've called Linda *Mom* since I was probably ten or so. It's just easier. Besides, any sentence starting with *Hey, Stepmom* automatically sounds like amateur porn.

"Bottom drawer on the left. Might be toward the back. I'm going downstairs to get a couple bottles of wine. Any requests? Reds? Whites?"

"Beer," Dad says.

I grab the cheese located precisely where she said it would be.

Being in the kitchen puts me in the center of the family's madness without having to participate as much. I find comfort in watching my family interact with one another. Camden, Hailey, and Alexis have always had each other. When our families merged, it wasn't like we immediately became the Brady Bunch. I've always been the black sheep, but they never treated me like it. They accepted and respected that I was quiet and kept to myself more often; they respected it but never let it stop them from making me feel included. A few years ago, Camden married Jordan, making her a Teller, so she's basically another sister. And now we have Kelly too.

It helps that the Teller love language consists of giving each other shit; it comes from the heart. I generally sit back and observe the chaos, but cooking allows me to focus on a task and still catch up on everyone's lives . . . and I enjoy it.

"Your mom wants to make this salad with mandarins or something," my dad says, shuffling around in their pantry, picking up cans and setting them back down. "I can't find the . . . the . . ."

"Okay, Sometimers," Hailey says with a chuckle.

"What are you looking for?" I ask.

"It's the, uh, what's that soup? You know, the square soup . . ."

Alexis blinks at me from the barstool across the island. "The fuck is he talking about?"

I smile and shrug, selecting a knife from the wooden block near the stove. The blade is dull as can be.

"I can hear you!" Dad says, still searching the pantry. "You know, the soup! It's beige and curly..."

"First you said it was square, now it's curly?" I ask. "Keep your story straight, man."

A few of us exchange glances. We all know it's ramen, but this is more entertaining. Also, for whatever reason my dad has always pronounced it "ray-men" instead of "rah-men," and it's something we'll never forgive him for.

"What are you talking about?" Hailey asks.

More boxes and cans get pushed around on the shelves. "They used to sell 'em for like a dime apiece..."

"Is it a new thing? Maybe we haven't had it before?" Kelly asks.

"No! Yes! Everybody has eaten this."

"I don't think I've had it," Kelly adds, winking at me. She fits in so effortlessly with my family.

"It comes in an orange packet. They have flavors!"

Alexis scrunches her face up. "Flavors?"

Dad groans. "Yeah, like beef, shrimp, chicken, Oriental—"

"Whoa, whoa!" we all shout in unison.

"Dad, you can't say that!" Hailey whispers loudly.

I shake my head at him while working the sharpening stone across the blade of my knife.

"No! It's not—it's a *flavor*! It's on the package!"

"The package of what?" Jordan asks.

Kelly hides her face in her hands to keep from laughing.

"The—the thing! I can't remember the fucking name!"

"Language," Camden reminds him, which gives an added layer of humor because he's usually the one Mom chews out for swearing.

I wash the knife in the sink before gliding it through the fresh mozzarella, dividing the white log into round discs. When we arrived, I noticed a bowl of fresh tomatoes Mom picked from her garden, and a basil plant in the window. Everybody likes caprese, and it's easy to throw together.

Dad's face looks more like a tomato the more frustrated he becomes.

Camden leans back in his chair, threading his fingers behind his head. "Not ringing any bells, Bruce."

Dad sticks his head out of the walk-in pantry and mutters, "I know you little shits are messing with me."

Mom walks into the room. "What is happening?"

"Linda." He stands in front of her and cups her face in his hands, his eyes pleading. The man is desperate at this point. "What is that stuff we put on top of the salad with the oranges?"

"Ramen?" Linda asks.

"Raymen!" he shouts, raising his hands toward the heavens, as if he just won nine hundred bucks at bingo.

"Way to ruin Christmas," Alexis whines.

"I can't find the ramen," he says. Sure enough, Mom goes into the pantry and exits with it less than a second later.

The smell of summer fills my nostrils as I cut into the plump red and orange tomatoes. I stack them onto the mozzarella rounds and arrange them on a platter, then sprinkle chopped basil and drizzle balsamic vinegar over top.

Everybody swipes up the snacks, and I get started on a new plate of them. They'll be gone by the time I'm finished, and then I'll begin on the Mediterranean pasta for dinner.

Kelly comes around to my side of the island and reaches across to steal a tomato, but I snatch up her wrist and pull her into me, then wipe my palms on the towel draped over my shoulder and slide a clean hand up her spine to squeeze the back of her neck a few times. She rises on her tiptoes like she's about to whisper something to me and I kiss her. In front of everybody, not giving a single fuck.

"Holy shit . . . Did I win?" Camden asks, a huge smile across his face.

Kelly's brows furrow, and she drops back down onto the heels of her feet. "Win?"

I roll my eyes. "Apparently, they had a bet going for when we got together." Kelly laughs and circles her arms around my waist.

"Wait, who had June?" Mom asks, looking around at the various family members patiently waiting. Camden clutches his phone, I assume pulling up the details of this whole betting pool they had organized.

"Linda!" Kelly laughs harder.

"Alexis!" Cam announces, pointing at her.

She jumps out of her chair. "Pay up, you bastards!"

"Damn, we should have gone in on it and stolen the pot." She takes the knife from me and cuts a couple narrow slices of mozzarella, then rotates and sneaks them to Chicken Salad and Odin while Alexis walks around and collects cash from everybody.

"About damn time," Dad says.

* * *

After dinner, Camden and I grab a six-pack and take the tram elevator from the outside deck down to the boathouse near the river's edge. We descend the bluff under the dark canopy of trees and are soon met by gleaming blue water as it flows on a gentle current. The late-day sun feels like a warm blanket when we emerge from the shady wooded slope. We step off the platform, our footfalls hollow on the wooden boards.

"So . . . You and Kelly." He gives me a big shit-eating grin. "And how's that going?"

I shrug, trying not to smile.

"You've been after that girl for years, and now it's—" He lifts his shoulders to mimic me. "Bullshit."

We cross the wooden wraparound deck of the boathouse, then prop our forearms on the railing to overlook the water and watch some of the boats pass by. I twist the top off one of the beers and bring it to my lips.

"She's a dream," I say, taking a swig. I need some advice. "But I was hoping I could ask you about something."

"Shoot." He pops off his bottle cap and pockets it.

"When you and Jordan first got together, she was having problems with her ex . . . I think we might be dealing with something similar."

"Fuck." He sighs. "What's going on?"

I give him the rundown of everything, from the weird messages on Instagram to the paper note left on the windshield in Bozeman.

"Who is it?" he asks. "Didn't you help facilitate the breakup with her ex?"

"It was inevitable, I just sped up the process."

"Good for you," he says. "So, you think he's stalking her?"

I shake my head. "No. I think it's Billy Akers. He was the guy who was cooking the books at Black Rabbit before I took over."

His brow furrows. "I don't think you told me about this."

I didn't. "He fucked Clyde over. While we were tending to him on his deathbed, Billy was cutting deals to sell Black Rabbit to the highest bidder."

"Holy shit. You told Clyde, I assume. Is that why he left you the shop?"

I shake my head. "He never left the shop to me, he left it to Kelly."

Camden turns to face me. "*What?*"

"Billy was the business power of attorney for Black Rabbit; he told Clyde he transferred ownership, but he never actually did it. What he *did* do was try to sell the shop to some faceless corporation who probably would have turned us into a cash cow, bleeding it out until there wasn't a penny left. Those weren't Clyde's wishes; it was supposed to go to Kelly. I never found the paperwork to prove it, though."

He brings the rim of the beer bottle to his lips and waits for me to continue.

"I spent two-thirds of my trust to buy the shop and kill the deal."

"What the fuck?" he shouts.

I glance over my shoulder and look up toward the house to make sure nobody heard his outburst. "Christ, keep it down!"

"Logan. There was close to three fucking million in that trust."

"I know. That's why I forged the papers to say it was left to me instead." I don't tell him that since we're married, Kelly and I both own it now. That crosses a moral boundary for Camden, and I don't need to involve him any more than I already have. But in order to explain why I think the stalker is Billy, I had to give him something.

He turns back to looking over the water. "Who knows about the money?"

I take a sip from my beer. "Dad knows. And Billy."

"How did you not kill that motherfucker on the spot?"

"I wanted to. *Fuck, I wanted to.* But between taking over the business, being there for Kelly after Clyde passed, not to mention my own fucking grief, I just didn't have the energy. I needed to put my focus into Black Rabbit to make sure we didn't go under."

"Well, what's stopping you now?"

"He was smart enough to take the money and run. Always talked about moving out west—"

I nod. "When he sent that letter, guess where the PO box was?"

"Bozeman," Cam answers.

"Not Bozeman, but a city less than two hours away." I let my beer dangle precariously over the water, holding on to the lip by my fingertips. All the work I've put in the last few years has left me in a similar position as the bottle in my hand, barely hanging on. "I've busted my ass to build Black Rabbit into something bigger. I had to in order to keep it afloat when Clyde Everhart was no longer the main draw. To keep his legacy going.

"We're worth more now than we were years ago . . . I think he's going to blackmail me for more money. He sent me a letter recently—well, he addressed it to Kelly—but it went to the shop instead of her house. I don't think those messages about being replaced are meant for Kelly, I think they're meant for me."

"Shit." Cam blows out a breath.

"He knows the best way to motivate me is through her."

"Yeah, and you've proved him right by handing over millions, you stupid fuck."

I shrug. In retrospect, I should have buried this whole thing. *Would have been cheaper to fund a second funeral.* I won't make the same mistake this time. "I didn't see any other choice, and I didn't have time to come up with something better. It's not like I could prove anything to his lawyers. I had to buy him out or we would have lost everything. *Kelly* would have lost everything."

He takes a drink and tips his bottle. "What else do you know about the guy?"

I grasp my beer in my palm so it doesn't fall. "Not enough. I'm hoping he's out west and staying there. I can deal with the fucking DMs until then, as long as it's nobody nearby who could hurt her. But I'm unable to do anything until I find out where he's living exactly."

Cam huffs. "Look, if he's far, then you've got a little leeway. Don't go all Lenny and the mouse on her. If she feels like you're trapping her, then she'll want to leave. I know your instinct is to protect, but you have to give her space to breathe, or you'll lose her entirely. She's probably freaking out as it is. It's safer to give her a leash."

I shake my head. I don't like those options.

"Have you installed cameras at her place?" he asks.

I don't tell him I've installed the attic door sensor. "Not yet."

"Might want to do that sooner rather than later. Just in case," he says. "Was Bozeman the last message you received?"

I nod. "Kelly is talking about going to the police in case it's just some asshole in the industry trying to fuck with her."

He shrugs. "She can go to the police, but . . ."

"But?"

"Stalkers are hard to nail down. You report it, get a case, and they investigate. It's an endless cycle of search warrants and requests for information; they can take weeks or months to gather that intel, and in most cases, those leads are dead ends. It's not that cops are lazy, it's that the procedural shit takes too much time. They can't do anything until there's enough to build a case, and stalkers are good at covering their tracks."

Casper is good at gathering intel. It might not be legal, but I don't need a clean case. I just need confirmation on who it is.

I scrub a hand down my face. "How did you deal with this with Jordan?"

"It sucked." He groans. "But I had her hidden for a good amount of time; that made it easier for me to breathe. You're dealing with a different animal, a stalker who knows where his prey is. He's tormenting both of you."

My jaw clenches.

"If you haven't gotten anything since Bozeman, maybe she's right and it was just some obsessed client or a rival artist or something."

I wipe some of the condensation off the cold amber bottle. "Maybe." I don't buy it.

"I'm really sorry you're dealing with that shit. Don't let it drive you crazy."

Too late.

Camden rolls his shoulders. "How's it going otherwise? Between you two?"

I smile. "So fucking good."

"I don't really have to ask, but . . ." He raises his eyebrows.

We exchange glances, letting the breeze do the talking. The water slaps against the wooden posts beneath the platform, causing it to creak. I don't answer him.

"Yeah, I thought so," he says. "I'm really happy for you. I know this is something you've wanted for a long time. You deserve it, especially after Piper died."

I nod. "How are you and Jordan?"

"Great." Cam looks around and lowers his voice. "We haven't announced anything yet, but we found out last week that Jordan's pregnant." He gazes up at me, already proud.

I pause mid-sip and my brows shoot up. "Holy shit. Cheers." I hold out my bottle, and he clinks his to it.

"Thanks." He smiles bigger than I've ever seen. "Weird, right? I'm going to be someone's father." He shakes his head in disbelief.

"It's terrifying."

"I feel so damn lucky. I never thought I would have a life like this."

I peer out over the water and smile. Camden and I are opposites in almost every way; we've always respected but never truly understood one another. Until today. We've found common ground in the prospect of permanence and family.

"Yeah, I know what you mean."

After a few beers, we head back up to the house. Kelly's eyes find mine from across the room, and it's subtle, but I see the look.

"Another message?" I sign from across the room.

She nods.

33

KELLY

"It's my house, Logan. I miss my space, my stuff." We've been arguing for the last ten minutes, and I'm digging my heels in.

His knuckles bloom with white as he grips the steering wheel.

"I love being with you, but it's been so long since I've been home. If I keep hiding at your place, I'm going to lose my mind."

He exhales slowly through his nose. "And what about your stalker? Your ex? Just going to leave the welcome mat out for them too?"

I cross my arms over my chest and angle my body in my seat. "I need my own space."

"I need you to be safe."

I roll my eyes. *I'll be safe at my house too.* "You've been hovering since this started, and I get it—you promised Dad you'd watch out for me. But it's *my* life. I need to have some semblance of control here."

The silence fills the truck cab. He doesn't look at me. I can't tell if he's considering it or has closed the door on the idea altogether. My gaze stays locked on him, trying to gauge if we're going to have a bigger fight about this, because there's no way I'm backing down. I need him to respect my wishes.

"Fine," he mutters. Though his tone tells me he's not at all happy about it. "You can stay at your place. For tonight." He glances over at me briefly. "You take Odin with you. Don't go anywhere without him. Keep the doors locked and answer my calls—if you don't, I'll come over and drag you back."

* * *

This was supposed to feel like solitude, but here I am side-eyeing every creaky floorboard and having staring contests with the shadow behind a door. *All because I "value my space."*

I hold my breath while opening my Instagram app and clicking my DM requests to see if any new messages have sprung up. "Please be nothing, please be nothing," I whisper while fully expecting another fake account giving me the same recycled, creepy line.

Odin snores soundly next to me, taking up half the bed.

Being home alone adds to my unease. Every groaning pipe and settling beam has me jumping. I've double-checked the locks twice and closed all my blinds, something I never used to care much about. It took me far too long to decide whether to keep the lights on. It might make people think I'm awake, but it will also let someone know I'm home. It's a double-edged sword. I shimmy deeper under my covers.

There are five new messages, all of them asking about my rates and when I'm opening my books again. I breathe a sigh of relief. I used to be able to ignore those messages so much easier. Ever since that physical note, it's been on my mind, taking up space and infiltrating my thoughts. I'm suspicious of every person who walks into the shop or past my house. Any one of them could be my stalker. It's a shitty way to live. I half hope it *is* Jason, at least then I know who to watch out for.

I tap out replies to each of the messages and commence my doomscroll, and then a new story pops up from Logan. It's not often he posts, so I click on it. It's a photo of him setting up his canvas to begin painting, and I can't help but smile. I wish I were there right now. I wouldn't be scared at his house.

Sleep evades me, trapping me with my paranoid thoughts and pounding pulse. Branches blow in the breeze outside my window, casting shadows onto my walls that resemble outstretched arms—reaching for me.

I considered taking a sleeping pill, but I don't want to sleep so soundly that I don't hear an intruder. It's the same reason I'm too afraid to turn on music or my TV. I need to be aware of my surroundings. Unfortunately, it makes all the ambient noises seem more threatening. I double-check that the baseball bat under my pillow is still there.

I told Logan we should spend a couple nights apart so we don't get sick of each other. There were some things I had to take care of around my house, like mowing the backyard, collecting my mail, and bringing home all the clothes he washed and folded for me.

After spending the weekend with him in Bozeman and another night at his place, I didn't want either of us to feel smothered. Our friendship and our work situation make our circumstance unique, since we already spend a lot of time together. I don't want to overstep any boundaries.

However, I've gotten used to his company at nighttime, but now the darkness feeds into my anxiety and worry. Suddenly, I don't like being home alone. Maybe I could just stop by his place and watch him paint for a little while. I won't stay the night. When I'm tired, I'll come back here and fall asleep. I'll maintain that boundary, I convince myself while typing out a text message.

Me: How is the painting going?

After a couple minutes, my phone dings with a reply. I'm filled with a sense of relief and instantly feel less vulnerable in my house.

Logan: Good evening, Chaos. Miss me already?
Me: Is your studio open to spectators tonight?
Logan: Depends.
Me: On?
Logan: If you plan on distracting me.
Me: Never. I was thinking I'd come over . . . sit real quiet . . . watch you paint . . . I won't disturb your work.
Logan: Aww. We both know you're not quiet.
Me: I promise to behave. I'll sit on my hands.
Logan: You'll sit on whatever I tell you to.
Me: Now that sounds like a distraction. You won't get any painting done.
Logan: Maybe not on my canvas.

I bite my lip while texting him back. Texting him is a good distraction for me.

Me: Between all the palm prints and teeth marks you left last time, I'm not sure there's any room left on this canvas for any of your "paint."
Logan: Some of my best work.
Me: You're making me blush.
Logan: Looks like there was room for pink.

The house settles, causing a shelf in my closet to pop, and I jump. Odin jerks to attention, releasing a loud threatening bark. My pulse climbs higher and my fingers fly across the screen.

Me: I just want to watch you paint. Please?
Logan: If you come over, you're not just watching.

I jump out of bed and stuff clothes into an overnight bag. Just in case. The sounds of this empty house are making me paranoid, and I'm not keen on returning. Fuck those boundaries, at least for tonight. I keep up the flirty banter, partially to keep my thoughts occupied.

Me: I can pose for you. Put me in whatever position you like.
Logan: Careful.
Me: Or what?
Logan: Or you'll end up more purple than pink tonight, sweetheart.
Me: I've always thought purple brought out my eyes.
Logan: Pack a bag.
Me: I don't need to stay the night.

I have to at least pretend that's not my objective.

Logan: Pack a bag.

As soon as I enter his house and lock the door behind me, all the tension and dread slips away. I'm finally safe. I sag against the door and exhale, taking a few steadying breaths. Nothing can get me here.

The lamps in the loft studio cast a warm glow on the floorboards, lighting my path toward the staircase where Odin starts climbing, eager to greet his owner.

"Hi," I murmur, toeing off my shoes and feeling humbled for showing up here after I put up such a fight earlier.

"Hey." The dry scrape of his palette knife carries from the loft as he mixes paint to the shade of his liking, blending with the aroma of linseed oil and just a hint of turpentine.

I take the stairs quietly, feeling the need to whisper, the way people do in places that feel holy. Logan isn't religious, but there's something sacred about the space where he creates. This is his sanctuary. A violin instrumental drifts from speakers above, it's slowed down, giving it an edginess that's dark and seductive—*very apropos.*

At the top, his open-air bedroom sits to the left, while his small studio for painting is to the right. He stands behind the canvas, barefoot and shirtless. The faded blue jeans slung low around his waist are well-worn with a hole in the right knee and splattered with paint from previous masterpieces. This is the hottest version of him, when he's in his element, creating and consumed in his work—but the thing that always gets me are those fucking glasses and the focused eyes behind them. Sexy doesn't even begin to cover it.

"Couldn't sleep?" he asks.

"No," I reply, landing on the top step.

"Come here."

I step closer, peeking around the easel to see what he's accomplished thus far. He has his backdrop completed; dark, moody navy blues fill every corner of the oil painting. A loose human silhouette has begun to take shape.

He quirks a half smile and wraps his arms around me in a hug. "I can't guarantee my bed will be much better."

When he releases me, I glance down at the small table beside him, littered with tools, paint, a glass of what I assume is Foxx Bourbon, and photographs of me, the ones from our photo shoot. It seems so long ago that he took them, so much has changed since then, so much changed that night.

"Wow." This is the first time I'm seeing the photos from our shoot. He hadn't shown me them. Wow. "These are kinda . . ."

"Hot?" he asks.

I nod. "Yeah," I say, my voice a little breathless. This is a side of myself I've never seen captured on film—until now. I remember the arousal I felt that night from his words, but didn't realize it was reflected in my eyes and worn on my face so brazenly.

"This is what you're painting?" I ask, peering up at him, still holding the images in my hands.

I flip through a couple more. Jesus Christ. *Is this how he sees me?* My confidence skyrockets when I see myself through his lens. I drop the stack of photos back on the table. "You're painting a nude, right?" I ask, peeling off my socks and sweatshirt.

"Yes."

He crosses his arms over his chest and cocks his head to the side, watching me.

With each article of clothing that falls, I'm left feeling more powerful. The craving for him returns, the same one I felt the night the photos were taken—it licks at my core. I know how good it is, I've had a taste, and I want more. I strip out of my leggings and underwear, standing naked before him—skin flushed, thighs aching, and a mind full of dirty thoughts.

He's mine just as much as I am his, and I don't want him painting some random woman's body on my modeled form. *Fuck that.* He won't paint anyone but *me*.

I reach for the stool behind him, but his palm lands heavy on the seat, keeping it in place.

"I told you I would sit on my hands and watch."

"And I said you would sit where I tell you," he says with a low voice. "You can't see the canvas if you're beside it."

He takes his seat and motions for me to climb onto his lap. I straddle one of his thighs, balancing my weight as he shifts to the side so he can reach the canvas. However, the warmth of his bare chest on my back is enough to keep me from squirming.

"I don't want you to paint anyone but me," I explain, jealousy coursing through me over a painting that isn't even complete. I'm well aware his artistic expression isn't indicative of his feelings toward me, but I still don't like it. Jealousy is rarely logical.

"Oh, Chaos," he says, pressing the lowball glass into my palm, encouraging me to take a sip. "You think I'd have your face permanently inked on my arm just to paint someone else? Don't insult me."

He takes back his drink, bringing it to his lips while keeping his eyes fixed on mine. Heat washes over my chest.

"It's healed really well," I comment, tracing my finger over the ink, feeling a bit foolish for being so territorial of paint.

He hums in agreement, setting down the bourbon. Sweeping my hair behind my shoulder, he leans in. "You gonna hold still for me?" he asks, his breath ghosting over my ear.

A smile eases onto my lips. "Depends on if you distract me," I state.

The dark chuckle from him has me soaked. It sounds like danger and sex. I will replay it a million times in my thoughts, of that I am certain. "I'll see what I can do."

He selects a tube of paint and squeezes a cold dab on my thigh, sending a wave of goose bumps over my flesh. Then after selecting a different tube, he adds another. And another. He mixes the paint with his palette knife against my skin, making me twitch, until the colors blend into that of a deep bruise.

"Told you I would paint you purple," he murmurs.

A shiver climbs up my spine. "I didn't know you were so literal."

He dips his brush into the oil paint above my knee, bringing it to the canvas.

Logan works with so much dexterity and skill it's mesmerizing to watch—*and sexy as hell*. He commands the paintbrush effortlessly, and his other hand snakes between my thighs, climbing higher. My chest rises and falls as he teases me with his touch, grazing the backs of his knuckles over the sensitive area.

"More," I whisper, opening my legs wider.

"Hold still," he says. His lips land on my neck and he sucks my flesh, biting, while his fingers trace faint circles over my inner thigh.

I exhale, a tremble building in my legs.

Lost to his art, he continues painting as if I'm not here. His forearms flex with every precise stroke, and I'm as fascinated by him as I am his talent. The hand between my legs toys with me relentlessly, moving so close to where I need him, and then pulling away—it's maddening. I release a frustrated whimper. The longer I watch him work, the more aroused I become. He rests his chin on my shoulder, occasionally praising me for sitting still, but I'm becoming restless as each minute seems to stretch longer than the last.

Just when I think he's going to keep me waiting forever, I'm rewarded by him brushing over my clit before his fingers penetrate me. I sigh, arching my back, and then he grips me from inside, tucking me close and massaging *that* spot. I writhe in his lap, wanting more.

"Hold still," he repeats. This time adding a corrective swat to my thigh with the paintbrush.

No.

My patience runs out. I twist in his lap, dragging his mouth to mine and licking the taste of bourbon and temptation off his lips.

"If you want to be my masterpiece . . ." he mutters, "then don't move."

I grasp his jaw firmly. "I want to be more than one of your many masterpieces." I shake my head. "I want to be your obsession. The muse you chase, the piece that torments you. Something you sign your name to and never let go."

His pupils blow wide, and something inside him comes loose. I see it—the moment he cracks.

He pulls out, wrapping an arm around my middle and yanking me up. The sudden shift sucks the air out of my lungs and my hand blindly shoots out for balance—smacking into the canvas. Wet paint slips under my fingers and I freeze, releasing a horrified gasp. I just smeared the piece he's been working on all night. I gape at the damage, unable to believe that just happened.

How could I be so clumsy?

I open my mouth, sputtering apologies, but he simply laughs. *He fucking laughs.*

He carries me over to the bed and rips off the comforter, throwing it aside.

"Paint!" I remind him. My thigh and palm are covered in it. He drops me on the crisp white sheets and I bounce, transferring a handprint. *Great, now I've ruined that too.* He tosses his glasses on the nightstand and towers over me,

Skating his hand up my thigh, through the paint, over my hips, between my breasts, he smears it all the way up to my collarbone and back to my stomach again. The oil spreads like grease, making one hell of a mess.

"Logan. I'm sorry. You worked so hard—" His mouth catches mine.

"I'm about to work much harder with you," he gruffs, unbuttoning his pants and shucking them off with his underwear. My eyes flick to his stiff length, glistening with pre-cum. *Fuck.*

He climbs up my body, bracing above me, every muscle straining as it tries to maintain a semblance of control. His hands clamp down on my thighs and he forces them apart. Our gazes lock, and for a brief second I drown in him—his stare dark and savage. He drives his cock inside me, stealing my breath. The growl that tears from his throat is menacing. My jaw slackens at the fullness he provides, my body accommodating his girth.

He runs his thumb over my bottom lip, smudging my chin with remnants of paint, and grins. "You want obsession? Look at my face," he snarls. "You're more than a masterpiece, more than a muse, or all the ways you torment me. You and I are more powerful than art, sweetheart—we're alchemy."

His words tighten every muscle, heat curling low in my stomach. I haul him to me, scratching my nails down his back with my own paint-covered palm.

He's right. When we come together, it's different, it's more than two people fucking. He makes passion feel like magic. His soul calls to something deeper, and he charms the darkness from my depths, bringing parts of me I didn't know existed to the surface.

It's those times I look at him and see myself reflected in his eyes.

I don't have to say a word because he already understands.

The once-clean sheets are streaked in blacks and blues, handprints and smudges that were painted with lust and longing.

"I've signed my name on you, you just haven't realized it yet," he murmurs.

He grabs my wrists in one hand, trapping them above my head, and sinks inside me with long, deep strokes, slowing his pace to a crawl that makes me want to scream. He cocks his head to the side, studying me with a dark fascination as I give in to him, like he's cataloging every gasp, moan, and shudder.

"You may know how to make me snap, but you break just as easily." I prepare to bite back with a quick retort, but I've got nothing. I can hardly think with the way his cock slowly drags in and out of me. The corner of his mouth turns up in a smirk. "You can be a smartass later," he says, knowing he's got me cornered. "Right now, you'll take what I give you."

Pinned beneath him, throbbing and desperate, I realize there's nothing left for me to do but obey and do as he says. He's dishing out his own torment—*and I savor every thick inch of it.*

"That's better." He nips at my lower lip. "How's that surrender feel?"

"So fucking big," I whimper.

"That's my good girl."

His forearm flexes above me as he claims me with untamed, inelegant thrusts. Sweat beads on his forehead, and his hazel eyes are unforgiving as he punishes my body in the most delicious ways. He fucks as if he has a personal vendetta against meaningless sex. He's feral. Uncontrolled. Exactly how I like him.

My gaze traces the ink up his blacked-out arm until it bleeds into delicate strands of hair. The piece I tattooed on him—the piece of me he will carry with him for the rest of his life. Fifty years from now, I'll still be inked into his flesh. *I'm permanent.* Few things in life make me feel more invincible than Logan, who seems more god than man, fucking me while proudly wearing my face on his arm.

"Give it to me, Chaos." He wraps his arms around my chest and rolls us so I'm on top. I straddle him with my knees dipping into the mattress as I roll my hips, sliding up and down his length.

"Goddamn it, sweetheart. You know exactly what you're doing to me. Driving me fucking mad . . ." His hand finds my throat, and I lean into it, letting him squeeze as I ride.

I groan, undulating and circling over him. My body is eager and begging, wanting not only my own gratification but his too. I want to make him come, see Logan vulnerable and helpless to the way I affect him.

"Slow," he says.

I shake my head. "I'm on top, I pick the pace."

"You're on top," he smirks, "but I'm the one fucking you." His strong fingers dig into my left hip, surely leaving marks that will turn into bruises by morning. He sits up, and I wrap my arms around his shoulders. My breasts press against his chest, smearing more of the greasy paint. He grips under my ass and bounces me on him like I'm a rag doll he's not done playing with.

I pull him closer, capturing his lips, and kissing him long, slow, and deep. This is the moment. This is what it's all about. This feeling right here.

"Please, Logan, make me come," I beg, my voice pleading, and he kisses me again. I kneel on either side of his hips, but he's doing all the work. Relentlessly filling me over and over. Hitting every spot just right.

He nods, burying his forehead into my neck, and pushes me onto my back, then sits above me and takes me with brutal thrusts, sending me into oblivion. His hand slips between us, and he circles my clit. "Fuck," I say between pants. "Don't stop."

My mind starts to empty, and the world falls away. Every worry evaporates until there's nothing but him. In this moment, Logan and I are the only two people in the world. My eyes find his and he nods, offering a silent permission. I clutch the back of his neck, arching into him, surrendering completely as my body seizes, every muscle locking before the release tears me apart.

"Oh hell, you were made for this. Good fucking girl."

His jaw sets and his strokes grow frantic; he looks just as wrecked as I feel. The sight of him makes me want to unravel all over again. His head drops to my shoulder, breath harsh against my ear, but he doesn't stop moving, he grinds deeper, rocking his hips into me and wringing every ounce of pleasure from the both of us. Logan growls, spilling into me—seeing this man lose control is its own kind of high.

Our chests heave ragged breaths in unison as the last shudders roll through us, racing pulses finally slowing as the tension leaves our bodies.

Not a noise is uttered between us; the thump of our racing hearts syncs together. There's no need for words when our eyes say everything.

Paint streaks where his hungry hands roamed over my body, a visual display of his physical lust and yearning. But what Logan doesn't realize is, his art has bled into my flesh, so deep that if they cut me open right now, I'm certain they would find his streaks of paint on my heart too.

34

LOGAN

Ruined sheets envelop our ruined bodies, spent and tired. Oil paint is smeared across her thighs, cheeks, chin, stomach, breasts, and neck. She's adorned with my fingerprints, each one tied to an action fueled by emotion. A grasp, a squeeze, a stroke, a kiss, a thrust. It's beautiful.

Her fingers trace the paint on my skin, her touch delicate and tender. She's covered me too; we're quite the sight.

Odin sits on the floor at the foot of the bed, blinking at us, his eyes filled with judgment and slight concern. He probably hasn't seen moves like that since he left the wolf pack he escaped from.

"Your mom's gonna be walking funny later."

"Logan!"

"What?" I gesture to him with an open palm. "He's a dog. He doesn't know what I'm saying."

"Yes, he does."

"Well, in that case, I hope you took notes, buddy. Tell your friends."

She covers my mouth with her hand, so I bite her palm.

"You're more of an animal than he is." She giggles and shakes her head. "Could you bring me my phone?" she asks, her voice raspy. "I want to document this."

Grinning, I walk over to the easel to pick up her discarded leggings, then fish the phone from the pocket. I walk it back over to her, flopping down next to her again. She snuggles up to my side and unlocks her phone, passing it to me with the front-facing camera ready.

"Your arms are longer than mine," she says.

I hold it above us and snap a few pictures of our work, then send the copies to my phone as well. I want to look at them whenever I like.

"We destroyed your sheets."

I chuckle. "Nah, we made them better . . ." I glance down and lift a lock of her hair with paint on it. It's already one a.m. *So much for that sleep.* "Go have a seat in the bathtub, and I'll meet you in there to get cleaned up."

I roll to my side, propped up on an elbow, taking a moment to appreciate the way her ass sways on her way to the bathroom. After gathering supplies from the kitchen, I meet her in the en suite with a glass of water, her favorite licorice, and a bottle of olive oil.

"Drink this," I command, handing her the glass of water. Her eyes grow wide when she spots the licorice while gulping down the water. I wait for her to finish drinking, then reward her with her treat.

"These are my favorite!" she says, tearing into the bag while sitting in the empty tub.

I know.

When I drizzle the olive oil over everywhere she's been touched by paint, she shivers. I climb in next to her and massage her flesh, loosening the paint until it thins and pulls away from her skin. She's putty in my hands. Her thighs, arms, breasts, neck, and countless other spots carry smudges. It's a time-consuming process to get it all.

By the time I'm finished, she wears a relaxed expression on her face, almost like she's drunk. She happily sighs, relaxed after the nearly full-body massage.

"Your turn," she says, slowly rotating.

I shake my head. "No, let's get you to bed—"

She pushes me away from trying to help, her eyes finding mine. "Let me do this, please."

I nod, allowing her to continue. She repeats the process on me, and I groan. Seeming quite satisfied with herself, she smiles. I understand the sleepy look on her face now; the way her thumbs dig into my muscles feels incredible. Come to think of it, I don't remember the last time I was taken care of like this. Even half asleep, she insists on pampering me.

She has me stand and turn around to make sure she's gotten everything. Then we turn on the faucet but don't bother filling the tub. We suds our skin with soap, then rinse off the oil and paint with the handheld sprayer, watching the blue-purple pigment circle the drain, and we repeat until the water coming off us is clear.

When we're dried off, I nab a fresh set of linens from the closet while she strips off the soiled ones and carries them downstairs; a garbage bag rustles as she stuffs the stained sheets inside. We work in tandem. By the time she returns, I've remade the bed.

I wash the paint off brushes, then turn off the Bluetooth speaker, pausing to look at the canvas propped on the easel, grinning at the colors and the way her hand smeared them together when she lost balance and reached out for purchase. The utter horror on her face afterward was adorable.

With a smile on my face, I flip the easel lights off, turning around just as she lands on the top step. Her gait is slow and deliberate. Then I realize she's carrying a cup, doing her best not to spill it. She gingerly sets it next to my glasses on the nightstand, then returns to her side of the bed and burrows under the covers.

I stare at her, then the cup, then back to her again.

She made me tea.

"Come to bed," she says, a yawn interrupting her words.

I climb in beside her, sitting up and resting my back against the headboard.

"You made me tea?"

"I always would have, but you never let me." She snuggles up to my side. "I want to take care of you too."

She rests her head near my hip. Her lips press to my skin, and I delve a hand in her hair, combing my fingers through the strands. She sighs and her eyes flutter closed. While stroking her hair, I bring the cup to my mouth and take a sip.

She put lemon in it. The *exact* amount of lemon. Kelly knows how I take my tea.

I slide my palm to the back of her neck and squeeze like I've done a million times before.

There's something about her small gesture that hits me square in the chest.

It's no longer my obsession, my possessiveness, my feelings . . . Kelly is making it whole, making it real. What we have is taking shape and transforming us in ways even I didn't plan for.

This is alchemy.

My wife is the most precious thing in my life. More than Black Rabbit, more than art itself. And I'll burn the world down if anyone dares to take her from me.

35

KELLY

The humming of his tattoo machine buzzes in the background, but my focus isn't on the piece he's doing, it's on *him*. His sleeves are rolled up to his elbows, giving me a great view of his forearms. When he tilts his head into the light, I can just make out the faint bluish-purple stain on his neck—it matches the one I have on my wrist, the one that's been peeking over my latex glove at me all morning, entertaining me with memories from the other night. We wear our private exploits on our skin not so secretly.

It's difficult not to glance at him, especially when he keeps looking back.

"*Stop staring at me,*" he signs.

I grin, moving my hands to reply. "*I'm not, I'm checking out that crooked line you just tattooed.*"

He shakes his head at me, sticking his tongue into his cheek to keep from smiling, then eyes me up and down. "*That skirt isn't HR appropriate.*"

I confirm the client's lids are closed before signing back. "*Good thing I'm fucking HR.*"

He glares at me, then roams his penetrating gaze over my body. "*You're asking for trouble.*"

I bite my bottom lip. "*Do I need to beg too?*" This man could bring me to my knees with one look, and he's all mine. *How did I get so lucky?*

"*Get back to work.*"

The bell at the entrance chimes, dragging me from my thoughts.

My client is deaf and coming in for a consultation regarding a tattoo we've discussed briefly over email. We're both stoked about the design.

I really want to do this piece, but I'm still inexperienced when it comes to communicating with my hands. Almost all of my signing is done with Logan, but signing with fluent clients is much more intimidating. What if I sign something wrong? What if he becomes frustrated? Shaking off the nerves, I step out of my station.

"Psst," Logan hisses.

I halt my steps at the entrance to his bay, worrying my fingernail. "Hm?"

"You're going to be fine," he assures me in a hushed voice. "Just tell him you're still learning and ask him to sign slower with you. He'll understand. I'm always here if you need help."

I nod and give a tight smile. "Thanks," I say, swallowing down some of the fear. My heart flutters as I continue to the front of the shop.

The thumbnail photo of him in his email makes him easy to spot. He's over six feet and wearing a white T-shirt, showing off a few other tattoos on his arms. I recognize one of them as Logan's work. "*Hi, Will,*" I sign in a greeting, then introduce myself—tacking on that I'm slow at signing.

"*That's okay. Thanks for telling me.*" He smiles wide, and his understanding floods me with relief.

I invite him back to my station where we sit and discuss the concept of his tattoo a little more thoroughly. It's a fierce, traditional-style tiger, soaring with tucked-in wings like it's picking up speed. In my peripheral, I can tell Logan is keeping an eye on our conversation in case I find myself in a difficult spot. I hold my tablet and scribble down the technical terms or draw out anything that's too difficult for me to describe. I'm slower, but my client is relaxed, which helps keep my thoughts calm.

Will is kind, engaged, and patient above all. After five minutes, I find myself grinning like an idiot at how easily my brain is translating what he's saying. It's amazing!

When I edit the rough sketch I had prepared for our meeting, he nods enthusiastically. "*You're very talented. This is exactly what I pictured.*"

I remember to express my excitement through my hands and not just my voice because I want to jump up and down.

We discuss placement on his calf and the sizing. It will probably take two sessions based on the work needing to be completed, one session for the outlining, then another for color.

He points to the spot on my wrist. "*Paint?*" he asks.

Logan snorts from behind me.

"*Yeah.*" I chuckle. "*I was painting last night.*"

Will tells me he paints too, and asks if I was working on anything special.

"*It's . . . A-B-S-T-R-A-C-T,*" I sign, spelling it out because I've forgotten how to sign it. His question catches me off guard and has me stumbling. "*Very messy. Lots of texture.*"

"*Cool,*" he replies.

I move off that topic quickly, explaining what our next steps would be, then bring him back up to the front so we can get him on my books. After getting his deposit, we say goodbye.

I return to my station and slump into the chair, clutching my tablet and adding a few extra notes to the sketch with a smile on my face. I did it.

"Told you you'd be fine," he says. I rotate my chair to find Logan standing in the aisle, leaning forward with his arms folded on top of the wall divider, wearing a sexy smile. "Nice save on the paint question."

He unfolds his arms to sign, "*Proud of you.*"

"*I like when you say that.*" There's something about his praise that's hot, even when it's for something as mild-mannered as a successful ASL conversation.

He waggles his eyebrows, signing, "*You like when I do a lot of things.*"

My mouth drops open, and he smiles to himself on the way back to his office. *Cocky bastard.* I'm shaking my head when my phone buzzes, so I glance down at it to see a text from Rosa.

Rosa: Hey! I'm going to be in town for work. Wanna grab drinks?

Oh good! I'm hoping I can introduce her to Thor at some point. She sounded down after we had our conversation about men.

Casper and Thor are single, but Casper at least spends his free time doing things he enjoys, like jumping out of planes or snowboarding off cliffs. The guy is an adrenaline junkie. Thor, on the other hand, doesn't do much outside of work. I can tell he's lonely, but with his past, he's afraid to settle down again. He and Rosa would be a great fit, they both avoid social media and are both stupidly attractive. I bet they'd hit it off.

Me: Yes! Thursday at nine? Where should we go?
Rosa: The Sable has a hotel bar.

The Sable is upscale. I could use a night of fun without Logan around. He has been hovering more than usual. Maybe if she's got time she can swing by the shop so I can introduce her to everyone.

Me: Perfect. I need a girls' night out!

I'm cleaning my station after finishing up with a client when Frankie tiptoes over with a vase of roses. The sanitizer nearly falls out of my hand.

"You got flowers," she whispers, smiling, and sets them on the desk. My heart hammers in my chest. *Are they from my stalker? Jason?* They seem similar to the crumpled ones I found in the trash that day he showed up at the shop. On occasion, I've received flowers from clients after finishing a big piece. Maybe that's all this is. *Unfortunately, I don't think I'm that lucky.* Regretfully, I reach for the note. I don't want to look. I break the seal on the envelope and prepare myself for those five fucking words I've come to hate so much.

Congratulations to the newlyweds. Till death do you part. XX

Relief floods through me. My shoulders sag and I laugh, slipping the card back into the envelope. Just a wrong delivery.

Spinning on my heel, I peer over at Logan, who is cleaning up after a client session, his eyes already fixed on me.

"Who is that from?" he asks, his voice low and threatening as he crosses the aisle into my workstation.

"Easy, killer. Wrong delivery," I explain, delighted it's not something from the stalker.

"We should really tell clients you hate flowers." He reaches for the card. "You always said flowers are for tattoos, apologies, and funerals," he recalls, huffing a laugh, and sliding the card from the sleeve.

"I love that you pay attention to those little details." I chuckle and nudge him with my elbow. "I need to call the florist and let them know they made a mix-up," I say, bending over in front of him to pick up a Sharpie—*not sure how high my skirt goes, but silly me, I forgot my underwear today*—getting his hackles up is my new favorite hobby.

Within seconds, his whole demeanor changes, the smile fades away, and every muscle in his body stiffens. "Where did they come from?" he asks. He flips the card over, stamped with the company logo.

"Lakeland Floral," I read aloud.

He snatches the vase and takes it to his office.

What the fuck?

I follow behind him. "Is something the matter?" He didn't react at all when I bent over for him.

He scrubs a hand down his face. "Nothing, I'm just going to call the florist and let them know."

I blink a few times. Okay? *Why is he so upset?* My head cocks to the side. "If there's something you're not telling me—"

"There's not."

We stare at each other for a moment, and I search his eyes for a lie, but he relaxes.

"Can you send Casper in here?" he asks, his voice more casual.

"Sure." Maybe I misread something. "Oh, hey, guess who I got a text from?"

He freezes. "Who?"

"Rosa! She's in town. We're going to get drinks on Thursday!"

"No." He locks his jaw. I'm not sure I've ever heard a firmer no. He said it like it's not even up for debate.

"I wasn't asking," I remind him. "I can go out for drinks with my friends."

"Absolutely not. I don't want you out with anyone."

I bark out a laugh. It was one thing to want me to stay with him, but not letting me go out at all? He can't be serious. "Logan. It's Rosa. We've been texting since the expo."

He shakes his head. "It's not Rosa that's the problem, my issue is with the person who is sending you messages and now gifts."

"What are you talking about?" I point at the flowers. "Those aren't even for me!"

He opens his mouth, then shuts it again, knowing I'm right, then takes a steady inhale and relaxes. "Look, how about you have her over to your house for drinks. I'll hang out in one of the bedrooms and read. You won't even know I'm there, you can still have your girl time, but I'll be around in case anything happens."

I shake my head. "I deserve freedom. I can't hide forever, ruled by fear. It already feels like it's taken too much control of my life. I don't want to be too afraid to leave the house. Besides, I feel safer being out and about. At home I'm a sitting duck."

Removing the vase from his hands, I place it gently on one of the nearby file cabinets, then spin to face him again and grasp his shoulders. "Logan. I'm fine. I love that you are being so protective. But please don't put me in a cage and take away my friends."

He scrubs a palm down his face and hauls me into his chest. "I'm not trying to put you in a cage."

"Just one night with drinks."

His eyes dart back and forth between mine. "I want to know exactly where you are going. If either of you gets a bad vibe or notices anybody hovering, you call me. I also want Rosa's number."

"Yes, daddy." I roll my lips together to keep from smiling.

He grumbles. "I'm just trying to keep you safe."

I rise up on my tiptoes, and he dips his head so I can plant a peck on his lips. "Your protective side is really fucking sexy."

The sound of a growl rumbles in his chest. "You are driving me crazy today, and I think you know it."

"Good."

He flicks his gaze upward and sighs.

"Still want me to send Casper in?" I need to leave his office before he changes his mind.

"Yes."

The moment I turn on my heel and step into the hall, the door swings shut at my back. *Jesus, what a grump.* I stop at Casper's station; he's disassembling his tattoo machine as I peek my head around the wall. "Logan wants to talk to you when you get a sec. Heads up, he's in a bad mood."

"He's always in a bad mood, Junior. What's new?"

"Well, this time he copped an attitude with me too."

Casper raises his eyebrows. "Damn. He must really be pissed."

I shrug and walk back into my bay. "Probably just needs a snack."

"Are you volunteering?" he asks with a wink.

"I put in my community service last night," I admit, giggling. "Maybe you should give it a shot?"

"If only," he says with a sigh. "Pretty sure y'all are the only ones around here getting laid, so if you could take care of his attitude, I'd be grateful."

36

LOGAN

"What do you mean you can't give out sender information? I don't care about confidentiality!" I shout over the phone.

"Easy, easy, easy," Casper says, prying the phone out of my death grip. "Christ, you have fucking zero customer service skills," he mutters under his breath.

Casper holds the phone to his ear and puts on a big fake grin. "Hi, I'm so sorry about that. Who am I speaking with?" he asks the florist. This dude thinks he can charm anybody. He'd flirt with a great white just for kicks.

"Gloria . . . Damn, that is a beautiful name." He's using the same voice he uses when he tries to pick up women. To be fair, it does have a surprisingly high success rate. He fake laughs at something the florist says.

Casper sighs, chuckling, and then locks his sights on me. "You're right, I am way nicer than that other guy. That was my boss. He can be a real asshole, huh?"

He laughs again.

I'm growing impatient.

"No, he's not mad at you. He's mad at me because *I* made a mistake with *his* flower delivery—Sorry, this might be incredibly inappropriate, but has anyone ever told you how sexy your voice is?"

I roll my eyes. Gloria sounds like she's smoked four packs a day since 1987.

He does that stupid laugh that women lose their minds over and then continues. "Oh, well I'm so glad I could make your day. Let's see if you can make mine, yeah?"

I fold my arms and give him a chin lift. "Hurry up."

He reclines in his chair, kicking his feet up on my desk and crossing his ankles. This is his way of telling me he'll take as long as he fucking pleases.

"Okay, I'm going to level with you, Gloria. This is my first week at a new job, and I was supposed to send out a bouquet of roses on behalf of my boss—the grumpy one, but I think I might have sent them to the wrong address . . . I know . . . Yeah, a dozen red roses were *supposed* to go to Kelly Everhart at Black Bourbon Distillery, but they said they haven't received them."

"Uh-huh . . . I see. Well, that's the crazy thing, I don't remember. No, unfortunately I can't find my confirmation number. Could you look it up by my name perhaps? Yeah, it's Jason . . ."

Casper snaps his fingers at me.

"Seleigh. S-E-L-E-I-G-H," I supply.

He repeats the name to the florist. "You're a godsend, Gloria. Thank you so much for looking into this for me." He covers his hand over the phone's speaker. "Jesus Christ, she would have been *Kelly Seleigh*?" he whispers to me.

Doesn't quite have the same ring as Kelly Teller. As much as I would love for her to take my name, it would be a shame to see the Everhart dynasty come to an end.

"I sent them to Kelly at Black *Rabbit*?" he says.

My eyes dart to his.

"Today, right?" he asks, and then Casper nods at me.

I'm gonna kill that motherfucker.

"You're an angel, Gloria. Well, suppose I still have a job after today, should we grab dinner sometime?" He pauses. "You're breaking my heart. Tell that man to appreciate you, or I'll have to swoop in." More bullshit laughter. "You know it . . . Okay, bye now."

He ends the call and throws my phone at me. "You're fucking welcome." I catch it on my chest before it falls to the ground.

"I knew it was Jason!" I smash my fist against the top of my desk. "He used a different message this time. Why?"

Casper shrugs. "This was more traceable. He might assume she's gone to the cops; if he put the same message as the others on this card, it would have been a dead giveaway. This might still be a coincidence."

"But how the fuck would he know about our marriage? That's something even Kelly doesn't know!"

He shakes his head. "That one I can't figure out. Unless he would have some connection to somebody in Bozeman? But even that's too big of a coincidence."

I gotta figure this out.

"Kelly is going out with her friend Rosa on Thursday. I need you and Thor to help me that night. I'm going to do some recon on Jason, but I want to make sure Thor has eyes on the girls. I'll have him hang out at the bar and make sure nobody fucks with them. While they're out, I need you to install cameras at Kelly's."

"I can do that," he says, shrugging.

"I need to do some intel before I make any move. This can't be sloppy. And I need to figure out what he knows—and how the fuck he knew about the marriage."

Casper stands. "Just don't be fucking stupid. You're no good to Kelly if you're sitting in a cell," he says, pointing a finger at me before he exits the office.

I sigh, leaning back in my chair and scrubbing a hand down my face. Jason is about to find out what it's like to be hunted. I need an outlet for the rage firing through my veins that I plan to take out on him. Until then, I'm going to be crawling in my skin.

I push out of my chair and open the door, and Kelly is passing by, but she turns and winks, wearing that devilish smile she's been teasing me with all day.

Fuck it.

Wrapping my fingers around her biceps, I haul Kelly inside my office, slamming the door behind her. She's been flirting with me all day, walking the line, bending over in front of me to pick up pens, flashing her pussy just to rile me up and test my patience—like it's cute. If she wants my reaction, then she's about to get it. I can put up with a lot of her shit, but that wink just sent me over the edge.

I shove her against the door.

"Logan—" She blinks up at me with wide eyes flickering with arousal and something wicked.

"What?" I ask. "Stop?"

She exhales, her breath hot on my palm. "No."

One hand covers her mouth while the other works up her trembling thigh and under the skirt she wore to fuck with me.

"No panties," I growl. "You knew exactly what you were doing, don't act coy now."

I slide my hands under her thighs, and carry her over to my desk in two strides, dropping her on top of the mess of papers. Grabbing her skirt at the hem, I shove it up around her hips and unzip my jeans, freeing my heavy cock. Her eyes widen when she sees how hard I am for her.

"You wanted trouble. You found it."

She bites her lip. "Promises, promises."

What a fucking brat.

I rut into her, hard and deep, her cry transforming into a moan. She clings tighter, eager for more. "You knew the second you provoked me that you'd end up flat on your back begging."

"You wouldn't have me any other way."

Fuck.

Her fingers curl into my shirt as I pound into her, rough and relentless.

The doorknob turns and clicks open. Kelly flinches and claws at my shoulders like she's trying to hide in my chest. *Too late for that.* I'm not stopping, not after those little quips to spur me on. I clench my jaw and power through, slowing my strokes but staying inside her.

Casper leans against the doorframe. "Christ," he says, chuckling. "You couldn't wait thirty minutes to clock out first?"

She nudges upright, burying her face in my neck while her thighs tremble against my sides.

"I warned her what would happen if she kept it up." I lick my lower lip and drive inside. "She chose to call my bluff."

"Guess she found out," he comments.

I pull out slowly, just to hear the wetness bounce off the walls, then press back in. Tangling my fist in her hair, I yank her head back to look at me. "Did you find out, Chaos?"

She nods, squinting her eyes shut. Her pussy tightens around my length; the way I'm soaked with her seems . . . *excessive*. She whimpers, and I expect her to recoil with shame after the slipped sound, but she doesn't. No, instead it's followed up by a sexy-as-hell moan, this time *louder*—she's into it. *She's showing off.*

My wife's a greedy little exhibitionist. She wants an audience while she gets fucked. Her body reacts, growing more slick and wet with each plunge into her tight cunt. She's feeding off the thrill, so I lean into it.

I chuckle. "She's trying to act shy," I say, "but twenty minutes ago, she bent over in this tiny skirt and showed me that she forgot her panties today."

Casper shakes his head and takes out his phone, staring at the screen. "You always lose your shit around her," he mumbles, mindlessly scrolling.

Kelly holds her breath as she comes, her body trembling. Even nuzzled in my shirt, she arches her back, giving in.

"Because she fucking loves it." I slap the side of her ass, and she flinches with a yelp. "She plays innocent, but she just came. Think she's embarrassed?"

He slips his phone into his pocket. "If she is, doesn't look like she wants you to stop."

"Pathetic, isn't it?"

He shrugs. "Nah. She's just a girl who knows what she likes."

"It's safe to say I think she's enjoying herself." Not once has she told me to stop or tried to push me away, she's only pulled me closer.

"Well, I'll let you finish up. Just wanted to tell you there's a car parked in the tow zone outside."

I nod. "Thanks, I'll take care of it in a bit."

"I'm sure." He laughs, then tilts his head to the side, glancing at Kelly. "Thanks, Junior, I appreciate you taking care of his attitude."

The door clicks shut and she smacks me. "You—you—"

"One more, sweetheart." I lay her back on my desk and thrust into her faster. Her spine bows and her groans fill the room as I slam into her. Her eyes are wild, full of fire and darkness—pupils blown, and it's more than arousal, she's high off the encounter. "You filthy fucking girl. You loved that, huh?"

The fact that she got off on being watched like that, seeing that other side of her, is enough to make me lose control of my own orgasm. I grunt as it tumbles out of me, spearing myself deep.

I lean down to whisper in her ear. "Next time you want to call my bluff, you better be prepared for the fallout."

Her chest rises and falls. "He saw me come." Her voice is half panic, half lust.

"So?"

"That's fucked up, Logan!" She chokes out. "I should have told you to stop!"

"Then why didn't you?"

"Because I didn't want to." She covers her face with her hands. "I don't know . . . It just—it made everything so much hotter. But now that it's over . . . He's never going to look at me the same again."

I kneel in front of her, and she props herself up on her elbows to stare me down, waiting for answers. I place a palm on each of her thighs, spreading them. "I respect you. Casper respects you. If he cared he would have flinched when he saw us." I press my lips to the inside of her thigh, placing a kiss to the tender flesh, then repeat the movement on the other side. "He's never going to mention it."

I know that look, she's overthinking, half present in her head. She needs to be anchored.

"Hey, you have nothing to be embarrassed about." Her glassy eyes refocus on me. "Don't turn what we just did into something ugly. You trusted me enough. You were honest with your body and emotions. You surrendered—and your surrender was beautiful. You are the most powerful woman I know. Never feel ashamed of what you want."

She nods, a small smile replacing the worry and unease that lingered in her gaze moments ago. I stand and lean forward, capturing her mouth. Her hand snakes behind my neck and brings me closer. *That's my girl.*

"One more thing . . ."

She stares back, with swollen, parted lips. God, she's gorgeous.

"Saturday night, you're mine. Frankie is going to reschedule anything on our calendars after five p.m."

She smiles wider.

"You deserve a night to be spoiled."

After all the bullshit with the flowers, I realize Kelly and I need a break. To be alone. Together. We need a night to forget all this shit. I need the distraction, and so does she.

37

KELLY

"It's so great to see you again!" I say, hugging Rosa at the hotel bar. The upscale bar is sequestered off the hotel lobby and below a large crystal chandelier. The lounge is swathed in gold and amber hues. Small clusters of upholstered high-back chairs and low tables are spread out across the space.

"Same!" We snag one of the intimate seating areas for ourselves, sitting side by side and leaving the love seat across from us empty.

The hostess drops off a couple of drink menus and announces their specials. We smile and nod until she departs. "What are you thinking of ordering?" I ask. "The cocktails look amazing."

She taps her red fingernail to her chin while flipping one of the pages on the menu. Then claps it shut. "Ketel One martini with ten olives. You?"

I've become more familiar with bourbon, thanks to Logan, the smell especially, and I think tonight calls for something strong. "That old-fashioned is looking pretty good," I say, closing the book and setting it on top of hers next to the small lit tealight on the table. Our server shows up right at that moment, and we place our orders. Service is speedy.

A buzzing noise has Rosa pulling her phone from her wristlet. "Logan just texted me," she says, chuckling. "The package . . . is . . . secure . . ." she mutters, tapping a message back out. "Hydration . . . en route."

I wince and cover my eyes with one hand. "Ugh, I'm so sorry about that!"

"As long as you're fine with it, I'm fine with it," she says, shrugging. "Wanna tell me more about what's going on, though?"

When I texted Rosa to ask if it was okay to give Logan her number, she was a bit apprehensive at first and wanted to make sure she wasn't enabling a controlling boyfriend. The optics aren't great, but he wanted to cover all his bases in case he was unable to reach me for whatever reason.

I reassured her this was a special circumstance. It's a little like being babysat, but I'd have agreed to any concessions as long as it got me out of the house. Thankfully, Rosa was very understanding, and I kinda love that she's giving him some shit about it; it makes the whole thing feel less crazy.

I sigh. "Yeah, it's a long story, so strap in."

I give her the rundown of everything that has happened thus far, right up to the stupid roses that may or may not have something to do with this? When I tried prying him for more information, he seemed to let it go. Who fucking knows.

"Wait, so you have no idea if the flowers are even part of this?"

I shake my head. "The flower delivery is an anomaly. I told Logan it was simply a mix-up. The message didn't match the others—it didn't even make sense! We're not married! I have a feeling the wrong card got put on the wrong bouquet and they sent them out for delivery."

"What about your ex? He gave you roses too, right?"

Our server shows up with our drinks, and I accept mine with a smile, taking a healthy gulp. I nod to Rosa. "Yeah. That's another issue. Logan seems to think Jason is behind all of this."

"Do you have any reason to doubt him?"

I shrug. "At first I thought it was Jason, but the longer this has gone on, it seems less likely."

"Have you gone to the police?"

With a long blink and deep inhale, I shake my head. "Not yet."

"Well, is he going to?"

I groan. "He says he wants to deal with it himself."

"Of course he does." She rolls her eyes. "How does he think he's gonna do that?"

I scoff. "Honestly, I don't know. He seems stuck on this whole Jason thing, but then it's like he doesn't do anything about it. I'm not sure if he's just waiting for more proof or what?"

"Who else knows about this? Do you have anyone else to talk to?" she asks.

"A couple of my coworkers, they're tight with Logan. Both of them are like older brothers, so they're on edge too. The whole thing sucks.

I'm so tired of this. I feel like Logan and I haven't had a chance at a normal relationship because all this other bullshit is taking up so much space." I sigh. "Logan is really struggling with it."

She takes a sip of her drink. "I mean, maybe you need to take a break, just allow things to calm down first. If it *is* your ex, your new relationship could be escalating his behavior. Especially if you're in danger, you don't want to risk your safety."

I shake my head. *No way.* "Logan is stressed. He cares deeply and is worried about me."

"He ought to do something about it instead of sitting around and waiting."

Lifting my shoulders, I ask, "What's he supposed to do?"

"Kick that guy's ass?"

Easier said than done. I chuckle and wave my hands as if I can erase the conversation we're having. "Let's talk about something else. This stalker drama takes up enough of my life as it is, I'm not letting it ruin my nights out with friends, those are rare enough as it is. I'm really happy you reached out so we could do this!"

She nods and wraps an arm around me, offering a half hug. "Me too! This is one of the first work trips that I could actually look forward to!"

"Oh!" I take a sip and set my glass on the table, then clap my hands together. "Okay, so there's a guy I'd like to introduce you to. One of my coworkers. He's really great, and I think you two would hit it off."

Her brows pop up. "Oooh, tattoos? He's an artist?"

"Yes, he's so talented!" I feel positive about them being a match. "He does incredible script and lettering work, watching him freehand is wild. He's gifted."

"Is he tall? He's gotta be taller than me, I want someone who can pick me up and toss me around." She waggles her eyebrows, making me laugh—something I haven't done enough of lately.

I nod. "He's got the height. He's also got muscles if that's your thing. Hang on, I have a picture." After taking out my phone, I go into my photos and scroll back to some from the Bozeman expo. I zoom in on his face and turn the screen toward her. "This is Hawthorne, he goes by Thor. He's a bit of a cowboy but very down to earth . . . There's just one thing. He's got a bit of a rap sheet. I know, not the greatest opener, but he's a good guy, truly."

"Holy shit." She takes the phone from me and blinks. "I don't care if he kicks puppies, this man is hot. Like, *hot*-hot."

"See?"

"Maybe I'll swing by the tattoo shop before I head out of town, then . . . introduce myself. Or we could go out Saturday night, see if he wants to tag along?"

I wrinkle my nose. "I'm sorry, I can't on Saturday."

"What? Why?" She pouts out her lower lip.

"Logan has a night planned for us."

She huffs a breath, rolling her eyes. "Come on. You can see him anytime. We can go clubbing. I wanna meet this guy!"

I laugh. "I know, I'm sorry—Logan's just worked so hard setting up this date."

She grumbles into her drink. "He probably hasn't worked that hard. Men don't put out serious effort like that. *Unless they want sex.*"

"Well, I'll take the sex too."

She raises her brows when I say that. "You slept with him?"

"Yes." I smile into my drink. "A few times." I shiver, relishing the memory of us in his office. I never knew humiliation could feel so secure. Like being laid bare and claimed with pride at the same time. It was sinful and delicious.

Rosa shrugs and raises her martini glass to her lips. "Cheers to you."

Maybe most men don't often put out effort, but mine does. He hand-painted an entire tarot deck, for fuck's sake. "He's my best friend. He put in effort before we even started dating."

She's a woman scorned, frustrated by the opposite sex, but she can't judge Logan's character based on other men. Logan is different, she'll learn that when she meets him. She'll learn that when she meets Thor too . . . *which is about to happen a lot sooner than she thinks.* My attention is drawn to the large hulking figure making his way through the door. Tall and tattooed, Thor carries a casual danger about him. He's like Logan in that way. A smile grows on my face. "Today is your lucky day, babe." I shoot my hand into the air. "Thor!"

His eyes fall on us, and he stops scanning the room.

He does that sexy smirk that makes women drop their panties, and Rosa instantly blushes. She fixes her hair as casually as she can, then turns her head to me and mouths *Oh my God.* She's wearing a tight red dress and looks stunning.

"Ladies," he says in that low, gritty voice.

"Let me guess, Logan put you on assignment?"

The corner of his mouth cracks into a smile. "He just wants to make sure nobody does anything stupid." His gaze flicks toward Rosa. "But he didn't say I couldn't join you."

I smile and arch a brow, gesturing to the unoccupied love seat across from us. He sits, and immediately their body language changes. Rosa tucks her hair behind her ear and angles her body toward him more, showcasing a softer, shy side of her. *That's new.*

This is interesting. I wish Logan were here to see this.

"I'm going to get another drink. Thor, what would you like? My treat."

He glances at me momentarily before fixing his attention back on her. "Just here to watch."

"If you say so." I wander over to the bar from our cocktail table, making sure to keep my eyes on them. I get a little frisson of excitement when Rosa sits next to him on the sofa. Holy shit, I knew they would be good together, but they are seriously clicking.

Thor leans in to say something to her, and she laughs. Logan may have sent a babysitter for us, but this is the most interest I've seen Thor take in a woman since . . . well, since ever.

I order another round and take a seat at the bar, leaning back to observe the show with gleeful delight as they get to know each other. Based on the way Thor is looking at her like he's already planning when to see her again, I don't think either of them minds.

38

KELLY

After work, I head back to my house to get my mail. It's been a few days, and I need some fresh clothes to take to Logan's. He keeps encouraging me to leave things at his house; at this rate, my name will be on the deed by fall. It's like he's got some covert operation to move me into his loft, one laundry load at a time.

It's great he wants me closer, especially because it makes me feel safe with him around. I sort through the ads, including offers for window replacement and blacktop sealing—two things I could probably use but can't afford—while ambling up my driveway from the mailbox. After entering through the back door, I step into the kitchen, standing over the garbage can, dropping the junk mail into the recycling as I sift through each piece. A couple are things I need to keep, but since all my bills are paperless, it's mostly junk. At the bottom of the pile is a manila envelope with my name on it and no return address. It's thick.

I grab my phone and consider calling Logan but shake my head and undo the metal tab on the back, holding my breath and shaking out the contents.

There's another envelope inside with a message scrawled on the outside.

These are better than selfies, don't you think?

I open it up.

Photos. Of us.

These aren't from last night, they're from before: the night I undressed for him next to his easel. The night we were covered in paint and having sex. Wrapped up in each other. The stack slips from my fingers, and they flutter to the floor like confetti.

We don't even look far away, they're zoomed in. As if they were taken right outside the window, which makes no sense, since he lives on the top floor.

With trembling hands, I clutch my phone and call him. He answers on the first ring. I open my mouth to tell him about the pictures, but only a sob escapes.

"What happened?"

I can't stop.

"Kelly, are you at your house right now?"

I nod, but he can't see that. My breath stutters as I try to catch my breath. "Uh-huh."

Last night was everything. It was perfect. My life was perfect.

Today was spent without a thought regarding the stalker. Even Thor commented on how quiet I was.

"Junior, you've barely said two words all day. I'd be worried about you if it weren't for how fucking smiley you are."

I laughed in response. Of course I did, I spent most of the hours dreaming about a future with Logan and what that might look like. Not just us, but the shop, owning it together as we grow old—and now that peace has been obliterated.

The night captured in these photos was special to me, the things he said to me were meaningful and sacred... but we weren't alone. It wasn't just an intimate moment between us; someone was lurking. Watching and snapping photos of us while we were too wrapped up in each other to notice.

"I'm on my way," he says. "Take a deep breath. Tell me what happened."

Odin bounds inside the house, and Logan is barely through the doorway before I'm crashing into him. He swallows me up in his big arms and tucks me into his chest where I fill my lungs with his scent. He runs his fingers over my hair, pulling a couple wild strands from the messy bun piled on top of my head. I exhale for what feels like the first time since opening that envelope.

"I'm so sorry," he whispers.

I withdraw from his embrace, picking up the stack of photos I collected off the floor and hand them to him. His jaw tenses with every image he flips through. There's a faint click as the bone pops, and I worry that if he applies any more pressure, he might fracture a molar. His temples flush. I've never seen him like this.

"They're really clear. I can't figure out how they took them, they're zoomed in—"

"They're from a drone," he says, dropping the photos on the counter and grabbing his phone.

"What are you doing?"

"I'm having Casper go to my place to sweep for bugs, cameras, anything that might be watching."

A tremor rolls up my spine, making my shoulders shiver. The possibility of more devices has me sick to my stomach.

"Then he's going to do the same thing here. For now, I want you to get your things. Whatever you need. You're going to be staying with me."

Odin leans against my leg.

"Hey, Odie," I croon, crouching down, wrapping my arms around him and squeezing. He rests his chin on me, almost hugging me back. "Oh, I have something for you . . . Just in case you forgot who your favorite person was."

I turn around and open the fridge door, then remove the dog-bone-shaped container and peel off the lid. He sniffs around the dish before gingerly taking bites of the peanut butter dog treats we made the night I attempted to stay home alone.

"I'm supposed to have dinner with my neighbor, Herb—"

"Kelly," he cautions, exasperated. "I'm not arguing about this."

I open my mouth and close it again, knowing it's the right move. "I'll reschedule the dinner," I say, standing again.

Logan hauls me into his chest, and I melt into the safety of his arms. His hand slides up to the back of my neck; he squeezes, then works his thumb into my shoulders where I'm carrying too much tension. "It's going to be okay."

He utters the words low and certain, as if he already knows the outcome of this situation and is sure of fixing it. He's protecting me in a way that feels like possession. The part of me that wants to cling to fear tells me it's hopeless—but I trust Logan because Logan doesn't gamble with what's his.

39

LOGAN

I did some ink for one of the head chefs at a nice restaurant downtown, and he was able to get us a great table last minute. I'm pulling every fucking string I have to give her a night worth remembering, including a dress I picked up for her from one of the boutiques downtown that she's currently changing into. It's a distraction.

"Ready to go soon?" I call up to her from the main level of my loft, tucking my hair behind my ears.

"Almost!"

According to my watch, we've got a few minutes before we have to leave. The click of her heels on the floor above has my pulse ticking. As soon as my eyes land on her, I am hypnotized. She walks down the stairs like it's a punishment—like she knows exactly what she's doing to me. I picked out the dress myself, and she still has my jaw dropping.

"Goddamn, Chaos." That's exactly what she is in that scarlet dress, pure chaos. A fucking menace. She's going to break necks tonight. I'm suddenly regretting the dinner reservation. Why the fuck didn't I just cook her dinner myself, I could have her half naked again by now.

"Thank you for the beautiful dress." She swallows. "Do you think he'll be watching us tonight?"

I spin her and press her back to my front, facing the wall of windows so she can see our reflection together, reminding her she's safe in my arms no matter what.

"I didn't buy this dress for you, sweetheart. I bought it so he could see you wear it with confidence. I fucking hope he's watching."

She inhales. Her fingers tremble as she clutches my arms. In the window's reflection, I spot her biting her bottom lip and even notice her cheeks flush.

"Are you sure we should leave him?" she asks, giving Odin some pets before we head out.

"We're only going to be gone a couple hours."

"I know, but we were gone all day," she says with a pout.

Her justification makes me frown. It's not like her to want to stay home when we have reservations at a nice restaurant. She needs this more than I realized.

"We gotta take him to the dog park. He needs more attention."

I laugh. That dog is exhausted from all the attention she gives him. "Think of how happy he'll be when you bring him home a doggie bag tonight?"

"Okay." She sighs.

She nods, more confident this time. Kelly turns toward the door, but freezes when she notices the new artwork I've hung on the wall. She didn't see it when she walked in earlier because it was behind her.

"Is that . . . is that what I think it is?" Framed on a canvas is the sheet our bodies painted the night she came over. That night was when things started to change between us and we became stronger, like metal.

"Wait, what did you scribble in the corner?" She squints to read the words. "My Obsession."

"Every piece of art needs a name."

She spins and threads her fingers behind my neck, dragging me down and teasing me with her lips in ways that have me regretting ever thinking we should go out to dinner. I could have had her spread out on my countertop and made a whole fucking meal.

On the way over, I made a rule: *No talking about the stalker.* No fear. No looking over our shoulders. Our attention is on each other. Jason can watch all he fucking wants from the sidelines—I'll even give him a show, but he's not going to interfere. Not tonight.

When we arrive at the restaurant, we're seated at our table and presented with two hand-bound leather menus outlining the chef's curated selections, and a third with the wine program. Tonight's special is recited like poetry, with great detail and plenty of lofty metaphors—*a rosemary-kissed lamb loin with truffle pomme puree, deceptively simple, yet prepared with uncompromising rigor.* Okay.

She listens. I don't.

My focus is solely on her tonight.

The server leaves us with a polite nod, and we relax into our secluded spot. The tables draped in white linens are spaced far enough apart, lowering the volume of patrons to a hum that fades into the background. It gives the illusion of intimacy in a very public place. This restaurant is the type that doesn't take walk-ins, and is packed night after night, and you either plan far in advance or you know somebody who can get you in. Being the head chef's tattoo artist has its perks.

The candlelit table illuminates her face in a warm glow as we peruse the offerings. I spend more time watching her than I do reading about the food. Kelly studies her options, considering each and every item before she makes a decision. She leaves much up to fate, but never when it comes to food. *The other things she puts in her mouth, however . . .*

"What are you thinking?" she asks, still scanning the page.

A half smile curls on my lips. "The things I'm thinking would make you blush."

Her eyes find mine, and she lowers her menu, nailing me with a chastising expression. "I'm talking about food."

"So am I," I say, returning to my menu with feigned interest.

Once we've made our selections, we close the leather books and place them on the table, and our server reappears with impeccable timing.

Kelly settles on the seared scallops with wild mushroom risotto.

"Excellent choice." The server nods and turns to me.

"I'll do the same," I say, adding on a bottle of Chablis.

With a polite nod and a warm smile, the server disappears with the leather menus.

"*Copycat,*" she signs.

"*How do you know you didn't copy me?*" I return.

"*Because I was the only one who read the menu.*"

I chuckle as a sommelier arrives at our table with the bottle of wine and pours it into each of our glasses before returning us to our bubble of privacy.

"This is quite the first date."

I narrow my eyes and cock my head to the side. "First date?"

"I mean, kind of." Her shoulders rise and fall.

"First dates are filled with unknowns. It's two strangers meeting. If it goes well, those strangers will carry smooth conversation for hours on end, it may ignite a spark, but often finishes with pleasantries and a smile," I explain. "We aren't strangers anymore, Chaos. And tonight will not end in pleasantries."

She grins. "Is that what we've been doing all these years?"

"It's what I've been doing," I say. "Getting to know you through late-night conversations at Black Rabbit. Observing your habits. Discovering your likes and dislikes. Admiring how beautiful you are. Stifling the attraction and obsessive thoughts while watching you work. Biding my time until you were ready for what I was prepared to give you."

I bring my glass to my lips, letting the bright, tart wine linger on my tongue.

She sucks in a breath. "And what was that?"

"Everything."

Even in the dim candlelight, I see the way her pulse quickens at her neck and the way her pupils dilate when she listens to my words. As much as I love her voice, her hungry silence is just as enticing.

She crosses her legs under the table, and I smile the way a wolf smiles at a fat rabbit.

Our food arrives and is placed in front of us. Three plump, mouthwatering diver scallops are perched on a bed of mushroom risotto. It looks almost as delectable as my "date." Kelly stutters out a thank-you to the server.

I raise my glass. "To first dates."

She delicately clinks her glass to mine. "And whatever comes after." This woman has no idea how much her words rattle my cage. Anticipation simmers under the surface as we sip our wine and take our initial bites. It's quite delicious.

"So if this isn't a first date, what would you call it?"

I resist barking out a laugh at her attempt to have the what-are-we discussion—*we're husband and wife*. "A continuation. An opportunity to spoil you for a night?"

"Do you often spoil the women you're in *continuations* with?" She lifts her wineglass, and my gaze drops to her left hand, wishing I could claim her there. If seeing her in the dress I picked out had me feeling possessive, I can't imagine what seeing the diamond ring on her finger will do to me.

I cock a brow and wipe my mouth with my napkin. "I enjoy spoiling you. I wouldn't know about any other women. There's no one besides you."

"What about the one who came before me? The last one."

I inhale and blow out the breath. *Ah.* I knew this would have to come out eventually. I set down my fork, rest my arm on the table, and twist the stem of my wineglass while I collect my words.

"Dad said she was a *piece of work*," Kelly prompts.

I huff a small laugh. Of course he minimized it that way. "Yeah. There was one other woman I was serious with. It was while you were away at college. I don't think you ever met her."

Kelly confirms with a shake of her head.

"Piper—that was her name—at first she was wonderful. Supportive, kind, and thoughtful. We were attracted to each other right away, and that only grew over time. I thought I loved her. I was even going to propose, but then I began to see the cracks in her personality."

She was bad for me. Clyde noticed, he always noticed these things before I did, and all he needed to do was see two people together to know whether they were a match. He had the real deal with Nancy, so he knew what love looked like—knew what soul mates looked like.

Clyde gently expressed his concern for me a few times when it came to our relationship. I brushed him off, assuming not everyone can have what he and Nancy did.

"She couldn't stand to see me giving anyone else attention, including your father."

Her brow furrows. "My dad?"

"I was his apprentice. You and I understand what kind of an honor that is. An opportunity to be mentored by Clyde Everhart demands hours of practice and focus. Your dad was patient and thorough with every lesson he taught, making sure I grasped and perfected every skill. He donated one of his most valuable assets—not only his knowledge, but his *time*. The least I could do is repay him with mine."

He didn't just teach me how to tattoo, he taught me how to be an artist.

"You were special to him. He loved you." She says it so casually, smiling into her wine before taking a drink, but it seizes the words in my throat. Clyde always made me feel like I mattered and what I created was significant. There was no better mentor than him.

"And Piper hated that."

"You were building your career."

I nod. "The week after I completed my apprenticeship and started out on my own, her dog became sick and she had to put him down. I canceled everything that week to be there for her. That week, things settled down and I saw bits of the Piper I fell in love with. But as soon as I went back to work . . ."

She hums in understanding.

I sigh. "The more controlling she became, the less I wanted to be around her. She blamed your dad." He was in her way.

Kelly purses her lips, cocking her head to the side as she listens.

"One day, I was taking trash out to the dumpster at work and found her tampering with your dad's old Buick. We got into a huge fight, and it was during that fight I started questioning some of the weird coincidences, like how quickly she got over her dog. She never admitted it, but I believe she had her dog put down so she could keep me home."

"Oh my God." Her back straightens and she presses the pads of her fingers to her parted lips. "What was she doing with the car?"

Piper lacked empathy but faked it very well. She saw people as possessions. In her eyes, she owned my time the same way she owned me. It was always about attention for her. It was her life source.

"Trying to cut his brakes. Everything in her life was something to leverage, including life apparently." I lift my shoulders. "I lost it. I reached out to her family, told them I was done, and they had her admitted."

"Jesus."

Piper was a different breed of chaos; she was disturbed.

"I was so ashamed of how bad I had let everything get, like a frog in boiling water. I should have seen it sooner, stopped it sooner. Instead, I had to get a restraining order and face your dad with the truth. That was the hardest part, explaining that I'd jeopardized his safety because my judgment couldn't be trusted." It makes me sick to think I could have been the reason to make Kelly lose her father even earlier than she did.

Kelly sits there stunned. "I never knew any of this . . . What did my dad say?"

"Nothing!" I chuckle. "He just hugged me. That was it." Clyde knew I was hurting. He never once gave me the told-you-so speech.

"Sounds about right. You were his golden boy. So, what happened to her?"

"It took a while for her to accept the breakup, but eventually, she stopped calling and texting, and I figured it was because we had the restraining order in place. Months later, I looked her up online but found her obituary instead. That was why she stopped calling." She took her own life.

I scrub a hand down my face, adjusting my posture. Up until a year ago, this was a story I couldn't speak out loud, but now I'm able to talk about those times and not feel the sting of shame and loss. Learning about her death threw me into a deep depression. It was abrupt, there was no closure.

"I blamed myself; I was too ashamed to even reach out to her family and apologize."

"Oh, Logan." Kelly reaches across the table to squeeze my hand. "Her parents knew you loved her."

But did I? I've asked myself that question a thousand times. I cared for her deeply, and I told Piper I loved her—believing it to be the truth. However, it wasn't until I began developing feelings for Kelly that I realized the magnitude of love and how vastly divergent the experience could be. It was the difference between a puddle and an ocean trench.

Piper didn't love me. She didn't possess the *capacity* to love anyone other than herself. She was tortured by it. That said, I'm not confident I loved her either.

Real love doesn't hesitate—it exists without question. But not loving someone is much harder to determine. That's when you have to ask, when you have to seek out signs that aren't there and beg for feelings that don't exist.

I don't ask with Kelly.

My fingers draw circles in the tablecloth. "Do you remember when you said you were feeling more serious about your relationships?"

Her fork pauses halfway to her mouth, as if she's slightly caught off guard by my change of conversation. I don't want to talk about the past with another woman, I want to talk about the future with the one in front of me.

She finishes the succulent bite and nods.

I slice off another piece of scallop. "Do you still feel that way?"

Her back straightens. "Yes."

"And how do you feel about us?"

Kelly chuckles. "Oh, are we doing performance reviews tonight?"

I smile. "Maybe."

"I feel very optimistic about our future . . . I'm very happy with you." She wipes her hands on her napkin. "Sometimes it's like I'm looked at by so many people, but you're the only one who sees me. The things you say, the way you touch . . . I can't explain it. It goes so much deeper than a physical level, though. You've been around for some of the most important events of my life, and in many ways, I can't imagine a life without you. Like we're—I don't know."

Soul mates. That's the word she's searching for.

"But..."

But?

"I can't help but wonder what our relationship might be like under different circumstances, you know?"

Fuck, I'm letting her down.

"I'm working on it," I say. It's a weak excuse. I haven't solved this problem yet the way I promised her I would.

She reaches across the table for me, but her smile is sad. "I know you are. This just seems to be . . . a lot. Even tonight, you're taking me out as a distraction. You made a special reservation at a nice restaurant just so we could forget about our reality. That's not how it's supposed to be. You shouldn't have to do that. It's not fair that you have to bear this burden too."

"We're not talking about that tonight, remember?"

She nods, silently chewing. She doesn't have to talk about it for me to know it's in her thoughts.

"We are going to get through this." I thread her fingers with mine.

"If it ever does become a burden, if I become too much—"

"You won't."

I'm a man of reason, but Kelly has me believing in more. We're fated.

It's time to go on the offensive; no more waiting for his next move. I'll search every dark corner until I find who has made her question our future. Her stalker's expiration is up.

40

LOGAN

When we get back to the loft, Kelly gives Odin a treat. I swear that dog has gained ten pounds since I brought him home.

"You're going to spoil that dog."

"Good." She winks at me from over her shoulder, then returns her gaze to the dog. "You could use some spoiling, huh, Odie?"

I can barely stand to watch her for one more second in that dress; as soon as the lock clicks behind us, I pull down the zipper. We're both done resisting. The tension is too high. She heads toward the stairs, with me stalking behind her. I shrug off my jacket, letting it fall to the ground, then get to work removing my cuff links. They clatter to the floor at our feet.

Kelly spins at the noise, spotting the shiny silver pieces on the floor, then begins unbuttoning my shirt with too many fucking buttons.

I loop my fingers under the delicate straps of her dress and slip them off her shoulders. As soon as she nudges my shirt down my arms, her hands drop to her sides, and the expensive fabric pools around her ankles. She's left standing before me in nothing but a strapless bra that pushes her tits up and a scrap of underwear. *Fucking hell.*

I hook my foot around the upholstered ottoman at my side and drag it in front of me.

"Get on your knees," I say, unzipping my pants. She kneels on the ottoman, and I stand in front of her as she frantically shoves down my boxer briefs.

"What if someone's taking pictures?"

I squeeze the back of her neck before sliding my hand below her shoulder blades, unclasping her bra. The cups fall away as she frees my stiff and aching cock. Those piercings of hers get me every time.

"Let 'em watch."

She wraps her fingers tight around me, stroking with a rhythm that makes my breath catch in my throat. My palm presses to the back of her head and I force the swollen crown past her lips, feeling her tongue flick as it travels over the underside of my shaft. She fists the base, holding me steady while she works her mouth, slow and zealous. I groan, relishing the sight of my hard flesh disappearing between her lips.

My head falls back as I succumb to her touch.

She pops off for a brief moment. "Look at me," she says. I meet her green eyes and can't help but fucking smile; she's so goddamn sexy. "It makes me wet when you watch."

"How deep can you take me?"

She ushers my tip toward the back of her tongue.

"Deeper," I command. Her fingers fan out over my ass, and her lids flutter closed. "Nuh-uh, I want your pussy drenched by the time I fuck you. Keep your eyes open when you take this cock down your throat."

She stares right into my soul and swallows. Holy shit. It sucks the air from my lungs. My unfocused gaze finds hers again, and this time she's wearing the hint of a wicked smile on her lips. The corner of my mouth tilts up, and I shake my head. "Look at you, so fucking arrogant while sucking me off. Why don't you prove it. Show me how good you are on your knees."

She moans around me, accepting the challenge.

"You want to show off, Chaos?" Smirking, I give her chin a lift and guide myself deeper.

"Choke on it."

She squirms, her throat protesting, and then she retches when I hit the back. Chuckling, I say, "Aww, struggling already? I thought you wanted to demonstrate that you were more than a pretty mouth for me to fuck?"

Gripping a fistful of hair, I hold her in place for a couple seconds and enjoy the view. She relaxes her throat as much as she can. "There you go. So proud of yourself, aren't you? Gagging and drooling like my beautiful whore."

I release her locks, and she turns feral, clawing at my thighs. She continues to work me over, and with minutes passing like seconds, I admire the way she indulges on my thick cock.

"Fuck, is that drool or need dripping from your lips? Hard to tell when you look up at me like you're starving." As much as I want to come down her throat, I've been thinking about how tight she is for the entire ride home.

"Oh, greedy girl, just like that," I croon. "All it takes is my dick in your mouth for you to forget how to think." I draw back, and she whimpers. "Deep breath."

She inhales through her nose and takes me again, gagging around me until mascara-filled tears streak over her cheeks, smudging the lovely makeup she spent so much time on.

"Christ," I growl through clenched teeth. Her unkempt midnight hair is tousled and wild, her lips wrapped around me. It triggers a primal need to fuck every last inch of myself into her until the only name she can remember is Mrs. Teller. I'm going to lose it like this.

"Up."

She stands, and I sink to my knees for her. "Turn around and bend the fuck over. Show me what's mine tonight."

She spins and I crook my fingers in the sides of her underwear, then drag them down her thighs and allow her to step out. I press my palm to the center of her back, forcing her to bend over the arm of the upholstered sofa next to us. She spreads her legs, giving me a delicious view, and I smack her heart-shaped ass that she's placed at eye level.

"You went through a lot of prep to make tonight memorable," she pants. "So did I."

It takes a second for my brain to comprehend what she's saying. A slow smile blooms on my lips and press my thumb to her asshole. "Is that so? You letting me fuck you here tonight?"

I grip her cheeks and spread them, which allows me to peek at her slick, wet, and pink entrance, and the ass I've been dying to take. Cocking my head to the side, I slowly drag my gaze over her delicious body.

"I trust you," she murmurs.

Trust.

It heals her words from dinner; even though I haven't solved this problem we're dealing with, she trusts I will—and I'll prove her right. However, if this is what we're doing tonight, I'm not going to do it rushed over the side of a fucking chair.

"You have such a pretty pussy."

She moans my name like a prayer.

I wedge my face between her cheeks and skate my tongue over her clit, climbing higher to her ass. Her legs tremble and I smile. One of my favorite things about Kelly is the way she responds to my touch. My tongue traces the knot before traveling back to her cunt, dipping inside.

"Make me come," she whines.

"Uh-uh," I say against her, nipping at her swollen nub. I sit back on my heels and spin her to face me, still kneeling at her feet. "If I wanted to get you off, I could have you gushing already." I dive between her thighs and wrap my lips around her clit, sucking. She cries out as I take my time, and her eyes soften. "But I'd rather watch your mind unravel as your body begs for more."

I flip her around again, smack her ass, and return to eating her from the back.

"You're . . . cruel," she says, choking out the breathy words. I keep it up until her legs lock and shake, the telltale sign she's about to come. I've memorized the way she responds to my touch.

My tongue slides up to her ass again. I pull away too soon, grinning when I hear that pathetic whimper. I crack my hand across her cheeks a third time and she jumps. It's not as rough as if she were receiving a punishment but enough to catch her by surprise.

"Why did you stop?" she asks with ragged inhales.

"Because . . ." I spit on her entrance. "It's time for me to stretch this needy pussy until it's dripping down my balls."

Getting to my feet, I stand behind her, cupping the back of her neck, and shoving her face into the cushion. She twitches when my tip presses to her opening.

I fill her to the brim. "This tight little ass of yours . . ." She tries to sit up, but I hold her in place, forcing my cock deeper while she fidgets. "Is going to gorge on every inch of me tonight, but your cunt gets fed first."

The couch rocks under us as I plunge into her from behind, with the sofa arm digging into her hips, but I keep her in place.

"You feel that?" I ask.

"So fucking good." Her words shake with each thrust.

She gasps, clawing at the smooth leather but unable to grasp it, which only makes me laugh. I jerk her back onto me harder, burying myself to the hilt. "Look at you, folded over and helpless, your tight body knows exactly how to take me, doesn't it?"

"Mm-hmm," she mumbles.

My hips drive into her, rough enough to rattle the frame of the couch; every so often I slow, just for the opportunity to see her writhe with need, then slam back in with a growl.

"Say it," I demand, fisting her hair and lifting her head up to speak. "Tell me your pussy is mine."

"It's yours," she rasps.

"Damn right it is." I push into her again. "And you're mine to fill. Always."

She comes without warning this time, her cunt milking me and making it difficult to maintain any control. Before finishing with her, I pull out and wrap an arm around her waist, then toss her over my shoulder and carry her up the stairs. I set her on her back onto the bed, part her thighs, and delve inside her again, and she fists the sheets. Resting her right leg in the crook of my neck, I press a kiss to her inner calf and graze my teeth across her soft flesh while rolling her clit between my fingers.

When she arches her back, I get to work, making her knuckles bloom white as I play with her. She groans and clamps down around my length. *Holy fuck.* I suck in a breath. "There you go, sweetheart. Be a good girl and come on my cock."

Kelly nods, her eyes desperate as she tips over the edge. I grin wide at the muscles tightening in her neck as her mouth drops open. Her messy tears from earlier are icing on the cake. *So gorgeous.*

Unwilling to force myself to wait this time, I withdraw and propel her legs forward before shooting ropes of cum across her pussy and cheeks with very little accuracy.

My heart thrums in my chest as I hone in on her. She's going to keep me hard and help me get through the refractory period. "We aren't done yet," I say.

I steal a pillow from the head of the bed, and she lifts her ass, letting me tuck it under her hips. Wrapping my arms around her thighs, I tug her closer, adjusting her position. She twitches when I work my cum over her clit with my thumb and shift it lower until I'm massaging her tight knot.

I insert a finger into her ass and her lips part. I sink down to the knuckle, pumping and spreading her for what's to come. She whimpers, and I pin her hip down while I add another, pulling a raspy moan from her throat. I pluck the bottle of lube from the nightstand, drizzling it in my palm and stroking my dick. It's not long before blood starts returning to my cock. *Fucking finally.* I push my thumb in, working around the perimeter, stretching her out one last time. "I want you to choose a safeword, just in case it gets to be too much."

"Red . . ." She smiles. "Thank you." It's not out of courtesy, it's cautionary. She's going to need this.

Sitting on my heels between her parted legs, I admire the way she's offering herself to me as if I'm a god—which is exactly how I feel. She lengthens her body, lifting her arms above her head and arching her back—giving me one hell of a view of her breasts.

"Please?" she says, grinding against my knuckles, and I add another finger. Fuck, she's going to be my undoing.

"Unreal," I mutter, shaking my head and pressing the swollen tip to her entrance. I lean into it until the head of my cock squeezes into her tight ass. *Fuck.*

Her lips part, and she blinks up at me.

"Still my good girl?" I rasp.

She nods, sighing as she says. "More."

I proceed slowly, pressing my hands on the backs of her lifted thighs, and I open her up to me more. "This is mine now," I say. "All of you."

I study her face, watching for any signs of discomfort.

"Take me, Logan."

A grumble vibrates in my chest. *Take it slow*, I remind myself. I add more lube, mixing it with the cum and sweeping it over the area until the resistance lowers. She's so tight I forget to breathe.

"Oh my God . . ." she sobs.

"You can take it, can't you?"

"Yes." She nods. "It's so good—*fuck.*"

I'm unsure if she's giving me a command or just an exclamation. She's wide-eyed and impatient, panting for more, so I sink deep until she's flush with the base of my cock.

She groans, and her chest rises and falls a little too fast for me.

"Shhhh. Breathe into it. Every inhale, I push deeper. Every exhale, you give me more. Understand?"

Kelly nods, allowing her muscles to soften. She follows my instructions and becomes more pliable under my palms.

"Perfect," I say with a smile. "You're so fucking perfect."

With messy hair and mascara, she clutches my wrists, her glassy gaze locked on mine with so much trust.

"Thank you for giving me this," I say, rocking into her.

"You own every part of me, Logan." *She knows exactly how to rile me up.*

I fold her knees to her chest as I grip her jaw firmly, taking her mouth like I own it. Holding her still as my hips flex. She moans, kissing me hard and deep. Her tongue swipes over mine like she's trying to make me lose control. It's working.

"Do you have any idea what you fucking do to me?" I ask against her lips.

"I do," she whispers, fully aware and smug.

I sit up and impale her on me, harder this time.

"Like that," she begs. "Fuck me like that." Her eyes flash, showing me glimpses of those dark corners she tries to hide.

I snap my hips again, holding her there as I rail harder and deeper than before. Her thighs tremble, and I snake my hand between her thighs and strum her clit with the side of my thumb while taking her ass.

"That's a good girl. You knew exactly what you were doing when you planned this out."

She's gripping me so tight, like her body is trying to swallow my length.

"I want you addicted to me," she says. "I want to make sure no one will ever make you feel satisfied like I do. I want to ruin you as much as you do me."

Christ.

"I've already experienced what it's like to be without you. I'm never going back."

I pull out nearly all the way, then surge forward again, forcing her to take each deliberate inch. "Fuck, I knew you could handle it."

I do it once more, observing the way her expression darkens slightly. There's that flicker.

A sinful, smug grin perches on her lips while her body stretches around me.

A scoff slips from my throat. "You want more?" I spit on her ass. "I'm taking everything, Chaos—and I'll fuck you . . . until there's nothing left . . . you haven't given to me."

"It's yours."

Those two fucking words. Sweat beads on my forehead as I make every effort to not come; she's bleeding out every ounce of control I have left. Every time I bury myself deep, she groans for more. She lights my veins on fire. Fuck mercy. Fuck control. I want my wife raw and untamed.

Kelly cries out my name, and I stare in disbelief at how perfect she is.

"Louder, I want to hear it over the sound of your screams while your legs are fucking shaking for me. While you're on the brink of shattering." I stuff my fingers into her pussy and stroke that spot.

"Logan!" Her voice trembles, senses overwhelmed. Her legs tense, and she mewls, raking my neck with her nails.

"Yes, sweetheart?" I tease, catching my breath.

Tears stream down her face. "I can't hold it." Her words come out like a plea.

I add another finger, pumping them in and out; she's going to be so sore tomorrow. I will never forget how beautiful she looks in this moment. How giving she's being, offering me her body, trust, and total submission. I will spend every second making sure I'm worthy of this moment.

"Break for me. Come on, pretty girl. Break and fucking gush all over my cock."

She sits up on her elbows, sobbing my name, and squirts all over my hand when she comes. *Oh fuck.*

"Good girl!" I draw out my praise, low and gritty. "That's it, let it wreck you. I want every messy, broken piece." I nod, encouraging her, her mouth open on a silent scream as she locks her eyes on mine and gives me every bit of herself.

Her body pulses, and the second she fractures, I lose it. I jerk inside her, filling her ass until I'm grinding down, forcing her to take every last drop. Every twitch, tremor, and delicious spasm of her body is mine. The fact that I brought her from sobbing to speechless makes my chest swell with pride, and I come undone right along with her until we're nothing but heaving chests and thrumming heartbeats.

After cleaning ourselves up, we ease back into bed. I gaze at the ceiling, smiling, with her tired body draped over mine under the sheets and one of her thighs resting on top of mine. Her warm, relaxed weight on me is grounding and fills me with a peace I didn't even know I needed. Kelly's ear is pressed to my chest as if she's listening to my heartbeat, while her fingers trace the tattoos on my neck. We're right where we belong.

"I wrecked your sheets," she says. "Twice."

My fingertips ghost up and down her spine. "No, you only wrecked the sheets once. This time you drenched the comforter."

She laughs and lightly slaps my shoulder.

I hike her leg up higher, then stroke behind her knee with my thumb. Kelly hums happily. "Yeah, I don't think you can hang that one on the wall."

I hum in agreement.

"Can I make you a cup of tea?" she asks.

The grin on my face widens, and I press a kiss to the top of her head. "No. I just want to hold you, take care of what's mine."

She does a little shiver, nuzzling into me. "I could stay forever like this. Wrapped around you and listening to your heartbeat."

I didn't know I could feel this much until her. A sense of calm hangs over us as we breathe together, our chests rising and falling, totally in sync as we come down from the high.

It's as if our bodies know exactly what the other needs and how to communicate with one another. But this part, the calm after the storm, after all the wreckage of breaking together, this might be my favorite. There's no high like holding her, knowing she's mine. Knowing she's safe in my arms where she belongs.

"I'm so sleepy, but I don't want tonight to end."

"Before you fall asleep, I want you to drink some water and take a painkiller," I say, reaching over to grab the glass of water and two small pills I set on the nightstand. She props up on her elbows, taking them from me and drinking from the glass until it's empty. I set it back on the table and drag a downy-soft muslin over us. She deserves all the softness after how rough I was.

I tip her chin up, bringing her relaxed mouth to mine before she falls asleep. There's no urgency when our lips brush, and she parts just enough to let me taste her. She sleepily sighs into me, and I kiss her again, more breath than lips. My fingers comb through her hair, untangling the strands one by one while holding her safely in my arms.

She's not only my chaos, she's my calm—and my obsession for her is as gentle as it is destructive.

41

KELLY

"So now," he says, plugging the orange extension cord into the living room wall outlet, "when you use your hair dryer, it won't shut off half the fucking house."

I clap my hands together. "Thank you!"

Logan groans, standing up off the floor like he's somebody's dad. "This isn't a solution, it's just a temporary bandage—and a shitty one at that. We're gonna need to have the electrical rewired sooner rather than later," he says.

"*We're?*" I ask with a smile.

The corner of his mouth tips up. "Did I stutter?"

I stretch up on my tiptoes and pull him down by his neck to kiss him on the cheek. "Ready to pick up where we left off in the attic?" I ask.

Yesterday, I expressed to Logan that I wanted to go through some of Dad's things. It's been weeks since I've been up there. As usual, he wanted to help—it's almost like a sixth sense, knowing when I'm working up there. Dealing with an emotionally charged task is a lot more bearable when he's around. He's strong enough to lift the heavy things I can't, physically and metaphorically.

"Let's do it."

"What if we put some of these sketchbooks in the shop?" I ask, thumbing through the pages of another sketchbook. We're getting a little sidetracked, enjoying the nostalgia of his penmanship and goofy drawings. "You know, like with the portfolio books in the front."

He shrugs. "Would you ever want to include them with flash? I'm sure some people will want them inked."

I flip a couple pages, revisiting the images. "Is that weird, though—tattooing his work posthumously?" I ask.

"Only you can decide that, but I don't think it's weird. I think he would love for you to be the one to continue his legacy. It might be a cool homage, a few small pieces from his private collection that you're willing to show the world."

I like the idea of having more of Dad's work featured at the shop he started so many years ago; it keeps him alive there. Black Rabbit has always had a heartbeat; the appreciation of art and history of ink run through its walls like a life source. Lines, love, and lineage.

There's some great work in these sketchbooks—there's some shit too—but I want to share his doodles and the artistic side of him that was more than flash. He was a talented artist of many styles, but most people only know him for the one.

"I'll pick out a few to set aside," I say, nodding and selecting four of my favorites. I carry them over to the attic ladder and set them beside the opening so I don't forget to take them down. Out of the corner of my eye, a small red light reflects off a mirror Logan moved earlier. It's just behind the attic hatch. I cock my head to the side, pushing off the floor of the attic, and walk over to the mirror, following the reflection to the source.

The hatch.

There's something electronic on the attic door hatch. It's hidden well, but it's not supposed to be there. I run my fingers over it, and there's another that matches it on the frame of the opening, but that one is painted over, so it's better camouflaged. *Holy shit.*

"Logan! Come over here." I gasp, pointing at the small shiny inlaid device. "Do you see this?"

He rubs the back of his neck, watching me, then takes in a long, slow breath before reluctantly standing and coming over to see what I'm pointing to.

"Is this some kind of hidden camera?" I ask. "Could the stalker have done this?"

"It's a security sensor," he says, stepping down the ladder and carrying the sketchbooks with him. When he reaches the main level, he sets the books on a small hallway table and motions me to come down the ladder. *Why is he not freaking out right now?*

"Logan, I didn't install a security sensor!" Someone came into my house and put that here. God, this is a nightmare that never ends. "Someone is watching me."

His shoulders rise when he takes a deep breath and releases it slowly. "Come down here."

42

LOGAN

Shit.

Kelly walks down the stairs and stands next to me, not taking her eye off the small sensor, as if it's a bomb about to detonate. I push the ladder up, shutting the attic hatch, then hit the switch on the wall, releasing the attic door. My phone dings, and I show her the notification on my screen: *Attic door open.*

"I installed it. It tells me when you go into the attic."

She blinks at me. Her gaze oscillates between the screen and me before gingerly taking it from my hands. "When did you do this?" she whispers, staring at the notification.

"A couple years ago." I peel the phone from her grasp, lock the screen, and tuck it back into my pocket.

She shakes off the shock. "Did you say *years*?"

I exhale. "Yes."

"Why?" she bites out. Here comes the anger.

"I wanted to know when you were going through his things. After he died, you didn't want anything to do with his belongings. However, once you were ready, you would lose yourself in this attic for hours, sometimes days. You weren't picking up your phone or responding to texts. Every Tuesday, you walked into work looking exhausted, like you had barely slept during your days off. What was I supposed to do? Just sit back while you buried yourself alive in his memories and things? I wanted to know when you needed help without being intrusive."

She barks out a fake laugh. "So you thought the answer to that was spying on me. Are you fucking kidding me?"

"My intentions were pure." *Ish.*

She walks away from me into her living room and sits on the edge of the sofa with her hands placed neatly in her lap. Her eyes are fixed on the floor. She's quiet, closed off. Something's wrong.

"I think it's time we contact the police," she says.

I kneel in front of her and take her hands in mine. "I'm close to figuring it out."

"You keep saying that." Her words sting. "You said you would take care of it. It's not just messages anymore, Logan—it's photos! I'm becoming paranoid. He's still out there."

I swallow. She's right. My head hangs between my shoulders before I blow out a breath and get to my feet, then pace back and forth in her living room.

"We still don't know who it is—"

Stopping midstride, I spin to face her. "It's Billy."

She presses her head into her palm and massages her forehead like I'm feeding her riddles. "Billy who?"

I stuff my hands into my pockets. "Billy Akers."

Her head snaps up, and she narrows her gaze at me. Kelly is all business when she says, "Start talking."

"The day Jason showed up at the shop, I was already in a bad mood because I had received a letter from Billy."

"So what? He retired years ago, I don't understand what he's got to do with any of this, he was a friend of my dad's."

"No, he wasn't," I argue, halting my steps and pointing at her. "No, he fucking wasn't."

Shit, this conversation is going to end up in the goddamn weeds. Here we go. She sits back on the sofa and crosses her arms, waiting for me to continue.

"You were supposed to get the shop when your dad died."

"*Me?*" She points to herself with wide eyes, blinking a few times. "I wasn't ready to run a shop. I didn't even have my license then."

I nod. "Didn't matter. It was still yours. That's what your dad wanted. Toward the end, I tried talking to Billy to make sure we had plans in place to keep Black Rabbit running. He was too quiet, something felt off, so I started digging. Billy had been embezzling money from the shop, slowly bleeding it without anyone catching on. So, while the rest of us were wrapped up with your dad's palliative care at the end of his life, Billy was cutting deals and lining his pockets."

"He embezzled money?" She winces; the look of betrayal on her face is obvious.

"Yeah, but that was the least of our worries." I wave my hand. "He tried to sell Black Rabbit. I'm not talking about the building or the chairs, I'm talking about the *name*. To some company out in L.A. They had plans to turn this place into a fucking reality show, come out with our own line of shitty ink, branded merchandise, it was a huge money grab. Not at all in the spirit of what this place was founded on."

She leans forward, burying her head in her hands. "I can't believe this."

"I knew your dad wasn't a sellout. In fact, your dad already had the paperwork filled out. He trusted Billy to file it, but he never did. He sat on it. Used the window between Clyde's trust and the legal handoff to try to sell everything your dad built right before he died. He was *not* your dad's friend."

"Okay, but we didn't sell." She drops her hands and sits up straight. "So what the fuck happened?"

I shrug. "I did what I had to do. I made him a better offer. I bribed him in order to kill the deal. Billy never *retired*, he ran."

"You *paid* the man who betrayed us?"

"To protect Black Rabbit and everything your dad built? Yeah, I paid him."

"How much?" she asks.

"That's not important."

"How much, Logan?"

"I had a trust fund."

"*Had?*" she asks. "Why didn't you just go to the lawyers? Why didn't you sue?"

I scrub a hand over my face. "There wasn't time. That deal had to go through before your dad died. I didn't have any paperwork to prove that it was supposed to go to you, all I knew was what your dad told me, and I believed him. I figured a company in L.A. probably had lawyers that would drain us while we tried to fight for it back. I just . . . I panicked. I was too busy trying to keep things afloat here while he was sick, all that baggage with Piper was still fresh, Clyde was dying. I just did the only thing I could think of."

"But you never put it in my name."

"Not at first." I rock on my heels. "I needed to make sure everything was stable and the shop wasn't at risk of going under before I put something like that on you. Besides, you were barely twenty-two, dealing with the death of your father, and spent most of your time in the attic. You had enough on your plate. I had thrown most of my trust into the place—it was an investment. I needed to make sure I wasn't saddling you with a failing business and losing everything I owned in the process."

She stares at me wide-eyed. "Oh my God."

"The story became that he left it to me and I would eventually transfer ownership when you were ready and Black Rabbit was in a good place financially. I didn't want you to know that your dad had been betrayed like that. I didn't want you to know about any of this. You were drowning in grief; the stress of something like this would have wrecked you."

She's silent while her brain processes the information, and then she furrows her brow and shakes her head. "But wait, back up, what makes you think my stalker is Billy? You think he's behind everything?"

I shrug. "I think he spent all that money and needs more. Maybe he's still mad I bought it from him; he'd be making more off royalties if I'd let them milk Black Rabbit like a cash cow. I don't think he's mad at you, I think he wants to hit me where it hurts, and he knows that's by going after you. I think that's why he sent that letter to the shop and not to your house directly. That was a message for *me*, not you."

"What did the letter say?"

I roll my eyes. "He made it seem like he was just saying '*How ya doin', Junior?*' Asking about what it was like being the boss, replacing your dad."

"He said *replace?*"

I nod.

"He thinks one of us replaced him?"

"That's what I think is happening. Remember where he always wanted to retire?"

She slaps a hand over her mouth. "Oh my God. Out west."

Exactly.

"But the photos?" she asks. "Would Billy seriously do that?"

"Blackmail," I say.

"Why wouldn't he have just asked for the money when he sent the photos?"

I shake my head. "He's letting us know he's got them. The more famous you become, the more they're worth. You're climbing the fame charts. Look at the way your Instagram has blown up over the last year."

"Fuck." She runs a hand over her hair, pulling more strands from the messy updo and tucking them behind her ears. "Why didn't you tell me this sooner, Logan?"

There's not a great reason why, other than trying to spare her from a massive headache and trust issues—which, in an ironic turn of events, is exactly what I've done. "I wanted to protect you. I didn't want you to think that I was trying to steal Black Rabbit or your inheritance."

She pushes off the couch and stands with her hands on her hips. "That's a stupid reason. That's such a stupid fucking reason. If I'm the owner of Black Rabbit, then I deserve to know what happened to it . . ."

Fair point. I keep my mouth shut, because for now, she only gets Black Rabbit if something happens to me. I haven't transferred it to her yet.

"So, what else don't I know?" she asks, closing the distance between us with clenched fists.

Shit.

She searches my eyes, as if all my secrets are buried right behind them. She's good at reading people when she knows there's something they want to hide, and right now, I'm doing everything I can to hold her stare because if I look away for even a second, she'll know.

Option one: Drop the big bomb right out of the gate and hope the blast radius takes me out before she does. After that, everything else will seem like mere bottle rockets in comparison.

Or option two: Feed her the small bullshit first, then slowly build up to the dramatic grand finale that explodes into a fiery chaos that can only be rivaled by her untamed fury and ability to throw things at me.

Do I want a quick merciful death? Or would it be fun to have a little edging first?

There is a third option . . . Presently, we're headed down a path that leads to me revealing whether she owns the shop. If I can throw her off the trail with a red herring, then at least I can dodge the whole proxy marriage thing.

I've got to distract her with a new reason to hate me.

"Odin wasn't a stray. I adopted him from a shelter," I blurt.

Her nostrils flare, and she backs away from me.

"I made him look like he was a stray because you're a sucker for that. Plus, that whole thing in your dad's letter, he set me up for that, I had to take advantage."

Her gaze darts to Odin. "What else?" she says, voice flat as she peers at our dog.

Sabotaged your last relationship . . . read some of your dad's letters to manipulate your feelings . . . married you. Minor infractions.

Kelly must pick up on my silence, so she slowly brings her attention back to me and narrows her eyes. "I *am* the owner of Black Rabbit, right? The way Dad wanted it to be?"

Well, fuck, so much for that strategy!

Careful . . . "We both own it," I reply.

She cocks her head to the side, crossing her arms again. "You're lying to me."

I shake my head. *Technically*, it's marital property, and in Minnesota, that means she gets half.

She throws up her hands and raises her voice. "Well, am I tits deep in back taxes, then? Why hasn't the government come around and asked me for money? Show me the paperwork that shows we own it."

She stalks toward me, and I back up.

Hard pass. "No."

Her raised chin tells me she's squaring up for a fight. "Why not?" she demands.

I rub the back of my neck. *She's got me backed into a corner.* "I can't tell you that."

She gives an exaggerated blink. "*What?*" Her tone is sharp.

My hands are tied on this one. I can't tell her everything, or I'll lose her. Our marriage is something that was going to happen eventually, and it allowed me to make sure she would get the business should anything happen to me. It killed two birds with one stone . . . It also ensured that if she ever tried to divorce me, I would still keep half of Black Rabbit. The tattoo shop tied us for life. She's too sentimental to walk away from her dad's shop—and so am I.

She buries her face in her hands. "I can't do this."

"Do *what?*"

I unclench my jaw and try to have a little perspective. She's dealing with information overload and just needs time to process everything. Her eyes glimmer as tears swell to the brim.

"This." Her body slackens, arms falling at her sides as if they're too heavy to hold up for even one more second. "You. Us. Installing sensors. Odin. Keeping secrets. All of it."

I step forward, my voice rising. "Stop. We're not doing that."

"I need space. A break. Not saying forever, but for now." My ears ring as the silence around us seems to pulse at the finality of her words.

A break? *A fucking break?*

The suffocation starts in my chest, spreading from my lungs and tightening every organ in its path. By the time it hits my mind, my thoughts can't even breathe.

She's giving up.

My spiraling thoughts eat away at the silence, filling it with raw noise as I search every possibility, every cause-and-effect outcome that will get her to stay. As my vision tunnels, there's a flicker of hope, like a shot in the dark.

It's almost too simple. *I'm fucked anyway, might as well have a little pre-party for the apocalypse.* My mouth tips up in a smile. I inhale deep and blow the air out smoothly, steadying my breaths as my heart rate slows.

Just because she wants a break doesn't mean I have to give it to her. *I won't let her.*

She doesn't get to give up on us. I didn't wait years to make her mine and risk it all just so she could throw in the towel when shit gets hard. Not a chance in hell. If Kelly wants a fight, then I'll give her one, but she better strap the fuck in because tonight won't be ending with one of us walking away.

I cross my arms and smirk. "No."

She cocks her head to the side. "That's not up to you," she fires back.

"Actually, it is," I say. "We're not done yet."

She sidesteps while keeping her wary eyes on me.

"No, no, no," I say, peering down at my feet. I chuckle and shake my head before meeting her gaze again. "Don't look at me like I'm some stranger you don't recognize."

"Honestly, Logan—" She swallows, backing up as I encroach on her space. "The man I know doesn't keep secrets. I don't know who you are right now."

The only thing keeping those words from gutting me is the knowledge that she doesn't mean them. If we're ripping off bandages, then let's do it. I'll go first.

"Yes you do." I take a few steps toward her. "I'm your fucking husband."

She sighs, rubbing her forehead with a palm as if exasperated by nonsense. "That's impossible."

"It's called a proxy marriage," I explain. "It's legal in Montana."

She quirks her head and raises her left brow, burying me six feet deep with a single look. "Logan, what are you talking about?" Her voice is calm and crisp.

"Remember the paperwork I had to submit in Bozeman?"

I see the moment her world tilts. Her lips part and she blinks at me. "Wait..."

My stomach growls; we should order a pizza. I have a feeling this is going to take a while.

She glares at me before words explode out of her. "We haven't even talked about marriage!"

Odin runs into the room and glances at me, so I keep my voice calm.

"And now we don't need to," I say. "I've already taken care of it."

Planting her palms on her hips, she walks in a tight circle while staring at the ground. The pieces are falling into place for her, but she's still not quite seeing the big picture. She throws up her hands, slicing me with a glare. "I don't even know what to say to you right now!"

"I mean..." I offer a small shrug. "A *thank-you* would be nice."

Her jaw drops.

"I needed to make sure if something ever happened, the shop would be yours," I explain.

And mine.

Togetherly ever after.

She shakes her head. "You're lying to me."

"I wouldn't lie about this."

She glares at me for a good ten seconds. "What the fuck?" she says, her voice going up an octave. With a red face and eyes that are practically bulging, she asks, "Why can't you just put me in your will like a normal fucking person?"

Easy. I'm not a normal fucking person. What in God's name gave her that idea? "Look, you've always been mine, Chaos. All I did was file the paperwork to make it legal."

"You cannot be serious right now. Do you understand how messed up this is?" Her voice pitches high at the end, and Odin's ears twitch at the shrill sound.

I shrug.

Her hand gestures are out of control. She's kind of adorable with her little fists flying around like that.

"A shrug? Your apology for acting *absolutely insane* is a fucking *shrug*? You don't even sound remorseful!"

I chuckle with a knitted brow. "What part of that sounded like an apology to you?" My mouth curves up in a smirk, and I shake my head. "I'm not sorry."

She gapes at me. Damn, she is *big* mad. "You!" Her voice is almost guttural, cartoonish; despite it all, my amusement is at an all-time high. I roll my lips together to keep from laughing.

Her eyes shoot daggers at me as she sweeps her arm to the side, pointing to the door. "Get out."

Odin hears "out" and hurries to the door. *She's not talking to you, dude.*

"No, thanks." I sigh and flop down on the sofa, threading my fingers behind my head. "I think I'll stay."

"Get the fuck out of my house." She takes a deep breath. "Now."

I kick my feet up on the coffee table. "I'm not leaving."

"Fine! Then I'll call the police," she says, whipping out her phone.

"Call them. I'm your husband. I live here. They aren't going to kick me out just because you're suddenly having buyer's remorse."

She spins in a circle as if something around here is going to help any of this make sense. Now it's her time to spiral. Poor thing.

Odin trots back into the room and jumps on the sofa with me. "Have you been letting him on the couch? I thought we decided on no furniture?"

"This is outrageous," she mutters to herself.

"Look, you can be mad all you want, but I am your husband and it's my job to keep you safe." I scratch Odin behind the ears while her sanity circles the drain.

Her arms fall at her sides, and then she raises the phone again. "I'm still gonna call the police and report what you did! I never signed any papers agreeing to this."

My arms stretch out across the back of the couch, and Odin rests his head in my lap. "You really wanna send Thor back to prison?"

She unlocks the screen. "What does Thor have to do with any of this?"

"He's your proxy, sweetheart. What do you think happens to felons who are involved in falsifying government documents?"

She gapes at me. "How could you put him at risk like that?"

"Hey, I'm not putting him at risk." I hold up my hands. "You are."

The phone clatters to the floor. *Crisis averted.*

"How dare you put this on me! You know what, fuck this." She jabs a finger in my direction. "And fuck you, too. If you won't leave, then I will. Come on, Odie."

Odin bounds off the sofa as she storms past me. I leap off the couch and cross the room in three giant strides to snatch her keys off the wall before she can reach them.

"Goddamn it. Give me those!"

The way her hands ball into fists at her sides makes me bark out a laugh. Does she really think she's in control right now?

She holds an open palm in front of me. "Please, Logan?"

Nice try.

"'Please' isn't going to work this time, babe. I made you a married woman without your permission. Do you think holding you here against your will is that difficult? Come on."

Her eyes well with tears. "Logan, how could you?"

She's faking. She's not sad, she just happens to cry when she's really pissed off, and now she's trying to use that side effect to her advantage. "Cute crocodile tears."

"Ugh!" she exclaims.

I stalk toward her and tuck a strand of wild hair behind her ear; her top lip curls and she swats my hand away. "I promise I'll give you the wedding of your dreams when you're ready. You won't miss out on anything. I'll buy you whatever dress you want, all the flowers, we can invite as many people—"

Her chin quivers before she grimaces. "You've never even said you love me." Her words hit me like a slap.

Damn.

I peer down at her while gently angling her face to meet mine. "Haven't I?"

"No." Then she *actually* slaps me, pointing up at me. "And don't you dare say it now!" She stomps toward the hallway while I'm left rubbing the sharp sting on my cheek.

"Oh, sorry, did you want to say it first?" I call after her, with a little attitude.

She spins on her heel. "You act like this is no big deal. How can you joke right now? Ugh!"

"*You act* like this wasn't inevitable . . . And I can't help it. Rage looks good on you." I'm also fired up after that slap. I'll give her a pass on the physical outburst. Honestly? I had it coming.

The tears fall, and she backs toward the hallway. "I hate you!"

No, she doesn't. "Aww. Is this our first fight?"

"It's about to be our last!" she shouts, spinning around and walking down the hall toward the bedroom.

"I sure hope not!" I yell. "You're kinda sexy when you're mad."

She marches back, only to get a good look at me smiling. "I've never been so angry with you, Logan Teller. When we get divorced, I'm taking the dog!"

Odin glances between us.

I laugh. "Why don't you go take a shower, and I'll order us a pizza. You'll feel much better after you eat."

She shakes her head at me in disgust. "This isn't over!"

"I know, Chaos," I mutter.

She clomps away. Then bolts back. *Again.* I plop back down on the couch and rest my elbows on my knees, waiting for her next shot at getting in the last word. It's like she can't decide whether she wants to slam a door in my face or keep berating me.

"I'm gonna bankrupt you seven times over with the diamond you're putting on my finger."

My grin stretches ear to ear, and I cluck my tongue. "It came pretty close." I'd already been saving for a couple years by the time I bought it.

She bares her teeth at me, unsatisfied by my glee at her statement. I can't help but laugh when she storms off for the third—or is it fourth?—time.

"And you're sleeping on the fucking couch!" she screams before throwing the bedroom door shut.

I lean back, kicking my feet up again and scrolling through my phone while selecting her favorite pizza toppings on the delivery app. "We'll see about that," I mutter. "*Wife.*"

43

KELLY

I'm still shaking with anger an hour later. He ordered a pizza and set it on the hallway table outside the bedroom door for me like I'm some fucking prisoner. He left other gifts for me: a bottle of bourbon, my favorite licorice, and a few bottles of water.

What an asshole.

He might be able to keep me inside the house, but the bedroom is mine tonight. That's where he's locked out. He doesn't get to sleep in this bed next to me, not after what he did. Not after keeping secrets and betraying my trust in a way I didn't even know was fucking possible.

Nothing says *fuck you* like making him sleep in another room. For someone as controlling as Logan, that's practically a death sentence. The only thing worse would be . . . *would be forcing him to listen to me having a good time when he's not allowed to watch.* There's no low I won't stoop to right now.

I storm over to the side of my bed, ripping the drawer out of the nightstand with too much force, and it clatters to the floor, sending a few of my vibrators flying. Whatever. I scan my modest collection of toys, opting for the least discreet one with the loudest buzz. Unlikely he'll hear it over the classical music he's playing in *my* living room. On *my* speakers. I'm so glad he's enjoying his evening.

He softly raps at the door. "Everything okay?" he asks. "I heard a crash."

I huff out a breath. *Crash. You're about to hear a lot more than that.*

"No, everything is not okay. You married me without my permission!"

"Really? Are we still doing this?"

My jaw stiffens at the audacity this man has. This is a side of Logan I've never seen before. He doesn't seem to care about any of this. His level of delusion is aspirational. It's certifiable.

I don't respond and simply remove my sweatpants and climb on my bed, pushing my underwear to the side and turning on the toy. It comes to life, louder than I even remember. My lips curl into a smug, pissed-off grin. Fuck you.

His footsteps grow quiet as he walks away. I'm getting off tonight, whether he hears me or not; it's not relief, it's retaliation. Slowing my inhales, I attempt to relax, rolling my shoulders back. Masturbating while angry is much harder than I anticipated. My thighs ache, and I'm too enraged by what he did to focus.

He *married* me.

Without asking. Without even telling me. And if I hadn't pressed him today, I still wouldn't know.

The music stops, and his stomps grow louder until I see the shadow of him blocking out the light through the space under the door. *Now I've got his attention.* I sigh breathlessly. Then a second time, louder again. Half fake.

He pounds on the door, making me smile. That's satisfaction. He's been mashing my buttons, mocking my anger to get me worked up. Two can play at that game. *I can incite violence too, you prick.*

"Kelly," he growls out.

God, I wish I could see his face. Jaw tight, eyes narrowed, fists balled, *dick hard.*

Now I'm getting into it. Arching my back into the soft duvet cover, I moan. Long and loud.

"You think you can get a rise out of me with your little show, Chaos?"

Ten bucks says I already have.

"Open the door," he demands.

"Fuck you."

I change the rhythm of the vibrator to a pulse.

"Open the door."

This time I hum his name.

"If you call my name one more time, I'll—"

"What? You'll come? Blow down my house?" I chuckle, rolling my eyes. "You're not the big bad wolf, Logan."

I trace the vibrator over my thighs and press it to my clit again.

"No, I'm worse." I hate how sexy that sounded. "You really think a hollow-core door and a temper tantrum are enough to keep me out?"

I whimper his name again, letting my lids flutter closed.

His dark chuckle on the other side of the door tells me I hit my mark. Eat your heart out. "Lo—"

Boom! The door splinters and swings open, bouncing off the doorstop with a rattle.

I flinch and scramble backward to the head of the bed, vibrator still buzzing in my hand. *Holy shit.* He just broke the door.

"Get out," I say, kneeling on the bed in my underwear and a T-shirt, trying to act like I'm unfazed by the fact that he just broke down my bedroom door.

"No."

"You don't get me tonight," I snarl.

He stalks toward me. "I get you whenever the fuck I want. I'm your husband, remember?"

I see red. Nobody talks to me like that, husband or not. *He thinks he can threaten my consent?* My hand is flying out to crack across his cheek before I can stop it. I've never slapped anyone in my life, and tonight I've done it twice.

He presses his tongue into his cheek and sucks his teeth. "I really wish you would stop doing that."

"Don't talk to me like that," I warn. "Ever!"

"Why?" He sharpens his gaze at me. "You used to love it when I called you mine."

I shake my head. "That was different."

"It wasn't. That's why you locked me out, Chaos. You wanted me to hear you moaning and coming. You wanted to make me suffer because deep down, you know you're still mine, and that pisses you off, doesn't it?"

It enrages me.

I spin around and pluck a pillow off the bed. "Couch. Now," I grit while hurling it at him.

He chuckles and catches it in his arms. "This is where I'm sleeping. And now that the cat's out of the bag, I'm not going another night without you by my side."

He tosses the pillow in front of me, stalking closer, so I snatch it up and shove it into his chest. "You want to be my husband? Practice doing it from the living room."

Logan smiles. "You're angry."

"No shit."

The room is silent, save for the loud-as-fuck vibrator stuttering around in between the pillows somewhere.

"I hate you," I sneer.

"You already said that."

I press my palms to his chest and shove him as hard as I can—hard enough to make him grunt. He doesn't move, so I budge him a second time, forcing him toward the door. He steps backward, letting me push him until his back hits the wall next to the exit. He doesn't fight it or remove my hands from him, though I'm sure he easily could, and then there's a flicker of guilt in his eyes.

I yell at him, I don't even know what I'm shouting, but I need to let it out. He just stands there and takes it, accepting my anger. He knows he deserves it.

I hate how unaffected he appears on the surface. I hate that he planned all of this. I hate that he used Thor against me. I hate that he bested me at every turn. I hate that I'm wet and wanting him. Mostly, I hate that no matter how much I try to hate him, *I can't*.

With my fists still curled in his shirt, I yank him off the wall and shove him backward onto the bed, where he waits motionless. Again, he doesn't smile or act smug . . . he takes it.

I tear at his belt and zipper, and he assists in helping me shove his pants down. Of course he's hard and slick with pre-cum. I tug the hem of his shirt, and he grabs the collar at the back of his neck and pulls his shirt off, then shimmies farther back onto the mattress and props himself up on his elbows. After dragging my underwear down my legs, I kick them off, then grip his jeans at the ankles and yank them off in two big swoops before chucking them into a corner of the room.

He hums when I climb onto the bed and straddle him.

"I want you," he whispers, lifting his hips so his cock presses into me right where I want it.

"I know." I press my fingers to his forehead and shove him, and he drops onto his back. "This isn't make-up sex," I say, removing his glasses. "This is hate sex. Pick a safeword."

"You want *me* to pick a safeword?" He laughs. "You think you can make me tap out?" A slow smile creeps onto his face, and I widen my eyes in warning. He schools his amusement and swallows.

"Matrimony," he spits.

"Cute." *This motherfucker.*

Straddling him, I grind against his cock, digging my fingers into his shoulders for leverage. He wants to own me, I'll own him right back and make sure there are marks to prove it.

He lies down, and I lean forward, brushing my lips over his. He kisses me, and I bite his bottom lip until he groans and I taste copper. Sitting up, I tug my shirt over my head and toss it on the floor. Let him stare. Make him wait. Make him watch.

He smirks at me, and that's all the evidence I need to know that I need to remind him who is in control right now.

"You look so—"

"Don't speak," I hiss. His voice is a weapon, one that can easily be used against me, and I'm not giving him the opportunity.

He rolls his shoulders and tenses, not liking that answer, but I don't give a single fuck.

"You aren't going to make a peep. You aren't going to touch me. You aren't even going to come. You are only here to get me off. *I* am using *you.*"

I slide over his pulsing cock and get into position, lining his tip against my entrance and lowering myself onto his thick length inch by inch.

He exhales, and a light sweat breaks out on his forehead. He clutches the sheets at his sides instead of my hips. I rock against him, and his hands twitch. It makes me feel powerful to watch his restraint fray. His gaze burns my flesh, but still, he obeys my wishes.

With my knees at his sides, I move up and down slowly and watch him unravel.

"You married me without asking."

He swallows.

"You took that moment from me. You stole my choice—*my agency*—the most valuable thing I have as a woman. You fucking took it."

He grits his teeth as I stretch around his size, sighing and squeezing his lids shut.

"Look at me."

He blinks open, his eyes all fire and lethality. "You're going to give it back. You're done running the show."

He fidgets as I reclaim my control, releasing an agitated growl.

"I trusted you, but you didn't offer me the same courtesy. You didn't trust me with information about Billy. Didn't trust me with Black

Rabbit. Didn't trust that I would have chosen you if you'd only fucking *asked*."

He opens his mouth—but my hands find his neck, squeezing. "Not a fucking word. You're lucky I'm letting you breathe." My other palm presses into his chest, and I sink my nails into his flesh.

"You know why you didn't?" I ask rhetorically. "Because you were afraid."

His abs spasm, but he's smart to know not to fuck with me right now. This isn't the time for his arrogance and cocky demeanor.

I lean down, pressing my tits against his chest, and whisper in his ear, my hot breath teasing his neck. "And you were right to be afraid . . . Do you really think you're the only one who's capable of crazy?"

I sit up, rocking against his cock, taking a few selfish seconds to just appreciate how fucking good he feels inside me.

The rumble in his chest is threatening, but I'm not frightened by him. He's already done the worst thing he could do by betraying my trust. Reaching back with both hands, I grasp his thighs and roll my hips. Fucking myself on him. He bites his swollen bottom lip, spreading some of the bright red blood.

His eyes widen as he takes me in, watching and painfully resisting.

I lean forward, prying the duvet out of his fists, and pin his wrists on either side of his shoulders as I bring myself closer to the edge. *Fuck, he feels good.*

He's holding on by a thread as I glide up and down his length.

"You thought marrying me would grant you ownership? More power over me?" I chuckle. "No, you just handed me the reins."

He groans. The pulse point in his neck looks like it might pop. I let go of one of his wrists to brush my thumb over the drop of blood, smearing it.

He whimpers—*fucking whimpers*—and I've never felt more fierce.

"Shhh," I coo. "This is what you wanted. You sealed your fate," I explain. "Next time, be more careful choosing the type of chaos you make your wife. I can be just as dark as you, darling." I lick the smeared blood from his lip.

His breath catches, and I turn his head, pressing his cheek into the mattress so he can no longer see me. "You don't get to watch me come," I say coldly.

I ride him hard, cruel and punishing. It's empty. I'm accomplishing a task. I don't stop or slow, I just move. The fizzling rage explodes into a million little pieces when I come. My hips undulate like I'm draining every last ounce of ecstasy he can offer me. My moan is raw and wild as I take everything he has. It's mine. *He* is mine.

The blinding euphoria subsides, and I'm left panting on top of him, coming down from the natural high of power, or pleasure, I'm not sure which.

He's still stunned into silence.

He's done.

I destroyed him.

I won—

His hand shoots up and seizes my throat. I cough at losing the inhale I didn't have a chance to take. Not enough to hurt, just enough to take back his control. I set my jaw and we have a stare-off.

"Do you feel better now?" His voice is hoarse and gritty.

With my nails digging into his chest, he flips us. He straddles my waist and dips his head to my ear, licking up my neck and biting the lobe before he whispers, "Remember my safeword."

Shit.

In less than a second, I go from ruler to ruled—but I'm not handing it over, he's going to have to earn it. He's going to work for it. *Hard.* I'm enraged all over again. Angry that he's turning the tables, and furious for knowing me so well, knowing I love it.

"You think I forgot who I am just because I gave you a turn?" he growls. "You think I don't know the woman I married?"

He slams into me, causing us both to groan. His hips snap with each thrust. White spots blink in the corners of my vision. He fucks like we're at war. Maybe we are.

He's reminding me just what kind of man I'm tied to. "You're the devil," I spit.

"Tell me, *wife*," he says, "how does the devil fuck?"

I gasp at the sheer arrogance he has . . . It's undeniably sexy. I don't care if that means I'm broken. He likes me that way. There's no response that won't stroke his ego, so I seal my lips shut.

"I know exactly what you are, Chaos. That's *why* I married you. I see the darkness you harbor, the violence you try to hide. But you can't hide from me. *I chose you for the parts you bury in the shadows.*"

He pins my wrists in one of his hands above my head and massages my sensitive clit with the other, his fingers torturously slow as he gives me a taste of my own medicine.

Logan is vicious and demanding of my body, but when I gaze into his eyes, they're filled with adoration. With pride. With *respect*.

"Your wickedness . . . Your depravity . . . they only feed the man who fucks you."

My body contracts around him as he nudges me closer to another orgasm. "The devil," I correct.

"Oh, sweetheart, I'm worse than the devil. *I'm your match.*"

I moan as he takes me, claims me, *chooses me*.

"Now," he says, his voice more agreeable, "you're going to come for me and get the rest of this rage out. We're not going to bed angry. I will fuck the fight out of you if I have to."

"You don't have the fucking stamina," I snarl.

"Try me," he snarls, putting his face in front of mine. He says it so quickly, with so much confidence, I think he'd do it just to spite me.

He kisses me softly, and I hate it.

Dipping his head, his lips graze over my neck. "Do you remember our wedding night in Bozeman? You wore my white shirt . . . the one that fit you like a dress."

That's why he made me wear it. Sick fuck.

"Don't," I threaten, looking away and squeezing my eyes shut, tears pricking at the corners. That night was special to me because it was the first time we had sex. But it's special to him for a different reason.

I'm jealous he has a memory that I don't.

"Fuck, you made a beautiful bride—"

I'm done. I want to stop. I don't want to come.

"Matrimony."

He freezes midstroke, and the tension in the room clears like somebody opened up a window. Before I even realize it, he's pulled out and is releasing my wrists. His weight disappears like he's vanished into thin air.

"Look at me," he says. "You're in control again."

I face him and see the reassurance in his eyes. "Was it the sex or the things I said? Are you hurt?"

I shake my head. "What you said. I just . . . I needed to stop."

He nods.

It's weird he's not fighting me on it; I would have expected him to.

"Do you want to talk about it?"

"We will absolutely be talking about it. But not right now."

He nods again, opening his mouth to speak, but then he closes it.

Whatever he's thinking pains him. His gaze searches mine. "Can I hold you?"

"I'm still mad," I whisper, looking up at him. It's not a total lie, but the fury I held earlier has quieted to a simmer. Sadder.

"I know," he replies. His brows still raised, he waits for my permission to touch me.

He settles in next to me, wraps his arms around my middle, and folds me into his chest. I don't have the energy to be stubborn. His fingers linger on my back, and his lips brush over my temple.

I close my eyes and allow myself to lean into him the way I want, melt into him, and accept the comfort he's offering. Somehow, that's enough for me.

For now.

44

LOGAN

She lets me take her to work, but the drive is silent. She barely even said any words to Odin when we dropped him off at my place for the day. I might be on thin ice in July, but we shared a bed last night, and for that, I'm grateful.

She's prepping her station when I enter my office and remove the wooden box from the shelf. The one with Clyde's letters for his daughter. This wasn't how I planned to give it to her, but this wasn't how any of this was supposed to go. Whether or not the timing is right, she deserves to have it.

WHEN KELLY GETS ENGAGED

I tap the corner of the envelope on my desktop until I finally get the nerve to stand up and walk it over to her station. I breathe a sigh of relief when she's not there, then set it neatly on the countertop where I know she'll see it.

I had a long session this morning, but we finished up at three, and I've barely left my office since. I looked up several times while tattooing, hoping to see her gazing back at me, but it never happened. She never glanced in my direction. Not once did I feel her eyes on me. It has me fucking rattled.

I open my desk drawer and peek at the black velvet box, then close it again.

Open the drawer.

Close the drawer.

Open the drawer.

Fuck... Close the drawer.

I've been dying to see her wear it for so long that it's on her finger in my dreams. But I'll own my mistakes. I fucked up on this one. She was right about what she said yesterday; I took her choice. Her agency. Something that is precious to her. I want to make it up to her. Not to apologize, but to respect her. To ask before taking. To give her the chance to say yes.

I gave her the letter this morning, and it wasn't there anymore while I was tattooing my client. I can't tell if she's just making me sweat or if I've truly broken something that can't be repaired.

The calendar on the computer screen shows she's wrapping up an appointment now. Which gives me twenty minutes before her next client comes in.

Twenty minutes.

Open the drawer.

This time, I allow my fingers to skim over the soft velvet as I pull it out and set it in front of me on my desk. Opening the box, I inhale. I had it designed over a year ago and finally made the last payment a few months back.

On a simple gold band rests a dazzling pear-shaped diamond, with a few smaller stones clustered around it. It's a beautiful harmony of effortless elegance and striking sophistication. I tilt the box, and the stone catches the overhead lights, ricocheting tiny sparkles across the wall. It's a unique design that is hers alone, made to exist on her finger or not at all.

I'll leave that up to her, give her that option, because I'm going to honor what she told me last night. I'm done making her decisions. I'm giving her agency back.

I close the box and take out my phone, sending her a text message.

Me: When you have a minute, can I see you in the office?

Air rushes out of my lungs after I hit send; I'm really doing this. I owe it to Kelly. I glimpse at the photo of Clyde on the wall; *I owe it to him too.*

When she walks in, I stand, hovering my hand over the velvet box and closing it in my fist. She shuts the door behind her with a soft click while I circle the desk. Kelly stands in front of me, arms crossed. Closed off and still pissed. *Valid.*

I hold the box between us, and her eyes turn into saucers. She opens her mouth to speak, but I go first.

"This isn't an apology. It's not to make up for what I did," I say. "It can't undo what I've already done."

She doesn't speak. She doesn't whisper. She hardly breathes.

"I married you without your permission," I say, admitting what I've done out loud. We both deserve to hear those words said without any excuses to follow. I don't regret marrying her, but I regret breaking her trust.

"I thought I was fixing something, but instead I broke something else. I didn't stop to think about what I was taking from you by making that choice for you."

She swallows. "You're proposing?"

"I'm giving you your agency back." I open the ring box. She blinks, and the sparkles from the ring reflect in her rich-green eyes. "Taking this ring doesn't mean you forgive me. I want to give you the chance to choose the future I forced you into. To choose the life I plan to give you. Maybe not right now, but in some version of our future together . . . you choose me back, the way I choose you. Not because I made the decision, but because *you* did."

A beat of silence settles around us.

"What if I say no?" she asks.

The question hollows out my chest. I gulp down my fear, not letting myself look down at my feet to hide from her glare. "If you say no, then you say no. I'll still be yours."

Her gaze leaves the ring and focuses on me. Like allowing me to look into her eyes is the last favor she'll ever grant me. She pins me with a glare. "Are you going to say it?"

I lower my chin. "Say what?"

"You know what."

That I love her.

Yeah, I want to say it. I want to say it so fucking bad it feels like it's going to crawl up my throat whether I like it or not. I want to fall at her feet and recite all the things I love about her even if it takes me all day.

"Not yet."

She nods, swallowing back tears. "Why not?"

"Because it's not fair to you. You're allowed to still be angry," I say. "Even if you feel the same way about me as I feel about you . . . We both know you don't want to say those words to me today. It would be forcing your hand again, and I refuse to put you in that position . . . And truthfully, I might be tough, Chaos, but I'm not strong enough to say those words to you and not hear them echoed back."

It would destroy me.

This has to be on her time, not mine. I won't do that to her twice.

"Thank you," she replies, her voice hushed.

She steps closer and takes the box from me and closes the lid with a soft click. She doesn't put it on but doesn't give it back. *And that's some fucking hope.*

"This isn't yes," she states.

I nod. "I understand."

She walks out and I let her. No more cages. No leashes. No binding documents. This time, she only comes back to me if she wants to. If she chooses me. It's up to her.

It's toward the end of the day when Casper knocks on my door and steps in, then shuts the door behind him and drops into the chair across from my desk. *Finally.* I've been waiting to catch up with him all day about the information he found, but almost every one of his back-to-back appointments ran long.

He gets right down to business. "Found him." He tosses his phone on my desk and I pick it up, staring at the screen. This can't be right.

"Hospice?"

"Billy's not our guy." Casper sits back in the chair, getting comfortable. "I ran background, checked care records, there's nothing. It's a dead end."

"You're going to have to sell me on that one," I say. "He could have somebody."

He shakes his head. "I did a deep dive on that fucker. He's an asshole, yeah, but he's been in hospice for like six months. The dude is on his deathbed. That letter you got? I think that's all it is. A letter. Amends. Whatever you want to call it."

I scrub a hand down my face. *No fucking way.*

"I looked into Jason."

My gaze snaps to his.

"I went over and talked with his neighbors, asked them if he was around the night those photos were taken."

"What are you, fucking Dick Tracy?" The guy knows how to find out information, that's for sure. Casper is skilled when it comes to digging up dirt, and his observation skills are unmatched.

"No, asshole. I'm just really fucking charming."

I roll my eyes. He does have a weird way of getting people to talk.

"Anyway, they said he was gone on a work trip. They collected his mail for him."

"So, it wasn't him?"

Casper shakes his head. "Not necessarily. There's a hotel straight out from you. With balconies. Guess what else the neighbors said? He has a fucking drone."

Leaning forward, I prop both elbows on my desk and massage my temples. "Wait, Kelly showed a picture of Jason to Rosa. She said it wasn't him."

There's a knock at my door. "Later!" I shout. Probably Frankie telling me she's heading out and asking if there's anything I need before she leaves. I've been waiting for this conversation all damn day, I don't want any interruptions.

"Well, maybe Rosa didn't get a good look at him! Maybe she doesn't remember. The height lined up. The description lined up. Clean cut? At a tattoo expo? Come on, man."

"Shit." Kelly had it right. It was Jason. I've let her down a second time.

Casper kicks up his feet on my desk like he owns the place. He doesn't, but he's earned the right to act like he does after getting this info.

"But what's his motive?"

Casper shrugs. "Revenge . . . What would you do if some asshole walked in and sabotaged your relationship with Kelly?"

I'd burn the world to ash.

Goddamn it. I chose the wrong guy and left her exposed to him. Vulnerable. I got so caught up in my own hatred toward Billy that I let it cloud my judgment. I swallow down some of the anger, but I can feel it climbing up the back of my neck like flames.

"You're sure it's Jason?" Figure I should double-check before I commit homicide.

"I'm sure enough that I wouldn't let Kelly sleep alone tonight."

I scrub a hand down my face. This should incite fear in me, but it doesn't.

It's fury running through my veins. Rage. Rage at Jason. Rage at myself for not listening to her, not seeing what was right in front of me.

"Okay, then," I say.

Casper cocks a brow. "You gonna tell her?"

"I'll tell her when I'm finished."

"Hey." He lowers his feet from the desk. "Are you going to do something you'll regret?"

That makes me chuckle. "I won't regret this. But will you stay with her until I'm done?" I stand, grabbing my wallet and phone. Shit, I missed a couple text messages.

"Sure thing."

"Anything else I should know?" I ask, hoping there aren't any surprises when I show up at his house to beat him senseless.

"Yeah," he drawls with a smirk. "What the fuck is on Kelly's finger?"

45

KELLY

I read Dad's letter one more time.

    Hey kid—

    If you're reading this, you've either found your soul mate, or are being incredibly reckless with your heart. Either way, congratulations.

    PS I'm not sure what condition Logan was in when he handed this envelope to you, but in my heart of hearts, I hope like hell he was smiling when he gave it to you . . . and if he wasn't, go easy on the man today.

    I'm gonna be real with you for a second. You're a lot like your mom. Beautiful, smart, and kind, but you also possess the same spark she did. She didn't just light up faces when she walked into a room, she lit the whole damn house on fire. That's a lot to handle for most people. So, I pray whoever you picked showed up with a box of matches and not an extinguisher. Don't fall for weak men who try to shrink you in order to make it easier on themselves. Extinguishers don't stand a chance with an Everhart woman. You want someone who will help you burn brighter and hotter, who will feed and fan your flames until the whole place burns to the ground.

    Remember what I said about seeing yourself in them? Who you choose to spend your life with matters not just on the day of your wedding, but every fucking day, because that's what love takes. You have to choose each other every day. Life will try to come between you. Choose each other anyway.

    If he's your soul mate—really your soul mate—then you'll always pick each other no matter what tries to pull you apart. Even when you're both full of piss and vinegar. Even when your pride is too great. Even when it hurts.

    Love you.
    Dad

I wipe my tears away. It feels like the two of them are conspiring against me. The velvet box is heavier than it looks. I open it and take another peek at the most beautiful ring I've ever seen. Delicate and dazzling. I should have expected this from him. Something with this kind of attention to detail, something so perfect and exactly what I would have chosen for myself.

Logan shouldn't have made that decision for me. He messed up. Badly. But we aren't done yet.

I remove the sparkling promise from the box and slip it on my left ring finger.

I'm choosing to wear it.

I'm choosing him. Even when it hurts.

Holding my hand in front of me, I bite my lip with a small smile. I can't help it. I'm still pissed, but not as much as I once was. One diamond ring—one really gorgeous diamond ring—doesn't wipe the slate clean, but it gives us a chance. And we're worth a chance.

We've done this whole thing in reverse. First marriage, then a proposal . . . but stunning diamonds and paper certificates are meaningless without his love. I appreciate him letting me have my emotions. Just because I'm not ready to hear the words today doesn't mean it's not the thing I've waited the longest to hear and what I've craved the most.

After folding the letter, I carefully place it back into the envelope, and then Frankie pops her head into my station. "Hey, I'm on my way out, but there's a Rosa up at the desk for you?"

Casper pauses outside my station, glancing down at my finger briefly and whistling. I tuck my hand into my pocket before Frankie sees and causes a scene. *She's going to lose her fucking mind when I tell her.* Casper heads back to Logan's office and shuts the door behind him.

"She's here?"

It feels like weeks since I saw her last after everything that's happened.

"Oh. Yeah! I'll be right up."

I head to the front and there she is, wearing a smile on her face and enormous sunglasses. "Hey!"

She wraps me in a tight hug, then pushes me to arm's length. "I know. I'm ambushing you. But it's my last night, let's go grab a drink. Happy hour. My treat. I won't take no for an answer."

I hesitate. Not because I don't want to see her, because I do—but Logan was going to take me home, and it's not like we have a shortage of things to talk about.

"Yeah. Yeah, just let me just go tell Logan. He was my ride."

"No biggie, I can drop you off afterward." She waves me off, backing out the door. "I've got the rental car out front. Just come find me when you're done."

I head back and knock on Logan's office door.

"Later!" he barks.

Yikes.

I'm sure Casper is in there giving him hell about the ring. Instead, I pull out my phone and text him.

Me: It's Rosa's last night in town and I told her I'd see her before she heads out. I'm going to have a couple drinks and then she'll bring me to your place. Promise. I've got my key.

I wait for three dots to pop up, but it's still unread. A car horn honks in the distance, so I clutch my purse and stuff my phone inside, then hurry out the front door. Just one drink. Two tops.

I already made my choice; the ring is on my finger. I'm sure he's not going to like it, but he needs to give me this. This will be a good way for him to show he can trust me. I'm safe with friends. He has her number. We're good.

Rosa honks again before I'm even off the curb.

I climb into the spotless car and reach for the seat belt to buckle up, and Rosa snatches my left hand.

"Oh my God!" Her grip tightens as she glares at the ring. "Is this—is this—"

I blink at her, wearing a guilty smile and shrugging. "It's a long story."

"I've got time." She scoffs, shoving me away from her. I'm not sure she has enough time for this one. "I just saw you! When did this even happen?"

"Technically—" I sigh. "We're already married. That's the long part . . . Remember when I was in Montana for the expo and we were out getting drinks? Apparently, I was also getting married."

"You know?" she asks.

I cock my head. "Know what?"

"I mean, he's *just* telling you this now? That was weeks ago! He didn't tell you until now?" she shrills.

I nod. "Yeah. It's called a proxy marriage, it's legal in Montana. Yes, yes, it's crazy. I-I don't know. It's a weird situation."

Her jaw unhinges, and she stares at me. But she's not really looking at me, she's looking through me. "And now he gave you a ring?"

"I didn't know until recently. Really recently," I say, trying to ease the weird vibe. "I was livid when I found out. I'm still mad. But . . ."

Her eyes focus on me again.

"So when is the divorce party?" she asks, putting the car in gear and pulling away from the shop.

I chuckle. "I understand it looks bad. But . . . I can't walk away. I'm not okay with what happened, but . . . I love him more than hate him."

"Kelly!" She barks out a humorless laugh; it's loud and strange, almost like a scream. "He's being controlling! You aren't in love, you have Stockholm syndrome!"

"It's not a flattering look." I unlock my phone, checking to see if he read my text. Not yet.

"Give that to me," she says, glancing down at it in my lap.

"My phone?"

She steals it off my lap. "Wait—" I reach for it.

"Chill out. I'm just checking something . . ."

I keep my attention on the road since hers isn't. She taps the screen a couple times and gasps. "Look!" She holds it out in front of me. "He's been tracking your location!"

I take my phone back and roll my eyes. "He's being protective. That's only because of the stalker stuff."

"No, he's being domineering. You need to know the difference. I really think you need to look into a lawyer."

An uncomfortable silence hangs between us. I totally understand where she's coming from. It doesn't matter how many excuses I make for him—saying *You don't know him like I do* isn't going to help the situation at all, it just makes me sound like a stereotype.

"Sorry, it's just . . . that's crazy. That's insane behavior. You know that, right?"

"I do," I confirm. She's right, it is crazy. "But he didn't do it for control." Well, not *all* for control. He was trying to save Black Rabbit and me. If he hadn't saved my dad's shop, there's no way I could have.

I explain some of the details but jump around a lot in the story because she keeps interrupting with more questions. I can't blame her, it's a lot to take in. After a few minutes, she turns onto Hartford Avenue. Wait a minute, this is a residential neighborhood.

I furrow my brow and look around. "I thought we were going out for happy hour?"

"After what you just told me? Absolutely not! I need to hear the rest of this story without any distractions or having to talk over people."

"Aren't you staying at the hotel?"

"What?" She pulls into a driveway and parks. "No, this is my Airbnb."

"We're really close to Logan's loft, I can practically see it from here." Damn, I can just walk home after this.

She reaches into the back seat and grabs a bottle of wine and a bag.

"Well, that's convenient!" she says with a chuckle. "You like reds, right?"

I nod.

"All right! Let's hear the rest of this shitshow!"

46

LOGAN

I'm in my truck when Casper calls me, so I pick it up over the Bluetooth. I'm headed to Jason's place.

"Hey," I answer.

"Slight problem. Kelly isn't here anymore."

"What?" I bite, checking my phone. I forgot I missed a text earlier. I pull up the message and groan. "Fuck, she went out with Rosa. I'll give her a call. I don't want her out at the bars until I know where Jason is."

"Copy," he says. "Just let me know where they are headed and I'll go babysit."

"Sounds good." I end the call and open up the tracker to find out which bar she's at. The dot isn't there. I zoom out. Nothing. I click her name at the top of the screen: *Offline*.

"Damn it."

I click the phone app and tap her name. It goes straight to voicemail. I don't like that one bit. I try again . . . Then thrice more.

"Why the fuck isn't she picking up?" I punch the steering wheel as panic rises in my chest.

I haven't even told her about Jason, so she doesn't know who to look out for. What if he was watching Kelly at the shop and followed her to a bar? My thoughts spiral with worst-case scenarios of him slipping something into her drink or sneaking behind her into the bathroom.

Wait, I've got Rosa's number. I call her up. It rings twice and then goes to voicemail. The fuck? Is she dodging my calls too? Did she just bitch-block me?

Casper said Kelly was wearing the ring. She can't be that pissed that she wouldn't answer my calls.

I promised I wasn't going to make these choices for her, but her safety is nonnegotiable.

I text Rosa.

Me: Where are you?

Fuck it, Jason is going to have to wait, my priority now is Kelly. I call up Casper.

I check the phone again. Rosa leaves me on read.

"I can't get a hold of Kelly or Rosa. I'm gonna need your help."

47

KELLY

The red wine swirls in my glass while I sit perched on a barstool behind the peninsula countertop, surveying the space. When I returned from the bathroom, Rosa practically shoved it into my hand. She poured it into one of those large plastic wineglasses that have cheesy wine puns on them like *Cabernet? More like Caber-yay!*

"This Airbnb is cute," I comment. Sort of a staged-and-beiged vibe. It's probably an interior design style with one of those oxymoron names like *boho luxe*, which really just means there's a macramé wall tapestry on an overpriced stick hanging somewhere on the premises. "I figured you were staying at the Sable."

"Nah, I just like their cocktails. My company is way too cheap to spring for five-star hotels." Rosa stands in front of the open fridge. "Should I make a cheese plate? I've got some leftover Brie and apples from the other day."

"That sounds excellent!" I haven't eaten yet today and was a little disappointed when she said we weren't going to happy hour because I had my heart set on some appetizers. I'm starving.

She pulls out the ingredients and begins chopping up the apples. "Can I help with anything?"

"No, no, I've got this!" she replies.

This wine is sweet—almost too sweet, and slightly . . . metallic? I'm not even through my first glass and can already feel the warmth spreading into my limbs. "What kind of wine is this again?" I ask, glancing down at my phone and checking the text I sent to Logan.

"Uh, Summer Rhino or something? Okay, let's get back to your story!"

That's when I notice the little plane icon in the upper corner of my screen. Did Rosa put my phone on airplane mode? Logan is probably losing his damn mind. I take it off and see a bunch of missed calls and texts.

"Oh shit. I gotta call Logan and let him know we didn't end up going to a restaurant. If I don't, he'll burn down the city."

"Seriously?" She spins around with the knife in her hand, waving it around while she speaks. "Yes, I mind! You just got here! What, he can't go two damn minutes without knowing exactly where you are? I told you, he's controlling!"

Whoa.

"I just don't want him to worry." *Why is she so upset about this?* I appreciate her concern; if a friend told me the same story, I'd have some reservations too. But I know Logan better than she does. He's my best friend. "I promise, he'd never hurt me."

She grumbles something under her breath, but I don't hear it.

"Don't call him!" she spits, pointing the knife in my direction. I really wish she would put that thing down. "I will drop you off at his place in like an hour. He can go without you until then."

I hold my hands up and set my phone on the counter in an attempt to de-escalate whatever the hell is going on right now. "Okay, you're right, you're right." My foot bumps into one of the suitcases neatly lined up under the countertop, and when I slide them aside with my foot, one of them falls over.

"Shit. Sorry about that." I climb off my barstool, my head feeling heavier than usual, and stand the suitcase back up in line with the others. They still have the Bozeman baggage tags on them, but the date of the flight is all wrong; this is old.

"No worries!" she replies "Okay. Storytime. Go."

I push the suitcase next to the others and that's when I notice the ID tag. The neatly penned capital letters are right there, clear as day.

Piper Nygaard.

Not Rosa, *Piper.*

Piper who is supposed to be dead.

Piper who tried to kill my dad.

Piper who killed her own fucking dog.

My breaths come faster as my heart slams against my rib cage. *She's my stalker.* I walked right into this. I have to stay calm.

"Hey, do you mind if I snoop around a little first? I love these little places."

"Go for it."

I take a step toward the living room; I need to get to the door. My limbs are sluggish and heavy. *There's no way one glass would do this.*

She spins around, holding the wine bottle. "Need a top off?" she asks.

I flinch, pausing midstep, and blink at her—looking my stalker right in the eye. "I'm good, thanks," I answer brightly, padding out of the room. I brace the wall for support. Oh fuck.

Focus. Just get out. One step in front of the other. I glimpse behind me to make sure she's not watching before I wrap my hand around the door handle.

The door creaks like a banshee when I pull it open, and her footsteps have my insides plummeting.

"Where are you going?" she barks, suddenly much closer to me and still holding that fucking knife.

My stomach sinks, and I swallow. I wave her off. "Just needed some air, this wine is hitting me." I can't tell her I know, not while she's holding that damn paring knife.

She sighs. "Look, I'm really sorry about the phone thing. Why don't you just sit back down in the kitchen. You can video chat with him and let him know you'll be home in an hour." The cadence of her speech is strange, like she's trying too hard to seem casual. "I didn't mean to be all crazy about it." *Crazy? No, crazy is impulsively tattooing your forehead.* She's way beyond that. I'm waiting for this lady to turn into Kathy Bates and *Misery* me.

"Okay." I give her a tight smile and nod.

"Come on," she says. "Come back and sit down."

She wants me to contact him through video chat so she can listen to our conversation and make sure I don't say anything I'm not supposed to.

I nod and follow her back to the kitchen, plucking a potted plant from one of the tables on my way. I set it on the counter in front of me and lean my phone against it. My hand shakes when I hit the video call icon near Logan's name.

He answers immediately. "Jesus Christ! I've been trying to get a hold of you."

Rosa leans against the countertop with her arms crossed as she watches me closely.

I clear my throat and drop my eyes to my phone screen. "Yeah, sorry I missed your calls. I'm just with Rosa at the house she's renting. We're having some wine." I hold up the glass.

That must appease her because she turns her back to me and begins slicing through the Brie.

I blink and my body sways. *Fuck*. Keep it together.

Then it hits me.

"Rosa is making us a snack, but what do you want for dinner tonight?" I ask while signing "*help*."

He cocks an eyebrow, and I shake my head while placing my index finger over my lips.

"How does tofu sound?" he asks. I hate tofu. He knows I hate tofu.

"I'd love that. Maybe a stir-fry?" I nod to him.

"What do you want on the side?" he asks. My thoughts are already foggy and now I'm trying to speak two different languages at the same fucking time. I relax my shoulders. The more relaxed I am, the easier the words will come. Not to mention my dexterity is clumsier, thanks to whatever drug is coursing through my system.

"Carrots," I say, while trying to remember the street name. The image of the sign flashes in my mind and I spell letters with my fingers "*H-A-R-T-F-O-R-D*."

"What else?" he asks. I think I see his pulse ticcing through the phone.

"Zucchini." *It was Hartford and Third.* I hold up my thumb, index, and middle finger, and twist my wrist for "*Third*."

"I'll pick some up from the store," he says. "Anything else you want?"

"Um . . ." I try to think of the house number, but I can't picture it. *Fuck, how do I tell him where I am?* Damn it, I can't even think of stir-fry ingredients to keep this bullshit conversation going.

"Mushrooms?" he asks.

"Yes! Mushrooms!" I press my index finger to my chin and curl it twice—"*Red*." Then I lift my hands, press my fingertips together in the shape of a roofline, dragging them down and apart at an angle, then straight down. "*House. Red house.*"

There were a few red houses on this block; he won't know which one. I try to remember anything unique about the exterior. I sign the letter *B*, then twist my wrist twice. "*Blue*."

"I can do that. When do you think you'll be home?" he asks.

I pinch my fingers together in front of my mouth. "*Bird*."

"Maybe an hour," I reply out loud.

Logan quickly signs back, "*What is blue bird? Street?*"

I shake my head in reply.

My thoughts are fuzzy, and I lean forward on the counter to keep from falling off my stool. Every blink becomes heavier.

How do I sign drugged*?*

I don't remember, so instead I sign *poison*.

"I can pick you up so she doesn't have to take you?" he asks, his voice cracking. "Ask Rosa for the address."

He scrubs a hand down his face. I've never seen Logan scared until this moment. It's strange seeing someone you've known for years exhibit a new expression. I've seen him angry. I've seen him anxious. But fear . . . Fear is new.

"*P-I-P-E—*"

I'm so focused on his face that I don't realize she's turned around. Rosa—Piper—whoever the fuck she is—sweeps her arm across the counter. My phone, the potted plant, and the glass of wine are flung off the tabletop and land with a huge crash on the floor. The screen on my phone goes black.

"You were signing my name!" she screams.

It's pointless, but I deny it anyway. "What are you talking about?" My words are weak.

Her laugh is unnatural. "Did you think I wouldn't fucking know sign language? He was my fiancé!"

Then she signs something to me; she's faster than I am. I only pick up a couple words, but I think she's signing, "*You think you were the first woman he taught how to sign?*"

What a cunt.

"What else did you tell him?" she screams.

"Nothing!" I shake my head. "Nothing!"

She shoves me and I lose balance, tumbling off the barstool. My hands shoot out to catch myself, and one lands on one of the broken pieces of the terra-cotta planter, slicing my palm and bleeding from the cut. *That's not good.* It doesn't hurt as much as it probably should. Whatever she drugged me with is dulling my senses.

"Wwhhat d-did you put in my wine?" Glancing over to the counter, I notice she hasn't taken a sip from her glass.

It's hard to know whether she actually poisoned me, but I'm not in pain, just sleepy. So I'm hoping it's only a sedative. A really strong sedative.

She's still screeching and yelling about something, something about telling him where we are and how stupid I am. If she's this mad, I figure it's a good sign. I did something she wasn't planning. Part of me wants to stay calm, and the other part wonders if I focus on how fucking terrified I am, if the adrenaline will keep me conscious long enough for him to get here. Her voice goes between shrill and echoing like she's far away.

I ignore whatever she's yelling and try to focus on staying awake. Logan will come for me. I just need to stay awake until he arrives.

Blood leaks freely onto the floor, the edges of the puddle slowly growing wider; it's the first time I've bled this much. Not a huge puddle, but last I checked, blood doesn't pool when things are going well. I stare at the rich-red color, it's the same color as the dress Logan bought me. The floor slowly tilts, but the puddle stays the same size and shape. It doesn't drip even though the white tiles on the kitchen floor seem to be stretched at an angle.

"He's going to be mad at you," I say, my words running together, and I reach for the white suitcases, grasping the tag.

There's a flash of white before pain flares at the base of my skull, but it doesn't last.

48

LOGAN

"Rosa never showed her face, there was no voice of another woman in the background," I say over the Bluetooth. Jason got to her. I wasn't fast enough. If he got Kelly, he might have Rosa too, which means I need backup, because my only focus is my wife.

"What else did you see?" Casper asks.

"I don't remember." I was so focused on Kelly and how she was doing, how sleepy she looked, that I wasn't paying attention to any other detail.

"Turning onto Hartford now," Thor says. They must have piled into the same car the second I said go. "She for sure signed 'blue bird'?"

"Yes." Colors and animals are basic beginner shit when it comes to signing; she wouldn't confuse those for something else.

As soon as the call cut out with Kelly, I called the guys to meet me at the red house on Hartford Avenue, near the cross section of Third Street. "Are you there yet?" I ask. I had driven out to Jason's house, so now I'm even farther away from the address she gave me. My foot presses the accelerator as I run a red light. The sound of a car horn fades when I whiz by.

"Mailbox!" Thor shouts.

"Bluebird is a mailbox," Casper adds. "House number 509!"

Fuck yes.

I adjust the address on my GPS. *What the fuck, this is only two blocks from my house.* "I'm a couple minutes away. Watch your fucking back, Kelly signed something about him having a pipe." The call ends, and I turn onto Hartford, but I'm still too many blocks away.

Technically, the GPS says I'm four minutes out, but I'm not driving the suggested speed limit down this road, so I get that number down to two.

As soon as I pull up, I expect to see Jason's car, but Casper's vehicle is the only one here. Thor throws his arm into the door, busting it open, and I jump out of my truck. I follow them in. They rush through the house, checking bedrooms, but I'm locked in place when I see the blood in the kitchen. *Please don't be Kelly's.*

"They moved," Thor pants.

Casper confirms. "There's nobody here."

I run both hands through my hair, gripping it at my scalp as I try to figure out what to do. I pull out my phone to check the tracker just in case, then see Kelly's phone on the floor near the pool of blood . . . which means it's probably hers.

There's a palm print of smeared blood on a cream-colored suitcase under the counter. The blood is on the address tag too. I flip it over and fear prickles the back of my neck when I see the name.

It can't be.

No.

"There's a phone over here," Casper says, picking it up. He hits a button on the side, and the screen lights up. "Oh fuck."

"What?" I bark. I don't need to hear *Oh fuck* right now.

He shows me the screen. Sure enough. It's an old selfie of Piper and me.

"You and Rosa?" Thor's brow furrows.

"That's not Rosa, it's Piper," Casper says.

It's always been Piper.

You'll never replace me. It wasn't Kelly's ex. It was *mine*.

My chest feels like it's in a fucking vise; the rooms are getting smaller. I need to find her, because every second I lose has another sick memory flooding my thoughts.

Piper poisoned Kelly. She poisoned *my fucking wife*.

"Where would Piper go?" I tear into the suitcases, but they're empty.

Fuck, where would she go?

"I saw security cameras outside," I say.

Casper runs down the hall, probably looking for whatever might give us access to see what's on them. This is taking too long. How long has it been since they left here?

I don't know.

I don't know anything, and it makes my fucking blood boil.

Piper hasn't lived in Minnesota for years—hell, the fact that she's living at all has me reeling. She's been here all along. Living in the shadows and waiting to ruin my life.

I scan the room for another sign from Kelly. The sign language, the suitcases. She's been leaving me clues. She's so goddamn smart, but there has to be something I'm missing.

My phone dings.

I know that ding.

I *love* that fucking ding.

Attic door open.

49

KELLY

The zip ties bite into my wrists as Piper drags me toward my own fucking house, like the dumbest criminal on earth. I stumble a few times on the way to the door; my head is throbbing. The ride over was spent drifting in and out of consciousness, and I remained slumped over the entire time, even when I was faking sleep. Every so often, I peeked to note what roads we were on. It's hard to stay awake with alcohol and sedatives swimming in your system, but doing it while keeping your eyes closed makes it nearly impossible.

I had to listen to her inane ramblings every waking second, and one thing I know for sure is that she doesn't plan to leave me alive. The only thing she hasn't figured out is what to do with my body. Apparently, my dead weight is too heavy, and she already wasted too much time getting me into the car after knocking me out and dragging me from her house—oh yeah, apparently that wasn't a rental. It was her actual fucking house. *No wonder it was so close to Logan's loft.*

I'm smart enough to know that secondary locations are bad news, however; as soon as I recognized the familiar roads and realized she was taking me to my house, I did everything in my power to start planning. I know my house better than she does. I was raised here. I've got home field advantage.

She shoves me through the back door, and I stumble in with exaggerated clumsiness, just enough to make me look weaker than I am. I pretend to trip over my feet and veer toward the hallway, smashing my shoulder into the switch that lowers the attic door. That fucking sensor I was so pissed about just might save my life. I'm leaving breadcrumbs in hopes Logan is picking them up.

Fuck, we should really bring back landlines.

I lie motionless on my side after falling, my elbows slightly bent as the zip ties dig into my flesh, and feign a loss of consciousness. Piper is too obsessed with herself to just kill me while I'm unconscious. She wants to teach me a lesson. If I can stay "asleep," it buys Logan more time. Logan is on the east side of town, and I'm on the west—we're about twenty minutes apart.

"Goddamn it!" She drops to her knees and yells in my face. "Get up!" I pat myself on the back for not flinching at the boom of her voice.

Buying time is my objective, it's all I have right now.

Just twenty minutes.

"Get up!" she screams again, then slaps me. I react without thinking; my fists, joined at my wrists, shoot out, slamming into her face. The diamond ring on my hand slices through her cheek. It's poetic, really.

This only pisses her off. She stands up and kicks me in the stomach. The blow to my ribs feels like it rearranges my insides. The painful impact isn't dulled by the drugs. I fold into the fetal position. She reveals that damn paring knife, and I freeze, keeping my eyes trained on her. She cuts the zip tie around my wrists while I visualize everything in my vicinity that could be used as a weapon. I brace my palms on the ground to push off.

"Don't move a fucking inch," she says, pointing the knife at me. "Or I'll let you bleed out in this fucking hallway."

I don't breathe.

"Roll on your stomach. Hands behind your back," she says, then shoves my face into the floor. "Get up slowly." I feel the point of the knife in my back, near the bottom rib that's probably fractured. She presses it deeper, then rips it lengthwise, slicing into my skin. It's not too deep, but it's deep enough.

I grit my teeth. "Fuck!" I wait for another slash, but it doesn't come. I lie still and catch my breath while my face is shoved into the floor.

"I said slowly," she says.

"I can't get up if you're holding my head to the floor," I growl through clenched teeth. My lips are numb, and my enunciation could use some work.

She retreats enough to give me room to move while keeping the knife pressed to my skin as a reminder. My reflexes aren't fast enough to snatch something without her burying that blade into my back. Now that she has me awake, I'm going to have to find another way to stall time.

She shoves me into a nearby wooden dining room chair. It belongs to my kitchen table, but I keep it over by the bookcase to use as a step stool. "Sit."

She zip-ties each of my arms to the rear posts of the chair, just above the seat. I saw a TikTok video once about how to break out of these, something with shoelaces. Unfortunately, my shoes don't have laces, and I doubt this bitch would just sit there and watch while I saw through my restraints with some half-assed MacGyver trick.

I shake my head. "It was never Jason." All the notes pointed to him. The flowers. The photos. And the whole time my stalker and I were out getting cocktails and giggling like it was a goddamn slumber party. She got me there, I'll give her that.

"It was sometimes Jason."

What? I blink at her, heat crawling up the back of my neck.

"He wasn't your boyfriend, he was working."

Memories of long conversations and uninspired sex flash in my brain. *He was a stranger.* I want to throw up when I think of the times I let him touch my body. Nothing was real, the sex was probably a perk for him. Bile rises up my throat in disgust. "It was always you."

She grins at me. "And it always will be," she snarls. She lunges for my ring.

I ball my hand into a fist, reopening the cut, and my palm fills with fresh blood. "No!" She cannot take this from me.

My strength can't compete with hers when I'm sluggish. She pries my fingers open, and I fight to keep them closed, but the slick blood helps the ring slip off easily.

Now I'm pissed.

"What's your plan here anyway, Piper?" She's been pacing the floors in a paranoid frenzy like an animal, bolting from one stupid plan to the next. Every few seconds, she's peeling back the curtains to peek out the window as if she's expecting red and blue flashing lights any second.

"Once you kill me, I'll be too heavy to move," I remind her.

She ignores me, wiping my blood off the ring.

I burrow deeper into her anxiety; it's her turn to feel afraid. "And you've got your fingerprints all over the fucking house because you keep touching my shit—is that my paring knife? Or did you steal that from your house—you know, the house with my blood all over the floor? Then there's the digital footprint . . ." I huff out a breath and wince at the pain in my rib. "You're getting sloppy."

Her hand twitches. "Who are they going to arrest? *Piper?* Piper is dead. I'm Rosa."

"Arrest?" I smile at her. The second Logan sees the blood on my clothes, she'll be *begging* the cops to arrest her. "You stalked, drugged, kidnapped, and slashed *his wife* . . . You really think he's going to just let that slide?"

"If Logan knew I was alive . . . he wouldn't be with you."

"He didn't want you before you were even dead!" I spit.

She backhands me, and I taste pennies. That's just one more punishment for later.

I hang my head between my shoulders and laugh. "You're only mad because you know I'm right. Tell me, how's it feel to be a fucking ghost?"

"I loved him first! I earned this!" She holds up my ring. "I deserve this!"

"Love isn't something you're entitled to, Piper, it's *chosen* . . . And Logan didn't choose you. Get over it."

Her breaths quicken as the pulse in her neck tics faster.

"You could leave right now and still escape—give yourself a fresh start. Forget Logan and the rest of the bullshit from your past," I offer. "Why are you even doing this?"

She stops her pacing to stare me down. "If I can't have him, no one can."

I roll my eyes—what a fucking cliché. "Real original. Your villain schtick is played out." I've seen television dramas with more subtlety. "These things never end well for the bad guy."

She jabs a finger into her chest. "I'm not the bad guy!"

"You're a fucking case file." I chuckle. "So, what've you got? Anything? You still don't have a plan, do you? You're running out of time."

"You can't do anything," she seethes. "I'm not afraid of you."

I bark out a laugh. "Yes, you are! You're fucking terrified," I say, grinning. I lean forward, letting the ties cut into my arms and ignoring the pain in my ribs as I stretch closer to her. I drop my voice to a whisper. "Because I know what keeps you up at night. You're scared to death that I'll replace you." I smile wider. "I'm your worst nightmare come true. I'm Mrs. Logan Teller."

Her expression contorts—filled with rage, or sorrow, maybe both. "Shut up!"

I laugh in her face because fuck her. "Which is worse . . . that he married me instead of you? Or the fact that he wanted to be my husband so bad he did it without even asking?"

She paces back and forth. Looking for something. Anything. "There's too much evidence," I say. She shuffles through the house, then walks out the door.

I hold my breath, waiting for her to return, but there's silence. No more incessant pacing and inane ramblings. She better drive fast because after Logan comes in and gets me, he's going to go after her.

The back door opens again, and she storms in with a big red gas can like it's filled with the solution to all her problems. I filled it up yesterday at the gas station. I was supposed to mow the lawn. Funny how tasks like cutting grass seem so absolutely pointless when you're watching your life flash before your eyes.

Defeat creeps in, and I swallow down my fear. *He'll be here any minute.*

She lifts the can, sloshing it back and forth, and sickening fumes quickly fill the space. *Don't panic, don't panic.*

Think.

I still have a lot to learn when it comes to home ownership, but one thing I do know is that gasoline is an outside toy. From everything I've heard, even looking at gasoline vapors the wrong way is enough to ignite them. Fuck, that damn extension cord is only a few feet away. Logan said it wasn't safe with my electrical.

There are no open windows, and with each second that passes, the fumes become more noxious. Any one of these outlets could spark and seal our fate. Hell, the static charge from the way she's zipping around the floor, sloshing her gas can of absolution like she's the Jackson fucking Pollock of insurance fraud, might be enough to barbecue us both. My main concern is that damn cord Logan rigged up for the microwave. Microwaves aren't meant to be plugged into extension cords because of the fire risk.

The can sounds nearly empty when she turns to me. I can see it in her smug smile. *She thinks she won.* Piper bends over and puts her face in front of mine. "He'll forget about you eventually."

Never.

"See, that's where we're different, Piper."

I've never been more terrified in my life, I've never come so close to facing my own mortality, but she's wrung enough fear from me, so I'm not giving her an ounce more—I'll be damned if I die without my words ringing in her ears from now until eternity.

"You're forgettable. But me? He can't forget me. How can he when my face is permanently inked on his arm? He'll think about me every day for the rest of his life. You might kill me, but seeing me on his body will haunt you for the rest of your miserable existence."

She seethes in front of me, her veins bulging. Straightening her back, she spills the gasoline onto my clothes, and I try to back up in my chair. The vapors near the collar of my shirt alone are suffocating.

Piper grabs my jaw with one hand, squeezing my cheeks together to part my lips. I twist and squirm away from her, but she grips me again, harder this time, pushing my head back. I thrash as the caustic gasoline enters my mouth. It tastes like acrid chemicals and hot steam, burning my tongue and robbing me of oxygen. I squeeze my eyes shut and kick with everything I have, trying to throw myself sideways to tip over in the chair.

I'm forced to swallow some to keep from inhaling it, and it coats my esophagus like acid. I can't tell if it's on fire or not. Breathing is impossible as the vapors shoot down my throat, blocking any air from getting to my lungs. She better fucking finish the job if she wants to live after this.

The front door explodes open, and the blur of a black T-shirt and his inked-up arm sprint past me. Piper is thrown into the wall, her head bounces off it with a sickening crack, and she crumples to the floor, lying motionless. Logan bends over, immediately starting on the zip ties.

"She has my ring," I croak, coughing and gagging. My shredded throat makes my voice hoarse as the chemicals burn my insides. It's agonizing. Nausea quickly sets in, and my stomach roils. I gag again, spitting to the side.

"Forget the ring," he says, splitting the zip ties with a pocketknife.

I extend my arm, reaching for her the instant one of my wrists is released. "I can't!"

My other wrist releases, and I scramble over her still body, stealing my ring back just as Logan tugs me away. She wasn't going to take this from me. I shove the ring onto my greasy finger, coated in gasoline and blood. He scoops me into his arms and heads for the back door.

I'm not sure if it's just the fumes making me hallucinate, but I swear I hear my dad's voice. *You have the same spark as your mom. She didn't just light up faces when she walked into a room, she lit the whole damn house on fire.*

I hear Dad telling me it's okay to let go, stop carrying the house I've clutched so tightly since he died. Dad doesn't live here anymore. It's time for me to say goodbye and start my new life, a life that fate doesn't decide, but one that I choose.

Logan is almost to the door when I spot the orange extension cord draped from the overhead microwave hanging down to the floor and around the corner in my living room. I dart my arm out to snag it in my elbow, and then I wrap it around my palm twice and clasp it as tight as I can. Logan barrels out the doorway with me, and the cord rips from the shoddy electrical outlet with the quietest little pop.

A snap. *A spark.*

I hear it before the door closes behind us. *The whoosh.*

A warm breeze hits our back as we step into fresh air that's no longer heavy with fumes and chemicals. The clean air soothes some of the burn in my chest.

He spins around, taking a few steps backward as the flickering orange glow climbs the walls of a house that's no longer a weight for me to carry.

Lifting my chin, I meet his gaze to find him already staring at me. He knows what I did, he saw me reach for the cord. He peers into my soul and claims me exactly as I am. His heart pounds faster, railing against his chest as he marvels at what I've done. The desire in his eyes is ravenous—this time I didn't hide my darkness, I chose to wield it.

50

LOGAN

With Kelly in my arms, I sprint down the driveway toward her neighbor's house. Casper flies down the street like a bat out of hell, with Thor in the passenger seat. They arrived less than two minutes after me. My driving was a bit more reckless than theirs on my way over.

They see Kelly in my arms and slow, so I signal them to keep going. An incinerated body in a burned-down house is going to raise some suspicions, so Thor needs to be as far away as possible from this.

I run to the neighbor's across the street and climb the porch. I don't bother pounding on the door, just walk right in. Her elderly neighbor, Herb, startles with wide eyes. He and Clyde were friends.

"Where's your shower?" I shout.

He shoots an arm out. "H-hallway, right side," he stutters. "Son, is that gasoline?"

I dash toward the bathroom, and after setting her in the bathtub, I drop to my knees and tear off her soaked clothes as quickly as I can.

"Watch her eyes!" he shouts behind me. "Don't let it get in her eyes!"

She squints, wrinkling up her nose and sealing her lips closed as I carefully stretch the neck of the shirt to avoid her face and slip off her head. Then I peel off the wet pants and underwear that stick to her skin, and finally my own shirt that absorbed gasoline while carrying her out of there.

The old man enters the doorway. "Give me the clothes," he says, reaching for them shakily while turning his head away from Kelly.

I plop the soggy pile of pants and shirts into his arms, and he disappears.

Kelly flinches when the initial cold shower spray hits her skin. "Keep your eyes closed, sweetheart." I instruct, gripping the shower head attachment and rinsing her face off, giving her intermissions to breathe in between.

The water mixes with the cut on her hand and circles around the drain with a light reddish-brown hue.

"I'm gonna throw up," she says, leaning forward on her knees, bracing one palm on the bottom of the tub and gripping the side of the basin with the other.

I gather her hair in my fist to keep it out of the way and gently brush my thumb over her white knuckles. Her weak body heaves up the liquid contents of her stomach. It looks like red wine but has the same smell as the gasoline fumes that have already eaten up the air in this small bathroom.

The memory of Kelly thrashing around while Piper clumsily tried to pour gasoline down her throat tenses every muscle in my body, filling me with unbridled rage. If Kelly didn't need me right now, I'd be racing into the inferno to take care of her myself.

"It burns," she sobs, her voice raw.

"How much did you swallow?"

She shakes her head. "Only a little bit." Her body heaves again, but nothing comes up.

"Can you bring us a glass of water?" I shout to Herb.

He returns with a large cup. "I'm not looking!" he announces, holding it out for me to take, and I pass it to Kelly. "Keep rinsing your mouth out," I tell her.

She nods.

Herb shuffles behind me, crossing the bathroom like a man on a combat mission, and shoves open the windowsill. Fresh air streams in. *Thank God.* I glance up at a shirtless Herb. His entire back is a collage of aged, once-vibrant tattoos.

"Where's the monster that did this?" he demands. He peers out the window, turning his head left to right as if he's going to find the suspect and kill them with his bare hands. I like Herb.

"They're still in the house," I reply with a flat voice, turning back to Kelly.

He quietly stares out the window, no doubt watching as Kelly's house is devoured by flames. The crash of windows shattering across the street is barely audible over the running water. Herb slowly hobbles while turning around. "Hot water and soap," he says. "You're gonna need to rinse her skin for a while to make sure you get it all. I'll see if I can find my phone to call 911."

I pull my cell from my pocket and hold it out for him to use.

"No, no," he mutters, giving me a firm look. "I'll find mine. Shouldn't take me too long to remember where I put it."

"Appreciate it, Herb," I say, giving him a nod.

"There's fresh towels in the cabinet," he calls, exiting the room. The air in here is finally smelling less like gasoline fumes—now it has a different smell. The acrid, bitter aroma of smoke and burning plastic.

"Look at me," I whisper, lifting her chin to check her eyes for signs of redness, and as soon as her gaze finds mine, I want to break down. She looks at me so trusting, even though the whole reason she's injured is because of me. I clear my throat, clearing away the emotion. "Your eyes look good."

"Very kind of you to hand out compliments when I'm this . . . unpolished," she says, her voice raspy.

"You fought for your life today; if you think that makes you less beautiful you're out of your goddamn mind," I mutter. "I'm sorry—"

"Don't start."

Kelly is quiet while I work, still rinsing her mouth out. Her cut hand is sealed around the plastic cup when she brings it to her lips, but the water circling the drain is that same reddish-pink color. I rotate her body to find the source, then notice the slash on her back. *What the fuck is this?* It's about five inches long and thankfully not any deeper than it already is considering yellow subcutaneous tissue is peeking out. I whip out my phone and dial 911. Had I known about the giant gash on her back, I'd have done it sooner.

"Where is your emergency?" the dispatcher answers.

Luckily, I spotted the number on my way up the porch steps in preparation.

"What's going on, sir?" they ask.

"We need medical services. My wife was attacked, she's injured. She has a large cut on her back and hand, she has possible chemical burns from gasoline, and has ingested some—I'm unsure how much. She has marks around her wrists as well."

I'm assured people are on the way. The dispatcher attempts to get me to answer a few more questions. I politely explain that tending to my wife's injuries is more important and I'll give my statement when the cops arrive.

"Oh, and the house across the street is on fire," I say before ending the call.

My wife's injuries.

Kelly shivers, so I turn up the temperature of the water. Her shivering quickly intensifies to shaking.

She's coming down from the adrenaline.

"It's gonna be okay," I mutter, brushing some of the hair from her face, and squeeze the back of her neck three times, telling her those three words I desperately want to confess. I should have told her sooner, it's just one more way I let her down. But I don't want the first time she hears it to be when she's groggy from sedatives and shaking. Instead, I say three other words. "I've got you."

But do I? I didn't have her when she was drugged or when the zip ties were digging into her wrists. I didn't even have her when she was being stalked. When I had the opportunity to protect her. I was too busy looking at the wrong people, not paying attention to the signs.

"Kelly, I need you to listen to me carefully," I demand. "I tripped on that extension cord."

She glances up at me, shaking her head.

"I tripped," I insist.

It was my past that caught up with her, and she was forced to save herself. I hate that. It never should have gone this far. Maybe if I had gone to the cops in the first place, things would be different, but I was selfish. This is one thing I can do for her.

I can't stop seeing her thrashing in that chair, fighting for her life while she was waiting for me to show up and be a shield.

Kelly nods, her teeth clacking loudly. She hisses while she moves into a sitting position, then leans against the side of the tub wall, tucking her knees into her chest. "I-if-f I have t-to go to the h-hospital," she says, "you're driving. We're not wasting our wedding money on an ambulance ride."

51

KELLY

After spending hours at the hospital, then several more in questioning, it's well past midnight by the time we drag ourselves through the door of Logan's loft. The exhaustion has left us barely standing.

When we step inside, Casper and Odin are passed out cold on the sofa—Casper sprawled on his back, one arm flopped out, one foot on the floor. Our pup takes up the rest of the space. When the door snicks closed behind us, both of them jolt awake.

We weren't sure what was going to happen after getting a lawyer and talking with police, so Casper was on house-sitting duty until we returned. Thankfully, we were released without issue but we'll need to stick around until the investigation is closed. I'm not concerned. There's enough evidence at Piper's house and her digital footprint is all over my phone. Besides, the extension cord was an accident.

"Everything okay?" he asks through a yawn.

I nod, heading for the stairs.

"How ya feeling, Junior?"

I give him a thumbs-up; I'm not using my voice unless I have to.

"Fill you in on everything tomorrow," Logan says. "You gonna crash here?"

He shakes his head, stands, and cracks his neck. "Nah, I gotta get home. Just glad you both made it out."

It's been two days, and neither of us has left the apartment other than to take Odin out for a walk. Logan shut down the shop temporarily, and Frankie is rescheduling all the appointments at Black Rabbit for the next ten days due to a "burst water pipe." I told him he should have said gas leak, but he didn't seem to find the same humor in it I did.

This is the first day I don't smell gasoline on me—finally we can lie in bed together without the slight, sick scent between us. We tried all the soap we had access to, then baking soda and vinegar, but in the end, it was lemons that did the trick. Logan was so careful while helping scrub it over my skin, avoiding my wounds. I see the way he looks at them, like they're taunting him, and it breaks my heart. He insists I stay in bed to let my body heal. Most of the time, he reads beside me, but I can tell he's distracted, it takes him too long to turn the pages.

I'm so grateful for him, more than I can put into words, but he's not been the same since we got home. He's been shuffling around the loft in silence, I've tried to cheer him up with jokes and memes, but he's gone to a dark place. I hate it.

Odin snores softly from his bed, soaking up the late-day sun streaming through the large loft windows. I plan ideas for dinner in my head while Logan reads. Cooking is usually his thing, but maybe if I take care of dinner tonight, he'll see I'm not as broken or helpless as he's been treating me.

Logan sets his book and glasses on the nightstand and wraps his arms around my middle, drawing me close. I wince when he makes contact with my injured rib and instantly kick myself for reacting. He flinches, snatching his arm back like I've burned him. *Shit.*

"No, it's fine. I'm fine," I assure him.

It doesn't make any difference, he still retreats to his side of the bed.

Every time it happens, that vein in his neck twitches, and then he jerks away. When I've tried to close the gap between us, he stands and leaves the room. It's been two days of this, and his rejection stings far more than my injuries do.

I strategically place a pillow under me to move into a comfortable position, then snuggle up on my side, my back to his front. I reach behind me and locate his arm to drape it over me the way he tried before, but he withdraws. And I let him.

The silence between us has never felt so suffocating.

I lie on my side, staring away from him, letting the room unfocus and the numbness eat away at my insides. Tears prick the corners of my eyes.

He sits up.

"Please don't leave," I whisper.

"What?" His voice is clipped, angry.

"Every time you pull away and I try to pull you back, you get up and walk away." I ease myself upright, careful to not let any pain show as I turn, but his feet are already planted on the floor. I shift to kneel beside him on the mattress. "*I need you.*"

He scoffs.

"Did I do something to make you mad?"

Logan glances over his shoulder. "I'm not mad at you. I'm mad at myself!"

I roll my eyes. He can't blame himself for what happened. "You didn't know."

"I should have."

A laugh bursts out of me. "You couldn't!" Neither of us knew until it was too late.

"I could have done more."

"How?" I snap.

He doesn't answer.

"Tell me, Logan," I press. "What signs did you have pointing to her? I'll wait."

I give him a few seconds to think . . . Nothing.

"Exactly." I cross my arms.

"My past almost killed you, Kelly," he says, his voice wavering. "I couldn't even save you that day, you had to save yourself."

"What the fuck are you talking about?" I uncross my arms. "You did save me!"

He picks his feet off the floor and rotates to face me directly. "She was pouring gasoline down your throat when I got there. I will never get that image out of my head." His gaze carries a sadness deeper than I've ever seen in him. "I never should have let you leave after work. I should have answered my office door when you knocked. I should have done a background check on the *woman you met in Bozeman*—"

"Logan." I cup his jaw in my hands and tilt his face so he's looking directly into my eyes. "I would be dead if you hadn't shown up." I don't know how to make this any clearer to him.

He gives a wistful smile. "You did such a good job, Kelly. You were so fucking smart every step of the way. It was the breadcrumbs you left that saved you, it wasn't me."

"You're starting to piss me off," I blurt. "Breadcrumbs don't mean shit if they're overlooked! Breadcrumbs didn't throw her off me, they didn't cut my zip ties or carry me out of the house before I caught fire. They didn't strip off my clothes and rinse the gasoline from my skin. They didn't hold my hair when I threw up, they didn't call an ambulance, and they certainly didn't take the fall for that fire! You act like you just stood by and watched from a distance. You were with me every step of the way. You paid attention to every sign I left without hesitation—you took action, and *that's* why I'm alive."

I push up on my knees and press my forehead to his. He palms my hips, his large hands heavy with intent. He doesn't pull away this time—he leans in. His touch sends warmth to the parts of me numbed by dejection.

"You saved me."

The tension leaves his body on an exhale, and he's finally letting go of whatever stupid guilt he's allowed to fester since we returned home. "Okay."

"Okay? That's it?"

He chuckles. "That's all I have right now."

"Is it?"

I lace my fingers behind his neck and squeeze three times.

The last time he'd done that to me was while tending to my injuries in a bathtub. It was so affectionate and tender that it made me question if I had actually heard him utter the words aloud.

For years he's given me assurances on the back of my neck. However, it wasn't until the other day that I understood their meaning. He didn't save his love for last, he gave it to me before our lips ever brushed. Logan has always spoken with his hands, and he's been giving his quiet love for years.

Our gaze tangles together, and we regard each other in silence; the anticipation has me holding my breath. We're both thinking it, but I want to hear him say it.

He inhales slowly, letting his touch drift from my hips, up my back, and finally clasping my neck like he's done a million times before, but this time it's different. His gruff exhale makes me smile. He knows what I want, and I'm calling his bluff. A smile crosses his lips—it's subtle, but it's there, filled with relief and reverence.

His voice is low and gruff, masculine and steady. "I love you."

The confession takes my breath away. Like he's been holding it right behind his teeth for years and finally can let it out. "I love you too."

His throat bobs once before he brings his lips to mine.

52

LOGAN

Our kiss is hungry. I steady her hands, and her mouth grows impatient against mine. I draw back just enough to take in her swollen lips and blown pupils. To see the way her half-lidded gaze begs me not to stop. "You sure?"

She nods and pulls me back in. Her kiss is rough, like she's been waiting for me to stop being so gentle and love her in ways that are raw, dark, and brutal.

Stripping off my shirt and sweats, I toss them behind us, but I'm much more careful while removing hers. Lifting the hem of her shirt reveals the deep-purple bruise that blooms near her ribs. I hate that bruise. Normally I like seeing her marked up, but the ones I leave on her come from a place of love and respect . . . These aren't mine, they stem from violence.

I swallow down the anxiety rising in my throat as I take in her wounds, trusting her enough to not blame myself.

She rushes to slip her arms out of the sleeves. "Slow down," I say with a chuckle. "If you end up more injured because you're too turned on, your doctors are gonna blame me first."

"They saw what you look like," she says, grinning. "They'll understand."

"Maybe I want to take my time with you."

Kelly bites her lip, filling her hands with her lavish tits and digging her black nails into the soft flesh. *Fuck.*

I catch her wrist and yank her into me, rougher than I probably should. Our mouths join together, and a growl spills from my chest as my tongue claims hers. She claws at the waistband of my boxers, shoving them down so she can wrap her fingers around my cock. *Goddamn.* I'm thick and heavy in her palm as she strokes me, spreading the bead of pre-cum down to the base. My need to be inside her ratchets higher with each heavy breath that escapes from her lips. Hooking my thumbs into her underwear, I drag them over her ass and down her thighs until there's nothing between us.

I guide her to lie on her side, then settle in behind and snake my arm under her neck. My other hand rests in the dip of her waist. The way my body protectively curves behind hers eases the tightness in my chest.

She's in my arms, safe. I sweep her hair over her shoulder and let my mouth brush across the birthmark on the back of her neck. "I love you," I breathe. Damn, it feels good to say those words out loud, but it's nothing compared to hearing her echo them back.

I'm conscious of her injuries and that I can't be too rough. "Tell me if it hurts," I whisper against her bare skin. She nods, then pushes her perfect little ass into my hips. She feels what she's doing to me.

"Greedy girl," I mutter.

"You love it."

I chuckle, gripping her waist firmer—territorial, yet tender. She's still bruised and healing, but the ache in me rages against the instinct to take her in a way that shows everyone who she belongs to. I don't want anyone to ever think they can take what's mine again.

I press a soft kiss to her shoulder, dragging my palm over her stomach and between her breasts. Her soft ass presses more firmly, wriggling against my cock.

"You're playing with fire . . ."

She sighs, her body melting against mine. "And who was the one who lit the match?" she asks, reaching behind and scraping her nails over my scalp. "If you can't take the heat . . ."

There's my Chaos. I encircle her left wrist, bring it to my mouth, and press a kiss to the bandage on the inside of her hand. "Keep talking like that and I'm going to forget how to be gentle."

Parting her with my fingers, I tease her clit until she twitches for me. A groan is pulled from my chest when I feel how wet she is. She hums softly, and I slip my index and middle fingers inside, curling them and stroking.

Her breaths quicken. "Your wife likes it rough," she rasps. *Fucking hell.* She's not making this easy.

I slap the delicate bundle of nerves between her thighs, earning me a yelp. While she's reeling from the sharp sting, my other hand creeps up to her throat, circles around it, and holds her in place.

I stuff three fingers in her. "This what you want?" I demand. She gulps, sending vibrations through my palm. As much as I love taking her with my cock, sometimes it's fun to just play with her pussy and watch her slowly unravel as she drowns in need.

"Yes." She makes a frustrated whimper, like she's trying to stave off her orgasm, but she can't fool me.

"Well, go on, then. Let's feel that needy pink cunt give it up."

Kelly moans, riding my hand and gripping the sheets while I pump in and out. She's so close.

I whisper. "You're doing great, almost there . . ."

She clamps down on me, and I release her throat, caressing her cheek as she pulses around me.

"Fuck," she pants.

I place a kiss on the back of her neck, scraping my teeth over the soft skin as her rapid breathing slows. My fingers traipse over her sensitive clit, making her twitch and grind. Christ, this woman.

"Logan?"

"Hm?" I reply, dipping inside her.

"Say it again."

A smile spreads on my lips. "Say what?"

"That you love me."

"I love you." I lift her thigh and sink into her until I'm buried deep where I belong. "Maybe not in the way good men do . . . but in a way that wants me to be a better one."

She responds with a sharp inhale. "I want you exactly as you are . . . for better or worse."

I hold her tighter, pushing deep until her mewls amplify to moans.

She nuzzles into my hand, and I cup her face. My thumb traces her cheek before drifting down to her lips. Her mouth parts, and she bites down on my thumb, playful and vicious. Her feisty side drives me wild.

"Fuck," I groan.

"Just didn't want you to forget you who you married. You don't have to be so careful with me."

"You think I don't want to fuck you harder? Flip you on your stomach and remind you exactly who you belong to?"

"Who do I belong to?" she teases.

I nip her shoulder. "*Me.*"

She hums like she wants more, and I want to give it to her, but I'm not about to injure her worse.

"Then prove it."

Goddamn it. I capture her throat, just enough that I can keep her body locked against mine. "You want me to brutally fuck you? Then you're going to keep still while I do it. Remember what the doctor said, no lifting, pulling, or twisting."

"I promise," she vows.

"You're my wife. Mine to care for, mine to protect, and mine to fuck . . ." I slide my fingers over her clit. "Now take it like an obedient fucking wife."

I fuck her with long, deliberate thrusts. Snapping my hips just enough to make her grunt. "This is what you do to me. This is what it means to belong to someone. This"—I plunge my entire length inside her—"is what it means to be my forever."

A broken sound escapes her throat, raw and begging.

"There you go, let it all out. Make those pretty noises I like so much."

She moans like it's the only way she can breathe.

Then she throws her head back as she comes, and I nearly lose my sanity. I drive into her harder, feeling her body break for me like it can't decide whether to fight for survival or become an offering.

"You're not fucking done," I say. "Give your husband another one."

I grip her thigh, hiking it up higher and spreading her open just a bit more, careful not to move her too much. She's already had more than enough roughness for my liking. I no longer pound into her but give her long, deep strokes that are slow and brutal. It's cruel torture. She clenches around me. There's already another one coming in behind the last.

"Oh, sweetheart, look how you take every slow inch so beautifully."

I massage every sensitive spot she begs for. Her back arches against my chest, and I release her trembling thigh. She collapses in my arms, sobbing my name as she comes. Shattering into a million little pieces—all of her edges as jagged as mine.

"Fuck, Kelly," I say through gritted teeth, barely keeping it together. "That's it. That's my fucking wife. Give it to me." I jut into her, not letting her come down, my thumb rubbing slow, firm circles over her swollen clit.

"Please, Logan," she begs. "I want every drop dripping down my thighs."

That's all it takes for me to let go. I bury my cock deep inside her and let the tsunami of pure fucking bliss tear through me like a storm until I can't see anything but her. Spilling everything I have as she wrecks me.

We lie tangled and breathless, our chests rising and falling in sync with each other. The need to kiss her has me gently rolling her under me. A soft smile curves on her lips when her hazy eyes find mine, and the fresh glow of ecstasy still lingers on her cheeks—damn, she's beautiful. I tip her chin toward me and kiss her until we're breathless all over again.

I sit up between her legs, prepared to retrieve a towel, but instead she parts her thighs. The carnal sight of my cum leaking out of her is so fucking hot, I pause to admire it. My thumb grazes down the length of her rosy swollen clit and catches the drip to stuff it back into her still pulsing pussy.

Instinctively, I press my hand to her stomach, knowing someday I'll leave marks here that aren't from my teeth. It's the first time I've ever truly wanted to leave something *good* behind. Perhaps she'll carry on her family's legacy with me.

She's tucked into me, my head nestled on top of hers. I remove the cold pack resting on her side, flip it over, and rewrap the towel around it before positioning it back on her ribs and holding it in place.

"How are you feeling?" I ask.

She sighs softly, humming approval. "You're very nurturing."

Nurturing. That's not a quality I hear about myself often, but for Kelly I'm very nurturing.

"For you I am."

She gives a subtle shake of her head. "Not just me, I've seen it with your family too."

I suppose that's true.

"Did you know Jordan's pregnant?" I ask.

"No! When did you find that out?"

I grin. "Last time we went over for dinner."

She pats my shoulder in a fake slap. "We agreed no more secrets."

"I forgot," I say. It's the truth, I've been mentally occupied with our stalker situation for the last few weeks. Somehow, having children never really occurred to me as something I wanted until I pushed my cum back inside her. I know almost everything there is to know about this woman, but this is something we've never discussed—as a couple or as individuals. The fact that I don't know her stance on something so important has been rolling around in my head since, and this is the perfect opportunity to bring it up.

"Do you ever think about that?" I ask. "Having kids?"

She remains still, not tense, but contemplative.

"You're thinking about babies?" she asks.

"I've thought about them with you."

"You? The guy who growled at me a little bit ago and was prepared to separate Jason's head from his body last week?"

"You're the one who said I was nurturing," I argue with a smile. She makes it sound like I don't have plans to take care of Jason. He was an accomplice and will be dealt with accordingly.

"I don't think there would be a dad more overprotective than you."

There wouldn't.

"I've thought about it," she admits. "Not daydreaming about cute little clothes or picking names or anything, but I've wondered if I was capable of motherhood. Whether I'd be a good mom. Growing up without one makes it harder to picture what that might look like for me."

"You would be a good mom."

She snorts. "You don't know that."

"Yeah, I do." She's far too compassionate.

"Is that something you want?" she asks.

"I used to not think so, but with you . . . I like the idea of having a family, and if that family ends up just being me, you, and Odin—that's okay too. However . . . if you ever decide it's something you want, or want to discuss more, I'm up for that. It's nothing we need to rush now."

"I think"—her finger traces figure eights on my chest—"I think I might want that . . . someday."

It makes me happy that she's leaving the door open on that conversation. That's enough.

"Then we'll talk about it more someday. We're not on any sort of timeline."

"Psh. Speak for yourself," she quips. "We've got a wedding timeline."

I chuckle. "Oh yeah? Did you pick a date?"

The smile in her voice is audible. "I may have . . ."

53

KELLY

Two months later

I end the call and collapse into Logan's office chair, relishing the moment. It's over, it's finally fucking over. I just got off the phone with the detective we've been in contact with for almost two months since the fire. Endless meetings and follow-ups. It seemed like we gave statements a dozen times and handed over everything we had related to her: phone data, photos, even the note that was on the windshield in Bozeman.

Sitting up again, I glimpse down at the phone that's still warm in my hands.

We're closing the investigation. Four words I've been waiting to hear for months. No more suspicion, no more questions, no charges being filed.

No more nightmares.

For nearly two months, Piper Nygaard has been haunting us from beyond the grave, but this time she isn't coming back from the dead. This is more than just an online obituary and deleted social media accounts. She's gone.

That house was filled with evidence, not just the charred grounds of my place, but the crime scene at hers. It was never a rental, she lived there. The place didn't look lived in because she didn't have a life. Logan was her hobby—*her obsession*—and I was getting in the way.

Once they got her laptop, it was pretty much over. She was good at keeping herself hidden but didn't extend that same stealth to her browser history. She had access to Logan's email and calendar. Always knew where he was going to be, knew what he was doing. Even going so far as to hire and frame Jason, making the flowers trace back to him just to fuck with Logan—who has assured me Jason will no longer be a problem . . . I didn't ask.

Most of the Instagram messages were sent while she was using the Wi-Fi at cafés and other public businesses. Much of the security camera footage was gone after thirty days, but Piper also purchased coffees and other items during her visits, leaving a credit card footprint. She truly believed she was invincible.

I step out of Logan's office feeling weightless for the first time in months. I walk down the aisle, listening to the familiar buzz of tattooing that has always lived in these walls, and toward his station where he's putting the final touches on a large eagle that spans across his client's back. The man lies on his stomach with headphones on. Logan glances up at me standing in the entrance to his work area, and I smile—really smile.

"Grant just called," I mutter, referencing the detective who has been managing this case. "We're cleared. Nothing is being filed."

His grin is as wide as mine.

He's been so stressed out since all of this went down. The cloud of suspicion hovered over us for weeks—a dead body inside a gasoline house fire was not a good look. If they had found either of us culpable in the fire, we would have been facing manslaughter charges. Logan admitted that until the investigation closed, Piper had enough power to destroy us.

"Celebrate with burritos later?" he asks.

I cup the back of his neck and squeeze three times. "You know my order."

He inhales as if he can finally breathe again, then nods and returns to his work, still smiling.

He's free of her. The years of her hovering over him are over. She remained dormant while he stayed single, building up the narrative in her mind that he was still hung up on her, too distraught from grieving her loss—his unhappiness was enough to keep her pacified. Until I started capturing his attention. When she saw the email from the Gallatin County clerk regarding our marriage license—that was when she made herself known.

The only thing left is dealing with my insurance company. Now that the investigation is closing, we'll be able to wrap that up too. Logan and I have already decided to not rebuild what was lost. Almost everything was destroyed with either fire, smoke, or water. Much of Dad's art had already been brought to the shop. Logan took pictures of everything when he made the tarot cards, so we have the records. We were able to salvage a few photos, sketchbooks, and small pieces of artwork that had been kept in lock boxes in the attic. After hearing his words in my head that day, I realized I don't need his things to feel close to him.

Fire is cleansing. It's time to move on, and now we finally can.

I return to my station and inhale. It's over. After holding my breath for so long, I forgot what it felt like to fully fill my lungs with air. I wipe down my worktable and wrap it in cellophane in preparation for my next appointment, taking a minute to look around the shop and relish the normalcy of it all. The beautifully mundane familiarity.

Thor's quietly piecing together stencils on the other side of our shared wall as Logan finishes up with his client and ushers him to the front desk, like he's done a thousand times before. I'm finally able to take in the sounds and sights of this shop, the details around me, without my fear or intrusive thoughts interrupting me.

Across the aisle, Anna sits quietly in Casper's chair, her arm propped up as he tattoos an intricate lotus flower. She's motionless except for a small twitch when he wipes down after a pass of ink.

Casper tries to draw conversation out of her, but oftentimes it's an exchange of nods before he's left to work in silence. He's a social guy, makes friends everywhere he goes, but no matter how friendly he is, she's the one he can't quite get to open up. He seems to have learned to interpret her silences, but he's also not giving up either; he doesn't know how. Anna is Logan's dream client—all tattoo and no conversation—but something tells me Casper wouldn't let anyone else touch her.

I continue prepping for my client, tearing the blue shop towels from the roll, then stacking them in a pile and folding them just right. My tray is wiped down and organized with tools, the little ink cups in a neat row like soldiers. Everything is in its place.

I reach for my tablet, eager to show my client what I've designed for them, but realize I've left it in Logan's office. I must have forgotten it when I took the phone call. I swear half my shit ends up in there now—sweatshirts, lip balm, hair ties, and every half-eaten snack that goes missing.

I slip out of my tattoo bay and hurry back to his office, finding it right where I left it. I pluck it off his desk and turn to leave, but Logan has my exit blocked. He quietly shuts the door behind him with a soft snick, staring at me like I'm his prey.

The quiet intensity in his gaze is a welcome one, because it's no longer wrought with stress or fear, like he's trying to memorize my face in case he never sees me again. This time, it's filled with a sense of permanence. It's home.

He doesn't say anything, simply steps into my space, claims my jaw, and kisses me. I melt into him, into the way he feels like home and security, trailing my fingers up his chest, then fist his shirt, needing to hold on to this moment. The moment we finally were set free to live again.

He pulls back slightly, our eyes locking, appreciating each other more than ever before. Grateful for this.

"It's finally over," I whisper.

He nods. "And this is where we begin." We didn't rely on fate for our survival, we relied on each other—*chose* each other.

We exit his office, into a world that looks the same but feels brand new. One we walked through fire for, a future we built from the ashes. We're not walking away from the wreckage unscathed, but we're walking away. Our love transformed into something permanent, dark, and born in the flames—forged of ink and alchemy.

EPILOGUE

CASPER

The Wedding

A single jagged-ass, half-charred tree sits alone, centered in an overgrown green lot where a house once stood. Like it grew out of a crevice in the sidewalk and kept growing stronger just to spite the concrete. Kind of like the couple who are getting married in front of it—well, getting married *again*. Logan promised Kelly a wedding, so here we are. In front of us, a beautiful couple and a fucked-up tree casting creepy shadows with its deformed limbs. Behind us, long tables filled with greenery and candles that I can only describe as an ethereal woodland Pinterest-fueled hellscape. Edison bulbs sway in the light breeze above us in the empty lot of land, where we sit on wooden benches while oohing and ahhing over the wedding vows.

The vows are short, intense, and . . . weirdly hot? After listening to Logan and Kelly declare their love for each other, I kinda get it. I think. Not the whole happily-ever-after part, but the person part. Finding someone who can see the worst in you and not blink.

There can't be more than fifty people in attendance. One of whom is my plus-one—Anna. She sits beside me, petite, and sharp around the edges in a way that warns others to never corner her. Fortunately for me, I love a good adrenaline rush, and there's nothing more gratifying than being in the presence of a wild animal knowing they could attack at any moment. She has soft-pink hair, the color of cotton candy, and sits beside me like she's just as sweet.

This is the first time I've seen her in a sundress, which is deeply cruel. When she comes in to get tattooed, she's hiding behind ripped jeans and loose shirts. But tonight, she's got that pink dress, strappy shoes, and *my* ink. There's something satisfying about the fact that no one else has ever tattooed her flesh. If I do my job right, no one else ever will either.

Tilting my head toward Anna, I whisper, "Do you see the way they look at each other?"

Her lip twitches, it's not a smile, but I'll take it. She gives a subtle nod.

"Do you think they'll start fucking before they finish their vows? Right in front of Nana Teller and the plates of bacon-wrapped dates?"

She rolls her lips together, trying not to laugh, and it makes me feel like I won something. She doesn't hand her smiles out freely, you've got to earn them. Strangely, I enjoy earning them, like a safe for me to crack.

Once the ceremony is over, we're left to our own devices at dinner. Long mismatched wooden tables are sprawled across the grass, decked out like an enchanted forest fucked a conference table. No seating chart, just *vibes*. Across from me, Thor sits, downing a glass of wine as if it might teleport him to anywhere but here. He showed up solo. Beside me, my date quietly eats like she's hoping nobody notices her at all—unfortunately for Anna, I do. With curiosity and a chub.

Then come the toasts.

First up is Clyde Everhart, the bride's father, which would be normal if Clyde weren't fucking dead. But he left a bunch of letters for Kelly to read at various milestones in her life, including her wedding day.

Logan stands and gathers everyone's attention—I grin ear to ear just thinking about how much he loathes being in the limelight.

"Before Clyde Everhart passed, he left me a box of letters addressed to his daughter for important days in her life. This is the first time either of us is reading this letter"—*Bullshit*. I am deeply suspicious he's read and memorized every letter in that whole damn box—"so, maybe cover small ears because all the eloquence Clyde possessed went into his art, not his words."

Small laugh. Classic.

"Hey kid . . . Well damn. You're really doing it. Wish I could be there to walk you down the aisle. This part hit harder than I expected. I had grand plans to look you in the eye and tell you that I love you, and look him in the eye and remind him that I'll bury him if he ever hurts you. But instead I'm writing you this letter because that's all the time I've got.

"You're a blaze, my girl, just like your mom. You've always been the best part of both of us. I'm sure you look beautiful today in your dress just like she did. I know you. You don't do anything halfway. Not ink, nor art. You go all in every time. And if you're with who I hope you are, your fire is an equal match for his deep water. Still, I hope you let him burn every once in a while. People think love just happens, like you could trip and fall into it—but the real kind, the kind that lasts, is raw and deliberate. I know you know how to love because I've seen it. Love him the way you deserve to be loved—loud, fierce, and unapologetic.

"You were always my best work, so I hope the one you chose knows what a damn honor it is to be your husband. And if he ever forgets, take after your mom and remind him.

"So now, I'm talking to your groom.

"Logan, take care of her. Not in the white-picket-fence kind of way. I don't care if you forget to open doors or say the right thing. But when she breaks, pick up the pieces and hold her. See her, the hard edges and the soft spots, and love them both, never ask her to sacrifice one for the other.

"I lived with her as a teenager; you can't tame her so don't even try. She's fierce. So if you're not ready to burn for her, you better step aside. If you're lucky enough to have her for a wife, then you need to be worthy of her as a husband—every damn day.

"Remember my promise if you ever hurt her. I meant it.

"I love you both. Make a beautiful life together. Love hard, choose each other, and raise some hell.

"Love, the father of the bride (Dad)."

It's silent when Logan finishes the note. Someone sniffles nearby. Goddamn it, I'm even getting choked up. I knew Clyde well; I had a short apprenticeship with him after moving over from a different shop. Hearing that letter is like hearing his voice again. The man was mostly quiet like Logan, but when he spoke, he never minced words.

Afterward, the Tellers give their toasts, poor bastards; I'd hate to follow Clyde Everhart. The Tellers' speeches are as neat and polished as the rest of the family is—sans Logan.

Then it's my turn, because I like talking and I'm an attention whore.

"All right, I'm up. I'm Casper. Friend of the bride. Friend of the groom. Award-winning tattoo artist. And tonight's designated liability.

"I've known Kelly well enough to know that she may seem precious and cuddly on the outside, but deep down she's a force to be reckoned with. She's got that cheerful, bubbly personality that makes everyone melt—and makes the rest of us turn into guard dogs in case anyone looks at her wrong. We'll sew your mouth shut just for interrupting her, which honestly, is the most *us* move ever."

She rolls her eyes at me, and I glance at the groom.

"And I've known Logan long enough to know he has feelings under that resting bitch face. Watching him fall in love was like watching a building collapse in slow motion. Impossible to stop, but something you wanted to watch with a bucket of popcorn. That man waited for her so long it was honestly uncomfortable to be around. But now? Look at you! Since getting together, you burn brighter and hotter together than you ever did on your own." I swallow to make sure my voice doesn't crack, then nod toward the tree behind them. "You've been through hell and back and have that charred cottonwood back there to prove it."

I clear my throat and raise my glass. "To Logan and Kelly. May your love stay wild and fucked up forever. And may the rest of us be lucky enough to find something half as real. Love you both."

It's the truth. I know there's a part of me that yearns for what they have. If I ever settle down, I want it to be a love as raw as theirs. I want romance with a dark side, in a window-watcher kind of way. Deranged, but *sexy* deranged.

I down my champagne and nod at Thor across from me. "Thor, you're up."

He flips me the bird while I drop into my seat next to Anna.

"I gave my toast at the first wedding," he grumbles. "Pass."

Okay, calm down, buddy.

"I totally killed it," I whisper in her ear.

She does that small lip twitch thing again. "You maimed it."

"Was that—Did you just make your first ever joke?"

She rolls her eyes at me.

"Careful, if you stay quiet for too long, I'll start to think you're mysterious," I warn. "That kind of shit always turns me on."

"Sounds like you're in trouble, then," she quips.

Is she flirting with me? I cock a brow and then my glass—just to her this time. "To getting into trouble."

She clinks her glass to mine. "And making it worth the consequences."

ABOUT THE AUTHOR

Sloane St. James is the award-winning author of the Lakes Hockey and Sky Ridge Hotshots series. She loves writing strong, witty women and the dirty-talking men who love them. In her free time, St. James enjoys spending time with her family, traveling, watching hockey games, and of course, reading romance. She resides in Minneapolis, Minnesota.

≋ Podium

FOR A GOOD TIME
follow us on our socials

 podiumentertainment.com
 @podiumentertainment
 /podiumentertainment
 @podium_ent
 @podiumentertainment